Southwest WI Library System
3 9896 01088 5057
WITHDRAWN
Dodgeville Public Library
139 S. Iowa St.
Dodgeville
W9-BRX-962

FIREBIRDS SOARING

FIREBIRD

WHERE FANTASY TAKES FLIGHT™
WHERE SCIENCE FICTION SOARS™

Across the Nightingale Floor Episode One: Journey to Inuyama	Lian Hearn
Across the Nightingale Floor Episode Two: The Sword of the Warrior	Lian Hearn
The Angel's Command	Brian Jacques
The Beggar Queen	Lloyd Alexander
The Beguilers	Kate Thompson
Beldan's Fire	Midori Snyder
The Bellmaker	Brian Jacques
Birth of the Firebringer	Meredith Ann Pierce
The Blue Girl	Charles de Lint
The Blue Sword	Robin McKinley
Brilliance of the Moon Episode One: Battle for Maruyama	Lian Hearn
Brilliance of the Moon Episode Two: Scars of Victory	Lian Hearn
Castaways of the Flying Dutchman	Brian Jacques
Changeling	Delia Sherman
The Changeling Sea	Patricia A. McKillip
The City, Not Long After	Pat Murphy
Clan Ground	Clare Bell
Dingo	Charles de Lint

The Dreaming Place	Charles de Lint
The Ear, the Eye and the Arm	Nancy Farmer
Ecstasia	Francesca Lia Block
Enchantress from the Stars	Sylvia Engdahl
Epic	Conor Kostick
Escape from Earth: New Adventures in Space	Jack Dann and Gardner Dozois, eds.
The Faery Reel: Tales from the Twilight Realm	Ellen Datlow and Terri Windling, eds.
The Far Side of Evil	Sylvia Engdahl
Firebirds: An Anthology of Original Fantasy and Science Fiction	Sharyn November, ed.
Firebirds Rising: An Anthology of Original Science Fiction and Fantasy	Sharyn November, ed.
Fire Bringer	David Clement-Davies
The Game	Diana Wynne Jones
Grass for His Pillow Episode One: Lord Fujiwara's Treasures	Lian Hearn
Grass for His Pillow Episode Two: The Way Through the Snow	Lian Hearn
The Green Man: Tales from the Mythic Forest	Ellen Datlow and Terri Windling, eds.
Growing Wings	Laurel Winter
Hannah's Garden	Midori Snyder
The Harp of the Grey Rose	Charles de Lint
The Hero and the Crown	Robin McKinley
The Hex Witch of Seldom	Nancy Springer

The Hidden Land	Pamela Dean
High Rhulain	Brian Jacques
House of Stairs	William Sleator
I Am Mordred	Nancy Springer
I Am Morgan Le Fay	Nancy Springer
Indigara	Tanith Lee
Ingledove	Marly Youmans
Interstellar Pig	William Sleator
Journey Between Worlds	Sylvia Engdahl
The Kestrel	Lloyd Alexander
The Kin	Peter Dickinson
The Legend of Luke	Brian Jacques
Loamhedge	Brian Jacques
The Long Patrol	Brian Jacques
Lord Brocktree	Brian Jacques
The Magic and the Healing	Nick O'Donohoe
Magic Lessons	Justine Larbalestier
Magic or Madness	Justine Larbalestier
Magic's Child	Justine Larbalestier
Mariel of Redwall	Brian Jacques
Marlfox	Brian Jacques
Martin the Warrior	Brian Jacques
Mattimeo	Brian Jacques
Mister Boots	Carol Emshwiller
Moon-Flash	Patricia A. McKillip
Mossflower	Brian Jacques
The Mount	Carol Emshwiller
The Neverending Story	Michael Ende
New Moon	Midori Snyder

Outcast of Redwall	Brian Jacques
The Outlaws of Sherwood	Robin McKinley
Parasite Pig	William Sleator
Pearls of Lutra	Brian Jacques
Piratica: Being a Daring Tale of a Singular Girl's Adventure Upon the High Seas	Tanith Lee
Piratica II: Return to Parrot Island	Tanith Lee
Primavera	Francesca Lia Block
Rakkety Tam	Brian Jacques
Ratha and Thistle-Chaser	Clare Bell
Ratha's Challenge	Clare Bell
Ratha's Creature	Clare Bell
Redwall	Brian Jacques
The Riddle of the Wren	Charles de Lint
Sadar's Keep	Midori Snyder
The Safe-Keeper's Secret	Sharon Shinn
Salamandastron	Brian Jacques
The Secret Country	Pamela Dean
Shadowmancer	G. P. Taylor
The Sight	David Clement-Davies
Singer	Jean Thesman
Singer in the Snow	Louise Marley
Singing the Dogstar Blues	Alison Goodman
The Son of Summer Stars	Meredith Ann Pierce
Spindle's End	Robin McKinley
Spirits That Walk in Shadow	Nina Kiriki Hoffman
A Stir of Bones	Nina Kiriki Hoffman

The Sunbird	Elizabeth E. Wein
Taggerung	Brian Jacques
Tam Lin	Pamela Dean
Tamsin	Peter S. Beagle
Tersias the Oracle	G. P. Taylor
The Tough Guide to Fantasyland	Diana Wynne Jones
Treasure at the Heart of the Tanglewood	Meredith Ann Pierce
Triss	Brian Jacques
The Truth-Teller's Tale	Sharon Shinn
Voyage of the Slaves	Brian Jacques
Waifs and Strays	Charles de Lint
Water: Tales of Elemental Spirits	Robin McKinley and Peter Dickinson
Waters Luminous and Deep: Shorter Fictions	Meredith Ann Pierce
Westmark	Lloyd Alexander
The Whim of the Dragon	Pamela Dean
The Winter Prince	Elizabeth E. Wein
Wolf Moon	Charles de Lint
Wolf Queen	Tanith Lee
Wolf Star	Tanith Lee
Wolf Tower	Tanith Lee
Wolf Wing	Tanith Lee
Wormwood	G. P. Taylor
Wren to the Rescue	Sherwood Smith
Wren's Quest	Sherwood Smith
Wren's War	Sherwood Smith

firebirds soaring

an anthology of original speculative fiction

edited by Sharyn November

decorations by Mike Dringenberg

FIREBIRD
AN IMPRINT OF PENGUIN GROUP (USA) INC.

FIREBIRD
Published by the Penguin Group
Penguin Group (USA) Inc., 345 Hudson Street, New York, New York 10014, USA
Penguin Group (Canada), 90 Eglinton Avenue East, Suite 700,
Toronto, Ontario, Canada M4P 2Y3 (a division of Pearson Penguin Canada Inc.)
Penguin Books Ltd, 80 Strand, London WC2R 0RL, England
Penguin Ireland, 25 St Stephen's Green, Dublin 2, Ireland (a division of Penguin Books Ltd)
Penguin Group (Australia), 250 Camberwell Road, Camberwell, Victoria 3124, Australia
(a division of Pearson Australia Group Pty Ltd)
Penguin Books India Pvt Ltd, 11 Community Centre,
Panchsheel Park, New Delhi – 110 017, India
Penguin Group (NZ), 67 Apollo Drive, Rosedale, North Shore 0632, New Zealand
(a division of Pearson New Zealand Ltd)
Penguin Books (South Africa) (Pty) Ltd, 24 Sturdee Avenue,
Rosebank, Johannesburg 2196, South Africa

Registered Offices: Penguin Books Ltd, 80 Strand, London WC2R 0RL, England

First published in the United States of America by Firebird,
an imprint of Penguin Group (USA) Inc., 2009

1 3 5 7 9 10 8 6 4 2

Introduction copyright © Sharyn November, 2009
Decorations copyright © Mike Dringenberg, 2009

"A Thousand Tails" copyright © Christopher Barzak, 2009; "Bonechewer's Legacy" copyright © Clare Bell, 2009; "Flatland" copyright © Kara Dalkey, 2009; "Dolly the Dog-Soldier" copyright © Candas Jane Dorsey, 2009; "The Dignity He's Due" copyright © Carol Emshwiller, 2009; "A Ticket to Ride" copyright © Nancy Farmer, 2009; "Something Worth Doing" copyright © Elizabeth Gatland, 2009; "The Ghosts of Strangers" copyright © Nina Kiriki Hoffman, 2009; "Singing on a Star" copyright © Ellen Klages, 2009; "Ferryman" copyright © Margo Lanagan, 2009; "Egg Magic" copyright © Louise Marley, 2009; "Fear and Loathing in Lalanna" copyright © Nick O'Donohoe, 2009; "All Under Heaven" copyright © Chris Roberson, 2009; "Court Ship" copyright © Sherwood Smith, 2009; "Kingmaker" copyright © Nancy Springer, 2009; "Little Red" copyright © Jane Yolen and Adam Stemple, 2009; "Three Twilight Tales" copyright © Jo Walton, 2009; "The Myth of Fenix" copyright © Laurel Winter, 2009; "Power and Magic" copyright © Marly Youmans, 2009

All rights reserved

CIP is available
Printed in the United States of America Set in Minister Light

Except in the United States of America, this book is sold subject to the condition that it shall not, by way of trade or otherwise, be lent, re-sold, hired out, or otherwise circulated without the publisher's prior consent in any form of binding or cover other than that in which it is published and without similar condition including this condition being imposed on the subsequent purchaser.

The publisher does not have any control over and does not assume any responsibility for author or third-party Web sites or their content.

for Lloyd and Janine Alexander

— I miss you —

contents

FIREBIRDS SOARING

Introduction

Here's a question: How does one write an introduction for the third anthology in an ongoing series?

If this is the first Firebird anthology you've read—welcome! If this is the second or the third—welcome back! Repeat readers already know the following:

- I hate reading introductions myself, so this will be short.
- I won't tell you anything about the stories.
- This book has been sequenced to allow you to read it all the way through in one sitting, although you probably won't.
- I want to hear from you, so my e-mail address is at the end.

But there's more to this book than four bullet points.

Each Firebird anthology sets the standard for the next, and, needless to say, each is a hard act to follow. This is the most substantial book yet. Its nineteen stories range in length from a few pages to almost one hundred; the settings range from 25,000,000 years ago to far in the future; and there are a number of stories that can't be classified as science fiction or fantasy, exactly. You might wonder why they're included. Simple. If someone has a wide range, I want to have the freedom to show it. It's more fun to blur the boundaries, anyway. Thus, the subtitle refers to "speculative fiction," which I consider more generous than "science fiction" or "fantasy."

The second bit of boundary blurring is visual. I asked the artist Mike Dringenberg if he'd like to be a part of the book, and to my delight he said yes. This meant that he became something of a collaborator; since he wanted to do "decorations" for each story, he read things right after I had selected them. More than a few times I was surprised by the images he'd chosen. But everyone sees a story differently, of course—especially a visual artist. (For those taking notes, he painted with powdered graphite mixed with water.)

You can't miss the third boundary blur—it's right in the middle of the book. If you've been keeping track of the list, you'll know that 2007 was Firebird's fifth anniversary, and we celebrated by publishing three short novels, each by one of Firebird's biggest names: Diana Wynne Jones, Tanith Lee, and Charles de Lint. Other people had written short novels, too; one of them was Nina Kiriki Hoffman, and I couldn't resist making it the centerpiece of *Firebirds Soaring*.

So what's next for Firebird? Well, more good books, of course—I am perennially looking for non-dystopian science fiction. Help me!—and more anthologies, if you'll have them, and surprises where I can fit them in.

Of course, I want to know what you think of *Firebirds*

Soaring. Please e-mail me at **firebird@us.penguingroup.com**. I actually do read all of the e-mail I receive and take your suggestions into account, so let me know what you think I should be publishing, what's missing in the marketplace, what we're doing right, and what we could do better. This is your imprint as much as anyone's, remember.

Speaking of which: you named this book. The acknowledgments in the back will tell you everyone who sent me *Firebirds Soaring* as a possible title. Thank you.

And, as always, thanks for reading Firebird books, and allowing me to publish more of them!

Sharyn November
January 2009

Nancy Springer

Kingmaker

Destiny, I discovered upon a fateful day in my fifteenth year, can manifest in small matters.

Tedious matters, even. In this instance, two clansmen arguing about swine.

Barefoot, in striped tunics and baggy breeches, glaring at each other as if they wore swords instead, the two of them stood before me where I sat upon my father's throne. "His accursed hogs rooted up the whole of my barley field," complained the one, "and there's much seed and labor gone to waste, and what are my children to eat this winter?"

"It could not have been my hogs," declared the other. "I keep iron rings in my pigs' snouts."

"Better you should keep your pigs, snouts and all, where they belong. It was your hogs, I'm telling you."

Outdoors, I thought with a sigh, the too-brief summer sun shone, and my father, High King Gwal Wredkyte, rode a-hawking with his great ger-eagle on his arm and his nephew,

Korbye, at his side. Meanwhile, in this dark-timbered hall, I held court of justice in my father's stead. No easy task, as I am neither the high king's son nor his heir; I am just his daughter.

My cousin Korbye is his heir.

But I could give judgment and folk would obey me, for I had been guiding my father's decisions since I was a little girl, sitting upon his knee as I advised him who was telling the truth and who was lying. In this I was never mistaken.

This is my uncanny gift, to know sooth. When I lay newly born, I have been told, an owl the color of gold appeared and perched on my cradle. Soundlessly out of nowhere the golden owl flew to me, gave me a great-eyed golden stare, and soundlessly back to nowhere it flew away, all within my mother's closed and shuttered chamber. "This child will not die, like the others," she had whispered from the bed, where she lay weak after childbirth. "This child will live, for the fates have plans for her."

If those plans were only that I should sit indoors, on an overlarge chair draped with the skins of wolf and bear, listening to shaggy-bearded men quarrel, I wished the fates had kept their gift.

The accused clansman insisted, "But it cannot have been my pigs! They can't root, not with rings the size of a warrior's armband through their noses."

"Are you telling me I'm blind? You think I don't know that ugly spotted sow of yours when I see her up to her ears in the soil I tilled? Your pigs destroyed my grain."

I asked the accuser, "Did you see any swine other than the spotted sow?"

"His sow destroyed my grain, then."

"Answer what I asked."

"No, I saw only the spotted sow. But—"

"But how could one sow root up the whole of a field by herself?" cried the other clansman. "With a ring in her snout? It could not be so, Wren!"

I scowled, clouds thickening in my already-shadowed temper. I possess a royal name—Vranwen Alarra of Wredkyte—yet everyone, from my father to the lowliest serving boy in his stronghold, calls me Wren. Everyone always has, I suppose because I am small and plain—brown hair, brown eyes, claydun skin—but plucky in my stubby little way. Although no one, obviously, is afraid of me, or they would not bespeak me so commonly.

"Wren, I am not a liar!" insisted the clansman with the ruined barley field.

I held up my hand to hush them. "You both speak the truth."

"What!" they exclaimed together.

"You are both honest." My sooth-sense told me that, as sometimes chanced in these quarrels, both men believed what they had said. "The real truth flies silent like an invisible owl on the air between you two."

"But—but . . ."

"How . . . ?"

But how to resolve the dispute? they meant.

Customarily, in order to pass judgment, I would have closed my eyes and cleared my mind until my sooth-sense caught hold of the unseen verity. But on this day, with my father and my cousin out riding in the sunshine, I shook my head. "I will sit in the shadows no longer. Come." I rose from the throne, beckoning dismissal to others hunkered against the stone walls; they could return on the morrow. "Show me this remarkable spotted sow."

Surely, striding out on the moors, I looked not at all like a scion of the high king, the sacred king, Gwal Wredkyte, earthly avatar of the sun. I, his daughter, wore only a simple shift of amber-and-brown plaid wool, and only ghillies, ovals of calfskin, laced around my feet. No golden torc, no silver lunula, nor am I royal of stature or of mien.

Nor did I care, for I felt like a scullery girl on holiday. Laughing, I ran along the heathery heights, gazing out upon vast sky and vast sea, breathing deeply of the salt-scented wind making wings of my hair.

"Take care, Wren," one of the clansmen called. "'Ware the cliff's edge."

He thought I had no more sense than a child? But my mood had turned so sunny that I only smiled and halted where I was, not so very near to where the heather ended, where sheer rocks plummeted to the breakers. Long ago, folk said, giants had carved these cliffs, playing, scooping up rocks and piling them into towers. Atop one such tower nearby balanced a stone the size of a cottage, rocking as gently as a cradle in the breeze that lifted my hair. It had teetered just so since time before time, since the giants had placed it there.

"Wren," urged the other clansman, "ye'll see my pigsty beyond the next rise."

Sighing, I followed.

KINGMAKER

A sturdy circle of stone it was, but no man has yet built a pen a hog cannot scramble out of. For this reason, and because swine require much feeding, customarily they roam from midden heap to midden heap, gobbling offal, with stout metal rings in their snouts to tug at their tender nostrils if they try to root. Otherwise, they would dig up every handsbreadth of land in search of goddess-knows-what, while the geese and sheep and cattle would have no grazing.

Laying my forearms atop the pigsty's stone wall, I looked upon the denizen.

The accused, doubly imprisoned. Tethered by a rope passed through the ring in her nose.

There she lay, a mountainous sow, unmistakable, as the complaining clansman had said, because of her bristly black skin splotched with rosettes of gray as if lichens grew on her. A great boulder of a sow, all mottled like a sable moon. Shrewd nosed and sharp eared, with flinty eyes she peered back at me.

I felt the force of something fey in her stare.

Almost whispering, I bespoke her courteously, asking her as if she could answer me, "Are you the old sow who eats her farrow?" For such was one of the forms of the goddess, the dark-of-the-moon sow who gives birth to a litter, then devours her young.

I sensed how the clansmen glanced at each other askance.

The great pig growled like a mastiff.

The clansman who owned her cleared his throat, then said, "You see the ring in her nose, Wren?"

"Yes. She looks disgruntled." Still oddly affected, off

balance, I tried to joke, for a *gruntle* is a pig's snout—the part that grunts—so *disgruntled* could mean a hog with its nose out of joint, as might be expected when a ring of iron—

I stared at the ring in the sow's snout, all jesting forgotten.

No ordinary swine-stopper, this. Despite its coating of mud, I saw flattened edges and spiral ridges like those of a torc.

"Where did you come by that ring?" I demanded of the owner.

"Digging turf one day, I found it in the ground. She needed a new one, hers was rusting to bits, so—"

"I want to see it. Come here, sow." Reaching for the rope that tied her, I tugged.

"She won't move for anything less than a pan of buttermilk."

But as if to make a liar of him after all, the sow heaved herself up and walked to me.

Reaching over the stone wall, with both hands I spread the ring and took it from her snout, feeling my heartbeat hasten; in my grasp the ring felt somehow willful, inert yet alive. It bent to my touch, so I fancied, gladly, then restored itself to a perfect circle after I had freed it from the pig and from the rope.

Still with both hands, as if lifting an offering to the goddess, I held the dirt-caked circle up in the sunlight, looking upon it. Pitted and stained it was, but not with rust. Rather, with antiquity.

"That's no ring of *iron*, fool," said the complaining clansman to the other one.

"Some softer metal," I agreed before they could start

quarreling again. And although my heart beat hard, I made as light of the matter as I could, slipping the ring into the pouch of leather that hung at my waist, at the same time feeling for a few coppers. I would gladly have given gold for that ring, but to do so would have excited the jealousy of the other clansman and caused too much talk. So with, I hoped, the air of one settling a matter of small importance, I handed threepence to the sow's owner and told him, "Get a proper ring to put in her snout. Then she will trouble your neighbor no more." To the other man, also, I gave a few pence, saying, "If your children grow hungry this winter, tell me and I will see that you have barley to eat."

Then I left them, striding home as if important business awaited me at the stronghold.

In no way could they imagine how important.

All the rest of that day I closeted myself in my chamber, with the door closed and barred, while I soaked the ring in vinegar, scrubbed it with sweet rushes, coaxed grime from its surface with a blunt bodkin, until finally by sunset glow I examined it: a simple but finely wrought thing made not of iron or copper or silver or gold, but of some metal that lustered even more precious, with a soft shifting green-gray glow, like moonlight on the sea. Some ancient metal I did not know—perhaps orichalcum? Perhaps this had been an armband for some queen of Atlantis? Or perhaps a finger ring of some giant who had long ago walked the heath and built towers of stone?

Such an ancient thing possessed its own mystery, its own power.

Or so my mind whispered.

Was I a seer as well as a soothsayer? The odd sort of recognition I had felt upon seeing the black moon-mottled sow had occurred within me at intervals all my life, although never before had I truly acknowledged it. Or acted upon it.

Perhaps I was an oracle. Druids said that the wren, the little brown bird that had fetched fire down from the sun for the first woman, possessed oracular powers.

I should feel honored to be called Wren, my mother had often told me while she still lived, for the wren is the most beloved of birds. It is a crime to harm a wren or even disturb a wren's nest. Except—this my mother did not say, but I knew, for I had seen—once a year, at the winter solstice, the boys would go out hunting for wrens, and the first lad to kill one was declared king for the day. They would troop from cottage to cottage, accepting gifts of food and drink, with the mock king in the fore carrying the dead wren. Then they would go in procession to the castle, and the real king would come out with the golden torc around his neck; the dead wren would be fastened atop an oaken pole, its little corpse wreathed with mistletoe, and a druid would carry it thus on high while the king rode behind with his thanes and retainers in cavalcade. Therefore the wren was called the kingmaker.

As I thought this, glad shouts sounded from the courtyard below: "High king! High king!" Gwal Wredkyte and his heir Korbye and their royal retinue had returned from hawking.

Although I seldom adorned myself, this day I took off my simple shift and put on a gown of heavy white silk edged with lambswool black and gray. I brushed my hair and plaited it and encased the ends of the braids in clips of gold. I placed upon my head a golden fillet. Around my neck I hung a silver lunula, emblem of the goddess.

For a long time I looked at myself in my polished bronze mirror that had been Mother's before she died.

Finally I took my newfound treasure—a ring the size of a warrior's armband, just as the black sow's owner had said—and I slipped it onto my left arm up to my elbow, where it hid itself beneath the gown's wide sleeve.

Then I went down to dine with my father and my cousin.

I found them in the best of spirits.

"Wren!" My father stood up, tall and kingly, his bronze beard shining in the torchlight, to greet me with a kiss.

"Cousin," declared Korbye, rising also, with equal courtesy if less enthusiasm. A comely lout accustomed to having his way with any maiden he fancied, he took it ill that his gallantries could not deceive me. Nevertheless, he held my chair and saw me seated at the small table on the dais, apart from the long ones down below where castle folk ate by the dozen. All could see the high king and his family, but none could hear what we said.

While the three of us ate mutton soup, pork in currant sauce, and oat scones with gooseberry jam, Korbye and Father told me of hawking, how well the ger-eagle had flown, and how Korbye's goshawk had taken a brace of hares. Not until the cheese and biscuits were served did Father ask me, "And what heard you today in the court of justice?"

"Little enough. A matter of swine."

A matter of a nose ring that had, I suspected, empowered

an old sow mottled like a black moon to destroy an entire field of barley.

In other words, to do what would otherwise have been impossible.

Facing the high king across the table, I drew a deep breath, looked into his eyes, and spoke: "Father, if your only living child were a son instead of a daughter, would he be your heir?"

And even as he opened his mouth to reply, my heart began to beat like a war drum, hard and fierce and triumphant, for yes, yes, it was true, the ancient ring thing hidden under my sleeve endowed me with a new kind of power: not just power to know truth, but also power to impose my will.

This I knew because my father, High King Gwal Wredkyte, answered me like a servant, whereas he should have rebuked me most angrily for asking such an impudent question at such an ill-chosen time. He should have risen and roared and ordered me to leave the table. But instead, without so much as lifting his eyebrows, he replied, "It is the custom that the king's sister's son should be his heir."

Indeed, such was the very old tradition, a reminder of the time when kinship was reckoned through the woman. But now that men also laid claim to their children, this ancient way of thinking no longer held force of law.

I demanded of my father, "And to this custom you cleave?"

"Yes."

He lied.

My sooth-sense told me: if I were a boy instead of a girl, I would be the next high king.

But letting no emotion show in my face, I nodded and turned to my cousin, the sister-son, the chosen one. "Korbye," I asked him, "when you are king, will you think more of the clansfolks' well-being or of your own pleasure?"

And quite tamely, as if I sat in judgment and he stood before me, he answered, "Of course I will consider always first and foremost the needs of my clans, my people."

He lied.

He would consider always first and foremost his own greed.

Why, then, should he be high king after my father?

Why not I? With this ring of power on my arm, I could make my father do as I pleased. I could claim the throne. I could be the first high queen, Vranwen Alarra of Wredkyte, earthly avatar of the moon, and no one would ever again dare to cry at me, "Wren *this*" and "Wren *that*." Embodiment of the goddess, I would rule my people for their own good. I would rid the clans of brigands and thieves, lying snakes such as Korbye—

Kill him?

Yes.

How best to have it done? Behead him?

Too noble.

Hang him?

Too gentle.

Torture first. The thumbscrews, the rack. Next, burn him at the stake or rend him limb from limb with horses—

And then such horror shook me that I am sure it showed on my face, for never before had such fancies manifested in me.

Enormities.

Cold as the moon.

My own thoughts unnerved me so that I leapt up from my unfinished dinner. Gasping, "Excuse me," I fled.

Through the dark-timbered doorway to the shadowy courtyard I ran, across the cobbles to the postern gate, out of my father's stronghold and away across the moors to the same place I had visited so sunnily earlier that same day, at the edge of the sea cliff.

There I halted, panting.

Not far away stood the tower of stone with the huge boulder rocking as gently as a cradle atop it.

Overhead a full moon swam like a swan amid scudding clouds. The sea wind blew strong, lifting my gown's wide sleeves as if I might take flight. Below, the breakers roared, gleaming silver-green in the moonbeams.

I snatched from my arm the ring of that same sheen, the color of the moonlit sea. I lifted that circle of mystery metal in both hands, presenting it to the goddess in the sky. Surrounding her, it shone like her dark and hollow sister.

It called to me.

My horror had passed, seeming of no account. More than ever, I yearned to cherish my treasure and be powerful. Destiny had given this ring to me to make me a queen.

"Wren?"

A man's voice, behind me. Turning, lowering my arms, I knew who it was.

"Father."

He strode forward to stand beside me, shining golden even in the silver moonlight. Quite gently he asked, "What is that you held up to the sky?"

I gripped the ring with both hands. Instead of answering my father's question, I said harshly, "Korbye should not be king."

"Why so?"

"He lied. He cares only for himself."

"Granted, he is a greedy young boar hog now, but do you not think he will change as he grows older?"

"Think you so?"

If he had said yes, he would have spoken untruth, and he did not dare. He did not know any longer what I would do, whether I might call him liar to his face. He knew only that something had vastly changed, and he guessed why.

He said, "Give me that thing you are holding."

"No." I stepped away from him so that he could not seize the ring.

Never in my life had I defied him so.

Always in his kiss on my face I had felt approval for my obedience.

Which did not necessarily mean that he loved me.

Or that he would not kill me if I threatened his power.

He scowled fit to darken the moonlight. With perilous softness he addressed me. "Wren—"

"Vranwen," I ordered, clutching the ring, feeling its chill metal awake and puissant in my grasp. "I am Vranwen Alarra."

I think he tried to stride toward me but could not move.

He gasped as if something strangled him. Three times he drew choking breath before he whispered in a ragged voice, "Vranwen Alarra, guard that ring well if you wish to keep your life."

"Seize it!" shouted another voice. Korbye's. He lunged from where he had been hiding, listening, in the shadow of the stone tower.

And because I had not known he was there, because I had not turned the force of my will upon him, he could have done as he said. Before I could face him he leapt toward me—

Then without making a sound as it left its perch, as silently as an owl in flight, the giant boulder stooped from atop the tower of rock.

Fell.

Thudded down upon him.

Flattened him within an eyeblink. Took him. No part of him to be seen ever again.

For all mortal purposes, Korbye was no more.

Father stood as if he himself had turned into a tower of stone. And I heard a sound like the harsh cry of a sea hawk. Maybe from him. Maybe also from me.

I know not how long we stood like wood before Father whispered, "Daughter, did you wish this?"

"No."

"Did you—power of that ring—"

"It acted of its own will." And in that moment I knew what it might make of me.

An avatar of the moon goddess, yes. One of whose forms was that of a black sow who devoured her own newborn babies.

Trembling, I flung the ring away. Off the cliff. Into the roaring, all-grasping breakers of the sea.

There I knew it would be safe. The sea needed no more power than it already possessed. Indifferent, it would drop the ring somewhere and forget it.

I turned, once more only a stubby dun-skinned girl named Wren.

Standing at the cliff's edge, I said to my father, "Kill me if you will."

He faced me for a long moment before he said softly, "Daughter, I could never do you harm."

I breathed out.

"But there is a fate on you that may kill you yet," he said, his voice as taut as a war drum's stretched dry pigskin. "What is it, my daughter? You wish to rule after I am gone?"

I shook my head. "Should I attempt it, some clan chief will slay me and take the throne." Just as someone might well have slain me for the sake of the ring.

"What then? What is this destiny that mantles you?"

I closed my eyes and let my mind search the night for the invisible sooth. And I found it.

Indeed, I thought as I opened my eyes, I should have known it before.

Slowly, gazing upon my father's sober face, I told him, "I am to be your kingmaker."

On the moonlit heather a shadow moved. I looked up: low over my head an owl flew. Just an ordinary brown owl, most likely. I barely glimpsed it before it disappeared.

At the same time something invisible winged between

my father and me, some understanding beyond words but not beyond awe.

And fear. Great fear.

But I loved my father. I whispered, "Somewhere, growing pure like a golden rose in some hidden place, there is a true chosen one who should rule after you. I will quest for him. And I will find him for you."

And also for myself, for he would be my prince, my true love, and I would wed him even though I knew that thereby death awaited me. As clearly as if I saw it in a mirror of polished silver, I knew that on the day they placed the golden torc of the high king on his neck, I would die. In childbirth. Of a daughter, who would someday be high queen.

Yet this was what I knew I must do. I told my father, "I will find him even if it means the oaken staff and the crown of mistletoe."

But Gwal Wredkyte did not, after all, completely understand, for he protested, "Some sacrifice, you mean, Wren? But already you have sacrificed—"

I took his arm, clinging to the warmth of his love, yet turning him away from the cliff's edge, guiding him past the boulder hunkering nearby like a mountainous dark sow wallowing in the night. "Bah. Nonsense," I told him. "I have sacrificed nothing. That thing I threw away was best worthy to adorn the gruntle of a pig."

NANCY SPRINGER is closing in on the fifty-book milestone, having written just about that many novels for adults, young adults, and children, in genres including contemporary fiction, magical realism, suspense, and mystery—but her first fictional efforts were set in imaginary worlds, and writing mythological fantasy remains her first love. Just to make life a bit more like fiction, she has recently moved from her longtime residence in Pennsylvania to an isolated area of the Florida Panhandle, where she lives in a hangar at a small, reptile-prone airport in the wetlands.

Visit her Web site at **www.nancyspringer.net**.

AUTHOR'S NOTE

Oh, give me a home where the water snakes roam, where the pilots and the alligators play. . . .

But "Kingmaker" was written years before any of that happened. The story developed from a fortunate fusion of a daydream I'd been having ever since my divorce—a fantasy about magically knowing whether people are telling the truth or lying; gee, wonder where that came from—and my long-time interest in legend and mythology, particularly Celtic. Too disorganized and enjoyable to be called research, my reading takes in many things odd and antique, such as the usages of nose rings in swine.

Given my Celtic bias, in "Kingmaker," the setting is sort of Welsh, almost Tintagel, with the crashing sea, the cliffs, the huge rocks left behind by playful giants, the logan stone balanced and rocking atop its pillar. I can't think of any detail in the story, including the sister-son as heir or the moon mythology of the old sow who eats her farrow, that did not come straight out of some nonfiction book I'd read sometime in the past, um, forty years. The legend of the wren is straight out of—somewhere; it's beyond me at this point to give credit where credit is due.

I can credit myself only with naming my youthful protagonist Wren, giving her the gift to know sooth, placing her in the judgment chair of her father the high king, and staying out of the story's way. In other words, don't ask me, I just live here. Now reading up on boiled peanuts, blue-tailed skinks, Catahoula curs, bromeliads, cottonmouth moccasins. Whatever.

Nancy Farmer

A Ticket to Ride

The lights in the library flicked on and off, and Jason knew it was time to go. The librarians already had their coats on. One of them, Mike, was waiting impatiently at the door.

Mike patrolled the stacks, pouncing on readers with cell phones or those who had too many books piled in front of them. "You're making work for the staff," Mike would say accusingly. "We have to reshelve those, you know." He prowled the library like a guilty conscience, taking books on sex away from teenagers, removing large-print novels from readers who had perfectly good eyesight, and evicting homeless people from the restroom.

Mike stood at the door with his keys. Jason slunk past, avoiding eye contact. He knew he was out after curfew and that Mike had the right to call the police. Twelve-year-olds weren't supposed to be on the street. But Jason had learned how to creep into his group home after hours. If he was lucky, he would miss getting beaten up by the older boys.

Rain was pouring down outside, and Jason pulled the hood of his poncho over his head. He knew he looked weird with his skinny arms and legs and the backpack of books sticking out like a hump. But the books were more important to him than anything. If need be, he would wrap the poncho around them and let himself get soaked.

He saw a dark shape under a tree and prepared to flee—but it was only old Shin Bone bedding down for the night. The hobo spent his days on the lawn of the public library, playing a flute and stopping people for conversation. He treated Jason seriously, speaking to him adult to adult, and the boy liked him.

Jason suddenly became aware that Shin Bone hadn't put up his tent. The rain had overflowed the gutters and the lawn was flooded. The old man lay in the water like a stone in a river.

"Wake up!" shouted Jason. He grabbed the old man's coat and tried to rouse him. A light in the library switched off. Now all the boy could see was the slick of a streetlamp reflected on the rain-filled gutter. Shin Bone's chest heaved and his breath rattled in his throat.

Jason ran to the library door. It was dark inside, but he pounded on it anyway. Mike was always the last one out, and he didn't go until he'd checked the locks. "Mike! Mike!" screamed Jason. After a long moment a light came on and the surly librarian approached the window by the door.

"I'm calling the cops," he said, his voice muffled.

"Yes! Call the cops! Call an ambulance! Shin Bone's dying!"

For a moment Jason was afraid the librarian wouldn't do anything, but at last he said, "Oh, bother," and picked up a phone.

The boy went back to Shin Bone, wishing Mike would open the door and help drag the old hobo inside. But perhaps it was dangerous to move him. Jason didn't know. He held the man's hand and felt a slight squeeze. "The ambulance is coming," he told him. "They'll fix you up. Just hang in there." Jason heard a siren wail in the distance.

A scrap of paper floated down the gutter, winking and turning in the light of the streetlamp. Points of light fizzed all around it like bubbles in a glass of soda. Jason felt a whisper of alarm.

It washed out of the gutter and swirled across the lawn. Jason reached for it and then drew back his hand. He didn't like the paper. It was up to no good, moving like a live thing, coming straight at them. It slid past his legs, turned two or three times in an eddy, and made its way to Shin Bone's side. The old man, with great effort, moved his hand. "I'll get it for you," said Jason, picking the paper out of the water.

The fire engine roared into the parking lot, sending out a tidal wave of water. The fire department was always the first at an emergency. The cops would be next, followed by the ambulance. Jason had seen the procedure at the group home, when someone had a drug overdose or got stabbed. He scrambled out of the way as the firemen bent over Shin Bone.

Mike came out of the library carrying a large black umbrella.

He could have done that before, Jason said to himself, thinking of the rain pouring down on the old man's face. The firemen were pressing on Shin Bone's chest. They shone a bright light on him and one of them shook his head. Then the police arrived.

"That's the boy who found him," Mike said, pointing at Jason. "It wouldn't surprise me if he was going through the tramp's pockets."

Jason was both shocked and outraged. He'd never stolen anything from the library. He'd kept every one of their rules, not even returning a book late. The library meant too much to him, the only place that was safe and warm, where he didn't have to constantly look over his shoulder.

"Hey! I know you," the cop said. "You're from that group home—"

Jason ran. It was a split-second decision and he regretted it at once, but by then it was too late. Once you ran, you were already guilty. You'd be sent to Juvenile Hall, where the boys were bigger and hit harder.

Jason climbed over a fence with the cop yelling at him to stop. He tore his plastic poncho and had to throw it away. He wriggled out of the backpack and the books splashed into a puddle. Now he'd never be able to go back to the library. He almost ran into the arms of another cop waiting at the other end of an alley. Fear gave him a burst of speed. He zigzagged, leaped a ditch, scrambled over a hedge—

—and found himself in a vast empty field. Jason was so

startled he skidded to a stop. He listened. There were no pounding steps behind him and no shouts. He couldn't even hear the rain because it had stopped raining. The sky had not a single cloud in it and was lit by a moon so bright it was slightly frightening. Jason had never seen such a moon.

In the middle of the field was an old-fashioned train. Steam hissed around its wheels and the clock-face of the engine, glowing in the brilliant moonlight, trembled with heat. The engine huffed gently as if talking to itself. It rolled slowly past and stopped.

Directly in front of Jason was a boxcar with the doors open on either side so that he could look through. He approached it cautiously. The floor was piled with what appeared to be empty flour sacks, and the space inside had a neat, comfortable look about it. It felt safe, as the library did when Jason had a good book and a whole afternoon before him. Almost without thinking, he climbed in and lay down on one of the heaps, pulling a flour sack over him for warmth. Soon he was fast asleep.

The engine quivered. The whistle gave a short, soft call, and the wheels began to turn. The train moved out. Long, low, and mournful it sang through the canyons of the city, past shopping malls and apartment buildings, until it reached the wilderness beyond.

Jason sat up. Sunlight was streaming into the side of the boxcar, and the wheels were going *clickety-clack* at great speed. Outside, a desert stretched away to distant purple mountains. At the far end of the car two men were playing poker, using beans instead of chips. One had a broken nose and the ruddy face of an alcoholic; the other resembled a wrestler Jason had seen on TV. They looked up at him at the same time.

"Feeling rested?" said the one with the broken nose.

Jason looked around frantically for a rock or some other weapon. In his experience, such men meant trouble.

"We let you sleep," the wrestler said. "You looked like death warmed up last night."

"Yeah, death warmed up." The other man chuckled. "But we've got to ask you questions now."

"Don't come near me!" cried Jason, inching toward the door.

"Whoa! Don't go there," said the wrestler, bounding over to pull the boy back from the edge. He carried him easily to the poker game, paying no attention to the blows and kicks Jason gave him.

"Settle down, kid. Haven't you seen a guardian angel before?" said the man with the broken nose. He swept the beans into a Mason jar and screwed on the top. "The kidney beans are worth a dollar, the pintos five, and the limas ten," he explained without being asked.

Jason crouched on the floor, sweating. "You don't look like guardian angels."

"That's because we watch over Shin Bone. These are the shapes he's comfortable with. Normally, we look like this." The wrestler turned into a towering Presence in a white robe, with huge, rainbow-colored wings sweeping from one end of the boxcar to the other. In fact, he looked *exactly* like the stained-glass window in the cathedral near Jason's group home. The boy covered his face and when he looked again, the wrestler was back.

"W-well," Jason said, trying not to be afraid, "If y-you're Shin Bone's guardian angels, you did a rotten job last night."

"See, that's what we've got to discuss," said the man with the broken nose. "By the way, my name's Chicago Danny, and that's Three Aces over there. We watch over people for the years allotted to them, and when their time's up, we call them home. Shin Bone was supposed to board the train last night."

"Only you showed up instead," said Three Aces. "I assume you have his ticket."

"Ticket?" Jason said faintly. He felt in his pants' pocket and pulled out the rectangle of paper with light fizzing around the edges. TICKET TO RIDE, it said in swirling gold letters, and in finer print, ONE WAY.

"Thought so," said Chicago Danny. "Problem is, it isn't yours."

"I didn't steal it!" Jason protested.

"Never said you did, but it puts us in a pretty pickle. Why don't you explain how it happened."

And so Jason told them about the storm and finding the old man under the tree, the scrap of paper floating down the gutter, and how he ran from the cops. "Can't we return and fix things up?" he asked.

"That's a one-way ticket," Three Aces pointed out. "Most trains go farther and farther into the past, until the bearer finds the place he was completely happy. That's where he stays."

"I can't remember ever being happy," said Jason, and he wasn't angling for sympathy. It was simply true. He'd been born addicted to crack and placed in one foster home after another. No one wanted him because he wasn't cute. As he grew older, he learned to spread his own misery around to make others unhappy. And he *did* steal, no matter what he told the angels, only not library books. That was how he'd ended up in the group home, one step away from Juvenile Hall. His life had been bad experience after bad experience, and there wasn't a bit of it he wanted to repeat.

"You're not reliving your past because that's not your ticket," explained Chicago Danny. "You're going to where Shin Bone was happy. Looks like the first stop is the town of Amboy."

The train pulled to a halt next to a cluster of houses and businesses. They got out and went into a café. Cowboys, truck drivers, and families on vacation crowded into booths with yellow plastic tables and vases full of yellow plastic flowers. A juke box played in a corner, with globes of colored light rippling around its edges.

"What'll ya have, gents?" said the waitress, pencil poised over an order pad.

"I don't have money," Jason whispered to Chicago Danny.

"Sure you do. Look in your pocket," the angel said. Jason pulled out a dollar bill.

"I'll, uh, I'll have a hamburger and a slice of apple pie—

with ice cream," Jason added, daringly. He was sure he didn't have enough money, but the hamburger turned out to cost thirty-five cents and the pie *with* ice cream was only twenty-five. He looked out the window and saw a car with enormous tail fins, and chrome just about everywhere you could put chrome, pull up. A man Jason had seen only on midnight television got out.

"Isn't that . . . ?" He hesitated.

"Elvis," Three Aces said.

"But isn't he . . . ?"

"Dead? Sure, and so is this town. They built the new freeway on the other side of those mountains, and one by one the businesses folded up. You're seeing Amboy as it was when Shin Bone was here. This was one of the best days of his life."

Elvis came in, and since all the other tables were full, he asked if he could sit with Jason and the angels. "*Sure*," said Jason, thrilled beyond belief. He sat in a happy daze as Elvis ate three slices of pie with ice cream.

But it seemed this wasn't the final destination for the train. Its whistle blew long and lonesome, and Jason, Chicago Danny, and Three Aces climbed aboard.

The next stop was Yuma, where they attended a rodeo and Jason rode a bronco for three minutes and won a prize. Then they went to Albuquerque and New Orleans, followed the Mississippi River up to St. Louis, and turned right to get to Chicago. "My town," said Chicago Danny, "when I was alive."

It was there Shin Bone had had the accident that ended

his career. He'd been a fireman for the railroad. "He was the best," Three Aces said. "He should have been promoted to engineer, but in those days a black man couldn't get that job. One night he fell between two cars that were being coupled and got his leg smashed."

"But he kept riding the rails," said Chicago Danny. "Once you get that wandering spirit, it never goes away."

At each stop Jason had a wonderful time, but sooner or later, no matter how much fun he was having, he would feel restless. He wanted to see what was around the next bend, over the next hill, beyond the horizon. Then Jason and the angels would get back on the train and travel on. Until they got to the farmhouse.

It was a rickety, falling-down structure at the bottom of a deep valley. Rows of scraggly corn grew next to lima beans, broad beans, and tomatoes. Chickens pecked their way through the vegetables, and a mangy hound lay on the porch. She looked up and thumped her bony tail.

"How can she know me?" whispered the boy.

"She knows Shin Bone," replied Chicago Danny. "He loved that dog Beauty, and when she died, he was heartbroken."

"I thought this was supposed to be a happy memory."

"This is *before*."

And now a skinny black woman came out onto the porch, followed by four raggedy kids and a pair of men, followed by a very old man and three more women with three more children, not counting the baby one of them carried.

"They can't *all* live in that shack," Jason said.

"They can and do," said Three Aces.

"Shin Bone!" the people called from the porch. "You've come home at last! We're all so glad to see you!"

"I'm not him," Jason said, shrinking against Chicago Danny. "I'm not even the right color."

"They see what they hope to see. Now run along and make them happy," said the angel. So Jason was swept into the middle of Shin Bone's family, and they made a big fuss over him. They fed him corn pone and fatback and many other things he'd never heard of but that tasted good. Best of all were the long, lazy evenings when everyone crowded together to tell stories. And nobody was left out, not even the great grandma, who never left her bed and who you had to shout at because she was deaf.

One night, very late, Jason sat on the porch with Beauty. Stars filled the gap between the mountains on either side. Mockingbirds sang as they did on warm nights, for it was summer here and had been for years. Jason heard, far off, coming through the mountains, the long, low whistle of a train.

He stood up as it chuffed to a halt, gave Beauty a last friendly pat, and climbed into the boxcar.

"Welcome back," said Chicago Danny from the shadows.

"We were counting on you," said Three Aces. The train went off through the mountains, away from the dog, the farmhouse, and Shin Bone's family sleeping inside.

"Counting on me for what?" asked Jason.

"To put things right. You see, most people travel only one way. They go into the past until they find the best time of their lives and there they stay. But not Shin Bone and not you. You're just naturally restless. You're happiest *on* the train, looking for what's around the next bend."

"What if I hadn't got restless?" Jason said.

"The train would never have returned."

Again they crisscrossed America, finding stops they hadn't seen before and revisiting some of the others. Clothing fashions changed; cars got longer, sprouted tail fins, and shrank again; the blue light of television flicked on behind window shades. And one night they pulled up in front of the library. The windows were dark, and frost covered the grass. Shin Bone stood under his favorite tree, waiting.

"What've you been doing since we left?" asked Jason, glad to see the old hobo look so healthy and happy.

"Haunting the library," admitted Shin Bone. "That's what happens to people who lose their ticket. They become ghosts. I amused myself by hiding in the stacks and flushing toilets. Mike drove himself crazy trying to catch me, but he never did. He's in a nice rest home now, I hear."

"I guess this is yours," Jason said regretfully, holding out the ticket.

"What are you going to do now?"

"Oh . . . I don't know." Jason looked at the dark city all around, at the ice coating the dark street. He had no idea how long he'd been gone or what would happen when he returned to the group home.

"Why don't you come with me?" suggested Shin Bone.

"I don't have a ticket."

The old man grinned. "I've been riding boxcars for fifty

years and never once—not once!—did I have a ticket. Stick with me, kid, and we'll go places."

They both climbed onto the train. "You made it!" hollered Chicago Danny, slapping Shin Bone on the back.

"Welcome home," cried Three Aces. "Just look at that view!"

The train picked up speed, and the countryside rolled by like life itself, field after valley after mountain range, with here and there the lights of a small farm. The air rushed past, scented with pine needles and sage.

"It never disappoints," said Shin Bone as the whistle sang its way through the sleeping towns and cities of America.

Nancy Farmer grew up in a hotel on the Mexican border. As an adult, she joined the Peace Corps and went to India to teach chemistry and run a chicken farm. Among other things, she has lived in a commune of hippies in Berkeley, worked on an oceanographic vessel, and run a chemistry lab in Mozambique. She has published six novels, four picture books, and six short stories. Her books have won three Newbery Honors, the National Book Award, the Commonwealth Club of California Book Silver Medal for Juvenile Literature, and the Michael L. Printz Honor Award. Her Web site is **www.nancyfarmerbooks.com**.

Author's Note

"A Ticket to Ride" was inspired by an elderly homeless man who camps outside our local library. He is clean and well spoken, doesn't take drugs or drink alcohol. Most of the time he lies in wait for library patrons because he loves talking and can do it for hours. But there is nothing wrong with his sanity. "Shin Bone" (not his real name) is simply one of those people who can't live too close to others. He has to be outdoors and he needs total freedom. He would have been perfectly happy living in the Stone Age, and I find him thoroughly admirable.

Christopher Barzak

a THOUSAND taiLs

When I was five years old, my mother gave me a silver ball and said, "Midori chan, my little *kitsune*, don't let Father know about this. He'd take it from you to sell it, but it's yours, my little fox girl. It's yours, and now you can learn how to take care of yourself."

"You mean I can learn how to take care of the ball," I said. Even then I was not polite as I was supposed to be. I was a girl who corrected her mother.

"No, no," said my mother. "So you can learn how to take care of yourself. That's what I said, didn't I?" She swatted a fly buzzing near her nose and it fell to the floor, stunned by the impact, next to her bare foot. The next moment she crushed it beneath her heel and continued. "A fox always takes care of itself by taking care of its silver ball. Don't you remember the stories I've told you? Well, I'll tell them again, my little one. So listen and you'll know what I mean."

My mother had always called me her fox girl, had always told me she'd found me wandering in the woods and brought me home with her. Father would laugh and say, "Your mother is always bringing home lost creatures. Soon we'll be keeping a zoo!" He'd stroked the back of my head like I sometimes saw him pet our cats: one long stroke and a quick pat to send me off again.

As a child I was often confused by the things my mother said and did, but it didn't bother me. It felt natural that life was mysterious and that my mother hid her meaning behind a veil of stories, as if her words were water through which truth shimmered and splintered like the beams of the rising sun. She taught me that some matters have no clear way to explain their meaning to others.

Children at school often remarked on her. How strange your mother is, they told me. And how alike the two of us were. "Why does your mother speak to herself? Why does she sometimes laugh at nothing? Is she crazy?" a small group once asked me at recess, forming a circle around me. "Why do you sit in class and stare out the window while we're playing *karuta* or Fruit Basket? Why don't you talk to us, Midori? What's the matter? Don't you like people?"

To tell the truth, they were correct. I was a strange child, and they sensed it. It was because, even then, people seemed so odd to me in their single-minded concerns and simple pleasures. I did not know at the time why, at the age of five—at an age before the world had had time to inflict many wounds on me—I felt this way. Somehow, though, I felt somewhere a world existed that was my true home, not the rice fields or the gray mountainsides in the distance, not the rivers and the fishermen standing along their banks, not the dusty fields where other children played games during afternoon recess, not the farm on which I was being raised, not the little town of Ami. And it was not that I felt I belonged in a radiant, carnivalesque city like Tokyo either. It was that I somehow knew I simply did not belong with people.

I knew all that at the age of five. But it was at nine years old that I discovered my true being in this world.

In fourth grade we read a book called *Gongitsune*. This is an honorable way of spelling and saying the name of the fox, the *kitsune*. Many of the new *kanji* we were learning that month were in this tale, and beside each new character the publisher had printed small *hiragana*, the simpler alphabet, to guide us to the right sound and meaning. I didn't need *hiragana* as much as the others, though. *Kanji* was easy for me. When *sensei* introduced new characters, it seemed I could look at them and, almost by magic, they would reveal their meanings to me, yet one more reason for my classmates to be suspicious. So when *sensei* gave us this story, I read for pleasure, I read without having to study our new words.

Gongitsune is about a little motherless fox named Gon, who finds a small village while he is out looking for food and begins to steal from the villagers. One day Gon steals an eel from a man named Hyoju. The eel was supposed to be for Hyoju's sick old mother. And because Gon stole the mother's meal, the old woman dies. When Gon discovers the consequence of his actions, he tries to repent by secretly giving things he steals from other villagers to Hyoju. But the villagers see that Hyoju has their things and they beat him up, thinking he's the thief. From then on, Gon only brings Hyoju mushrooms and nuts from the forest. Hyoju is grateful, but doesn't know who brings him the gifts, or why. Then one day he sees a fox in the woods and, remembering the fox that stole the eel for his dying mother, he shoots, and Gon dies. It's only afterward, when the gifts of mushrooms and nuts stop showing up on his doorstep, that he realizes it was Gon who had been bringing them all along.

"And what is the moral of this story?" our *sensei* asked after we finished our reading.

We waited with our eyes open, our mouths sealed tight. We knew that she would deliver the answer the very next moment, that our input was not important.

"The moral is that there is an order to the world, that everything is as it is for a reason. Gon's mother dies, Hyoju's mother dies, Gon is shot while he tries to make amends for his mistakes, and Hyoju feels guilty after realizing he's killed the creature that's been helping him. But nothing can be done about this. Everyone must accept their own fate."

We stayed silent. A few children nodded. But I didn't like what the *sensei* said. I didn't think the story was about accepting fate. I thought it was about how stupid Hyoju was for not trying to find out who was leaving mushrooms and nuts. Gon wasn't that clever really. Hyoju, if he wanted to know, could have discovered Gon at any time. Instead he chose the human way. He chose the path humans almost always choose. The path of ignorance.

Poor Gon, I thought as I sat at my desk. *Poor little fox.* I stroked the picture of him struck down by stupid Hyoju's bullet, his fur glowing white as moonlight.

And there, in that moment, I realized it was Gon's tribe that I belonged to, not the human family. I was a *kitsune*, I realized. I was a fox.

Every *kitsune* has a silver ball that contains part of its essence. Why hadn't I understood this when my mother gave it to me years before? I'd thought she was just telling me another of her stories, the kind she was always telling me, the kind that I hadn't really, until that day, believed. The silver ball holds a piece of the *kitsune*'s spirit so that when it changes shape it's never entirely separated from its original form. It made sense now. It all washed over my mind like a clear spring rain, and I stood and walked to the back of the room to gather my things. *Sensei* turned around when she heard me shuffling the backpack onto my shoulders and cried out, "Midori chan, what are you doing?"

"Going home," I said. I slid the door of the classroom open and walked down the hallway. *Sensei* rushed and caught me by my shoulder as I was walking out the front entrance, but I shrugged her hand off and stared up at her, making the most defiant face I could summon, and said, "Never touch me in such a way again."

She slowly took her hand off my shoulder. Her face dropped, all the muscles relaxing, and in this way she revealed the fear I'd instilled in her. When you are a *kitsune*, you can use your powers to persuade and affect human emotions. It's a simple trick really, especially because most humans have little control over their own emotions anyway. So even so soon after realizing what I was, I knew how to use one of the powers that is a right of all *kitsune*.

At home I put my school things away and pulled my futon from the closet, unfolded it, and sat down, folding my legs under me. I took the silver ball from a box of toys and rolled it around in the palms of my hands, pressing it against my cheek occasionally. It was as warm as my own flesh, and when I held it to my ear I heard a pulse and a thump, a heart beating over and over.

When my mother came in from hanging out the wash, she found me with the ball held against my ear and said, "Midori chan, what are you doing home already? School isn't over."

"I left," I said.

"What?! Why did you leave?" she asked, her face creased with worry. It was the face that I would watch over the years as it became her final mask, it was the face that would make her an old woman before her time.

"I was sick," I lied. "I phoned, but you didn't answer. They had me lie down in the clinic, but I left when no one was looking. I wanted to come home."

"Oh my," she said, and left the room to call the principal, to let him know I'd arrived home safely. When she returned a little while later, she said, "Midori," and her voice dripped with disappointment. "You trust me so little that you lie to me now?"

I nodded, but did not say any more. After all, why was I in the care of these people anyway? Simply because my mother had found me lost in the woods one day and brought me home? They were my jailers, for all I knew. Such was my thinking at that moment.

"Well then," she said, "now that you've gone and done it, you'll have to clean up your own mess at school. But don't tell Father! If he knows, I'm not sure what he'll do."

"I won't tell," I said, taking the beat of my own heart away from my ear finally. "But you must tell me more about myself," I said. "About my true nature."

"Your true nature?" she said. "What do you mean?"

"I am a *kitsune*," I said, "aren't I?"

She frowned and laughed a little, and put one hand against her face and shook her head. "Midori chan, I should never have told you that story. You're getting a little old for that now, aren't you?"

I stared at her, my face burning, but did not answer.

"Midori," she said. "Really, you are an impossible child."

My mother—or my human mother, as I came to think of her more often after that day—suddenly had very little to tell me. So for the second time that day, I snuck away. Out the back door I went, taking a small trail that lay between my father's cabbage fields and a persimmon orchard. It was autumn and the persimmons were growing to ripeness, their golden-orange globes fattening day by day, weighing down the tree limbs. Mother always picked baskets of them to bring back and cut into slivers for dessert.

When I reached the end of the persimmon orchard and cabbage field, there was a small road that led out to the main road in town. On the other side of the road was a forest of bamboo and pine trees. I looked both ways, and when I was satisfied that all was safe, I hurried across the road, into the forest.

I was not certain where I was going, but I stepped with certain strides, as if I knew the path like the inside of my heart. The forest floor was mostly clean. Only a few branches littered the ground. Light filtered down through the treetops like shafts of molten gold. When I finally stopped, I stood in a clearing before a tiny house on a small wooden platform beneath a fir tree. The house's miniature double doors were locked, and there were little steps leading down to the platform it sat upon. Coins and colored strings and bottles of tea had been left on the steps. It was an old shrine, dilapidated, the wood gray and moldy. A home for the spirits of this place. I looked around, staring up at the canopy of trees surrounding me, and thought, *Yes, I remember. These woods are my home.*

My father's father had made this shrine many years ago, to honor the spirit of this land, and I was that very same spirit. My mother had found me lost in the woods and brought me home with her. This land belonged to me. I was a *kitsune*, as I'd realized, and this was the land to which I was bound.

How, then, had I come to be a human child? That was a much more difficult story to put together. But, oh, I was one smart fox.

My father had worked this land for many years, as had his father before him, with a decent enough crop each year, until suddenly one year a blight plagued his cabbage and persimmon and anything else he tried to grow. He was baffled, but he never thought to honor the spirit of the land as his father had. It was my mother who must have reminded him. She was always saying how he'd forgotten his ancestors, how he'd forgotten the spirits of the land. Yes, I thought, she had to have been the one to remind him of this shrine his father had built years ago.

So he restored the shrine to appease whatever gods may have been roaming nearby, and soon the land gave forth again. But this only angered him more. He didn't like that his land did not truly belong to him. So he waited and watched until he saw a small fox visiting the shrine at dusk, sniffing around the steps where he'd left his offerings. "A *kitsune*!" he shouted through the house that night. And soon he was plotting. "They are the trickiest of all," he told my mother, "but their weakness is that they're in love with their own cleverness."

This is true, unfortunately. This is very, very true.

So he began to leave even more offerings at the spirit house, until its steps were full. I could imagine him as he left the door of the shrine open one evening, and sure enough, when the little fox came by, it stood on its hind legs to pull itself up the steps, knocking off the other offerings to see what had been placed inside. And when the fox poked its head through the doorway, my father jumped out from his hiding place and pushed the fox in the rest of the way. Then he barred the door, locking it. The land would be under his control as long as he held me in his power. But it was my mother who would find the silver ball.

Days later, she visited the shrine to tidy it up. She couldn't stand the idea of what had happened, and wanted in some way to let the *kitsune* know that she was loyal to it. She could not speak of her feelings to my father for fear of being thought disloyal, or to others for fear of being thought crazy, so while she arranged offerings on the steps and chattered to the spirit locked in the house about how she couldn't help it even if she wanted because he had the key, she noticed a silver ball sitting on the forest floor, just beneath the platform the house stood upon. She knelt down and picked it up, and that is when I told her how she could help me.

She would bring me into this world as her child, so that I could eventually free myself. Do not worry, I told her through the ball. I will be the source of my own liberation.

I did not see my human father as my enemy, as some may think would be my natural feelings toward the man. Instead I thought him very clever to trap my spirit. Not clever enough to remember a *kitsune* has tricks up her sleeve even in the worst of conditions, but clever nonetheless. I also felt indebted to him, for it's a rare opportunity for those born in the spirit realm to receive the chance to be human, and it's through human suffering that one can enter nirvana most easily. I decided to welcome this entrapment as a step on the path to eternity. The Buddha himself is said to be like a lotus flower, growing upward from the mud at the bottom of a pond, for the time he spent in the world allowed his bright wisdom to flow forth. Instead of despising my conditions, I would learn from others, I thought. Now that I knew my position in the world, I could carry on with life, with fate, more easily. I would grow into a young woman and try my best to please my teachers and parents.

Later, when I returned from the woods, I told my mother

not to worry. That all would be well. I told her I would apologize to *sensei* and make everything right at school again, that Father would never have to know what had happened. She stroked my cheek and said, "Now that's my good girl, Midori. That's my good girl."

When I went back to school the next day, *sensei* didn't say anything to me. She pretended as if nothing strange at all had happened. I could have allowed her to remain in fear of me forever, but I decided that, as I was a human for the moment, I would go to her and apologize for my behavior, as humans do.

"*Sensei*," I said, "about yesterday, please excuse me. I'm so sorry. I myself don't even know why I acted in such a way. I am truly sorry."

"Midori chan, I was so surprised!" she said. "But it's all right. This sort of thing happens sometimes. Especially in the fall, when the wind from the mountains is bearing down on us." She looked out the classroom window then and said, "Winter is coming."

We did not speak of this matter again, and I appreciated her easy forgiveness and the way she turned the discussion away from the matter of my guilt to the change of the season. I decided I would not give her so much trouble in the future. I would do my best to be a model student.

The chime for class to begin sounded and all of us took our seats. I listened intently and volunteered to help in any way possible that day. After lunch, it was time for all of the students to clean the school. I was on hallway duty with a girl named Kazuko. She was from a good family in town. Out of all the children in my class, she was the only one who never made fun of me or my mother. But she was so quiet I wasn't even sure how her voice would sound if she said something. Usually we wiped our section of the hall floor facing each other on hands and knees, her feet braced against the wall behind her, mine braced against the wall behind me, saying nothing. We had never spoken before, but on that day, while we wiped the dust and dirt away, Kazuko stopped working and looked up at me. I looked back and smiled. It was the first time I had tried to be friendly to someone. When she smiled back, I was thrilled. I had done this thing right.

"Yesterday," she said in a voice like a trickle of water, "what you did was amazing. I couldn't believe it. I thought, This can't be! But you did it! You walked out and *sensei* couldn't do anything about it. You're so strong. I envy you."

"It wasn't anything," I said, shrugging. "I regret it. It was too much. I apologized to *sensei* this morning."

"That's what's even more wonderful," she said. "You showed her how you felt, and because it was rude you apologized—but you weren't afraid. It's all the same, don't you see? You have no fear. I wish I was more like you."

I wanted to reach out and touch her face, to stroke her cheek like my mother stroked mine. *I have a friend*, I thought. "I wish I was like you, too," I told her. "Why don't we teach each other how?"

She grinned and nodded, her bangs bouncing on her forehead under the red bandanna wrapped around her head. "We'll be good friends for sure," she said.

"And even when we're no longer near each other one day,"

I said, unable to stop myself even then from predicting the future, "we'll never be alone again."

From Kazuko I learned many things. How to tell a girl that her hairstyle was pretty, how to tell a boy that he was smart or funny, how to tell a teacher that he or she has been a great help to me, how deep I should bow according to a person's status, how to seem excited about playing silly games like Fruit Basket when the foreign teacher from Australia came to teach us English. And later, after we began to grow fast and went to junior high, how if I wore my hair in two braids and smiled with my teeth I was the cutest girl in our class, how if I pretended to daydream while sitting at a picnic table in the school courtyard during afternoon recess, others would think I was poetic.

When I went to Kazuko's house, her family was so normal. Her mother was always cooking or cleaning or mending clothes; her father was always working or, on Sundays, watching sports on television; her older brothers constantly arguing while they played video games in a back bedroom. I could hear them back there even with their door slid shut. I learned from Kazuko and her family how to be human. I learned what it felt like to love others, to be loved, at least a little bit, even though I was not a member of their family. And from all that, I learned how to feel a great absence in my life when I was with my own mother and father, in my own home, wondering why I could not have the kind of life Kazuko's family gave her.

My self-pity never lasted long. I couldn't allow it. I knew why my mother and father couldn't love me in that way. My father because his wife didn't give him the son he longed for. My mother because when she looked at me, I could see in her eyes his disappointment pressing down on her. None of us could give the other what they needed. We were doomed from the beginning.

So in the end the universe had exacted a price for our cunning behavior. My father thought he'd tricked me by trapping me in the shrine, and I thought I'd tricked him by becoming his daughter. But all of our trickery was for nothing. Since my spirit was not truly trapped in the shrine, my father's crops were still often blighted. And for me, what I'd thought would be an escape from the spirit world was instead an education in the sorrow of mortality. I learned how everything slips away in the moment we hold it. I learned from the beat of my human heart how we are forced to live in a world that will inevitably fade.

This is not enough, I thought one day as I was hanging the laundry on the line for my mother. *This is not enough*, I was thinking still, when suddenly I heard a strange choking sound come from the nearby kitchen window. I dropped the sheet I was hanging and ran inside shouting, *"Okaasan! Okaasan!"* There was a pain in my heart before I even reached the kitchen, a throb in my chest as if someone had reached inside my chest and squeezed hard. When I arrived I found her on the floor, one arm across her chest.

This is not enough, I had thought.

And Death replied:

"But this is what you have."

I was a third-grade student in high school that spring,

seventeen years old and preparing to go to college in Tokyo with Kazuko. We had remained friends throughout the years, drawing closer and closer until we were more like sisters. My mother knew of our plans to go to university together in Tokyo. There would be trouble with Father, she'd told me, but she would take care of it. There was no need to worry.

Now she was gone and I wasn't sure what would become of the plans Kazuko and I had made together. Over the years my father had grown to dislike me more and more, especially when it became apparent he'd have no son to inherit his blighted farm, in which he took a spiteful pride. And with my mother dead, he'd taken to drinking sake every night until he was drowned in his and its misery. When he drank, his dislike for me grew into a hatred that brought forth curses that shook the walls. That spring, I often found myself running from the house, my hands clapped over my ears to shut his voice out behind me. Without my mother to protect me, I didn't know how to proceed with my plans to leave. I'd become so human that I'd forgotten I could challenge his belligerence with the strength of my own will. I'd become such a proper Japanese girl that I'd forgotten I was stronger than him.

One day, soon after our graduation ceremony, I told him my plans. "I'm moving to Tokyo with Kazuko," I said. "We're going to room together and go to college."

"College?" he said, as if it were another planet. "College? How can you think about college? Your mother has died!"

"She died three months ago, Father."

"I need you here," he said. I could see his muscles tense with frustration. "Besides," he said, "you've graduated.

You don't need to go to school any longer."

I could hear the rest of his meaning unspoken: that I did not need to go to school because one day I'd marry a man who would take care of me. That, until then, I'd help him take care of this home.

"I'm sorry, Father," I said, "but I've already decided. I'm going to Tokyo. You must learn to take care of this house on your own. I want a different life than the one you see fit for me."

I felt the back of his hand strike my cheek before I actually saw him moving. For a long stretch of time, I could feel the knobs of his knuckles pushing my face to the side after his fist struck. I saw a bright flash of light behind my eyes and my jaw rattled. I thought I was seeing a dream, the way I sometimes dreamed my teeth were all crumbling and falling out of my mouth. Soon they would all be broken and fall out covered in blood, I thought, when I felt them scrape against each other. There was no pain immediately, but as soon as the white flash of light faded and my vision returned, I felt the sting and the piercing flow of blood flooding through my cheek. What's more, I saw his hand rise again, come down at me again, moving toward me like the scythe moves toward a stalk of rice.

My cheeks, my mouth, my nose, my shoulders, my chest. His rage was like the rage of a demon as he pushed, grabbed, shook me. I cried, pleading, but he could not hear me. When his rage was spent, he stood above me, crying like a child, his hands over his face. "Why this?" he said. "Why this?"

I stood up slowly, gingerly, my head bowed, one arm held in front of it to protect me from further blows. "Why can't you be a good girl, Midori?" he said as I walked past him to my room. I passed a mirror on the way and caught a glimpse of the bloody meat of my face. I stopped for a moment to get a better look. My bottom lip was split and my cheek was swelling so that it seemed it might tear open. I was fascinated. The blood seeped out, and in my blood I saw a glimmering. When I looked closer, it seemed like tiny beads of mercury, and then I remembered the silver ball my mother had given me years ago. I'd put it in a toy box and hidden it at the back of my closet after I became friends with Kazuko and no longer needed the comforts of my secret origin.

Now I crawled on my hands and knees to the back of my closet to find it. When I opened the lid, the ball seemed to glow, faintly illuminating the dark. I picked it up and heard the same heartbeat inside it I'd heard nearly ten years before. That was me in there, I remembered. Kazuko had made me feel so human that the silver ball had become something I dreamed about over the years, and forgot each morning when I woke. I had become someone else. I had forgotten myself.

I fell asleep in the closet, listening to the silver ball's heartbeat, feeling its warmth in my hands. When I woke several hours later, my father had fallen asleep on the floor in the living room. I crept back to my room and picked up the phone to call Kazuko. When she answered, I was already crying. "*Ne, ne,* Midori chan," she said. "*Doushita no*?" What's the matter?

Through clenched teeth, I told her what had happened after I told my father our plans. When I finished, she said she was calling the police. I told her not to, that I would take care of this myself, but within a half hour the police were at my house and my father, crying, was explaining how his wife had just died and now his daughter was going to leave him to go to college in Tokyo. "I didn't intend to hurt the child, you see, it just happened, she is abandoning me."

I stayed in my bedroom and when the police officers were done speaking with my father, they came back through the hallway to my room and knocked. I slid the door open, lifted my face to them. They were both men. They squinted at the sight of me. Then, as if shaking off a bad dream, they regained their stiff composures. They said in kind tones that my father was having a difficult time right now, and that I should be a good girl, take care of him now that my mother was gone, that I should help him. "There's a university right here in town," one of them said.

"That is the agricultural college," I reminded them. "I already know as much about farming as I want to."

"You can go to secretarial school," the other suggested.

I nodded. "You are right," I told them. "Thank you for your help."

They excused themselves from my room and I watched their backs as they went down the hall, back to the living room, and talked more with my father, telling him to control himself, or else they would return and that they'd not be so kind the next time. Minutes later they were gone and he was in my room, angry again. "What person of importance do you think you are?" he said. "Calling the police on your father!" He shook his head as if I were the one who should be ashamed. "Such willfulness, even as a child," he complained. "I blame your mother."

"I did not get my willfulness from her," I told him, staring straight into his eyes. "I did not get anything good from either of you."

"Bah!" He threw his hand in the air, as if he were throwing away trash. "No good has ever come of you either, and nothing ever will."

When he had passed out for the second time that evening, I called Kazuko again. I thanked her for being concerned, for being my friend, but said that I wouldn't need her help any longer. "Midori chan," she said, "you're acting as if we're never going to see each other again."

"I won't be going to Tokyo with you," I explained. "But please don't worry. Really. I'll be fine. I'll be more than fine. I hope you'll be happy, Kazuko."

"Midori—"

But quietly I disconnected.

For a few days I kept to my room, barely coming out to eat, barely sleeping more than three hours in the night. My father knocked on my door from time to time, and called my name weakly from the other side, but I didn't answer, and eventually he'd drift away. The phone rang sometimes, but neither he nor I moved to answer it. It was probably Kazuko calling. *But I've already said good-bye,* I thought. I held the silver ball in my hands, cradling it against my body while I considered my fate. There was a reason for everything, I'd been told, but I was not at peace with this. I was finished, I decided on the fourth day. I was through with this world. It was time to reclaim my proper identity.

I took the silver ball and placed it inside my mouth, holding it there, a pearl in an oyster, and finally swallowed it with much effort, choking, my throat swollen with it until my body filled with its terrible rhythm and I fell—that *body* fell to the floor, I should say, but I remained standing above her, looking down at the girl I'd been for nearly eighteen years. Midori Nakajima. *Such a pretty child,* I thought, kneeling down to look at her more closely. Even with bruises, she looked like an angel. "Good-bye," I said, and kissed the flesh that had been home to me for so long. "Good-bye," I said, and walked out of that room and out of that house, into the woods to the shrine, where I broke the lock he had placed on the doors so many years ago, and reached inside to retrieve my true skin.

It's been a long time since that moment of discovery. I can still remember in detail, and still wince at the memory, how I reached into that old, rotten shrine in the forest and found nothing but dust, the dried husks of insects, and empty air. And then what? Then I looked around the forest with my eyes wide open without a story to go along with it. It was a forest of bamboo and pine trees with an old shrine at the heart of it, and me standing in the middle of it, my hands empty, and no way to undo my choices.

I ride the trains at night now, staring out the windows at the lights of passing cities and towns and villages, thinking back to that moment, the point that I'd thought without any doubt would be my exit to salvation. I'd thought so far ahead in the story, had imagined all of it happening in a particular way. *Midori,* I think as I stare at my face in the glass of the train window, *you silly girl.* I truly had been a *kitsune* in spirit, clever as an old nine-tailed fox, cleverer maybe, clever enough to have grown a thousand tails over my brief history of living. But the only person I'd managed to trick with the stories I'd been telling for so long had been me. A *kitsune.* Indeed.

I walk the streets of Tokyo sometimes, and wander through its parks and subway stations, watching all the people that fill the city with their fragile bodies, their feathery breath, their fleeting dreams. The buildings are so tall that when I look up I get the sense of falling backwards, as if I'm flying. When I look down again, though, the streets still surround me, the neon glares in the puddles, and the people continue doing whatever they're always doing. Laughing, arguing, reminiscing, cursing the day they met each other, holding hands, walking together, remembering their childhoods, their school days, and then, when they come to an unfamiliar intersection, they realize they've forgotten their intended destinations, and look around wondering how they got here.

I like looking at their faces, at their smiles and frowns, at their brows furrowed in confusion. And when they return home for the evening and the streets begin to grow empty, I go down into a train station and select a destination. There are so many paths to choose from, and no one ever tries to stop me. But I always travel alone. That's the price of my ticket.

In fifteen years, I've seen everywhere the trains of Japan can take me. I've climbed Mount Fuji in the dark of a stormy night, lightning cracking the sky open around me, and when I reached the top I saw the sun rise clear and bright. I've visited Nara, where the deer roam through the cemeteries and parks like lost children, and I've been to Kyoto, the old capital, where the trees are already beginning to change colors as the summer closes and autumn draws near. At the Golden Palace, even weak sunlight is more than enough to set the walls of that place aglow. I lingered in the shadows of its great walls on days when my spirit's body, instead of growing bent and wizened, grew thin and light as the flame of a candle. I looked up at the golden phoenix perched on the rooftop and wished that one day it would show me a different sort of trick than the one I played.

I've stood upon the wooden bridge of Kiyomizu Temple, where the water is purer than anywhere else on this planet, and held my arms out like the wings of a crane, looking up into the sky and waiting for Buddha to make me light enough to fly up into the blue air, to see Japan grow smaller and smaller below me until I am so far above everything that I can see people walking the busy streets like ants tumbling through their tunnels, living obliviously or else noticing far too much, living contentedly or in frustration, unhappily or ridiculously happy, as they always seem to be doing. People. Higher and higher still I'll go, until the island I call home is a stone surrounded by water. I'll wave with both hands as Tokyo and Nikko and Sapporo and Osaka and Nagoya and the rice fields of my youth fall away from me. "*Sayonara*, Japan!" I'll shout, and even then I'd fly higher.

But, no, this is just another story I tell myself, even now. I never did leave that bridge, or any other high place I've visited. I can stand on tiptoe and reach, stretching my arms out like a beggar, but the sky will not open for someone who does not truly want to leave.

In fifteen years, I've seen so many things, enough things to last a lifetime. But I don't want to stop watching people on their way to their destinations, loving and saying good-bye to each other as they go wherever they must go.

I don't travel far from home any longer. After a day spent walking along the Sumida River, watching a foreign family taking pictures of each other in front of Tokyo Tower, after an evening of wandering through the brightly lit game centers and their bubbling noises of winning and losing, I take the train home, back to Ami, of all places. It's a long ride, but it's never long enough if you ask me.

I sit and watch my fellow travelers while they read novels and newspapers, drink coffee or beer, and send messages from their cell phones to someone they're leaving behind in the city or to one of their friends sitting beside them. Sometimes I'll stand and hold on to a strap in a crowded car, swaying back and forth with my eyes wide open while everyone else has closed theirs tight, pretending they're not among so many others, trying to be alone.

Back home in Ami, the streets are quiet and you can hear the wind blow down them and around the tiny houses, on its way to wherever it is going. I walk along the banks of the slow moonlight-rippled river, along the rice fields on the outskirts of town. I stand in front of my father's house and watch his hunched shadow pass by the frosted windows. The farm often gives good crops now, though it's nothing to do with me so much as the man who rents his fields from him. I stand in front of the gate of the schoolyard where the other children once asked if I didn't like people, and sigh at the memory of the obstinate silence I gave in return. It's strange to remember I used to think I'd do anything to leave here. Now I can't get enough of people. Now I can't get enough of this place. The moon is always right in front of me or just beyond the curve of my shoulder. I can hear the cicadas scream all day in the summer, their soft whisperings in the night, and they are a kind of consolation, the closest things I have to living. I could give it all up again and walk away knowing what that really means this time, but I won't. Not yet at least. Just a little bit longer, I tell myself. Just a little.

The fireflies glow off and on in the mist-covered fields, calling out, *Here I am,* waiting for another light to appear in the darkness. *Here I am,* one calls to another. *Come find me.*

Here I am.

❖ ❖ ❖

After two years an English teacher in Japan, **Christopher Barzak** has returned to his home state of Ohio, where he teaches writing at Youngstown State University. His stories have appeared in the anthologies *The Coyote Road, Salon Fantastique, Interfictions,* and *The Year's Best Fantasy and Horror,* among others. He is also the author of *One for Sorrow,* his Crawford Award–winning debut novel, and *The Love We Share Without Knowing.*

Visit his Web site at **christopherbarzak.wordpress.com**.

Author's Note

When I was living in Japan, I was given a children's book as a gift by one of my fourth-grade classes. Everyone in the school system where I taught—a small rural community outside the suburbs of Tokyo—knew I was trying my best to learn Japanese, so the book *Gongitsune*—a staple for fourth-graders in Japan (which happened to be my reading level in Japanese at that time)—was a perfect gift. I fell in love with the story of Gon the fox, as he's called affectionately in Japan, and the lessons he learns and that he teaches others. The artwork was some of the most fabulous depictions of a fox—an animal thought to be a magical creature in Japanese mythology—I'd ever seen. It made me curious, and my curiosity led me to read further into fox lore, and the further in I went, the more

I wanted to write about a young girl who is, in fact, a fox spirit but does not know her own origins and powers immediately, the way we're all born into our lives here without knowing where we come from, why we're here, or where we're going.

I modeled the young woman in the story on two girls from my classes—one was the young girl in that fourth-grade classroom who'd been selected to present me with the book, and the other was her older sister, one of my ninth graders. They were both feisty and rule-challenging, which is sometimes a rare quality in Japanese girls, who are encouraged to be quiet and well-mannered. Writing about Midori in this story, I kept these two sisters in my mind and hoped they wouldn't ever lose their challenging spirits as they grew older and began to make their own lives.

Chris Roberson

ALL UNDER HEAVEN

Lu Yumin stood on the Ting township dock, waiting for his grandmother to arrive, as the sun rose over the still waters of the Southern Sea. A skink skittered over his foot, breaking his concentration on the red-and-gold object in his hands. Skin crawling, he shook all over and cursed the little gray-green aquatic lizards that swarmed the dock.

A junk had just put out from the dock, motoring away from shore, the hands scrambling in the rigging to unfurl its square sails, each emblazoned with the image of a stylized red lantern. One of the crewmen was aft, and he cupped his hands around his mouth to shout over the motor's noise. "Get moving, Grandmother Lu! Or would you prefer we bring you back some fish when we're done?"

The other crewmen of the junk laughed raucously. Yumin sighed deeply and turned to see the old woman coming up the dock toward him, a heavy mesh bag slung over her shoulder, a pipe clenched in her teeth.

"The stage suffered the day that Ling Jun chose to become a sailor, no?" Grandmother scowled and made a rude gesture with her free hand toward the retreating junk. "The idiot. Ten years as first mate on my boat, and he takes a post with the Red Lanterns scrubbing decks. If he'd stuck with me, he'd have his *own* boat by now."

Yumin shrugged and turned his attention back to the device in his hands, trying to work out what was preventing it from operating.

"Ever since you found that thing in the rubbish pile last month," Grandmother said, drawing nearer, "I think you've scarcely been without it."

"It's something to do with my hands, I suppose," Yumin answered sheepishly.

"Now look, Daughter's-son." As Grandmother shooed a few skinks out of the way with the toe of her boot and dropped the bag to the planks of the dock, Yumin's nostrils caught the strong scent of ginger that followed her everywhere like a cloud. "I've never stood in the way of your tinkering, and God knows that I'm grateful enough for it when the junk's engines give out, but you've been spending more time at your hobby than your job, and it's got to stop. I've cut you some slack since your mother died, but now I need your head and hands both back at their jobs. It'll just be you and me on this trip."

From the deck of Grandmother's junk came the sound of wet flesh slapping wood, and they turned to see a pair of otters, their forelegs propped up over the boat's railing. One, with a nick in his ear, waved his paws, signing furiously.

Grandmother sighed. "Yes, Genius, just me and Yumin and you and Recluse, of course."

Recluse, the other otter, nodded his small head, signing the gestures for laughter, while Genius ran in a tight circle, slapping the deck with his paws and tail.

"Clowns." Yumin shook his head.

A squawk came from overhead.

"And you, too, Great Sage," Grandmother called up to the cormorant perched atop the mast, "you feathered pillow, you."

The cormorant clacked its beak, an avian sort of laugh, and then returned to preening its feathers.

"Here, take this, boy." Grandmother pushed the bag of supplies over to Yumin with the side of her foot, and then vaulted nimbly to the deck of the junk.

Yumin tucked the device inside his tunic, and then handed the bag over, careful not to let the supplies fall into the cold waters.

"Hurry up now. We need to get on the open water before midday, or else the Red Lanterns will have caught all of the fish before we catch a one." To Yumin's surprise, Grandmother said the name of their rivals with scarcely a moue of distaste.

Yumin untied the junk from the dock and, with a final glance back at the town, jumped the gap, landing on the deck with a thud. He had just five more days before he needed to be back, or so the recruiting officer had said. Five days to spend one last trip with his grandmother, and then break her heart.

Once they'd motored far enough away from the shore, Grandmother cut the engines and let the sails catch the wind, propelling them out into the waters of the Southern Sea.

At the wheel, Grandmother puffed on her pipe and called over to Yumin, tinkering with his device in the prow. "I want to drop anchor near the Sunken City by nightfall and be in position to release the nets before dawn."

The Sunken City, Yumin thought. Would this be his last time to see its faint lights?

"You hear me, Yumin? Or have your brains fallen into that little red box of yours?"

"I heard you, Grandmother." Yumin tried not to sound like a petulant child, but succeeded only partially.

The Sunken City had a name, once, but no one used it now. Before the water levels of the Southern Sea had risen to their current height, when it was only a lake a few hundred meters deep, the Sunken City had perched at its shores. It was a port city, a hub for travel and home to fishers, and also the place where all of the creatures of the Southern Sea were first hatched and adapted for life on Fire Star. Most had originally been aquatic strains brought to Fire Star once the red planet had been sufficiently terraformed to support aquatic life. Many of the species had been modified over the generations, their genes twisted and turned until they were better suited to survive on the red planet, and some, like Grandmother Lu's otters and cormorant, had even had their intelligence and aptitudes boosted. When the water levels rose even higher, as the red planet grew ever warmer, the Sunken City was claimed by the waves, and as the coast migrated inland to the borders of Ting township, it had become the new port.

"You know, Grandmother . . ." Yumin said, at length. "About the Red Lantern Families . . . ?"

"Yes, what of them?" Grandmother answered, guardedly.

"Well, it seems to me that the main reason they're so successful is their automation. If you were to automate your operation, you wouldn't need to hire extra hands. In fact, if you sprang for one of the mechanical intelligent central controllers that are now available, you wouldn't have to go out on the waters at all, but could instead stay at home and relax while the automated systems did all of the work for you."

Grandmother blew air through her thin lips, making a sound like flatulence. "That isn't real fishing. And besides, it's automated systems like the Red Lantern Families that are fishing the Southern Seas empty. That's why the fish have been so scarce. Machines that don't need to eat and sleep, that catch more fish than the market can buy, driving down prices for everyone else. Besides, I've got the otters and the cormorant and you to help me, so why do I need to spend a fortune on automata just to haul in the nets? We'll do just fine, as we always have."

Yumin sighed, and turned back to the red-and-gold brick.

That night, they dropped anchor, and Yumin was so tired that he went straight to sleep after their evening meal, climbing into his bunk in the hold before the sun had completely set.

How long he slept, Yumin wasn't sure, but sometime in

the middle of the night he was roused from his slumber by the sound of something large bumping the bottom of the boat. Yumin scrambled out of his bunk and up on deck, but Grandmother was already there, smoking her pipe and peering over the side of the junk.

They could see nothing in the dark waters except glittering lights far below the surface.

"The Sunken City," Yumin said. He knew that the lights were just bioluminescent algae, cultured and engineered when the submerged city had been a living metropolis, but still, seeing them by moonlight, he couldn't help but be reminded of the bedtime stories of his grandmother, before he claimed to have outgrown such things, about the Land in the Sea, a glittering kingdom at the bottom of the ocean, ruled over by a magical dragon.

Grandmother puffed her pipe, the burning ember in the bowl glowing red like a hot coal, casting an eerie red light on her careworn features, but said nothing.

They were back at work before sunrise. The cormorant wheeled overhead but squawked that it couldn't see any sign of shoals beneath the water.

"That's a bad sign," Grandmother said, but she didn't have to explain what she meant. Fish had always congregated around the structures of the submerged city, finding shelter to feed, and to reproduce, in buildings that once housed humans and their machines. If there were no fish to be found here, it was not a promising indicator that they would have much luck in other locales.

"What do we do, Grandmother?"

"Well, there's nothing to be gained from standing here and gawking. We'll send Great Sage out to range a bit farther afield"—she flashed a few signs at the cormorant, who squawked in response, then flew off in a wide arc, heading toward the east—"while we start trawling here. It'll be only for individual fish, at best, but it beats waiting around on our backsides."

With Grandmother's help, Yumin released the nets, two large sets of mesh hooked to strong lines that ran over pulleys on a high gantry in the junk's rear, ending in wide spools attached to a motor. When the nets were in place, Grandmother took the wheel and started up the engine. The boat moved in wide circles, marking out the limits of the Sunken City far below. If there'd been shoals in these waters, the otters would have been put to work, herding the fish in their dozens and hundreds into the nets. With only scattered fish to be had, their talents wouldn't be needed, so they sat on the prow of the junk, leaning into the spray, luxuriating in the warm sum.

When they'd made a full circuit, Grandmother cut the engine, and Yumin kicked the lever that started the motor spooling in the nets. When the nets had been reeled in and were hanging from the gantries overhead, Yumin was dispirited to see only one or two fish sporadically flopping in the heavy mesh.

"Keep heart, Daughter's-son," Grandmother said brightly. "We'll catch them yet."

Yumin sighed. He'd hoped to fill the hold with a big haul

right away so they'd be forced to head back into port sooner rather than later. Then he could tell Grandmother his news when they were nearly in reach of home, and there'd be less chance that he'd miss his transport.

"Look there." Grandmother pointed overhead with the stem of her pipe.

The cormorant came angling in from the east, frantically flapping his wide wings, and gracelessly landed on his perch at the mast's top.

"Well?" Grandmother shouted impatiently up at the bird.

The cormorant shivered, and squawked in his simple syllables that he had sighted something in the water to the east. It seemed to Yumin that the bird was agitated, even nervous. "Grandmother, does Great Sage seem . . . distressed, to you?"

Grandmother looked from Yumin to the bird overhead and back again, and shrugged. "That may be. He's probably just excited, eager for the treat he'll have earned when his directions lead us to a good catch."

Yumin nodded, and looked up at the shivering bird, unconvinced.

After a few days of relaxing, the otters were eager for some exercise. They slid out through their bolt holes, one on either side of the boat, and coursed along beside the junk as they traveled eastward.

Yumin was in the prow, fiddling with the red-and-gold device. He was worried but found that he was more concerned about what his grandmother would think of his present than of what she would say when he told her his news.

And worried that she'd try to keep him away from shore for so long that he'd miss his transport. The officer had told him to report in six days, and it had already been three. Grandmother wouldn't intentionally keep him away once she heard his plans, would she?

He reassembled the device, but its screen remained dark, flat black in its ornate frame of gold. He toggled the switches that initiated the internal diagnostics, but when the cycles were complete, it emitted a sequence of tweets and whistles that meant no fault had been found. To all indications, then, the original persona was intact, deep within the red-lacquered shell, but it still did not communicate or respond to stimuli—awake, but unresponsive.

Yumin's deep concentration was shattered when he was pelted on the side of the head with a dumpling, leaving a greasy spot in his hair.

"I've been calling your name forever, boy," Grandmother hooted. "Where are you, anyway? Your body is here but your mind is somewhere else."

"Sorry, Grandmother," Yumin said, and couldn't help but think that soon, his body would be elsewhere, too.

The junk reached the spot that the cormorant had indicated, and the bird perched on top of the mast, nervously preening.

Yumin released the nets while Grandmother fired up the engine, and they began to drag the nets behind the boat. The otters dropped back, allowing the junk to course ahead. They gave a little salute and then dove beneath the waters.

Grandmother was at the wheel, and she called over to

Yumin at his post at the nets. She told him about chores they needed to look after when they got back, errands she needed him to run. Yumin felt an uneasy fluttering deep in the pit of his stomach and tasted betrayal on his tongue.

Far behind, the head of one of the otters crested the surface of the water. From its nicked ear, Yumin could tell immediately it was Genius. Absently, without waiting for the otter's signal, Yumin kicked the lever that started the retraction of the nets. But after a few moments, Recluse, the other otter, still hadn't surfaced, and its companion, Genius, wasn't giving the affirmative salute, but was instead motioning "Fear" and "Danger," frantically.

"Hey, Grandmother," Yumin called, and the old woman looked back. "Could Recluse could be caught in a net, do you think?"

Grandmother rubbed her lower lip between thumb and forefinger, and nodded, slowly. "It's possible."

"You think I should stop the nets' retraction?"

"No, let them keep reeling in. If Recluse is in a net, bringing the nets onboard will be the best, and perhaps only, way of getting him loose."

"Fair enough." Yumin glanced back and eyed the otter trailing behind them. "Something's got Genius spooked, though."

Grandmother came to stand beside him. "Will you look at that?"

The otter was still on the surface, still signing "Danger," and "Fear," and "Big." Then he began to sign "Fish," followed quickly by "Not Fish." He dove, was gone for a long moment, resurfaced and signed again. "Fish, Not Fish."

"What does he mean, Grandmother?"

"Nothing good."

There came a high-pitched squeal, as the motor pulling in the nets began to strain.

"Yumin, take the wheel." Grandmother switched places with Yumin, going over to lean low over the spools. From the wheel, Yumin could see that the line was taut, the motor still pulling, but the nets weren't coming in.

Yumin looked back, past the aft end of the boat, to where the lines of the net cut V-shaped wakes into the cold water. Genius the otter was nowhere to be seen.

The motor squealed and strained, and then suddenly the junk lurched forward as the lines momentarily went slack before going taut again. But now the line was spooling in, and the nets were slowly being hauled out of the water.

"There we go!" Grandmother shouted, clapping her hands.

The nets flapped onto the deck. There were fewer fish than they'd hauled in over the Sunken City, but, more surprisingly, there was a huge rent in the mesh of one of the nets.

"What did *that*?" Yumin said, mouth hanging open.

Grandmother narrowed her eyes and shook her head, without saying a word.

Night fell, and the otters never resurfaced.

Yumin and Grandmother sat on the deck, laboriously mending the nets. They hadn't spoken much since the loss of the otters. The cormorant, Great Sage, refused to come down from his perch atop the mast.

The stars were out overhead, and the moons moved across the sky. There was a shooting star moving toward the north, and Yumin realized it was a ship leaving stationary orbit at the top of the orbital elevator. Yumin was momentarily worried that his transport had left without him, but he calmed himself, remembering that it had only been four days, and he had two more to go.

Yumin looked up from his mending. "Grandmother, I suppose we'll have to head back into land, come the morning, right?" He tried not to sound too eager, but he couldn't prevent a trace of excitement, mingled with fear, from creeping into his voice.

Grandmother was looking at the net in her hands. "I've never see the like. Just never."

"What about the stories you told me as a boy? The old stories of fish with razor teeth, or otters who carried swords, or dragons from the Land in the Sea."

Grandmother waved his words away. "Those were just stories. Not flesh and bone."

After a long silence, Grandmother began to talk, quietly, her voice so low that at first Yumin wasn't sure whether he was only imagining it. "My husband, your grandfather, used to love those old tales. He seemed to know more of them than anyone could count. And as much as he loved telling them, your father, well, he loved listening to them."

She paused, and Yumin felt a sting of some strange regret, like a hunger, but thought it strange to feel such a pang of loss for his grandfather, a man he'd never met, and his father, who had died while Yumin was still a babe in arms. He'd never known either of them, not really. But still, when Grandmother would mention them, Yumin couldn't help but feel that he was missing something deep inside, something vital.

"It is a dark thing to outlive your children," Grandmother continued, after a long moment's silence. "Darker still to be left behind, when everyone you know has gone away into the long night."

Yumin remained silent, trying to think what to say.

"The Red Lantern Families have made me an offer."

"An offer?" Yumin asked.

"On the junk, on the business, on everything."

"What did you tell them?"

"I told them they could take their offer and use it to plug their bungholes." Grandmother paused, and turned her eyes to the moons overhead, sailing one toward the other. "But now. . . . Now, I just don't know."

A long silence followed. In the dim light of the moon, Yumin saw Grandmother sit up straighter.

"But enough stargazing and woolgathering, yes? We have work to do, after all!"

Grandmother and Yumin slept on deck and, before sunrise, were awake and back at work, the engine chugging and belching black smoke, the nets dragging behind. Yumin was concentrating on the red-and-gold object in his hands. If he only could find a way to make the persona within communicate.

Grandmother scolded him for lollygagging. Yumin slipped the little machine back into his belt and turned to face their wake.

The V-shapes the nets' lines made as they parted the water

were joined by another. The cormorant overhead squawked profanity and flew away.

"Um, Grandmother?"

Just as the old woman turned back to look, a triangular head parted the waters, grayish-green with black spots, and was lifted on a long, sinuous neck. Baleful, moist eyes regarded them coolly.

"What . . . what is it?" Yumin said, eyes wide. It looked to him like one of the skinks from the Ting township dock, but grown to enormous size.

"It is a dragon," Grandmother said simply, her voice low.

A stunned silence followed. The huge bulk of the thing lifted farther out of the water, and Yumin could now see that it was caught in the net.

"Cut the nets loose!" Grandmother yelled, but Yumin stood stock still, unable to will himself to move.

Grandmother rushed over and hit the release, sending the lines whipping across the deck.

The junk lurched forward. The dragon roared, then shook the nets loose and dove beneath the waves.

The junk plowed on without a hand at the till.

"That . . . that thing . . ." Yumin found that the words in his head spun faster than they could be forced from between his lips.

"The dragon," Grandmother said simply.

"That . . . dragon . . . must be the offspring of lizards who got into the chemicals and supplies buried in the Sunken City."

"That's as may be," Grandmother said, absently. Then she blinked, repeatedly, and shook herself for a moment, like a dog trying to get dry. Her composure regained, she clamped her pipe between her teeth and lit it. "I believe I'll be selling out to the Red Lantern Families now. And I'll thank you to take the post you've been offered with the Fleet, and leave me to enjoy my retirement in peace."

Yumin stammered, dumbfounded. "I can't . . . I can't believe you knew about that."

Grandmother scoffed. "And *I* can't believe you thought anything could go on beneath your grandmother's nose know without her knowing."

A beeping sounded from Yumin's belt, and he pulled out the red-and-gold device. On the little screen, now lit up, was the semblance of a human face.

"*Waking up now,*" the device chirped. "*Persona coming online.*"

"This . . . this is for you." Yumin held the device out to Grandmother. "I've been trying to get it to work, but I couldn't get it to communicate."

"Communication has never been a strength in our family," Grandmother said, smiling slightly, her hands folded in her lap. "But I can see why the Fleet wants you. The first voyage to the stars will need someone to keep their artificial brains and machines up and running while the crew sleeps, won't they?"

"I scored higher on the entrance exam than any applicant they'd had," Yumin answered, chest swelling with pride, "and if I joined up, I'd be taken aboard as an apprentice. By the time the crew went into deep sleep for the interstellar voyage, I'd know more about automata and artificial intelligences than I could ever have imagined possible."

Grandmother smiled and, still reluctant, took the proffered device. She looked it over, cautiously, as though half convinced it might bite her.

"What is—?" Grandmother looked at the face on the screen and fell silent, taken aback.

It was the face of her husband, long years dead.

"Greetings, Grandmother Lu," the face on the screen said in an approximation of his voice. *"How may I be of assistance today?"*

"The persona is just an off-the-shelf model," Yumin said quickly, "but I've customized it with data taken from your old family recordings, to look and sound as much as possible like Grandfather."

Grandmother looked from the device to her grandson. She then turned and looked over the waves. The cormorant was wheeling back toward them, hesitantly.

"These aren't my waves anymore. This is someone else's sea, now. Soon it'll all be automated, and the people will stay ashore, fat and lazy, with their ghosts and memories." She paused, and a smile spread slowly across her face. "But you know what? That doesn't sound so bad, anymore."

The cormorant squawked an interrogative.

"Get down here, you idiot bag of feathers," Grandmother shouted. "We're bound for dry land, and we'll leave these waters to monsters and the machines."

She looked at Yumin.

"Besides," she said, "Yumin has a transport to catch. That Fleet won't wait around forever, now will it?"

Halfway home, they dropped anchor, and Grandmother fixed their evening meal, roasting all but one of the fish they had caught on their journey, giving that one to the cormorant for his dinner.

The sky was growing reddish orange with the setting sun in the west, still crystal blue overhead, and growing dark as night in the east. Two bright stars shone over the eastern horizon, one faintly blue-green, the other small and white.

"You know, when I was a child, and you told me about Earth"—Yumin pointed to the blue-green star, rising in the east—"I thought it was just another place where adventures happened, like the Land in the Sea. And when I learned that there was no such place as the Land in the Sea, I assumed that Earth was just in stories, too."

"Hmmm." Grandmother sipped from her bowl of broth, salted fish on the broil, humming absently.

"But then I learned that Earth was a real place, the planet from which people originally came. And not only were humans living on Fire Star, but on the moons of Wood Star, and in orbit around Ocean Star. And not just in stories, but in reality."

"Mmmm," Grandmother hummed, nodding, her attention on her cooking.

"I wondered where else humans could go, where else we might find someday to live." Yumin straightened and looked up as the stars came out overhead. "And now I'll be among those who go out into the heavens, one of the first to travel to another star, searching for a new home."

Grandmother set down her ladle, and then walked over to the railing of the junk. She motioned Yumin to join her. "Daughter's-son, come over here."

When Yumin reached her side, the old woman pointed over the side of the boat, down into the dark waters.

"What?" Yumin said, and leaned over the side. There, deep beneath the cold waves, he saw the glittering lights of the Sunken City.

"Remember this," Grandmother said. "There *is* a Land in the Sea. And as we have seen, it is ruled by a mighty dragon. Things in stories can also be real. But what you will find, out there among the stars . . ."

The old woman paused, a proud smile on her face as she looked up at the night sky. She reached out and took her grandson's hand. Yumin felt safe with her calloused fingers wrapped around his.

"The things you will find, Daughter's-son, we don't yet know about, even in our wildest stories."

They stood, the old woman and the young man, looking up at the heavens, as the blue-green star that was Earth rose slowly in the east.

❖ ❖ ❖

Chris Roberson's novels include *Here, There & Everywhere, The Voyage of Night Shining White, Paragaea: A Planetary Romance, X-Men: The Return, Set the Seas on Fire, The Dragon's Nine Sons, End of the Century, Iron Jaw and Hummingbird,* and *Three Unbroken.* His short stories have appeared in a wide variety of magazines and anthologies. Along with his business partner and spouse, Allison Baker, he is the publisher of MonkeyBrain Books, an independent publishing house specializing in genre fiction and nonfiction genre studies, and he is the editor of the anthology *Adventure Vol. 1.* He has been a finalist for the World Fantasy Award three times—once each for writing, publishing, and editing—and a finalist twice for the John W. Campbell Award for Best New Writer, and twice for the Sidewise Award for Best Alternate History Short Form (winning in 2004 with his story "O One"). Chris and Allison live in Austin, Texas, with their daughter, Georgia. Visit him online at **www.chrisroberson.net**.

Author's Note

I accidentally created a world, several years ago, and have been writing about it ever since. I'd been trying without much success to launch a career as a writer, but despite having written six or seven novels and dozens of short stories, I'd sold exactly none of them. I finally gave up doing it the "right way," started a webzine with a few other writers, and posted my stories online for free, thinking to build an audience and a career that way, instead. Which, of course, didn't work either, but it at least got me the attention of an editor, Lou Anders, who asked me to submit a story to an anthology he was putting together. On a plane flight home, I cooked up an alternate history story that took place in a world dominated by Imperial China, a world I eventually decided to call the "Celestial Empire." I knew only as much about Chinese emperors as I'd seen in Bernardo Bertolucci's *The Last Emperor*, so the Celestial Empire and its history in that first story were little more than set decoration, but the story worked well enough for the editor to buy it, for a few reviewers to comment on it favorably, and for it to be nominated for a couple of awards, winning one of them. Having written that first story, I didn't really expect to revisit the Celestial Empire again, and went to work on other things. Then Lou asked me for another story set in the Celestial Empire, and Sharyn November at Viking asked for a novel set in the same world, and George Mann at Solaris asked for a whole *series* set in it. Needless to say, I had a *lot* of research to do, and I gradually fleshed out about twelve centuries' worth of history, from the fifteenth century in China to the far future on a terraformed Mars. Without meaning to do so, I'd created a world.

Now there are something like a dozen short stories and a handful of novels to the Celestial Empire, with more on the way. I've written about other worlds from time to time (including our own, on rare occasion), but the place to which

I return most often is the Celestial Empire. I suppose the moral to the story is that you should be careful what you cook up on plane flights, since you might end up involved with it for years afterward. Which isn't much of a moral, I'll admit, but what can you expect from someone who creates worlds by accident?

Ellen Klages

Singing on a Star

I'm spending the night with my friend Jamie, my first sleepover. She lives two doors down in a house that looks just like mine, except for the color. I'm almost six.

My father walks me over after dinner, carrying my mother's brown Samsonite travel case. Inside are my toothbrush, my bear, a clean pair of panties (just in case), and my PJs with feet. I am carrying my Uncle Wiggly game, my favorite. I can't wait until she sees it.

Jamie answers the door. She has no front teeth, and her thick dark hair is held back by two bright red barrettes. My hair is too short to do any tricks. Her mother, Mrs. Galloway, comes out from the kitchen wearing an apron with big daisies. The air smells like chocolate. She says there are cookies in the oven, and we can have some later, and my doesn't that look like a fun game! My father pats me on the shoulder and goes into Mr. Galloway's den to have a Blatz beer and talk about baseball and taxes.

There is only a downstairs, like our house. Jamie's room is at the end of the hall. It has pale pink walls and two beds with nubbly green spreads. Mrs. Galloway puts my suitcase on the bed next to the window, where Jamie doesn't sleep, and says she'll bring us some cookies in a jiffy.

I know Jamie from kindergarten. We are both in Miss Flanagan's afternoon class. We share a cubby in the cloakroom, play outside with chalk and jump ropes, and are in the same reading circle. This is the first time we've been alone together. It's her room, and I don't know what to do now. I put Uncle Wiggly down on the bed and look out the window.

It's not quite dark. The sky is TV blue, and if I scrinch my neck a little, I can see the edge of the swing set in my own backyard. I feel a little less lost.

"It's time to listen to my special record now," Jamie says. She holds up a bright yellow record, the color of lemon Jell-O. I can see the shadows of her hands through it.

She opens the lid of the red-and-white portable record player on her bookshelf. I'm jealous; I'm not allowed to play records by myself yet, because of the needle. Jamie plunks it down on the spinning disk, and the room fills with the smooth crooning of a man's voice:

You can sing your song on a star,
Take my hand, it's not very far.
You'll be fine dressed just as you are . . .

"We have to go before the song ends," Jamie says. "So we can see Hollis."

Jamie is not this bossy at school. I nod, even though I don't know who Hollis is. Maybe it's her bear. My bear's name is Charles.

Jamie points to a door in the pale pink wall, next to my bed. "We have to go in there."

"Into the closet? Why?"

"It's only a closet sometimes," Jamie says, as if I should know this. She opens the door.

Inside is an elevator, closed off by a brass cage made of interlocking Xs.

"Wow." I have never been in a house with an elevator before.

"I know," says Jamie.

She pushes the cage open, the Xs squeezing into narrow diamonds with a creaking groan. "C'mon."

My stomach feels funny, like I have already eaten too many cookies. "Where are we—?"

"Come *on*," says Jamie. "The song's not very long." She grabs the sleeve of my striped shirt and tugs me through, pulling the brass cage closed again behind us. To the right of the door is a line of lighted buttons, taller than I can reach. Jamie presses the bottom button, *L*.

A solid panel slides in front of the brass cage, shutting us off from the room with the pink walls. There is a clank, and a whirr of motor. I close my eyes. The elevator moves.

In a minute, it stops with another clank and the rattle of the brass cage squeezing open.

"Hi, Hollis," says Jamie.

"Why, hello Miss Jamie," a voice answers. "What a delightful surprise." It is an odd voice, soft and raspy, a bit squeaky, like a not-quite-grown-up boy. I open my eyes.

I don't know where we are. Not in Jamie's house. Not anywhere in our neighborhood. Outside the elevator is a tall room with a speckled linoleum floor and a staircase with a wooden railing, curving up and out of sight. A rectangle of sunlight slants across the tiles.

I remember my swing set in the almost-dark. I feel dizzy.

"C'mon," says Jamie. She tugs at my sleeve again. "Come meet Hollis."

I step out of the elevator. The room smells old and dusty, with a sharp tang, like they forgot to change the cat box. At first I don't see anyone. Then I notice a little room under the stairs. The floor inside is bare wood, and a man is sitting on a folding chair, reading a magazine with a flashy lady on the cover.

"Two surprises!" says the man. "What a great day this is turning out to be." He smiles as he closes his magazine, but his voice sounds sad, as if he's about to apologize.

"This is my friend Becka," Jamie says. "She's very good at jacks."

"A fine skill, indeed," Hollis says. "I'm pleased to make your acquaintance."

"Me, too," I say.

I'm not sure I mean it.

Hollis looks as odd as his voice sounds. He is not young, and is very thin. The skin under his eyes droops like a bloodhound. His hair sticks out in tufts around his head, like cotton candy, but the color of ginger ale. He's wearing gray pants and a red jacket with a bow tie. On the pocket of his jacket is a black plastic bar that says HOLLIS in white capital letters.

"I want to go up to the roof today," says Jamie. "Will there be trains?"

"A most excellent question," Hollis says. "Let me check the schedule." He pulls back his cuff and looks at his wristwatch. The face is square and so yellowed I can't see any numbers. "Yes, just as I thought. Plenty of time before the next arrivals. And a good thing, too. I'm feeling a bit peckish."

I don't know that word, but Jamie laughs and claps her hands. "I was hoping you were," she says. "But—" She shakes her head. "But you can't leave your post."

"No," he says, even more sad than before. He looks around the empty lobby like he expects someone to appear. "No, I can't leave my post."

"I could go," Jamie says. She sounds as if she just thought of it. But I think they are telling each other an old joke, one I don't know.

Hollis snaps his fingers. "Why, yes you could. You're a big girl." He turns to me. "Are you a big girl, too?"

I don't feel very big at all. Too much is happening. But I hear my own voice, telling my mother, "I'm a big girl now," when she didn't think I was old enough for a sleepover. "Yes," I say, louder than I mean to. "I'm a big girl."

"So you are," says Hollis. "So you are." He pulls a green leather disk out of his pocket, about the size of a cookie, with the top all folded over itself, and pinches the bottom. The folded parts open like a flower. When he holds it out to Jamie, I see that it's a coin purse. Jamie takes out two nickels.

"And one for your friend," Hollis says. He holds the purse out to me, and I take a coin. The leather petals refold around themselves.

"The usual?" asks Jamie. She sounds much older here.

"But of course," he says. "Farlingten's best."

Jamie leads the way. The front door of this building is glass and wood, with a transom tilting in at the top. I've never seen one before, but I hear the word in my head. *Transom.* I say it under my breath, and I can taste it in the back of my throat. I've never tasted a word before. I like that.

Out on the sidewalk, a white-on-black neon sign buzzes above our heads and stretches halfway up the tall brownstone building. HOTEL MIZPAH. WEEKLY RATES. This is a noisy place. Cars and trucks honk their horns under the viaduct, and men are yelling about money at a bar next door. I hear a clang and turn to see a green streetcar clattering down tracks in the middle of the street, sparks snapping from the wires overhead. The lighted front of the car says FARLINGTEN.

"What's Farlingten?" I ask Jamie.

"It's where we are, silly."

"Where are we, though?"

She huffs a sigh and puts her hands on her hips. "In *Far*lingten." She seems to think this is enough of an answer and skips a step ahead of me.

I want to go home. I don't know how to get there from this street.

My neighborhood has trees and front yards and driveways and grass. Here all I can see is dirty bricks and stone buildings, black wires crisscrossing everywhere. We come to the corner of the block. Above a wooden rack of magazines and paperback books is a faded green awning that says SID'S NEWS.

"This is Sid's," Jamie says. "It's my favoritest place."

Sid's isn't exactly a store, more like a cave scooped out of the corner, with shelves on both sides. On the left are a hundred different magazines, all bright colors and pictures. My parents only get *LIFE* and *TV Guide*. On the right are rows and rows of cigarettes in white and green and red packs, and boxes of cigars with foreign ladies on their lids. The slick paper and tobacco smell spicy, dry, and a little sour. I almost sneeze.

In front of us, a woman in an orange cardigan, her glasses halfway down her nose, sits on a stool behind a counter full of more candy and gum than I've ever seen in one place in my whole life. Hersheys and Sky Bars, Jujubes and Paydays, twenty flavors of LifeSavers in a rolled-log metal display—and dozens I've never seen before. I think about pirate gold and jewels, and Ali Baba, every treasure story I've ever heard. This is better.

"Wow," I say.

"See," says Jamie.

The woman behind the counter looks up. "Hey, kid. It's been a while."

"Hi, Mrs. Sid. How's business?"

"Can't complain," she says. "Whad'll it be today?"

"The usual." Jamie drops her two nickels onto the rubber

OLD GOLDs mat that is the only clear space on the counter.

"Raxar it is. Can't say that I blame you. Two?"

"Three. This is my friend Becka. She's never had one."

Mrs. Sid raises an eyebrow.

"It's her first time here," says Jamie.

"Ah."

I shake my head. "No thanks, I want a Three Musket—"

"You can get those anywhere," says Mrs. Sid. "Try this." She reaches over the counter and picks up a candy bar with a pale, steel-blue wrapper, thicker than a Hersheys, not as thick as a Three Musketeers. On the front, in shining silver letters, it says RAXAR. The *X* is two crossed lightning bolts. "Trust me. You've never had anything like it."

I take the bar and hold out the nickel in my hand.

Mrs. Sid shakes her head. "Keep it, kid. The first one is free." She rings open the cash register and rattles Jamie's nickels into the wooden drawer.

Back on the sunny sidewalk, the silver *X* winks bright and dull, bright and dull as I walk. *Farlingten Confectionary Company*, it says on the side. I start to pull open the paper wrapper.

"Not now," Jamie says. "Hollis doesn't have his yet."

I stop. I'm her guest, so I have to be polite.

When we get back to the door below HOTEL MIZPAH, Jamie puts her hands behind her back. Hollis is waiting by the elevator.

"What did you bring me?" he asks.

"Raxar!" Jamie says, and holds her hands out in front of her, a blue-gray bar flat on each palm.

"Hoorah," says Hollis. "It's the same forwards and backwards." His voice sounds like he's very disappointed, but he's smiling and his droopy eyes are bright. "Now on to the penthouse."

Hollis hangs an OUT OF SERVICE sign on a nail by the elevator door and holds the brass cage open for us. He presses the very top button, and the elevator clanks and whirrs for more than a minute. I don't know *what* to expect when the doors open, but it's just a hallway, with the same dingy linoleum and stairs as the lobby.

We climb eight stairs. At the top is a metal door that Hollis opens with a key. "Watch your feet," he says.

I step over the raised sill out onto a roof of gravel-embedded tar. A stone wall about a foot wide runs along all four sides. My sneakers make crunching sounds as I walk over to the nearest corner. Standing on tiptoe, I can rest my arms on the gritty top and look out almost forever. It is the highest up I have ever been, and I feel like I'm flying, standing still.

From here, the world is made of boxes—straight-sided rectangles of brown and gray. Walls and streets, windows and doorways, rows of brick and stone ledges on buildings that look so small I could hold one in my hand. Below me are other rooftops with chimneys and water tanks and laundry flapping, and the flat black top of the buzzing MIZPAH sign.

I don't know how long I stand there, taking in all the lines and angles. When I look up, Jamie is waving at me from the opposite wall.

"It's almost time for the train!" she calls.

I crunch over to where she and Hollis stand. There are

more boxes on this side, but also trees in the far distance, and the curve of a river. The light is golden, late-afternoon, as if the city has been dipped in butter.

Jamie points her Raxar bar at me. "When you hear the train, open yours and take a bite."

"Okay." I take it out of my pocket and, like the others, cock my head and listen.

After a minute, I hear the faint rumble of heavy wheels on invisible tracks, and the long, low notes of the train's whistle.

"Now," says Jamie.

I slide my finger under the glued flap. The steel-blue wrapper is heavy paper, lined with a thin foil, and crinkles as I unfold it. The bar inside is the same color as the afternoon light. I bite into one corner of it, and my mouth is flooded with magic. It tastes like toasted butter, malted milk, brown sugar, and flavors I have no name for. The bar is solid at the first touch of my teeth, then crumbles and melts onto my tongue.

I look at the glittering lightning *X*, then at Jamie.

"Well?" she says. There are golden crumbs at the corner of her mouth, and her bar is already half gone.

"It's, it's—it's great," is all I can manage.

"I told you," says Jamie. She takes a huge bite of hers, most of what remains.

The train whistle sounds again, a little closer now, louder.

"What does the train say to you?" Hollis asks me.

"Let's have an adventure," I answer after a moment. I nibble at my Raxar bar. Tiny bites, making it last.

"Ah," he says. It is a long *ah*.

"What?"

"That means the people inside are going to the right place. They'll have a fine, merry time there."

"Where are they going?"

"It's different for everyone."

I nod. Another minute, and there is only one bite of candy left. I put it in my mouth and hold it in my cheek, like a hamster, letting my new favorite flavor melt away until it is only a memory. Hollis holds out his hand for the empty wrapper.

"What does it sound like to you?" I ask.

He tilts his head, considering. "Like a saxophone," he says. "Mournful. A little tarnished."

"So what does *that* mean?" I lick my lips and find one more golden crumb.

"It means those people are going into the wrong future," he says, shaking his head. "They're all coming to Farlingten, and none of their dreams will ever come true."

My arms get all goose bumps. "Does Jamie know that?"

"No," he says. "I don't think she does." He reaches over and touches the red barrette in her hair, sliding his hand down to stroke her cheek, the way my mother pets the cat. Jamie is looking out at the trees and doesn't seem to care.

"I'd like to go home, please," I say. My voice sounds very small.

"The light *is* fading," says Hollis. "I suppose it's time."

"Can we stay just a few—" Jamie starts.

"No," he says. "You're not safe here at night." He moves his hand to her shoulder and gives it a little squeeze. "Not yet."

He follows us across the gravel and inside, pausing to lock

the metal door behind him. The stairwell is dark after the sunlit roof.

The elevator is waiting for us. Hollis opens the brass gate and pushes a button I hadn't noticed before, a squiggle between the 6 and the 7. Then he steps back out into the hall.

"Good-bye, Miss Jamie," he says as he closes the gate. "I'll see you again soon." He looks at me. "It was nice to meet you, Miss Becka."

I nod, but I don't look up until the metal panel slides shut, and Hollis is gone.

The elevator clanks and whirrs. I cross my fingers—both hands.

When the door opens, the voice is crooning the last lines of the song:

. . . you can stay put, right where you are,
Or sing your song up on a star.

But that's not possib—

My legs shaking, I step out of the elevator into the room with the pale pink walls and my game lying on top of the nubbly green bedspread. I am so glad to see Uncle Wiggly. Jamie closes the gate and then the closet door.

She walks over to the record player, where the yellow disk is now going around and around, hissing like static, and lifts the needle.

"Isn't that the *best* place?" She slips the record into its cardboard sleeve. "We can play your game now, if you—" We hear footsteps in the hall, and Jamie turns to me, her eyes fierce.

"You *can't* tell. Not ever."

"But what if—?"

She grabs my arm, hard. "Promise. Or I can never go back."

"Okay." I pull my arm away. "Okay. I promise." I sit down next to Uncle Wiggly and look out the window.

Mrs. Galloway opens the door and comes in, carrying a plate of cookies so warm I can smell them. A cleaner's bag is folded over one arm. "Who's ready for chocolate chips?"

"I am," says Jamie. She takes two cookies and bites into one.

"How about you, Becka?" Mrs. Galloway holds the plate out to me.

I shake my head slowly. "My stomach feels funny."

"Oh?" Mrs. Galloway sets the plate down on the bed and puts the back of her hand on my forehead. "You don't have a fever," she says. "Do you want some Pepto?"

"I don't think so."

"Hmm. Would you like to go home, dear?"

I nod.

"Well, I'm not really surprised. Five *is* a little young for a big adventure like this." She pats my shoulder. "Let me hang up Jamie's good dress, and I'll walk you back."

She reaches for the knob of the closet door.

No! I want to shout. But when she opens it, nothing's inside except clothes on hangers and three pairs of shoes on the floor.

"The record's over," Jamie says. "And it's dark now." Her voice is cool, matter-of-fact.

"I'll see you in school," I say.

Jamie turns and closes the lid of the record player. "Maybe."

Mrs. Galloway walks me home through the last moments of twilight, and my mother fusses over me and puts me to bed. When she folds my pants over the back of my chair, a nickel falls out of the pocket.

"Where'd this come from?" she asks.

I don't know how to answer that. "Um, Mrs. Galloway. In case the ice cream truck came. But it didn't." I've never lied before. My stomach squirms. Nothing else happens.

"That was nice of her." She puts the nickel down on the bedside table and tucks me and my bear under the covers. "Big day, honey. You'll feel better in the morning." She kisses my forehead.

When she's gone, I pick up the coin. It is smooth and round and nickel-shaped, but the man on it is not Jefferson. On the back, F-A-R-L-I-N-G-T-E-N curves around a picture of an animal that's not a buffalo. I feel goose bumps again and I want to throw it away. But I don't. I think of pirate gold and Ali Baba and butter-light on tall, square stone. I can almost taste a Raxar bar. I get up and put the coin in the box on my dresser, under the felt lining.

Just in case.

In the darkness, lying in bed, even my own room seems strange now. A car drives by. A slanting square of light plays across my ceiling, corner to corner, glass and chrome reflecting the streetlight outside. My closet door leaps into the light for just a moment. I turn my head the other way. But when I close my eyes, I see the Xs of an impossible elevator and taste *transom* in the back of my throat.

Monday starts the last week of kindergarten. Every day Jamie puts her things in our cubby and sits on my right in reading circle. She watches me, but I don't want to talk to her. At recess I play Red Rover with other kids.

On Tuesday, we return our library books after snack. I wait until Jamie is over by the biographies, and ask Mrs. Gascoyne if she knows where Farlingten is.

"Far-ling-ten? No, dear, not right offhand. But if you want, I can look it up."

Except she can't. There's no Farlingten in the phone book, or on the state map, or even in the big atlas of the whole world. No Farlingten anywhere.

Thursday night, the air is hot and thick. Thunder rumbles far away, but rain hasn't come to our house yet. I toss and turn, sweaty under just a sheet. Through my open window, I can hear the murmur of my parents' voices from the back porch, smell the sweet, acrid waft of smoke from my father's pipe.

Then I hear the music. Not from the hi-fi in our living room, but from outside, a few houses down. I jump, like I've been pinched, and the smooth crooning glides faintly over the distant thunder.

You can sing your song on a star . . .

It seems to go on forever. I look out my window and wonder about Jamie. I shudder when a train whistles somewhere in the distant darkness, all grays and browns. It does not sound like an adventure.

Jamie is not in school Friday afternoon.

My mother picks me up at three o'clock, because I have a box with my rest rug and paintings and papers to bring home for the summer. We are at the front door when Miss Flanagan calls from my classroom.

"Becka! You left this in your cubby." She hurries down the hall. "I'm glad I caught you," she says, handing me a stiff cardboard sleeve.

It's a record. On the TV-blue cover is a cartoon of a little girl with dark hair. She is sitting with her legs dangling over one arm of a bright yellow star. Across the top, in magic marker, it says *BECKA.*

I stare at it. That's not how I write my *K*s.

"I've never seen that one before," my mother says. I can hear the question in her voice. She buys all my things.

I can't explain. I don't even know how it got into the cubby. "It was sort of a present," I say after a minute. I'm not sure I want it.

"Who—? Well, never mind. I hope you thanked them." My mother slips it under my rest rug, then puts the box into the back of the station wagon. I can feel it through the back of my neck as we drive.

She pulls into the parking lot of Ackerman's Drugs, six blocks from our house. "I need to pick up a few things," she says. "So I thought we might celebrate with a sundae, Miss First Grader."

Ackerman's smells like perfume and ice cream mixed with bitter medicine dust. The candy counter is next to the red-and-chrome soda fountain. While my mother buys aspirin and Prell shampoo, I look at every candy bar in the display. No lightning bolts. "Do you have a Raxar?" I ask the counterman when he is done making a milkshake.

"Raxar?" He wrinkles his forehead. "Never heard of it."

I'm not really surprised.

When we pull into the driveway, there are police cars parked two doors down. My mother frowns and carries my box to my room before she walks down to the Galloways' to see what's happened.

I put the record on my dresser, next to the box with the nickel.

That night my mother checks the lock on the front door twice after dinner. At bedtime, she tucks me in tight and kisses me more than usual.

"Can I have a record player for my birthday?" I ask.

She smiles. "I suppose so. You're a big girl now."

So you are, echoes Hollis in his odd, sad voice. *So you are.*

"I am," I say. "First grade."

"I know, honey." My mother sits down on the edge of my covers. "But even big girls can—" Her hand smoothes the unwrinkled sheet, over and over. "When you were out playing, did you ever see your friend Jamie talking to a man you didn't know?"

I think, for just a second, then shake my head and keep my promise.

"Well, you be careful." She strokes my cheek. "Don't go anywhere with a stranger, even if he gives you candy, okay?"

"I won't," I say. I don't look at the record on my dresser, and wonder if I'm lying.

Ellen Klages was born in Ohio and now lives in San Francisco.

Her story "Basement Magic" won the Nebula Award in 2005. Several of her other stories have been on the final ballot for the Nebula and Hugo awards, and have been translated into Czech, French, German, Hungarian, Japanese, and Swedish. A collection of her short fiction, *Portable Childhoods*, was published in 2007.

Her first novel, *The Green Glass Sea*, won the Scott O'Dell Award for historical fiction and the New Mexico State Book Award. It was a finalist for the Northern California Book Award, the Quills Award, and the *Locus* Award. A sequel, *White Sands, Red Menace*, has recently been published.

Her Web site is **www.ellenklages.com**.

Author's Note

This story came out of my oldest, strongest memory.

I'm in bed, in the yellow bedroom of my parents' house. (I moved out of that room when my sister Mary was born, when I was three and a half, so I'm younger than that.) It's dark, and I'm listening to a Disney record narrated by Sterling Holloway, the story of a little taxi, sad and desperate, set in a seedy, Damon Runyon city. A Will Eisner city. *The Naked City*.

Vivid, inexplicable images, outside the realm of any possible nursery-school-age experience: a tangle of concrete struts arching over alleys, soot-stained brick, corrugated metal garbage cans, neon over a distant doorway, jazz filtering out. And it is always bound to that yellow bedroom, which is as accurate as carbon dating in my family.

All my life those images sat in the back of my mind, dimly lit and seductively creepy. Where did they come from? I'd occasionally ask someone my age if they remembered a Disney record called *The Depressed Little Taxi.* Ha. No. At flea markets, antique sales—and much later, on eBay—anywhere there was an accumulation of late 1950s children's records, I thought—*What if?*—and looked. I never found a trace of its existence.

Then one night last fall, in the wee hours, I was playing on my laptop, a glass of wine at hand, tired, but not quite ready to sleep, following odd links to other odd links. I typed "Sterling Holloway" into Google's search bar; it is his voice that is most evocative, that instantly conjures my preschool room, shadowed with loss and regret.

I went from site to site to site to site and at two in the morning, on YouTube, I may have found it. A cartoon, not a record, but if it *was* the source, it would permanently overwrite the elusive images that had lived, for fifty years, on the borders of fantasy, dream, and memory, and I would lose—forever—that sense of noirish magic.

I had to watch it. I had to find out.

But I had to write this story first.

Louise Marley

egg magic

Tory lingered in the chicken pen in the September sunshine, watching her flock scratch through the grass, spreading their feathers in the morning breeze. The banty, Pansy, trotted to Tory to have her glossy black and red feathers stroked. She chirkled under Tory's fingers. "Silly Pansy," Tory said. "You act more like a puppy than a chicken."

Most people, she knew, thought chickens were dumb. The kids at school, except for the 4-H Club, thought her hens were stupid, smelly animals who didn't care a bit about people. Tory knew better. Pansy loved to be petted, to be scratched right at the back of her short neck. The stately leghorns followed at her heels when she filled the feed dispensers, when she poured out the scratch or corn or scattered the grit. The pair of Black Jersey Giants pecked around her toes as she filled the water dispenser, hoping for the kitchen scraps she brought out in plastic bags. The Barred Rock layers waited for Tory to come through the gate every morning, and then dashed ahead of her into the coop, making a game of pretending to protect their eggs. Her single Araucana, tufted head looking as if someone had stuffed her ears with cotton, preened beside her nest each day, making certain Tory knew who had laid those azure eggs.

Only Rainbow kept a haughty distance, patrolling the far side of the pen.

The school bus rumbled around the corner and turned into their lane. The boys, five-year-old twins and twelve-year-old Ethan, boiled out of the house and down the gravel drive to the bus stop. Rosalie, Tory's stepmother, stood on the porch steps, calling her name.

"Rainbow!" Tory said. "Come say good-bye. I have to go to school."

The hen turned one black eye in Tory's direction. She gave a single sharp cluck, a sound that would have been a snort in another kind of animal. The banty chirruped. Tory murmured, "Never mind, Pansy. Rainbow's just cranky. It's because she's so much older."

Not even Henry, Tory's father, knew how old Rainbow was. She was older than any of the other chickens. Pansy might live ten years if she were lucky, if she didn't get sick or get nabbed by the boys' border collie. But Rainbow, tall, thin, and long necked, had been left behind by Tory's mother when she left. That had been sixteen years before.

Rainbow's plumage changed colors with the seasons, from gold and black, to green and black, to rusty brown and black.

She fit no breed or crossbreed Tory could find in any catalog, and she mirrored Tory's own mysterious heredity—her sharp black eyes, her long neck, her narrow hands and feet. Tory looked nothing like her father, who was big and sandy haired. Tory had a faint memory of her mother, an ephemeral impression of a thin face, long fingers, lank black hair. Henry had spoken to Tory of her mother only once. A gypsy, he said. A traveler. He would not say how they had met, or why she had left.

"Victoria! Hurry, you'll miss the bus!" Rosalie waved to her. She was wearing that awful old apron again, pink, with a bedraggled ruffle around the bottom. Her round face was pink, too, and her hair, an indeterminate brown, stuck up in every direction.

Victoria gathered up her egg basket and her backpack and let herself out of the pen.

Rosalie called again, "Victoria! Give me your basket and run!"

Tory didn't run, but she did hurry across the yard to hand over the egg basket.

"Don't forget your 4-H meeting, dear."

Tory rolled her eyes as she turned toward the bus. Rosalie tried too hard. If she were only thin and mean, she would be the perfect wicked stepmother from the fairy tales, but Rosalie went overboard in the other direction, watching over everything, interfering in everything. She had bought Tory's first bra for her before she asked for one. She fussed over Tory's hair, suggesting awful hairstyles, and she nagged at her to wear colors other than black. She made her clean her fingernails every day when she came in from the chicken coop, and she constantly reminded her of things she already knew, like her 4-H meetings. Tory wished she would just devote herself to the boys and let Tory take care of herself.

The boys were already in the bus when Tory climbed up the ribbed rubber steps. The bus lurched forward the moment the doors closed, and she grabbed seat backs as she worked her way to her usual seat. Three seats back from the driver. Not too far forward, which would be weird. Not too far back, where her half brothers could torment her. She sank onto the bench seat, her backpack under her feet, the *Catalog of Contemporary Poultry* on her lap.

Newport was a small town, and the bus carried little kids as well as high school students. Ethan and Jack and Peter sat in the back. The older ones sidled between the seats in twos and threes, sitting together, giggling and talking. Tory always sat alone.

Alison Blakely climbed on the bus, flipping her long blond hair with her fingers as she came up the steps. She looked like the classic fairy-tale princess, but she had a sharp tongue. She grinned pointedly at Tory's catalog. "Not more chickens?"

Tory kept her eyes down, but her cheeks warmed. She shook her head.

Josh Hudson was waiting for Alison. He scooted over to make room for her, and she leaned close to whisper something in his ear. He laughed, and Tory glanced over her shoulder. The prince and princess, fair and beautiful. Tory looked away from them. She was nothing like them, she reminded herself. She was dark and dangerous. Solitary. A mysterious and magical future awaited her when her mother returned. Her mother, the gypsy queen.

"Hey, Tory," Josh called.

Tory pushed ragged black strands away from her forehead. "What?"

"One of the eggs you brought us last week was really weird," Josh said, more loudly than necessary. "It was blue!"

Alison made a face. "Ooh, blue eggs. Ick! I'm glad we get ours at the store."

Tory bridled. "He means the shell, Alison. The shell is blue, not the egg!"

Alison shivered. "Still!" she cried.

Tory glowered, and her cheeks burned. "I have an Araucana hen. She's very rare, and she lays blue eggs. And all my eggs are better than the ones from the store!" She was embarrassed at the tension in her voice, and she wrenched herself back to face forward again.

Alison wasn't being fair. Tory's hens laid eggs in a palette of colors—white, tan, speckled, and blue—but they all had beautiful dark yellow yolks and a full, rich taste. Her flock ran free in their pen, in fresh air and sunshine. They ate a good laying mash and drank water from a scrupulously clean tank.

Tory knew what eggs from the store looked like, with their pallid yolks and runny whites. She wished she had said that. She should have shivered, like Alison, as if the very thought of eggs from chickens who never saw the sky made *her* feel sick. But it was too late now.

She tried to focus on *Contemporary Poultry* as the bus rattled along.

She was surprised to see Charlie Williams jump up into the bus. Usually he drove his father's pickup to school. His long legs took all three steps at once, and he grinned at her as he came down the aisle. Charlie was tall and thin, even thinner than Tory. His knobby wrists stuck out of his shirt sleeves, and his sneakers seemed enormous. "Hi, Tory."

She nodded to him awkwardly and murmured, "Hi."

He stopped beside her seat. "My mother says she hopes you have lots of eggs this week. She's baking for Christmas already."

Tory lifted her face to see his eyes. They were a nice clear brown, not the glittery black of her own. And Rainbow's. "There should be plenty. All my hens are laying well."

"That's great." Charlie nodded. "I'll tell her."

"How many does she want?"

"She said she'd call your mom when she knows."

Tory stiffened. "Rosalie's not my mom, Charlie."

"Well—yeah." His thin face reddened. "I know. I just meant . . ." He dropped his eyes. "Sorry." He shifted his backpack and stumbled a little as he worked his way back to his seat.

Tory bit her lip as they rolled into town toward the cluster of school buildings. She hadn't meant to embarrass Charlie. She just didn't want him to think—or anyone to think—that she was Rosalie's daughter, plain and ordinary. She was different, a changeling, mysterious. And one day, when her mother came back, they would all see.

It was when Tory was eleven that her life changed. Until then, Tory and her father had lived alone in the rambling country house with its wide yard and wraparound porch. Tory had invented an entire history for herself, turning the big old house into a castle, with a king and a princess, and a gypsy queen mysteriously gone missing.

Rainbow, the old chicken, was all that was left of the vanished queen. Tory treasured the solitary hen despite her arrogant ways. She spun stories in her head in which her mother returned for Rainbow, and for her daughter. She imagined a gypsy caravan trundling into town, the way they sometimes did during the county fair. She pictured her mother stepping down from an elegantly painted wagon to restore the kingdom, king and queen together, happy daughter basking in their affection. But something completely different happened when she was eleven.

Henry married Rosalie. And Rainbow laid her first egg.

On the day Henry brought Rosalie and seven-year-old Ethan home, Tory fled to the chicken coop to crumple onto the floor and sob out her resentment and dismay.

Rainbow sat on her perch, watching Tory cry. When her tears subsided, Tory sat crosslegged on the floor, rubbing her swollen eyes with her sleeve. The old hen hopped down from her perch and came to stand next to her, one yellow three-toed foot poised above the floor. She bent her long neck and pecked at Tory's arm.

"Ow! Rainbow!" Tory exclaimed.

For answer, the chicken pecked her again, and then hopped up with a little flutter of feathers to stand beside her nest. Tory stared at her. "What's wrong with you?"

Rainbow tilted her head, her scarlet comb drooping to one side, her black eye unblinking. Tory sighed, pushed back her hair, and got up to see what Rainbow wanted.

In the nest was a single narrow egg.

Tory stammered in surprise, "Rainbow! You—did you do this?" She stretched out her hand to the nest, wary of Rainbow's hard beak, but the hen moved back, out of the way. Tory picked up the egg and cradled it in her palm.

It weighed nothing, as if it were filled with air, like a balloon. It was the color of a cloud at sunset, pink and lavender and gray, and oddly elongated. It almost didn't look like an egg. Both ends had the same pointed shape, and the middle was slender. And it was so light! Tory stared at it in her hand, wondering.

"Victoria? Victoria, dear, may I come in?"

All of Tory's resentment came rushing back to her at the sound of this intruder's voice. For a long moment, she didn't answer.

The door opened, and her new stepmother, Rosalie, put her head in. "Victoria?"

Tory turned, holding the egg close to her chest.

She couldn't see why Henry had married this woman. She couldn't understand why he had to marry at all, why things had to change, but why this Rosalie? She wasn't even pretty. She was plump, and she had scraggly brown hair and round brown eyes. And that awful boy!

"Victoria? Did your chicken lay an egg?" Rosalie's eyes widened at the sight of Rainbow's pink-and-gray egg in Tory's fingers.

Ethan was there, too, loudly demanding to know what was

in the little barn. Rainbow, with an angry squawk, dashed out past Rosalie, between Ethan's legs, and off to the farthest corner of the pen. Tory also stalked out of the coop and back to the house, the egg between her palms. Her father was waiting in the kitchen doorway.

"Honey? Rosalie was worried about you, and . . . what do you have there?"

And suddenly, the first egg Rainbow had ever laid was everyone's business. Henry took it from Tory's hand, exclaiming over its lightness. Everyone gathered around the table to look. It was Ethan who began demanding that they crack it and see what was inside.

"No," Tory said, giving him a withering look. "It's mine, and I'm not going to break it. I'm going to keep it just like this."

"Come on, honey," her father said. "Don't you want to know why it's so light?"

Rosalie said, in her soft voice, "No, no, Henry. Victoria's right. It's hers, and if she wants to keep it intact, we should respect her wishes."

This was too much, the intruder speaking on her behalf. Henry was her own father, after all. He was the king, and she was the princess. These other people had no role here.

Tory spoke to Henry as if no one else were present. "Okay, Dad. Get a bowl, will you?"

Henry and Rosalie exchanged a look but neither spoke. Henry brought a glass bowl, and Ethan climbed up on a chair, without even asking permission. Tory pulled the glass bowl to her, as far from Ethan's hot curiosity as she could. She held the colorful egg in her right hand and struck it on the bowl's edge.

The narrow oval split lengthwise, as neatly as if it had been perforated. Tory held one half in each hand, gazing in wonder.

Rosalie said, "There's nothing in it!"

Tory said slowly, "Dad—there's a—there's something painted on the inside."

Ethan crowed, "Let me see! Let me see!" Tory snatched the shells away from his grasping hands and held them up where her father could see them.

The two halves of the eggshell made an image, cloudy and vague, as if painted out of fog, but unmistakable. It was a woman, with narrow dark eyes and long hair and one long-fingered, slender hand held to her throat. The image made Tory feel disoriented, as if she were upside down. On the inside of Rainbow's barren egg was the faintly remembered image from her babyhood.

It was her mother.

"Magda," Henry muttered, and then shut his mouth hard.

"Who? What did you say, Dad?" But he shook his head. Again, Tory saw her father and Rosalie, the interloper, look at each other.

Fresh tears welled in Tory's eyes as she fit the eggshell back together and held the whole egg protectively to her chest. "Dad?" she whispered. "Is her name Magda?"

Henry pressed his lips together.

Ethan demanded, "What? What?"

"I didn't see anything," Rosalie said. "An empty eggshell."

Henry muttered, "Old hen never did lay any eggs."

They had all seemed to lose interest then, except Tory. Amid the fuss of suitcases and boxes and things, Tory carried Rainbow's strange gift up the stairs to her room. Ethan stared hungrily after her, but she ignored him. She stood beside her window, pondering the image in the egg. Her mother had a name now. It was Magda, a perfect name for the magical queen of her dreams. She would come soon, in her painted wagon, and carry Tory away. She would take her to a real castle, and Henry, too, and the king and princess and the gypsy queen would live happily ever after.

Rainbow met Tory at the gate when she got back from school, stretching her neck and scolding. Her feathers shone their autumn gold and black, her ruffled comb gleaming scarlet.

Tory dropped her backpack outside the gate and slipped inside. She knelt to offer Rainbow a morsel of oatmeal cookie saved from her lunch. The hen pecked at it until it was gone and then cocked her head at Tory as if demanding to know what happened to the rest of it.

The other hens came running, and Tory scattered a handful of corn for them. They pecked at it happily, chortling among themselves. Tory ducked into the coop to check the nests.

She savored the sweet smell of fresh wood shavings. Some chickens smelled awful, but hers, with their spotless coop and generous pen, smelled of clean feathers and good food and healthy bodies. Most of the hens laid their eggs in the hours of darkness, but there were always a few in the afternoons.

Tory's egg business was thriving. Every weekend she sold several dozen eggs, brought back egg cartons to reuse, and collected discarded newspapers for the laying nests.

There were four eggs today, two large white ones and two tiny speckled ones, Pansy's efforts. Tory cupped them against her middle, enjoying their smooth warmth against her palm.

"Good girls," she said as she made her way back through her little flock. "Especially you, Pansy! You try harder, don't you?" Pansy waddled at her heels, clucking mournfully when Tory went through the gate. "Don't cry," Tory told her. "I'll be back soon."

She went up through the screened porch and into the kitchen. The boys were seated around the table, arguing and poking at each other. Tory passed them on her way to put the eggs into the refrigerator, where a shelf was set aside for the purpose. Rosalie, immersed in setting out milk and sandwiches, greeted her, but Tory could hardly hear her over the boys' racket. She murmured some response and dashed up the stairs toward her own room.

She glanced back from the landing, noticing the flush on Rosalie's cheeks, her hair curling in sweat-tendrils around her face. She looked tired. The kitchen counter was lined with jars of freshly made preserves, blackberry and raspberry and currant. The hot-water bath still steamed on the stove. Tory paused, supposing she should offer to help her stepmother.

Just then Peter upset his milk into Jack's lap, and Jack jumped up, knocking his chair to the floor. Ethan squalled some insult, and Rosalie exclaimed in exasperation. Tory groaned and escaped into her bedroom.

⊠ ⊠ ⊠

Tory had just turned thirteen when Rainbow laid her second egg.

It came the day she started her first period. Rosalie gave her a cup of tea for her stomach and a Midol for the cramping, and let her stay home from school, lying on the couch eating toasted cheese and chicken noodle soup. For once, Tory let Rosalie fuss over her, bringing her magazines and a pillow for her feet. She lay there most of the day, reading, until Ethan came home from school and the twins, then eighteen months old, got up from their nap in their usual noisy fashion. Tory wandered out to the chicken coop to get away from the din. She felt fragile and headachy, tender all over.

By that time there were nine hens in her flock. Her first layers had come when she and Henry went to the feed store in Newport to buy scratch and grain for Rainbow. The feed store owner took her in the back to show her some leghorns that had come in for a Newport farmer, and Tory begged Henry to buy her one. He bought three, and Tory's little egg business began.

In the next year, she acquired Pansy from a woman who was moving into a retirement home, and the first of her Barred Rock layers from a man Henry met at the barbershop, who had heard of Tory's enterprise, and had more chickens than he wanted. More Barred Rocks came from him a few months later, at the same time Tory discovered the joys of the *Catalog of Contemporary Poultry* and the satisfaction of showing her hens in 4-H shows. Her Black Jersey Giants were a birthday present from Henry—well, the card said Henry and Rosalie—and her single, prized Arucana she bought with some of her own egg money. She was proud of every hen.

She spread fresh grit in the pen and pulled a handful of corn from her pocket. Pansy came running, chirping. The other hens were spread out around the ramp to the coop, and at the top of the ramp, Rainbow stood with both feet set, claws curled around the joist. As Tory watched, one of the Barred Rocks tried to come up into the coop, but Rainbow, with a single ominous cluck, warned her off.

"What are you doing, you crotchety old thing?" Tory asked. As she approached the coop, Rainbow stepped backward and waited just inside. The Barred Rock stepped up on the ramp, bringing another warning from Rainbow.

"Okay, okay," Tory said. The Barred Rock chirped plaintively as Tory moved past.

Rainbow had jumped up beside one of the nests. And there, on the shredded newspaper, was another sunset-colored egg.

This time Tory hid the egg inside her sweater, and after finishing with her chickens, she smuggled it up to her room. Rosalie called as she passed, "Victoria? Are you feeling better, dear? Do you need anything?"

"I'm fine," Tory answered, and hurried on. She pretended not to notice that Rosalie had followed her out of the kitchen and was standing at the foot of the stairs, gazing after her. The twins were banging pot lids on the floor of the kitchen, and Ethan was watching cartoons with the volume up to drown out the banging. Tory felt her cramps coming back, and she wished everyone would simply go away and leave her alone.

She sank onto her bed and gazed at the pink-and-lavender

egg in her hand. Like the first, it was long and narrow, with symmetrical ends. She set it on her pillow, and went to her desk drawer to get the shards of the first egg, and laid them beside the new one. The image inside the first had faded to grayish blotches.

Tory picked up Rainbow's new offering and cracked it on the edge of the lamp.

Like the first, it fell into neat halves. And like its predecessor, it held an image.

It was the same, the woman's vague face, long black hair, dark eyes, a narrow hand. Narrow, like Tory's own. Dark eyes, like her own. Magda. The missing queen.

Tory stared out of her bedroom window at the yard, the neat chicken coop, the pen with its wire covering to keep the hawks away. Rainbow marched at the outer edge of the pen, her neck craning this way and that, her comb shining in the sun. As Tory watched, she tilted her head up to the window. Then, imperious as always, she turned her back and strutted away.

And now Tory was sixteen. The other high school kids called her "the chicken girl," which she had learned only when Ethan announced it to everyone at the dinner table.

"You—you little troll!" Tory shouted before she dashed to her room to sob on her bed. Henry, in a rare display of temper, had ordered Ethan to his room without dinner. Rosalie had tried to make it up to Tory with the offer of a shopping trip into Spokane, but Tory only shook her head. Rosalie made Ethan come to her room to apologize, and Tory slammed the door in his face, just missing his fingers on the doorjamb. She told herself she didn't care what the other kids thought. She didn't need them.

The Jones house hummed with activity. The twins were in kindergarten every morning, and Henry was busy at work, staying late each evening, leaving early each morning. Rosalie seemed tired all the time. Tory buried herself in her schoolwork and her hens, scouring the catalogs for new ways of increasing her egg production, for sources for replacement hens when one or the other of hers quit laying, reading the mailings from colleges with animal husbandry programs.

She didn't tell anyone, not even Henry, that she had the third of Rainbow's eggs, unbroken, hidden in the back of her desk drawer.

Two awful things had happened on the day she found it.

She'd been excused from study hall in the library to work with the 4-H advisor. When she came back, handing her pass to the teacher and looking for a seat at the long tables, Josh Hudson looked up as she walked past him. He took a long, noisy sniff. "Mmm," he said, just loudly enough for all the kids at the table to hear him. "I smell chicken."

Alison Blakely was next to him. She laughed, and then everyone else at the table laughed, too. Tory was so humiliated she could hardly see. She blundered into a chair, like some toddler just learning to walk, her backpack banging against the person sitting in it. Her hair fell into her eyes, and her feet felt as if they no longer knew where the floor was. Charlie Williams leaped up to help her, putting his hand under her arm, grabbing her backpack as she stumbled forward. He meant to be nice, she knew that, but somehow that made it worse.

And Josh clucked. Clucked!

Giggles rippled up and down the study table, until finally the teacher left her desk and walked over to see what the disturbance was. Still, Tory knew they were laughing behind their hands, passing each other notes, avoiding her eyes. Charlie pointed out the assignment in the history book, and she stared at it, but she couldn't make sense of the words on the page. Her face felt hot enough to melt right away from her bones.

And it was at dinner that same night that Rosalie and Henry made their announcement.

"But you can't be!" Tory wailed at her stepmother. "You're too old!"

Her father growled, "Victoria!" Even Ethan sucked in his breath.

Rosalie stared at her, her eyes round pools of surprise and hurt.

The twins gazed around the table, chubby faces beginning to pucker for tears.

And then Tory realized that Rosalie had finally taken off the hideous pink apron and was wearing a maternity dress. Her dress bulged in front, a sign Tory knew she should have recognized. She felt tears of shame and despair starting at the back of her throat. "Excuse me," she whispered. She shoved her chair back and ran to the solace of the chicken coop.

It was just too much. There were already too many children in the house, too much noise, too many demands.

And it was disturbing to think of Henry and Rosalie . . . No, she wouldn't think of it. It was gross. She raced up the ramp into the dimness of the coop and leaned against the wall, crying into her hands. "I hate it here," she sobbed. "I hate it here!"

For long minutes she stood there, wishing she were anywhere else but here in this stupid house, in this stupid town, in her stupid school, where she didn't matter to anyone or anything.

Something stabbed at her shin. She gasped and dropped her hands.

Rainbow had come into the coop and was pecking at her leg with her sharp yellow beak. When Tory crouched down beside her, Rainbow pecked at her arm. With a shuddering sigh, Tory held out her empty hand. "Nothing here, Rainbow," she said brokenly.

Rainbow ignored her hand and pecked her leg again. Tory stood up. "Rainbow, you old crank, I don't know what you want! I never know what you want!"

Beyond the tall hen, she saw Pansy hovering in the doorway, fearful of Rainbow's beak but wanting to be petted. The other chickens were happily scratching in the grass outside, in the twilight. Rainbow pecked at her again. "Ouch! Rainbow!"

Pansy, with a nervous chirrup, dashed away down the ramp. Rainbow craned her skinny neck up at Tory and took a few hops toward the nests.

"Oh," Tory said softly. "Oh, Rainbow—did you—?"

She scanned the lower nests, seeing nothing, and then

stood on tiptoe to see into the upper ones. There it was. Rainbow's third egg.

It glowed like a sunlit cloud in the semidarkness. Tory lifted it out of the nest. As before, it seemed to weigh nothing, and it was cool in her palm.

Rainbow gave a loud, satisfied cackle and swaggered out of the coop. She paraded through the rest of the flock to the far end of the pen. Pansy dashed in to cluck at Tory.

"Look at this, Pansy," Tory said. She held out the egg. "She left me another." Pansy made a mournful chirp. "I know," Tory told her. "I don't understand it either."

Carefully, she wrapped the egg in a fold of newspaper, and tucked it inside her sweater. She shooed the hens into the coop for the night and then went into the house, hoping to slip through the kitchen unnoticed.

Rosalie was still at the sink, washing dishes. Tory's job. She looked up when Tory came in, and Tory saw that her eyelashes were wet, her round cheeks blotchy. She pulled off her rubber gloves, and came to put her arms around Tory. "Victoria! Won't you talk with me?"

Tory felt the hard swell of Rosalie's stomach against her, and she pulled away, revolted by it. "No," she said. "I'm sorry about the dishes." She turned toward the stairs.

"That's okay, Tory," Rosalie sighed. "I know you're upset."

Surprised, Tory stopped on the second step. Rosalie had never used her nickname before. Rosalie looked up at her, her lips trembling. Hesitantly, she said, "It's perfectly natural, you know. For us to have . . . for there to be another baby."

Tory nodded. "I know. I'm sorry I acted that way."

Rosalie stepped closer. "Dear, I don't want you to apologize. I . . . I just wish . . ." Her lips trembled again, and she pressed her finger to them.

Tory put her hand inside her sweater to touch the newspaper-wrapped egg and wished she could just disappear.

"Never mind," Rosalie said in a choked voice. She turned back to the sink, her shoulders slumping. Tory, aching with confusion, went on up the stairs.

She unwrapped the egg on her bed and stared at it. The others, in the back of her desk drawer, had faded. This one, she supposed, had another image, but if she broke it to see, that image too would fade. She was too old to be imagining castles and princesses now, but she still dreamed of her mother's return. And suppose there was never another of Rainbow's eggs?

Tory picked up the egg and went to stand beside her window. Stars had begun to twinkle, and the shreds of cloud glowed a misty white. Tory held the egg to her cheek as if she could feel the image through the shell, imprint it on her skin. Everything was changing. If her mother didn't come soon, it might be too late.

Two days before Christmas, Tory woke to the sounds of tense voices in the kitchen. She sat up and peered out her window. It was still dark, but snow had fallen during the night, and it glowed with starlight. Her bedside clock read 5:10 in big red numerals.

Tory pulled on her robe and went to the top of the stairs to peer down into the kitchen.

Her father was speaking into the phone. "Yes, yes. Okay, Doctor. We're on our way."

Tory hurried down the stairs, her feet bare, her hair tumbled in her face.

Rosalie sat at the kitchen table, her hands on her belly, her face haggard. She tried to smile at Tory, but it was a pale attempt.

"What's wrong?" Tory asked. A chill ran through her, from the bottoms of her feet on the cold linoleum all the way to her fingertips.

Henry was helping Rosalie up, pulling a coat around her. "Rosalie's having contractions," he said hoarsely.

"But—but it's too early, isn't it?"

Rosalie leaned against Henry, but her eyes met Tory's. "It is, dear," she said, her voice rough with pain. "I have—" She didn't finish her sentence but bent forward with a groan, as Henry supported her.

"We're going to the hospital, Tory," he said, already turning toward the door. "We need you to—to take care of things—" His voice, too, trailed off. He looked over his shoulder at her, a look of mute, frightened appeal on his broad face.

Tory had never seen her father frightened. She stood glued to the kitchen floor as if roots had grown from her feet. She stared at her father, at Rosalie's hunched figure. "Me?" she breathed. The darkness beyond the kitchen window, the gleam of the new snow, the nighttime chill in the house all took on nightmarish qualities.

"Please," her father said. And before Tory could think of something to say, Henry and Rosalie were gone, the car roaring down the driveway, turning into the road toward town with little rooster tails of snow rising behind its wheels. For a long time she stood there, wondering at the empty feel of the house with her father gone. No, that didn't make sense. Her father was gone every day, at work. The emptiness came from Rosalie's absence.

A strange thought crept into Tory's mind. Did the castle have a queen, after all?

She thought of all that would need doing, the things Rosalie did every day. The boys would want their breakfast. The twins would need their clothes picked out. Ethan would need to be told what chores to do, would need permission if he wanted to go somewhere with his friends. There would be lunch, and dinner if Henry and Rosalie weren't back . . .

Tory shivered, trying not to think of Rosalie not coming back. She didn't know how bad this might be. Babies came prematurely, she knew that, but—two months? How serious was it?

When the phone rang, she jumped a foot.

It was her father. "We're in the emergency room, but we have to go to Spokane," he told her. "To Sacred Heart."

"Spokane?"

"Yes. The doctor says they have better equipment there."

"But when will you—"

"Honey, I have to go. The helicopter is here."

"Helicopter?" Tory's voice sounded thin in her ears.

Her father's voice was tight. "Tory, they want to get your mom there in a hurry. I'm going to follow in the car. You'll be all right, won't you?"

"Dad—"

"Yes, honey? I have to go now."

"But Dad—please, I want you to tell Rosalie—"

But Henry was gone before she could squeeze out the words.

Helicopter. Why did they send people to hospitals in helicopters?

Tory was suddenly very, very frightened. Her knees felt shaky, and she sank into one of the kitchen chairs, her head in her hands. She didn't realize till later that she hadn't corrected her father when he referred to Rosalie as her mom. She hadn't even noticed it.

She felt a bit braver when the sun came up, the darkness shrinking back slowly, reluctantly, from the snowy landscape. The twins came clamoring down the stairs not long after that, with Ethan behind them. Carefully, trying not to alarm them, Tory explained that their mother had gone to the hospital in Spokane.

"Where's Dad?" Ethan asked. He had never resisted calling Henry his father. But then, he knew his real father—*biological* father, Tory corrected herself. And he didn't like him much.

"Dad went to Spokane, too," she told him. She left out the helicopter. They might think it was exciting, but they might just as easily find it scary.

"What about breakfast?" Peter asked pragmatically. Tory set about making oatmeal. She scorched the pan, but she managed to produce three bowls of cereal. The twins tormented each other at the table, banging spoons, spilling milk and sugar, until Tory couldn't stand it anymore. She let them take their bowls into the living room, to eat in front of the television. She set the pot to soak and wiped up the mess from the table. When she went to the sink with the sponge, she saw that a few hens were outside, scratching through the powdery snow, cackling among themselves. Rainbow was nowhere to be seen.

Tory pulled on her coat and her lined boots and took the egg basket from its hook. Cartoon music blared as she let herself out onto the porch.

Before she reached the screen door, a hysterical squawking began in the chicken coop. Tory froze.

It was Rainbow, of course, but she had never heard the hen make that noise. The dog leaped up from his porch bed and began to bark, frantically, scratching at the door. The other hens scattered and ran across the pen, this way and that, as if something were chasing them, but Tory saw that they avoided the coop.

Ethan came running. "Tory! What's going on?"

Tory said, "I don't know," as she hurried off the porch. Over her shoulder she called, "There must be something in the coop!"

"Tory, wait!" Ethan cried. "What if it's a coyote or something?"

Tory paused, her hand on the gate to the pen. Ethan was right. If it was a coyote, or a raccoon, she didn't want to be in that coop with it. But Rainbow and the other hens . . . they were her responsibility. There was no one else to call on. She lifted the latch, the metal icy under her fingers. Just as she stepped through the gate, the rest of the hens came scurrying out of the coop. Rainbow gave one more loud squawk, and then there was silence. The border collie barked twice more, as if in query, and then he, too, fell silent.

Ethan stared across the yard at Tory, and she stared back through the wire fence. "Are you going in?" he finally asked.

"I—I guess I have to."

"Maybe you should wait! Let's call somebody!"

"But, Ethan, what if—" The idea of losing her hens, or losing Rainbow, was too much. She turned toward the coop. The dog nosed around the outside of the pen, mercifully quiet now except for his snuffling.

Tory jumped at the slamming of the screen door. Ethan had gone back into the house. *Cowardly troll!* she thought. He could at least have stayed to see if she was all right. Rosalie, she knew, would have stayed with her.

Slowly, Tory approached the coop. All the hens except Rainbow now clustered at one side of the pen, as far from the border collie as possible. Feeling cold despite her warm coat, Tory walked up the ramp and peered in.

Rainbow was on her perch, head tilted, watching her with a glassy eye. Tory saw nothing else, no other gleaming animal eyes in the dimness. She heard no scrabble of claws or hiss of panicked breath. She flipped on the overhead light, and the shadows receded to the corners.

Tory approached the nests, where she could see several eggs. As she lifted the first of them into her basket, she felt a prickle on the back of her neck, as if someone had drawn a feather across it. She had tied her hair up in a sloppy ponytail, and the exposed short hairs at her nape rose as if static electricity had drawn them upward.

Tory whirled, the egg basket before her like a shield.

She opened her mouth to call to Ethan, but no sound came.

The woman's face was just as she had thought it would be, narrow and sharp featured. She smiled, and she lifted one hand to push back the long black hair that fell over her shoulder. Her fingers were long and thin.

"Hello, Tory," she said. Her voice was slightly hoarse. "Do you know who I am?"

For a long moment Tory couldn't draw breath into her lungs. Rainbow, behind her, shifted her feet on the perch and fluttered her feathers.

The woman took a step forward, not quite into the light. She wore a loose caftan in a shiny material, and her eyes . . . her eyes were as dark as midnight. As dark as Tory's.

"The eggs," Tory breathed.

The woman smiled again. "Oh, yes," she said, with a ghost of a laugh. "The eggs."

"I don't understand them."

The woman waved a hand. "I didn't want you to forget me." She laughed again, lightly.

"Are you—" Tory hardly dared ask it. She felt Rainbow's beak on her shoulder, pecking hard once, twice. "Are you my mother?" she breathed.

The woman nodded. "I am. In my way. I haven't been much of a parent."

Tory gazed in amazement at the woman she had wondered about for so long. She found, now that she was face-to-face with her, that she couldn't think of her as her mother.

"Magda," she said. The woman nodded again. Tory blurted, "Why did you leave me?"

Magda lifted the heavy hair from her neck with both hands. Her sleeves floated around her slender arms. In the shadows she looked fragile and beautiful. "My kind don't have children, in the normal run of things," she said.

"But—but Dad . . ."

Magda shrugged. "Poor Henry. He just couldn't understand."

"He's married now."

"Oh, I know, Tory. I know all about it."

Tory adjusted her grip on her egg basket. "How?"

Another shrug. "I've been here once or twice. Well, three times, actually. Don't you have three eggs?"

"Yes."

Magda grinned and moved forward into the light. Tory saw that she wore heavy gold hoops in her ears and a gold choker around her neck. There were lines around her eyes, and her lips were painted a harsh red. Her fingernails were dirty.

"What are you?" Tory heard herself ask the question she had held in her heart since Rainbow's first egg had showed her the image.

Magda gave a throaty chuckle. "Come with me and find out."

Again Rainbow pecked at Tory's shoulder. "Come with you?" Tory's voice cracked, and her mouth felt dry. This was what she had wanted, what she had dreamed of, but . . . "Now?"

"This is the perfect time." The woman came closer. She smelled of something like woodsmoke and musk, utterly unfamiliar. "Come with me," she said.

"I can't." Rainbow pecked her shoulder, and Tory stepped out of the hen's reach. "I have responsibilities," she said.

"Oh, responsibilities!" Magda's tone was light, but there was an edge to it. "Just why I left, Tory. I hate responsibilities."

Tory stared at her mother. "Everyone has responsibilities," she muttered. She sounded, she thought, exactly like Rosalie. This wasn't going at all the way she had imagined it would.

"We don't!" Magda laughed and waved her hands, making her sleeves flutter.

"We?"

"We!" Magda winked. "The witches!" she hissed.

Tory gasped. It was as if this woman had read her mind, as if she had dipped into it and picked out her thought. "You're not a witch," she protested, her voice faint with dismay. "You're a gypsy. Dad told me."

"Are you sure?" The woman stepped past Tory and lifted a cloud-pink egg out of the nest beside Rainbow. She held it out on her palm. "Do you know how old this stupid hen is?"

Tory gaped at the egg. All she could think of to say was, "Rainbow's not stupid."

"Oh, I think she is. She wouldn't leave with me! Insisted on staying here, with you, in this silly, boring place."

She laid the elongated egg neatly on top of the other eggs in Tory's basket. "You're going to come, though, aren't you, Tory? You don't want to stay with these dull people!"

"No, no, I don't, but right now . . . I can't leave."

Tory heard Ethan calling her name. He must have come back outside. She stared down at the patterns of rose and gray swirling on the surface of Rainbow's egg.

Ethan called again. "Tory! Tory?" She took a step toward the door and stopped.

"This is our chance, Tory. There's no time to waste!" Magda seized Tory's wrist with cold, strong fingers. "They're waiting for us!"

Rainbow cackled and jumped off her perch to strut at Tory's heels.

Tory stared at the chicken and then at Magda. Ethan called again. Tory pulled her arm free. "I can't leave the boys," she said weakly.

Magda lifted both hands, palms up. "Yes, you can," she said. "Who's to stop you?"

Tory took a shaky breath. "It's wrong. They need me."

Magda leaned close to her, her dark eyes widening. "Who needs you, Tory?" The smell of musk intensified. "Come with me, travel, see the world. . . ."

A horn honked from the driveway, and Tory heard the slam of a door. She backed to the door of the chicken coop and looked out. Rainbow followed.

Charlie Williams came around from the front of the house and was just going up the steps to the porch, where Ethan was waiting for him. Tory saw Ethan talking, gesturing to the chicken pen, and Charlie turned and started across the yard.

Charlie's tall, thin figure, so familiar and normal, gave Tory courage. She turned back to Magda. "My brothers need me," she said haltingly. "My—their—Rosalie is in the hospital."

"She'll be fine," Magda said with confidence.

"How do you know?"

Magda shrugged her thin shoulders, making her caftan ripple. "It's the sort of thing I know." She laughed again, and the sound was suspiciously like a cackle. "You need me, Tory—need me to take you away from this!" She gestured at the chicken coop, but somehow Tory knew she meant all of it, the house, the town, the school—the family.

Tory shook her head. "I've needed you lots of times, Magda," she said. "When I started to walk, when I learned to ride my bike, when I started school! Where were you then?"

Magda's smile faded, slowly, and her dark eyes glittered. She looked a bit like Rainbow at that moment, Tory thought, thin and old and mean. "I told you, Tory," she said in a low tone. "My kind aren't good with children."

Tory lifted her chin. "Not my fault," she said.

Magda gave a slow nod. "Quite right." She looked down at Tory's heels, where Rainbow glared back at her. "You stupid chicken," Magda said. "Are you coming with me this time?"

Rainbow craned her neck, opened and closed her beak, and took two mincing steps backward.

Magda waved a dismissive hand. "I guess that settles it," she said. She pointed a finger at Tory. "But I'll see you again. When you've had enough of all this."

"Tory!" It was Charlie, coming in through the gate. "Are you okay?"

Tory hurried down the ramp. Snowflakes had begun to fall again, dusting Charlie's hair as he frowned up at the chicken coop. His face relaxed when he saw her. "Tory! Gosh, your brother was really worried. I came as fast as I could. Everything okay with your hens?"

Tory crossed the pen to meet him. "Yes," she said. "Thanks for coming, Charlie."

"What's going on in there, Tory?" Charlie looked past her to the coop.

Rainbow strutted slowly down the ramp, alone. There was no sign of the visitor. Rainbow marched to the wire fence and stared out. In the lane beyond the driveway, a dented, multicolored van rumbled past on its way to the county road. Tory turned her head to watch it until it disappeared, and then she smiled up at Charlie.

"Oh," she said quietly. "Oh, nothing, really. Just my old hen raising a fuss."

Louise Marley is a Campbell Award and Nebula Award finalist, and a two-time winner of the Endeavour Award. Three of her novels have been named ALA Best Books of the Year. Her Singers of Nevya series, which includes the novel *Singer in the Snow,* reflects her first career as a classical concert and opera singer. Her novels *Airs Beneath the Moon* and *Airs and Graces*, about girls who fly winged horses, draw from the experiences of her country girlhood.

She lives in the Pacific Northwest with her husband and son. Visit her Web site at **www.louisemarley.com**.

Author's Note

I grew up on ranches in northern California and western Montana, riding horses, milking cows, and stacking hay bales in the summers. Three years ago, I met a young farm girl who raised her own chickens and sold their eggs to neighboring farmers to raise money for college, and I wanted to write a story about her and about her beloved chickens.

Chickens are animals full of surprises. Different breeds have different personalities, and they lay eggs of all different colors. The eggs of one breed taste quite different from those of another, and the eggs of chickens who are lovingly cared for are the best of all. They're almost magical!

Kara Dalkey

Flatland

Appomattox Kim leaped out of bed the instant her alarm began to shout, "Eat my dust!" in Mandarin. She didn't bother waiting for her mind to get in gear. Bathroom first. On the way, she hit the hotkey at her workstation that sent an e-mail to the coffee shop on the ground floor of the mod-tower. She went to the toilet in the tiny bathroom, pausing a moment to stare at herself in the mirror in all her dark-haired, bedhead glory. "I am so goddamn lucky," she said in the usual morning affirmation. Funny how she'd been hitting the "goddamn" harder than usual lately.

By the time she emerged, the light by the little dumb-waiter door in what passed for a kitchen in her high-tech "cubio" was blinking. Appie extracted her cup of hot liquid intelligence and took a few steps more out onto her deck.

Older residents of the mod-tower called theirs the "holo-deck" based on some old television show. Unlike decks in traditional apartments, this one was probably nowhere near the outside of the building. Three walls of Appie's deck were flat-panel displays linked to her workstation. Most cubio dwellers had scenery like Mount Rainier or Hawaii or Paris as their default, but Appie liked the feed from the Worldtree Agency's satellite. Right now it showed a ring of dawn emerging behind a darkened Earth. It made her feel like she was sitting on top of the world. But lately that feeling had a taint of loneliness—as though she were adrift out in space, alone and forgotten. She felt old. She was all of eighteen.

Appie sat in the plastic ergo-chair and put her feet up on the picnic table, allowing herself fifteen minutes to sip at her extra dark coffee-plus-whatever-other-stimulant-the-agency-could-legally-acquire-this-week. She felt the effect hit after six sips this time, like a door bursting open in her brain. *Yowza! Good stuff this morning,* Appie thought, blinking and sighing in appreciation. *Props to the barista.*

She glanced at the time glyph in the corner of the screen to her right. 7:25 A.M. Pacific Standard Time. Good—she could still have a little wake-up time and log on well before eight. That would look good to Worldtree. Every bit of edge counted. Appie was already a three-star employee, but it still wasn't wise to slack. Ever. "Yep," she sighed, "lucky."

Lucky that she had been plucked right out of high school. Colleges were full up, all the time, and you had to know someone or have the bucks to get a spot. But the smart megacompanies had their own plans, were forming their own schools, and had built the towers of modular cubio apartments to get their employees young, eager, trained their way, and working all the time. Training came with the job, and for a business-minded kid, was tons more relevant than what you got in college. For the young person who could hack it, the cubio gigs were the best—highly paid independence and the best resumé entry you could ask for. *If* you could hack it.

Because an agency like Worldtree demanded *all* your skills. Anything you could do, sell, be. Whatever you could offer as value added, they'd find a project that needed you. Appie had been hired because, at school, she'd been a Harbinger. She'd just try out odd combinations of clothes from her closet and a week later other kids were wearing the same things. She'd do her makeup or hair in some freaky way, and she'd see copycats all over school the next day. It had really bugged her. But the guidance counselors had also noticed and given her name to the Worldtree headhunters. Her Korean father was all about hard work and making the most of opportunities. He had urged Appie to take the gig. The rest was history. Now Appie had her own life, her own cubio, with a prime app of marketing and design consultant and a bigger salary than anyone in her family had ever earned.

Appie had been in heaven the first six months in the Worldtree tower. Fashion and manufacturing honchos all sought her advice and sent her samples. She hadn't bought her own clothes since moving in. She'd even been an advertising model for some of Worldtree's tech partners, for print media in Asian markets. Somewhere in Shanghai there was a poster with her 3-D image holding a digital camera the size of a Corn Chex square.

But despite the achievement, Appie had been antsy lately,

worried, jumpy at nothing in particular. It concerned her, and she hoped management hadn't noticed.

At 7:50, Appie bounced up from the table and went to her workstation. Her cubio mod came with state-of-the-art IT, replaced every six months by Worldtree. The screen showed the rotating logo of a tree with fractal branches and roots. It represented their reach, which was everywhere. Worldtree seriously believed in "insourcing" and had their employees working seamlessly with other companies around the globe. It was hard to tell where one company ended and another began.

Appie placed her right hand on the screen, feeling the familiar tickle as an electrical charge flowed from the tips of her fingers to the base of her palm.

The screen flickered and words appeared: "What value do you bring to Worldtree today?" These faded, replaced by the Chinese character for "ambition." Then a pleasant-looking female Asian avatar appeared. "Good morning, Appie. It is seven fifty-five A.M. Pacific Standard Time, April twenty-seventh, two thousand seventeen. How would you like to begin your workday?"

"Calendar."

"Certainly." The screen changed to show her schedule. Appie studied the entries closely. Fortunately it looked the same as it had the night before. That was not always the case. The agency operated around the clock, and a mod-dweller's schedule belonged to the agency, to mess with at its whim. Today was mostly a video conference with a client needing marketing advice. Appie figured she wouldn't even have to change clothes or comb her hair. Having that carefree look was a plus when manufacturers wanted to brainstorm with an ambassador from the much-desired eighteen- to twenty-five-year-old demographic.

Appie clicked for details and her heart skipped a beat. She leaned closer to the screen to be sure. Yes! Julio Tanaka. *Wow. A good day after all! I think.*

She'd done one marketing conference with Julio before and had never forgotten the experience. It had been so damn hard to concentrate with his stunningly hot face in her vid-screen. Ever since, she'd kept an eye out for the chance to work with him again. Here it was.

She jumped up from her ergo-chair and pogoed around the room for a few moments to shake off the nerves. *Julio! I'm going to see Julio!*

A chime from the workstation spoiled her fun. Appie sat down at once—it was Carolyn Madrona, her manager and floor warden, messaging her. Carolyn's thin face surrounded by an untidy mass of dark curly hair appeared in a corner of the screen. "Morning, Appie. Hope I'm not interrupting anything."

Appie cringed inside. They *said* they never vidcammed the cubios but rumors persisted. "Uh, no, just doing some warm-ups. What can I do for you?"

"I noticed you had a couple of hours open coming up tomorrow, and I wanted to set you up for more CAD training and another hour of Global Economics. Okay if I just fill in your calendar?"

"Um, sure." A part of Appie died inside. She'd hoped to

kick back those two hours to relax and try out a game demo.

"Great. You're a three star now but you've been with us nearly a year and we'd like to see you at three and a half by this point. By the way, Mercator Mercantile really liked the job you did on their sales database. They sent a recommendation."

"Cool." It had been make-work, really boring, but there hadn't been any other projects available that day and you had to keep busy.

"So they've sent a new packet for you to work on as soon as you have time. It's great that you're so diverse and responsive, Appie. That'll take you a long way."

Appie wanted so bad to sigh deeply, but she did not, *not*, let herself. Attitude was half the game. "Thanks."

"Thank you. Have a good time at your conference. Mercator has budget issues these days, so don't expect much joy if you recommend something extravagant. Still, they paid their fee in advance, so we can't complain. Besides, it's all good when you have Julio on the team, right?" She winked.

Appie kept her face strictly neutral. "Yeah. He's a sharp dude. Good to work with."

"Riiiight. Anyway, send me a report when you're done. I see they've moved up the start time to eight thirty, so you might finish up early. If you do, we have another project to send your way."

"Uh, cool. I guess business is booming."

"That's because we make it boom," said Carolyn sardonically. "Good luck. Later." Her image disappeared from the screen.

Vidcam or no vidcam, Appie sighed loud and long. She rubbed her temples and muttered, "I need a break," then immediately wished she hadn't spoken. She quickly clicked on her e-mail page. There were lots of messages but none urgent, and she didn't have time to answer any at the moment. She clicked over to her private e-mail. There were fewer and fewer messages here each week, as high school friends, discouraged because Appie never had the time to call or see them, forgot her and moved on. At least her mom and dad wrote almost every day. There were sidebar ads on this page, for companies that Worldtree owned or had a big stake in. One, flashing on the right, was for the White Bison Resort in North Dakota, offering weekend packages of "Open Spaces for Open Minds" at a great bargain rate for cubio dwellers. *That sounds really nice*, Appie thought.

She glanced down at the time glyph. "Omigod!" She had ten minutes until the meeting started. She wanted to log in early, just in case Julio was early too and they might have a chance to chat before business. Appie rushed to her one little closet and changed out of her oversized T-shirt into an oversized black hoodie and dark blue stretch pants. She squirted hair gel into her hand and mussed up her short hair some more. Then she grabbed her coffee and sat at her deck table. Appie took three deep breaths before tapping the conference code into the remote.

In a blink, the deck became a well-appointed conference room with a huge picture window showing a beautiful, sunny spring morning over Puget Sound, the Olympic Mountains sparkling with snow in the distance. But Appie's attention was caught by something else. Julio was in the room.

"Hey, Appie, another early bird. Howya doin'?" He smiled and stretched, showing off some very fine biceps and pecs beneath his short-sleeved polo shirt.

Boy works out, Appie thought. "I'm good. You?"

"Never better. You're rockin' the casual look today."

"Yep. And you're . . . you." Appie knew her eyes were giving away too much admiration, and she cussed herself for it.

"Like it? Look me up on buymyface.com. You can download it onto your comfort-bot." Julio winked.

Appie fought down a blush. "You're outrageous, you know that?" Appie was all too aware every meeting *was* recorded. Did Julio have too much rank to care?

"Value added, dude. I'd sell every nonessential organ in my body if it didn't mean too much downtime."

Appie cringed inside but there was no doubting the boy's ambition. Julio was gunning for five stars if he wasn't there already. "Good for you. Anyway, I don't own a comfort-bot."

"Should look into it. Han Robotics has got amazing stuff. Their stock is going orbital. You could sell your own image, you know. Bet you'd get some buyers." Julio smiled.

Feeling flattered swirled with all kinds of wrong in Appie's gut, leaving her totally flustered. To imagine strangers doing . . . things to a simulacrum wearing her face. "Uh, thanks, but that's not the business model I want to develop for myself."

"Old-fashioned girl, eh? Suit yourself. Oops. Here come the clients."

The remote beeped as someone tapped in their code

and suddenly two people, a man and a woman, thirtyish and dressed conservatively, appeared in the room.

They exchanged introductions and made the usual business-type small talk. All the necessary little rituals. Appie noted that the clients had a hungry stare in their eyes. This opportunity was important, perhaps vital, to their company.

Mercator finally began their pitch. The woman began, "We're considering a line of clothing expressly for cubio dwellers like yourselves. Clothing that's comfortable to work in, sleep in, whatever. We have a supplier for a fabric that wicks away sweat and always has a fresh scent."

"Or whatever scent you want," the man added quickly.

"And here are the styles we're developing," the woman said, opening up a new window on Appie's vidscreen to display sketches and prototype outfits. There were simple unisex tops and bottoms and a jumpsuit. Appie was not impressed. Julio wore a dubious frown as well.

"What colors would these be available in?" Appie asked.

"Well, light colors like pastels dye best on this fabric, but we've been trying to talk the manufacturer into trying out some patterns, like this kicky stripe design." She let one of the sketches cycle through a variety of colors.

Julio stifled a laugh. "I'm sorry, but those . . . look like kids' jammies."

"Well, that's the idea," the woman persisted. "We know you people work under mountains of stress, so we thought comforting clothes would be the way to go." She displayed the jumpsuit design and let it cycle through bright colors and stripes.

"Yeah, jammies . . ." Appie agreed. "Or prison uniforms."

There was a glint of recognition, of irony, in the woman's eyes, and suddenly anger flashed up from Appie's gut. "You're dissing us," Appie growled. "We are not children, and we are not prisoners or new slaves like some in the media claim. We work our butts off every day, all day. We give all we have to give, all the time. You want to sell to us? Don't patronize us. Give us something we can use, that helps us. We don't need comfort, we need . . . inspiration! Don't give us pastels. How about . . . cloth covered in facts, figures, wise observations—"

"Yeah, like 'no I in team' stuff," Julio tentatively put in, trying to follow her lead.

"No, not stupid corporate affirmations," cried Appie, warming to her subject. "Stuff from the latest GAAP edition, reviews of the current movie hits in China and India, what are the top-selling toys in Mexico, demographics on where the displacees from the shrinking coastline states are going and what they need, and if you go high-tech enough, have these printed on something like e-paper so you can download updates through your workstation. Inspire us! Cubions are competitive. Give us something that promises to give us an edge. *That* will be unique. *That* will sell." Appie realized she'd been pounding the table with her fist, and she self-consciously returned her hands to her lap.

Moments of silence passed. The clients stared at her. Julio stared at her. Appie realized her suggestion would triple the cost of manufacturing, and Carolyn had said Mercator was tight on budget. *Oh god, I just blew it big-time.*

The man leaned over and whispered something in the woman's ear. "Um," said the woman, "wow, that gives us a lot to think about. Um. My partner and I need to have a little discussion. We'll be right back." She leaned forward and touched her remote. Their images vanished.

Appie covered her face with her hands. "I suck."

"No, no, those were great ideas," said Julio. "They'd be idiots not to take them up. But the negativity scares me. We're supposed to be helping clients, not yelling at them."

"I'm sorry. I just saw that thing that looked like a prison uniform and—"

"Touched a raw nerve, huh?"

"I guess. I mean, I don't feel like a prisoner. I wake up and I love the smell of challenge in the morning. But . . . it's funny. I just saw an ad this morning for the White Bison Resort. It looked . . . really good."

"You should go," Julio said, an earnest tone in his voice. "It's Worldtree owned, so there's all kinds of ways you can biz-spin a vacation there. Besides, the restaurant there, the Brownhorn, is one of the few places left you can get beef steak at a reasonable price."

Appie almost never ate beef, but she suddenly found her mouth watering at the prospect. She looked up at Julio. "You're a Harbinger too, aren't you?"

He grinned. "Worldtree hires the best. Oops. Here come the clients again. Whatever you do, don't apologize."

The clients popped into view once more. They looked sheepish. The woman began, "My partner and I have discussed this and we want you to know we are terribly sorry if we've inadvertently shown disrespect for you people and what you do. Obviously, it is our goal to offer only the best and most appealing merchandise. That said, we think your ideas are fantastic and a much better way to go. We have a couple of lines of apparel that we're not wild about that we might be able to shut down to bring this into budget. We're going to give your 'idea-wear' a chance. We'll come back, if you don't mind, and show you our new prototypes when they're ready."

Appie was stunned. Everyone said their thanks and good-byes and the clients couldn't seem to get off screen fast enough.

Appie sighed, blinking, and turned to Julio. "Well, that went better than expected. Good job."

"Hey, you did all the work, I was just backup. All the props should be for you."

"Thanks. Well. Anyway, I hope we get the chance to work together again sometime."

Julio smiled. "Hope is for wimps." Then, shifting his voice to sound exactly like the voiceover to the company training vid, "At Worldtree, we make the future happen!" He tapped his remote and blipped out.

Still grinning, blushing, and shaking her head, Appie walked over to the workstation and sat down. She had to give Carolyn a report anyway. But asking for vacation time was dicey. Taking a deep breath, Appie messaged her manager.

Carolyn's vid appeared in the upper right. "Oh, hi, Appie. That was fast. Your score is coming in just now. Wait for it . . . oh, wow! Mercator gave you four and a half stars, Appie! Good job!"

"Thanks, I—"

"Exceeded expectations. And Julio sent along a good word, too. I'm impressed. Takes a lot to get a compliment out of that boy."

Appie was really hoping her blush couldn't show up in pixels. "Um, thanks. I wanted to ask, Carolyn, about vacation? I'd like to take some?"

"Oh, thank God!"

"What? You . . . you're okay with that?"

"Appie, the company gives you a week's vacation for a *reason*. You've been here a year and you've only taken two days!"

"Thanksgiving and Christmas, yeah. But I was looking at the White Bison Resort and thought it sounded good."

"Excellent. So, did you want to go soon?"

"If I could . . ."

"How about this weekend? White Bison's got a springtime weekend special for Worldtree contractors. I can even set up a cheap flight for you—we get a good deal with Pacifica Air."

"Um, cool. Great." *Wow, is this a great company to work for or what?* thought Appie.

"Okay, I'll move your project schedule around and get you all booked. I'll e-mail you the details this afternoon. This is a great idea, Appie. I'm glad you're taking some downtime. Gotta run. Bye."

"Bye." Carolyn's image vanished, and Appie leaned back in her chair, blown away. *That was easy. Carolyn's being really helpful. So . . . why am I still worried?*

⊠ ⊠ ⊠

Two days later, the airport shuttle out of Fargo let Appie out in front of the White Bison Resort Lodge. Though it was just the beginning of May, the air was warm and full of scents Appie hadn't smelled in a long time. Grass and sage, earthy and animally, made her nose tingle. All around her, the land stretched out for miles and miles, and the indigo sky arcing above her seemed huge. It was thrilling and unfamiliar, like a visit to an alien planet.

Appie went inside to the faux rustic interior of the lodge and registered. There was a nearby connecting doorway to the dining room of the Brownhorn Restaurant and, because she'd foolishly forgotten to bring food onto the flight, Appie was famished. She sent her weekender bag up to her room with a well-tipped bellhop and went right into the restaurant.

Appie showed the maître d' her employee ID and was seated at a great table on the second floor. She had a fabulous view of the sunset over the plains. She'd scheduled a drive and hike tour for tomorrow that she was really looking forward to. Nevertheless, she put her small laptop on the table and opened it. It was a company resort, after all, and you never knew who'd be watching. She tried to think of some suggestion useful to the airline industry, but ever since the gas crisis of twenty eleven, the airlines were stripping as many services as they could. It had been years since anything but water was offered to passengers except on intercontinental flights, and already most flights under two hours were one-third stand-up passengers. Appie just couldn't think of what more could be done.

"Excuse me, is this seat taken?"

Appie looked up. "Julio!"

"I'll take that smile as a no." Julio Tanaka sat down across the table from her.

"What are you doing here?"

"You're such a good Harbinger, Appie. I heard your idea for a quick weekend here at White Bison and decided it sounded fantastic."

Appie laughed. "And I heard your idea for steak and decided to try this restaurant."

"Here's to great minds thinking alike," said Julio, raising his water glass. "Um, that is, I hope you don't mind sharing some of your weekend with me."

"Mind?" Appie clinked her water glass with his, feeling supremely silly. *Well, so much for a* relaxing *weekend,* she thought. But she didn't mind.

They talked restaurant biz over dinner. They talked music biz over dessert, noting how techno-mash-ups had made it into Muzak. They let their bodies do the talking as they danced into the wee hours of the morning at a resortified version of an old-school rave in the White Bison Auditorium.

Appie semi-awoke in panic the next morning because she had not heard the alarm. The next few moments she blundered around the hotel room, searching for the workstation, until she woke up enough to calm herself down. She was on vacation. It was okay.

She glanced at the bed. Julio wasn't there, nor was there any sign he had been. Appie then remembered how she had pointedly turned him away when he escorted her back to the room. *Turned down a hottie like that. What's up with me? Hope he isn't mad.*

But the bedside clock showed she'd better hustle if she was going to take the little ecotour she'd signed up for. Appie threw on clothes and brushed her hair and dashed out the door. She stopped by Julio's room, fully expecting him to still be asleep or, worse, refuse to answer her knock. But in moments he opened the door, already dressed, looking wide awake. A phone rig hung in his ear and, looking past him, Appie could see his laptop open on the bedside table.

"Hi! You're up," Appie said in surprise.

"The early bird gathers no moss," said Julio, grinning. "Already got two more projects lined up for when I get back. How'd you sleep?"

"Like a rock. *Did* you sleep?"

"In my own fashion. So what's up today?"

"Got an ecotour. Um, I suppose you're too busy—"

"No, not at all. This is vacation, right? I'll be right there."

A couple of minutes later, Julio joined her, wearing an armtop and still sporting the Bluetooth. They got down to the "duck" truck and found there was still an open slot, given that it was off season, so Julio paid and got on.

It was a glorious, sunny morning. The tour truck went by wetlands filled with geese and ducks, and prairie now repopulated with bounding antelope and great herds of lumbering bison. Eagles and hawks circled overhead, as well as vultures searching for scraps left behind by wolf and coyote packs. Appie took it all in, wide-eyed, but Julio seemed rather bored, mostly tapping something into his armtop.

The ecotour stopped at a low range of hills on which a nature trail had been constructed. Appie eagerly hopped out to hike around a bit, but Julio stayed in his seat.

"Aren't you coming?" Appie asked.

"You go on ahead, I'll be right after you."

So Appie loped up the trail over the hill ridge. One arm of the trail led out onto open prairie. The rest of the tour group stayed on the hills for the view, so Appie went the way no one else was going. After about a quarter mile, she stopped. The only sounds were the hissing of the long grasses and birdsong. The sun was warm, and the wind was gentle. Appie closed her eyes and held out her arms to take it all in. She felt a part of herself opening up that had been closed for so long—

Something slapped the back of her head. "Stop that," Julio said behind her.

"Hey!" Appie spun around, rubbing her scalp, and glared at him.

"Don't look at me like that. I was rescuing you."

"Rescuing me? From what?"

"From what I call the rapture of the void. You think you're getting all spiritual and connecting to the earth. Don't fall for it, Appie. It'll make you lose your edge."

"Isn't that what vacations, what this place, are *for*?" Appie demanded. "Aren't experiences like this what living is for?"

"Don't go all Opt-Out on me, girl. You're better than that."

"Opt-Out" was almost a dirty word in the cubio world. It was what cubions called folks who, despite being well educated, rebelled against the life of the mod-towers. People who chose to work few hours at simple jobs, live poor, spend little, and base their life around home and family. They were forming themselves into a movement called the Frugalists. A noted right-wing blogger had recently proclaimed that such people should be charged with treason for allowing the United States to "fall behind" India and China.

"No," said Appie, "it's just good to see that there's more of the world out here. This is what we're working for, right?"

Julio snorted. "This is what I'm working to avoid."

"I don't get you. Why did you come out here if you don't like it?"

"Because I like to be reminded, too, but of something else. When I look out at all this, I see nothing, emptiness, a wilderness. The only worthwhile landscape is a place where humans have built things, or where the natural resources are being harvested. Where we've made our stamp of achievement. This land is not being productive. Out here, there's nothing worthwhile for you or me. Nature is not some kind, warm mother, Appie. You, as a woman, should realize this. Can you imagine life like the ancient Native Americans, giving birth without hospitals, getting sick without modern medicine? Pure misery, Appie. We're working so that humanity never has to experience that again."

"Okay, I see your point, sort of. But, don't we lose something in the process?" Appie protested.

"Stuff well lost, in my opinion," said Julio, staring narrow-eyed at the horizon. He checked his armtop, then held out his hand to Appie. "Come walk with me."

Uncertain, Appie took his hand. She felt so confused, admiration for his ambition mixed with revulsion.

He led her several yards away from the hills where the nature trail lay, to an outcropping of rock. Behind the rock they were hidden from anyone's view. Julio glanced once more at his armtop, glanced overhead, then pulled Appie into a tight embrace, with a long kiss that went straight to her groin.

Well! thought Appie, *at least part of him is human. He wanted to come out here for some romance. Shame he didn't think to bring a blanket.*

Julio's hand moved down to her butt. And then Appie was aware of him slipping something small and rectangular into her back jeans pocket.

"You don't have to give me your card. I know how to find you," Appie murmured in his ear.

"Shhh. It's not mine. It's a lead. A hot one."

Appie drew back, appalled. "You're talking biz—"

"Shh! Kiss me! We might still be in view of the satellite," he whispered loudly.

"Sat—oh." As his lips fell hungrily on hers again, Appie realized that given Worldtree's fleet of satellites, one was rarely not potentially viewable. After a long while, Appie finally drew back to catch her breath.

"If it's such a hot lead," she whispered, "why aren't you handling it?"

"Plate's too full," Julio whispered back. "You need it more than I do. This could make your career, Appie. We Harbingers stick together, right? I wanted you to have it."

"Aw, and here I thought you were kissing me because you liked me."

"I *do* like you. I like you lots." And the kissing continued so long, they nearly missed catching the ecotour truck back to the lodge.

One thing led to another, and the next morning when Appie woke up, Julio was in bed beside her. She watched his chest rise and fall as he slept, her feelings in vague turmoil. It had been good; Julio was skilled. But his eyes had been closed most of the time.

Appie got up, put on the flimsy bathrobe the resort provided, made a tiny pot of the weak coffee that came with the room, and strolled out to the deck. As the sun rose higher over the eastern horizon, Appie noted that not once did she wish for a remote. She wondered if she could download this scene for her cubio deck.

Appie heard Julio stir behind her as he got up to go to the bathroom. Minutes later he strolled out to join her, wearing only a bath towel around his waist and holding an open cell phone.

"Good morning," Appie said, eyeing the phone with concern.

"You're looking happy and rested," said Julio cheerfully. "What do you say, did I show you a good time?"

"Well . . . sure . . . what, are you calling somebody?"

Julio managed to look annoyed and embarrassed at the same time. "I'm making a vid. A souvenir, to remember the weekend. C'mon. Give me a smile and tell me we had a good time, okay?"

Appie rolled her eyes but then remembered the better parts of the day before. She smiled and said, patiently, "I had a very good time with you, Julio. Thank you."

"Excellent." He snapped the phone shut. He walked up to her and kissed her lightly again. "When does your flight leave?"

"Not until four. So I have most of the day to kill, if you—"

"Got a better idea. The restaurant, Brownhorn, needs a courier the first week of every month to take legal documents to their headquarters in San Francisco. I bet I can get you on a flight out of Fargo by eleven."

"Oh, *Julio*," Appie sighed in annoyance.

"It'll show initiative! Besides," he added in a whisper, leaning close, "it will give you a chance to check out the place I gave you." He patted her butt. "They're in SF too."

Appie felt her hard-won happiness drain from her at cutting her vacation short. On the other hand, Julio's go-getter attitude was getting on her last nerve. "Okay, okay. I'll get back to work."

"Stop grumbling. We're the lucky ones, remember? We've got the best jobs in the world."

"Yeah," said Appie with one last, regretful glance at the view. "So goddamn lucky."

Appie let her mind drift as she rode in the taxi from the San Francisco airport. She gazed at the hybrids, ethanols, and electrics sharing the road, tried to read the faces of the drivers as she had the passengers on her crowded flight from Fargo. What did these people want, need, hunger for? What could Worldtree and its innumerable associates sell them? Appie sometimes told herself she was helping people in ways they could never appreciate. But sometimes she felt like she was preying on her own species.

After dropping off the legal papers at the headquarters

for Brownhorn Restaurants Ltd., Appie directed the taxi to the address on the card Julio had slipped into her jeans. The taxi let her off in front of a tall, narrow pink storefront with an iron-gated door and a quaint cupola on the second story, similar to its neighbors in the Haight-Ashbury neighborhood. There was only a small sign in the window to show this was the location of Mindportal, Inc. It stood near the crest of a hill from which one could glimpse the downtown. Appie saw a couple of new mod-towers going up that would rival the Transamerica Pyramid for attention. She rang the doorbell and heard a chime somewhere inside.

The iron gate slid aside and the door was opened by a tall, slender woman with short-cropped gray hair. She was wearing a loose, long, white dress and her large eyes were a startling shade of blue. "May I help you?" the woman asked in a mild, throaty voice.

Appie hadn't called ahead, paranoid fears of being overheard on her company cell phone having held her back. "I'm Appomattox Kim from Worldtree. You had requested a marketing evaluation of your . . . product." Appie was seriously winging it, as Julio had given no indication of what Mindportal produced, and the business card he'd given her was merely the company name and address. Appie assumed it was some sort of software . . . maybe competition for one of the major companies Worldtree already handled, and that's why the job was so touchy.

The woman gasped, her hand flying to her throat. "You . . . Worldtree actually sent someone! Oh, please, come in! We'd been hoping but since we hadn't heard . . . I must have overlooked your e-mail. I'm so sorry, please come in!" The woman held the door open.

Appie walked in, trying not to appear as sheepish as she felt. "Actually, I expect there was no e-mail, Ms. . . ."

"Please, call me Grace."

"Um, Grace. I was only just given your contact information, and as I'm on a six-hour layover, I thought I would take the opportunity to make first contact and get to know your company."

"Wonderful! We were so worried, and we weren't sure where else to turn. Thank you for coming. Right this way." Grace guided Appie down a long, white-painted hallway whose only decoration was a large flower arrangement in the Wafu style of Ikebana on a side table. Appie admired its circular structures of pine and bamboo before she was ushered into a plain, white-walled office with IKEA desks and Herman Miller chairs. Serious money was clashing with frugality here. She sat and opened up her laptop.

Grace sat behind the desk, steepling her fingers. "I suppose you have all the background on the service we hope to provide. Frankly we're not sure if we should be applying for FDA or AMA approval yet, so I'm afraid we haven't begun that process. We're hoping Worldtree can help us on that end."

"I see." *Whoa, a drug or medical device? A service?* Appie thought, keeping her face neutral. "Yes, but I like to hear first from the company's own perspective what they believe they are offering before giving any feedback."

"Well, that makes sense. Here at Mindportal, Ms. Kim,

we believe we are offering, quite simply, a religious experience."

Appie's hands paused above her keyboard. "Say what?"

"Oh, I know, we can't use that in the brochure. Religion has such heavy connotations, and none that we want to imply. Our device is a helmet that, using electricity and magnets, provides the same sort of experience that monks strive for years to achieve and that has inspired prophets through the ages. One five-to-ten minute session under the helmet, and one comes away with the feeling that All Is Connected. The universe is one and filled with a numinous purpose of which we are all a grand part."

After a pause, Appie said, "Um, wow." *No wonder Julio hadn't wanted to touch this.*

"Yes, I see you understand the implications. But we have no interest in using this device to create a cult or enhance a church organization. We could all become billionaires if we did, but we don't want to start the next Scientology. Our founding engineers came from the University of California, and we want to ensure this device is used under careful supervision."

"I see," Appie said. "Then, who, exactly, do you see as your target market?"

"Well, eventually, everyone. We hope. But in order to become established, we'd like to place ourselves first as a business productivity enhancement tool."

"A productivity enhancement tool," Appie echoed dubiously. She shifted uncomfortably in her chair. Were these people wingnuts in clever disguise? Was this an elaborate practical joke on Julio's part? She wanted to glance around surreptitiously for webcams. "But wouldn't a state of . . . religious ecstasy interfere with one's work productivity?" *Jeez, I'm starting to sound like Julio.*

Grace smiled and shook her head. "It's not like that. The experience doesn't rob your mind of the capacity to think, quite the opposite. It simply . . . opens you up." Her hands fell palm outward, like the wings of butterflies. "You have a feeling of oneness with all Creation, a general feeling of well-being, of serenity, that everything will be all right. Some of our test cases have reported enhanced creativity. And as the zen saying goes, 'Even after the enlightenment of Satori, one must chop wood and carry water.'"

"And you believe this will be of service to people like me, who work in mod-towers?"

"Well, we have read of the stress and intensity of your work lives," Grace said. "We've heard you even have a room in the towers called the 'Hug and Cry,' where you go when it gets overwhelming."

"Yes, there is such a place," Appie said, hearing some defensiveness in her voice, "but it's rarely used. I haven't been to it once the whole time I've worked at Worldtree." *Cubions don't dare use the Hug and Cry often,* Appie thought, *because your room card opens the door and HR can tell who's cracking by how often you check in.*

"Well, perhaps our device can provide what your Hug and Cry cannot. True peace."

"Is that your ultimate goal with this service?"

"Well." Grace smiled and looked down at the floor. "Some of us have hippie grandparents. We like to think that our device could eventually lead to better understanding between people, perhaps even an end to war. But that's thinking years ahead. Right now we just need to find acceptance somewhere, and we believe the business community is the best place to start. After all, if people believe it will help them make money, it's bound to catch on, isn't it?"

"Isn't that a cynical approach?" asked Appie.

"We like to think we're being realistic. Now, would you like to see the device?"

There wasn't much to see. Grace led Appie to a glass partition. In the room beyond, a young woman in T-shirt and jeans lay in a big, plush recliner with what appeared to be an oversized football helmet on her head. Wires led from the helmet to a box being monitored by a bespectacled middle-aged man. He looked up and waved at Grace. The young woman under the helmet twitched a little as if in deep REM sleep. After five minutes, the man removed the helmet and the young woman sat up, smiling. A tear ran down her cheek.

"Are the experiences always positive?" asked Appie.

"Mostly, although some report uncanny feelings—like one volunteer who felt stretched in different directions, which he interpreted as a tug of war between angels and demons. Another felt weightless, like floating in space, and had a trace of nausea afterward. But the end result is one hundred percent positive. There's always a feeling of connectedness to the universe, the sense that everything is going to be all right. Would you like to try it for yourself, Ms. Kim?"

"Uh, no, thank you," Appie said hastily. "I think it would be best to approach this from the aspect of one who hasn't experienced it and needs to be convinced."

"I understand," said Grace. "But you're always welcome to try it if you're ever curious. Free of charge."

"Thank you," said Appie. "I assume . . . you've experienced it yourself?"

"Of course," said Grace, with a serene smile.

"Do you ever . . . need a refresher?" Appie asked. "I mean, is there reuse potential for this service?"

"Ah, I see what you mean. How do you put a price on transformation? One could use it again, but neither I nor our subjects need to 'refresh' often to remember the experience. Once or twice a year might be all that's needed to sustain the feeling."

Appie nodded and glanced at her watch. "Oh dear, I should be getting back to the airport," she said, even though she had hours to go until her flight.

"I'll have a cab called for you." Grace left to go into her office.

Appie watched as the middle-aged man escorted the young woman who had been under the helmet to the door. The young woman was wide-eyed and all smiles, like a child on Christmas morning. *Only, her mind is the present that has been opened,* thought Appie.

Grace returned. "The cab will be here in ten minutes. You seem . . . disquieted, Ms. Kim. Are there any other questions I can answer for you to set your mind at ease?"

"You've never worried that this might be dangerous?" Appie asked.

"Do you mean physically? It's a very gentle procedure, really, with no more brain stimulation than a lengthy cell-phone call. Roller-coaster rides are more dangerous to the brain than our service, yet people gladly jump on those for no other purpose than entertainment. I can e-mail you the test results. I can't be too specific about the structure of the device itself as our patent is still pending. You understand."

"Yes, of course," said Appie, frowning, "but people are very . . . culturally sensitive about this kind of experience. Couldn't they claim that, because it's physically, deliberately induced, it's not real?"

Grace frowned quizzically. "People have been deliberately inducing this sort of experience for millennia, whether its through hunger fasts in the desert or climbing mountains or years of meditation in a temple or taking LSD in the sixties. Not that I want our service compared to recreational drugs, but people seem willing to go to extreme, even illegal lengths to have such mental experiences."

I only went as far as North Dakota to almost have one, thought Appie.

"We hope to make them accessible, reliable, and legal. Perhaps you are hesitant because it is a technological innovation."

"Well, maybe. But if you tell people, 'Hey, I can make your brain do this' and then do it, won't people discredit the effect, claiming it's fake?"

Grace shrugged. "Therapeutic hypnotists are straightforward about their technique, and yet they have been able to use their technique to effect positive change in their clients' lives."

"Yes, hypnosis," murmured Appie, "that might be a good place to start. Used to be thought of as crackpot and now it's been accepted for decades. But it's not quite the same.

Hypnotherapists, to my knowledge, stay away from religious sensitivities."

"True. We know we are dealing in sensitive territory. Perhaps Worldtree can help us navigate those waters."

"I think we have a cultural anthropologist on staff, as well as a couple of doctors of philosophy," said Appie. "But I'd like to hear from you, since you've used the device, what you believe. What do you tell someone when they ask you, "Is the experience *real*? Or is it just something all in your head?'"

Grace stared at Appie for a long moment. "I think I know what you're grasping at. Naturally we advise each client to decide for him- or herself. But I look at it this way. You know those studies done by brain surgeons who poke at parts of people's brains to evoke a certain movement or feeling?"

"Yeah, I've read about things like that."

"Well, a surgeon could poke your brain and make your hand feel like it was dipped in ice-cold water. But your brain has that capacity because, on occasion, you may really dip your hand in ice water. Your brain's capacity reflects an external reality. Why would our brains have this capacity to sense the oneness of the universe, a sense that can be induced in many ways, even technological, if that capacity did not reflect an external reality? So, yes, Ms. Kim. I believe the experience we provide is the perception of something real. Ah. Here's your taxi."

They shook hands and said good-bye, Appie claiming she would send along a preliminary proposal within a couple of days. Grace looked hopeful but also resigned. *She knows the device has long odds of acceptance, at least right now,* thought Appie. She got into the cab, her mind spinning on options and possibilities.

Her mind was still spinning that night as she bumped her little wheeled suitcase down the long corridor back to her cubio in the Worldtree Seattle mod-tower. She swiped her room-card through the lock and went in. Her cubio looked smaller, somehow, and in some strange way unfamiliar. *Jeez, I've only been gone two days.* She let the suitcase fall to the floor and she collapsed onto the bed, staring at the blank ceiling. She felt exhausted. *If Mindportal succeeded, people wouldn't need vacations.* Wouldn't need resorts or church or therapy or Hug and Crys. They'd work happily on and on. Win-win situation, right? If Worldtree sponsored this, billions could be made. It could be huge. *So why am I really nervous about this job? Maybe because, if I don't approach it just right, the bosses will laugh in my face and I'll lose stars. Worldtree is a big company and big companies are conservative about some things. No wonder no one else has touched this job. No wonder Julio had to slip it to me on the sly.* Thinking of Julio made Appie remember the long kiss out on the prairie and the loving that followed after. She couldn't help but smile.

"Security alert," chirped her computer. Appie sighed. Cubions weren't allowed to turn their workstations off. There were so many constant updates and new software installs that your computer kept working even when you weren't.

Appie dragged herself out of bed, feeling like a zombie rising from its grave. She tottered to the workstation to see a security warning on the screen. "Warning: door to Cubio 709 has been accessed. To authorize proper resident, type in code below."

"Damn, forgot," Appie muttered. She typed in her password, SOFINE09, created in happier times, and hit enter. The security screen took a moment, flashed "accepted," and vanished beneath her usual desktop picture. Appie staggered back to the bed and flung herself on it, trying to get her mind back on what to do about Mindportal.

But there came a knock. At her door. Appie frowned. Cubions never knocked on doors. They sent e-mails or called. Maybe it was an instant message summoning sound. The knock came again, louder. It wasn't coming from the computer.

Appie sat up, then went to the door, excited. *Maybe it's Julio, come to welcome me back and ask about how it went with Mindportal. We'll have to be careful though. Don't know who's listening here in the mod.* Ready to put on her best sexy smile, Appie opened the door.

Carolyn Madrona of HR stood there in all her curly-brown-haired glory. "Hey, Appie, I saw you were back. Can I come in?"

"Sure." Appie stepped back in confusion as Carolyn walked in. Human Resources was visiting in person? *Am I in trouble?* was the first thought to cross her mind.

"So how was North Dakota?"

"It was great, just great. I had a great time. Um, why are you here? In person, I mean."

"Well, we got a notice from the White Bison that you

checked out early and that you changed your flight. I just wanted to make sure you were okay."

Wow, they do *keep tabs on you*, thought Appie, her worry growing. "Yeah, just fine. Julio told me about the courier job for the Brownhorn so I flew some papers out to their office in San Francisco."

"Yes . . . Julio . . ."

"Omigod, is that the problem?" asked Appie, suddenly feeling a spike of panic. "I mean, it's okay for coworkers to, um, get together off the job, isn't it?"

Carolyn rolled her eyes. "Yes, it's okay, Appie. You're over eighteen and all. But there's something about Julio you ought to know."

"Look, I know he's a player, and I'm not expecting a big romance with him, so you don't have to worry about downtime or a big drama."

"That's good, but still—"

"I mean, we just had a good time, all right? I mean, can't that stuff just be private, you know, do you have to be here asking me about it? We were just having a good time!"

"I know," said Carolyn, holding up her BlackBerry. She thumbed a few buttons and on the screen played a tiny image of Appie in her bathrobe with a North Dakota sunrise behind her, saying, "I had a good time, Julio, thank you."

"How did you get that?" Appie asked, feeling a slow burn building.

"Julio submitted it. With his report."

"His report?" Appie remembered him working on something yesterday morning when she met him before the ecotour.

"So he filed this with other proposals on the road?"

"No, Appie. Julio's developing a new Worldtree service as a traveling companion. *You* were the job."

"I . . . was the job? You're shitting me, right?"

"Do you want to read his report?"

"No! I mean, pardon me, but I thought prost—call—gigolos were illegal!"

"Sex wasn't part of the . . . original business plan. I guess you could call it value added."

"*Value added?*" Appie exclaimed.

"See, this is what we were afraid of—"

"*We?* How many in the company know about this?"

"Just those people Julio reports to, and us in HR."

"How many is that?"

"See, this is why Julio's going to get his proposal shot down. He didn't do the proper preparation, or choice of test subject—"

"Test subject!"

"Okay, I'm going leave and let you have a cool-down. Besides, you're still, strictly speaking, on vacation for another twelve hours." Carolyn turned and strode to the cubio door.

Appie folded her arms across her chest and scowled at the HR floor warden. "Thanks a *lot*, Carolyn. I get to spend the rest of my so-called vacation thinking about what a sham it was!"

Carolyn paused at the door. "You *should* be thanking me," she said with exaggerated patience. "Office crushes and romance can cause a disastrous amount of downtime. Take a few hours, get past it, and you'll be ready to work in the morning. I'll send over an e-mail with your new schedule so it'll be ready when you log on. Good night." The door slid open and Carolyn left.

Appie stood unmoving, fuming, her mind whirling. She tried to remember if there had been any office gossip connecting Carolyn and Julio, any reason why Carolyn would make up cruel lies. She couldn't remember any. Appie's breathing became raspy; her chest felt heavy. A large, fat tear rolled down her cheek. *No, oh no, I'm not . . . oh, hell with it!* Appie hit the button to open the door and made a run for the Hug and Cry.

Down the hallway she ran to the elevators. She passed only one coworker on the way—no one she recognized, but Appie turned her head away just the same. There was nothing more embarrassing than bursting into tears on the job. She flung herself into the elevator and agonized as the door took its sweet time to close. She wondered if there were cameras in the elevators and decided there probably were. Appie held her tears back until she got off on the fourth floor, where all the employee services were. She walked fast, head down, past the company gym and weight room and slashed her room card through the Hug and Cry lock as though slicing her resume with a knife. She dashed inside.

A fat young woman with red hair set down a paperback book and stood. "Well, hello there!" She opened her arms wide.

Appie fell into the woman's embrace, sinking into her soft shoulder and sobbing harder than expected.

"There, there. Do you want to talk about it or just cry?"

"Muft 'ry," Appie gasped. But as she wept, the business side of her brain reminded her that this young woman consoling her was being paid to do so. And work in the Hug and Cry was considered one of the least desirable and glamorous jobs in the company, as it didn't bring any new revenue. Appie found herself wondering what her consoler had done to deserve or require this placement and this took Appie out of her emotion storm. She pulled out of the embrace.

"See, it's not so bad. Tissue?" The redhead held up a box, and Appie obligingly snatched a tissue and blew her nose loudly.

"I'm sorry I couldn't offer a more full-contact hug," the woman went on. "I'm still recovering from surgery and my belly is just a little tender."

"Surgery?" Appie asked from behind the tissue.

The redhead smiled. "Worldtree accepted my ovaries for donation! Both of them!"

"*Both* of them?" Appie echoed, appalled.

The redhead nodded. "I was afraid they wouldn't because, well, you know . . ." She looked down at herself.

Appie didn't see what the deal was. Most cubions were either too fat or too thin.

"But my genes tested good. Apparently carrottops are in demand, especially in Asia. So I lucked out—the proceeds will go into my 401(K) and I'll be set. I can't tell you, I was *so* worried."

"But don't you ever want a family of your own?" Appie asked.

"The way I look at it," she replied, smoothing the hem of her blouse, "is that I'll have lots of children. I just won't be the one raising them. Besides, dating and families create too much downtime. I have a comfort-bot and that suits me just fine."

Appie couldn't help wondering if that comfort-bot ever wore Julio's face, but she Did. Not. Ask. "Well, hey, congratulations, then. Good for you."

"Thanks. Oh, I'm sorry. I shouldn't have made this about me. This is your time. Is there anything else you want to talk about?"

"Um, no, actually, you helped pull me right out of my funk."

"Oh, I'm so glad! Um, would you be willing to fill out one of those survey cards by the door when you go, so that HR can know that? You know how it is. I'm gunning for two stars by Labor Day."

Oh, you poor thing, thought Appie. "Sure," she said. "I'd be happy to." She stood to go.

"Thanks! It would mean a lot coming from you. I mean, with you being a Harbinger."

Appie froze. "How did you know that?" She was quite certain she'd never met this woman before today.

The redhead smiled sheepishly. "I'm one of those geeks who actually reads the company online newsletter. The latest issue has a little squib about you and your work with Mercator. They had your picture, too, so I recognized you when you came in."

"Oh," Appie said, feeling stupid for her paranoia. "I've been so busy, I hadn't seen it." She never read the company newsletter.

"I'll bet. I'm a Conduit. I read everything and pass it on. I'm in so many forums and newsgroups that—" Suddenly she glanced up at the ceiling. "Well, anyway, it's my only serious addiction. It's so cool to meet someone who's really on the way up. Here's my card. If you ever need anything, I can probably find the right place to ask." She pulled a Worldtree card from the cardholder on the table in front of her and handed it out to Appie.

Omigod, she's turned this into a networking opportunity, thought Appie, taking the card and reading, REBECCA FORTIN, ADMIN. HUMAN SERVICES. "Um, thanks. I'll keep you in mind, Rebecca. I, um, gotta run. I have a report I have to get ready for tomorrow."

"Of course you do," said Rebecca with naked admiration. "Good for you. I'll be looking for your name in future newsletters."

"Thanks, yours too. Um, bye." Appie dashed for the door, though she did pick up one of the survey cards on the way out. Her hurt at feeling used was now numb. Everyone was using everyone at Worldtree. Why should she be special? She decided that burying her nose in her work was the best way to get past it.

Back in her cubio, Appie sat on her bed, tapping notes about Mindportal into her laptop, so it wouldn't be accessible on the company system. If the Mindportal data were accurate, and the helmet truly created a mental reset, the amount of employee downtime it could save Worldtree would be considerable. No need for fancy resorts and special flight packages, no need for two-faced, lying travel companions. No need for wide-open spaces for inspiration. No need for churches or psychotherapy. Just magnetize the mind, work, and smile. Thousands of contented minds working away, secure in the knowledge that cosmologically, existentially, everything was going to be okay. Win-win-win, right?

A lingering doubt hung at the back of Appie's mind, but she was unable to crystallize it into recognizable form. She wondered if it was just habit, playing devil's advocate, trying to see the issue from all sides. A headache threatened like storm clouds on the horizon, so Appie set the laptop aside. She put in her earbuds and turned the sat-radio to the old-school New Age channel to fall asleep by. It worked.

She woke, unsettled, not to the alarm but to distant strings, surf, and whale songs. Appie sat up and pulled the earbuds out. The silence that followed was off-putting; the cubio seemed dark and strange. Appie sensed that she'd had disturbing dreams she could not remember.

The digital display on the clock beside the bed showed 6:10 A.M. Her body was still on Central Time. Not wanting to descend back into whatever discomforting visions she'd been wandering through in her sleep, Appie decided to start the day. She walked slowly to the bathroom and did her stuff. She didn't bother to look in the mirror, perhaps a little afraid of it. She shuffled out to the deck and picked up the remote. And realized there was nothing she wanted to see. It would all be just pixels, even if it reflected something real at the other end.

Realizing she had something precious, time, in her grasp, Appie left the cubio and actually, physically, went down to the coffee salon on the ground floor. She was vaguely aware of other people checking out her sleep-rumpled clothing and bedhead, but Appie let it bounce off her shell of prewakeful introspection. She showed her employee ID, ordered a mocha, and took it to sit at one of the little round metal tables on the sidewalk.

From where she sat, Appie could smell the sweet sea aroma drifting up from the Sound; it blended well with the coffee. The added faint whiff of urine on the sidewalk from last night's drunks didn't blend, but it did add a sense of place. From her seat, Appie could just glimpse a sliver of slate blue sea beyond the buildings, and the white of the snow-capped Olympics beyond that. She remembered someone telling her that in certain Eastern philosophies, an expanse of water to the west facilitated the dissolution of the ego. You really could lose your sense of self overlooking a vast expanse of flat water. She remembered reading a Web article praising the fact that Puget Sound still had a couple of surviving pods of orca. Appie wondered if she'd ever get to see any in the wild. Just a few blocks away was Pike Place Market, and Appie wondered if she could conjure some excuse to go there instead of back to her cubio, to go and smell the flowers and eat some pot stickers and pretzels, to watch the salmon being tossed by lively young men, to discover some tiny boutique in the uneven old levels of the market, someplace magical like in a fantasy story. A copy of the local city weekly sat on a nearby chair. Appie picked it up (market research, she reassured herself) and began to read about local musicians striving to get noticed, a tiny urban park that desperately needed money, a favorite neighborhood strip club closing down. None of which she'd been aware of, locked away in her cubio.

When she got to the raunchy want ads in the back, she

resurfaced and set the paper aside, leaving it for the next casual reader. Appie sauntered back into the shop, tossed her empty cup away, looked up at the clock. It was 8:20.

"Omigod!" Appie ran for the elevator, tapping her foot in impatience as it seemed to take forever to crawl up the shaft to her floor. She swiped her card and ran into her cubio, flinging herself into her workstation chair. The screen was flashing its "Warning: Unauthorized Entry" again, and Appie tapped in her password, grumbling, "Shuddup, I know, I know." *Damn, Julio was right*, Appie thought. *Rapture of the Void makes you useless for the routine.*

As soon as she logged on, there was an IM from Carolyn. "Appie, where have you been? Are you okay?"

Appie's hands hovered over the keyboard. She was about to claim her alarm didn't go off, but the company could check that sort of thing. So she stayed vague. "Sorry, lost track of time. I'll work through lunch. Give me the schedule."

Appie groaned as the day planner appeared on the screen. Database work this morning. Training in the afternoon. Several side tasks for "if you have time." One of them was labeled "New designs from Mercator." Pleased for any delay from the doldrums ahead, Appie clicked on it.

Another window opened to display two-piece unisex sets in black, gray, or white. They still looked like pajamas or gym gear, but as promised, they were covered with writing. Appie zoomed in for a close-up to read some of it.

"Goodness without wisdom invariably accomplishes evil."—Robert A. Heinlein

"Every individual strives to grow and exclude, and to exclude

and grow, to the extremities of the universe, and to impose the law of its being on every other creature."—Ralph Waldo Emerson

"If I am not for myself, who is for me? When I am only for myself, who am I? If not now, when?"—Hillel

Appie didn't find it fun to read these, rather they annoyed her, like being nagged by an erudite parrot. She signed off on the project with a "Great, good job. Send me samples." Just to get it out of her work queue. Then she descended into the slough of database hell.

She came up for air around ten A.M. Normally, Appie never took "breaks," but with a shortened lunch coming up, a break seemed infinitely desirable. She could justify it by noodling some more on her notes regarding Mindportal. She looked around. Her laptop was gone.

Panic rising in her chest, Appie searched the area around her bed. No laptop. She stood on her toes and surveyed the cubio like an alert meerkat. There just wasn't any room in the place for a laptop to be hidden. She remembered the security alert this morning and her panic deepened. Security was tight at Worldtree, but thieves were ever innovative and workplace theft still happened. *Someone knew I had left the cubio this morning.* It would be a bad blot on her record if she had to report it stolen and get it replaced. But it was Worldtree equipment with Worldtree software and data, and *not* reporting the loss would be worse. Worst of all, of course, was that it contained her notes on Mindportal.

Hands shaking, breathing rapidly, Appie sat down again at the workstation. She IM'ed Carolyn and willed her fingers to type the hardest words she'd ever written. "Carolyn, I think I've lost my laptop."

The reply came back almost immediately. "No, you haven't. Didn't you read your e-mail this morning? IT took all the marketing laptops for a software upgrade. You should have it back tomorrow. Can I help you with anything?"

Appie sighed a long sigh. "No, thanks. Much relieved." Well, that explained the security alert . . . except . . . wouldn't IT have had the proper code so the alert would not have been triggered? Maybe it was a new guy. Appie returned to working on Excel spreadsheets, finding the marching numbers a soothing relief from panic mode, though the adrenaline coursing through her blood made concentration a challenge.

As noon rolled around, Appie felt more in control, more on an even keel again. Everything would be all right. She'd get her laptop back tomorrow and work on the Mindportal notes then. There was no rush, after all, since the project wasn't on any company timetable.

She finally went to her e-mail page. Lots of messages. The one from IT this morning. A note from Rebecca, reminding Appie to send in the survey form. *How did she know I hadn't?* wondered Appie. And then a new message appeared, with a bright red, flashing exclamation point beside it. From the VP of Marketing. Not a mass company mailing. It was only for her.

"Please come to my office as soon as you can." That was it.

Appie read it three times to verify its reality. She numbly typed back a reply. "I'm on my way." Everything was not going to be all right. She logged off, got up, and walked out the door, heading for the elevator like a convict headed for execution.

The VP's office was on the forty-fifth floor. Appie stepped out into a lobby filled with light from floor-to-ceiling windows that looked out on a genuine, excellent view of the city. The VP of Marketing had a huge corner office that was remarkably bare of furniture—a long desk, chairs, one filing cabinet, one set of wall cabinets, and that extraordinary view.

As soon as Appie entered, the man behind the desk got up and strode toward her, hand extended. He was gym tanned and ripped and wore a navy cashmere V-neck, khaki pants, Rolex watch. "Suits" never wore suits anymore. "Appomattox Kim? I don't think we've formally met. George Huelva. Good of you to come right away. Have a seat."

Appie pasted a smile on her face and sat down. "What is this about, sir?"

"Please, call me George. Sorry to call you in on your lunch hour. I was thinking of calling down for teriyaki. Want me to order something for you?"

"No, thanks." Appie's stomach felt like a black hole of fear. She couldn't possibly eat.

George sat behind the desk again, leaned back in his ergo-chair, crossed one leg over another. He picked up a pen off the desk and began to play with it, turn-tap-turn-tap. "Appie, knowing the way gossip runs wild in a company like this, well, any company, we felt it was best to let you know officially, so that you wouldn't get the wrong impression."

"Let me know what?"

"This morning we decided to let Julio Tanaka go."

Appie's stomach seemed to jerk sideways. This was not the particular bad news she was expecting. "Julio? He's been . . . fired?" Her first thought, of course, was, *Did I have something to do with it?*

Anticipating her thought, George said, "We understand you were just on vacation with him, and I want to assure you it had nothing to do with that. Per se."

Per se? Slowly, Appie asked, "If I may, George, why was he . . . terminated?"

George gazed aside out the huge windows, raised the pen to his upper lip, and twirled it horizontally beneath his nose in unconscious imitation of a melodrama villain's mustache. "Obviously it would be inappropriate to comment on the details. But suffice it to say that Worldtree has no place in it for cowards."

"Cowards," Appie echoed without inflection. She couldn't possibly think of any way that Julio matched the description of coward. If anything, she thought he was recklessly bold. "But I thought he was almost a five-star, sir—George."

George nodded and returned the pen to the desk. Turn-tap-turn-tap. "A grave disappointment, certainly. But I expect you're wondering what this has to do with you."

Appie's turn to nod. "Of course."

George sighed and looked again out the window wall. "There was a project we had assigned to Julio. A very important project. We have learned that he chose to hand that project off to someone else. It has turned out that someone was you."

The pit in Appie's stomach sank deeper. As if that were

possible. No need to dispute the fact or ask how Worldtree knew this. "Yes, he did," Appie said softly.

"May I ask why you didn't tell anyone about this?" Turn-tap. Turn-tap.

There was only one possibly acceptable answer. "Ambition. He told me it could make my career. I believed him. I wanted to wait to make the big splash. So I wanted to wait until I had developed a proper assessment before telling anyone."

George nodded again. He pushed back in his chair and crossed his arms on his chest. "Well, I want to assure you right away, Appie, that you're not in trouble. Julio may have chosen to do the wrong thing, but we think his instincts may have been right. We've been watching your progress, and we think you show great promise. Great promise."

"Thank you." Appie still didn't dare breathe.

"So. The Mindportal project is yours. And I have to tell you, Harold is very interested in this client. *Very* interested." Tap-tap-tap-tap-tap.

Harold would be Harold Staffer, conservative, brilliant, quirky CEO of Worldtree, who had taken it from a small consulting office to the global spiderweb it was today.

"Oh. Wow," was all Appie could say in reply.

Suddenly all smiles, George sat up and leaned forward on the desk. "So tell me—I know you've met with the people at Mindportal and made some notes—tell me what you think. Give me your preliminary assessment."

"But . . . I'm still working on the notes," Appie said, delaying for time to think.

George shook his head, waving the pen around. "C'mon,

c'mon, this is marketing! The first impression is always right. Tell me what you think."

"Well," Appie sat back. For some reason the quotes on the clothing came back to haunt her. *Goodness without wisdom . . . impose the law of its being . . . If not now, when?* Her hands, gathered in her lap, opened up, as if holding an offering. Sunlight, tinted golden by passing clouds, spilled through the window wall into her open hands, momentarily dazzling her. She felt strangely removed, sitting as if hovering in space. Some combination of fear and awareness that this moment was Very Important joined to create a mental space of its own. A dizziness that was not dizziness momentarily took her, as if she were suddenly weightless, as if magnets moved against her mind. She felt it, the Connectedness-of-All-Things. She understood that she sat at a fulcrum of a mutable future, dependent on her action in this moment. And then the moment passed, leaving behind a feeling of calm, courage, and certainty. She looked up at George, knowing what she had to say. "It's a bad idea."

His smile turned to a scowl instantaneously. "What is?"

"The intention is that Worldtree will use the Mindportal helmet as a morale booster for employees and the Mindportal company is looking at this application as a way to gain user acceptance, right?"

George sat back, still scowling. "In a nutshell. But your notes seemed overwhelmingly positive."

So they had seen the notes. Damn them. "The notes were incomplete. I hadn't gotten to outlining the downside yet."

"What downside?"

She ticked off on her fingers. "One. It's lawsuit hell. As soon as the first employee has an epileptic fit—"

"But the stats say the device is no more dangerous than a cell phone—"

"And you might recall certain wireless companies paid out millions in settlements. Doesn't matter how safe the helmet actually is. We'll have to spend bundles proving it isn't. Two, religious rights."

"What? This has nothing to do with religion!"

Appie shook her head like a stubborn bull. "Even the people at Mindportal implied there was a spiritual element. A certain number of employees will refuse to use the device on religious grounds. Again, lawsuits may ensue. Legal can tell you how sticky those will be. And if there's *any* impression that Worldtree is trying to create a corporate cult"—*As I suspect they may hope to,* Appie added to herself—"the media would have a field day. Stock would tank. Stockholders would flee in disgust."

"But—"

"Three!" Appie announced, taking a deep breath because now she would have to lie, even though it was for a good cause. "The Mindportal device will not create more productive workers. Julio saw this, and that may be why he didn't want to touch the project. He called it Rapture of the Void, falling in love with nature, what have you. It takes you out of the mundane. You feel more calm, yes, but then the last thing you want is to go to work. You're more likely to dwell on big-picture questions."

"Big picture?" echoed George, undoubtedly imagining Worldtree as the only big picture worth discussing.

"Yeah. Family, environment, poverty . . ."

George blew air out between his lips in disgust. "Opt-out shit."

"That's my point," said Appie. "And remember the marketing truism that Happy People Don't Buy Stuff. The people at Mindportal confided to me that they hoped this device could eventually bring world peace, an end to war." Take that, Harold, who was reported to have major investments in military-industrial companies. She hoped he was listening in.

"Hah!"

"They have their own agenda, George, and it's not the same as Worldtree's. It's a bad idea, George. *Especially* if it works as Mindportal claims." And that Appie was able to state with absolute conviction.

George stared at her, biting his lower lip, arms folded again across his chest. "That's your assessment?"

"Yes, it is."

His nostrils flared and he stared out of the window for long moments. He stabbed the pen into his desk blotter once. Twice. "All right. Thanks. Write me up a full report and I'll send it on."

Appie quoted another aphorism she had seen on Mercator's clothing. "The truth will set you free. But first it will make you miserable."

"Yeah, yeah. Go on. We'll be in touch."

Appie left his office and got into the elevator feeling . . . immense relief. It was all going to be okay. Just not in the way she'd expected. She returned to her cubio and typed up the points she had just outlined to the Marketing VP. She then e-mailed the report to George, with a blind carbon copy to

Rebecca the Conduit, who read everything and passed it on. "Ooops," Appie said with a smile. *Worldtree might take our time, our lives, our ovaries. But they will not take our souls.*

She didn't know if she'd be "let go" or if she'd resign first. Either way, the end was near. Appie checked her bank account online and found she had a good start on a nest egg, given that she almost never bought anything. And her available credit was through the roof. She'd heard there was a sizable opt-out community on Orcas Island. Maybe there was one in North Dakota, too. The world, her future, felt limitless, like a flat endless prairie stretching out the horizon, vast as the sea. She wondered if there were fresh lilies down at Pike Place Market. She'd always liked lilies. Appie logged off her workstation and walked out the door to go find out.

Kara Dalkey is the author of fifteen novels, mostly historical fantasy, and about a dozen published short stories, both fantasy and SF. Her most recent release is a reprint of her novel *Euryale*, a fantasy set in ancient Rome, published in the paranormal romance line of Juno Books. When not writing or being an office drone, she has lately been taking courses in boat piloting so that she and her sweetie can explore the islands of Puget Sound in their mini-yacht.

Author's Note

This story came about as a reaction to the best-selling nonfiction book by Thomas Friedman, *The World Is Flat*. This eye-opening, highly influential work about the progress of globalization and what it means for American companies and workers basically says that young people in America had better be prepared to give their all for the sake of their jobs in the future, since they'll be in competition with Chinese and Indian youth who are eager to do so. Friedman himself seems to dismiss the question of whether the lives of American youth, caught up in the globalized treadmill, will be worth living. But that is precisely the question young people need to ask themselves as they think about college and career: "What can I do, who can I be, in order to have a life worth living?"

So "Flatland" is about that question. I believe our culture

will be facing some increasing contradictory stresses in the years to come, around the old concerns of work vs. family and work vs. self. How much of yourself and your life are you willing to sacrifice to the success of American business?

The Mindportal device is based on an actual invention used in a university research study. I predict that eventually such a device will find its way to a hi-tech gift shop near you. What it gets used for, however, and the results, will be very interesting to see.

Candas Jane Dorsey

Dolly the Dog-Soldier

You do a job, you want to know why, and how it turns out. Here are the things that happened to Dolly.

1. The Colonel picked her out from all the ones in the litter. She remembers it only slightly. It was a long time ago. She remembers that then, all of them used to run together like wolves and tumble together at noon and night like puppies. When the Colonel came to the arfenedge with his wolven eyes and his sweet talk to the Sisters, soon the litter went to live at his halfway house out in the country.

Halfway to hell, Dolly thought later. Not much later. How she learned the word *hell* was this: a teacher came to separate the litter out into ones-at-a-time. She knew he was a teacher because he said so.

"I am Wayne, and I'm here to try to teach you little savages a thing or two. That means you call me Teacher, or sir, or

Mr. Wayne if you think I'm feeling friendly, and you listen to what I say, and you learn something."

"You look like an Airedale to me," said Tezzy, who liked this new tool of words and liked to bite, too.

"Dammit to hell," said Mr. Wayne. "You wash out of this programme and you're back on the sidewalk, and probably with some scars to show for it! It's in your interest to listen to me now, and not be a mutt."

"Sir, we were in the arfidge," said Terry. He was Tezzy's littermate, from a mom who'd liked her needle too much when he was about six, people years, and he'd dragged Tezzy out of the path of cars ever since. He'd troubled to learn to talk before then. "Wun't they take us back?"

"Let me tell you all something," said Mr. Wayne wearily. At least, he looked weary to Dolly as he sat down and gestured the litter—Dolly guessed she better start calling them a pack now—to come 'round him and shush up. "This Colonel we work for doesn't let anybody go. I came here seven years ago for a three-month contract. Am I teaching in the countryside? No. I'm here in an armed camp surrounded by a pack of little street wolves, trying to turn you into something the Colonel can use."

Dolly huffed politely, her nose turned away. He'd said they were a pack! It was official, then. She thought she detected a bit of street dog on him, under the fine clothing and the good grammar. And indeed, at her sneeze, he looked at her and said, "Unless you have a summer cold, I'll assume you want to speak."

Dolly could hardly get her tongue out of the way of the

flood of words. "What is *dammit* and what is *hell*? What is *contract* and what is *assume*? How will use and how much will hurt?"

So maybe it wasn't the Colonel who picked her out later for special training. Maybe the Colonel just noticed somehow from his God-eyes, what Dolly soon learned to call surveillance, just how Mr. Wayne's eyes focussed on her dully at the start of her speaking, then sharpened and looked back, like he finally had something to listen to properly. The other littermates—pack kids now—were laughing and making fun like usual, but Dolly was modelled on a different breed from them.

"Shut up," said Mr. Wayne to them, and then to Dolly, "Hell is a place of punishment. *Dammit* means people are stuck there like they were in prison. It's from the word *damned*, which means 'condemned' or 'sentenced.'"

Tezzy started to speak, and Mr. Wayne turned to her. "Shut up and learn something. You need a real bone to chew on, and you'll get one. You'll get the world according to Colonel Quartermaine. That ought to be enough."

He went on to all of them, but Dolly knew he really continued to speak to her. "And the use is unclear, but I think it goes without saying that it will hurt. Sometimes.

"As for contracts, a contract is a deal between people. This pack and I had better make one now: I contract to tell you the truth as best I know it, and you contract to pull up your socks and learn something, so you can take some kind of control of your own lives. Knowledge is power."

"What is 'power'?" said Dolly.

8. Soon after her capture, Dolly had some surgery. It was painful and took a long time to recover from, but when she had, she looked very different from how she once did. The only visible sign was a scar at her lip, which she learned to say was from a violent incident in her childhood.

2. Okay, so she didn't actually *see* the Colonel for months. It all mushes together in memory, until recently when she has tried to sort it out. Long before then they realised Mr. Wayne really was a nice man, just trying to stay toughened up like them. Much later Mr. Wayne turned into just Wayne, but that was for Dolly and is in another part of the story.

Also, that was long after the dormitory, and the staff up there who punished them all if any of them were caught talking in the dark with each other, a pack's best time; punished them for creeping into each other's beds in little heaps—like the puppies they so wished they still could be; punished them for putting their front paws under the covers; punished them if they said "paws" or "pack" or "dog" or "pup" even though the angry shouted commands and reprimands sounded a lot like barking and growling to the resentful pack; punished them if they barked back.

It was lonely in the dorm, but with the help of Mr. Wayne, everybody remembered that they all, even a street pack's lowest member, knew you can eventually make a dog do what you want, even if all you do is hit it, because that's Nature. All Nurture does is add to the power of the command, because the pup is so eager for the puppy love it can't get from the litter anymore that it grovels and cringes toward any hand, hoping this one will be the one to deliver the pat of approval. Mr. Wayne tried pretty early to teach them to give their own pats to themselves.

They were pretty young then. Even at the time, Dolly remembers, she thought, *What's the approval of a young pup like me worth?* And she knew the others had trouble with it too, from the way the skin creased above their eyes when they were trying. The way their paws—hands, that is—would come up involuntarily toward their heads, like when you pat a real dog on its belly and its back foot thumps; they were trying to deliver their own *positive reinforcement*, but their hands seldom got all the way to their faces or hair.

Finally, Mr. Wayne said, "Do it like this," and he put his own hand over the centre of his chest. "Protect your heart. The ancients thought the liver was the seat of the soul, but we assign soul and love to the heart. Put your little paws over your little hearts."

And with protection, they may survive to become big hearts, Dolly thought, but she put her little left hand over her breastbone, trying to get it exactly as far from each nipple, and hoped for survival. By now, Tezzy had started believing in being a Good Dog, so Dolly had no one with whom to talk revolution—except, perhaps, Mr. Wayne, but she thought that would take a bit of planning, and the learning of some special words she didn't know yet.

That was before the day the Colonel came to their room. The Colonel was tall and bulgy, not because of his pants with their balloon sides (called jodhpurs, she later learned), but around the belt and the lower buttons on his shirt. He had sparse hair in a pitiful comb-over, and broken blood vessels in his cheeks, and the stale smell of old booze coming out of his skin like the street rubbies the litter sometimes had shaken down for their pocket-pools of spare change. Despite all these, he was surrounded by an aura that educated Dolly and the others instantly about *power* and brought to all their hearts the terrifying knowledge that they would never get away back to their dens on Rynam Avenue, so in fear and shock as he walked in, his military boots shining and his outfit out of some old cheap movie like they'd sneaked into the Dreamland Theatre to see, they all stood, shrinking back, and placed their paws protectively over their hearts, and he thought they were saluting him.

He stood and looked at them, and they looked at him sideways, trying to take his measure, pressing their self-esteem against their chests hidden under tiny paws, shrinking everywhere else into their trademark cringe. They all tried to keep from trembling.

"Well done, Wayne, old boy," said the Colonel.

Mr. Wayne's fair skin flushed, but he said, "Sir. They're a good bunch. A good group, sir. They do as they're taught."

Dolly was the only one, she found out later, who understood the hidden meaning in that, as the pack stood there with hands frozen to their sternums, mesmerised by this tall, delusional figure—ah, but Dolly didn't know that word then: she just looked at his antique outfit and listened to the strain in the upper registers of his voice, like dogs know how to do, and she resisted the impulse to whine at his terrifying foolishness.

She wasn't going to like any of this from here on in, she thought, and it was going to hurt a lot.

10. Dolly had a hard time adjusting to her new life. But she decided, finally, that it was going to be better than the old, if she had to use her last breath making it so. *Going to be happy if I die trying? Well, something like that.*

3. Dolly was wrong about the possibility of pain—at first. They spent most of their time with Mr. Wayne, and when they were with the Colonel, at first, they did a lot of things that Dolly liked.

She liked the gymnasium with its barres and hanging rings and stripey wood floors, but better still she liked running and jumping through the forest around their house, and most of all, she loved what the Colonel called "the burn" as the pack worked hard to develop strength, agility, and endurance.

The sessions with the Colonel grew both harder and more difficult. Harder was no problem to Dolly. She had been born to that wiry readiness and resilience that the Colonel prized. What was more difficult was keeping her hand over her heart as she learned why the Colonel wanted them.

They were a Noble Experiment, he told them, in the Reclamation of Humanity from the Depths to which Decadence had Driven the Race. They were one pack, which he called a cohort. There was a cohort from Rio, where they were all jaguars and could tear out your throat with a swipe of their claws, and one from Thessaloniki, who were Rom and could sell you their own shit, so appealing and appalling they were with their ragtag filthiness and their sad greeting-card eyes.

The Colonel had a lot of money. He paid for everything. Gradually most of the pack came to love him. Why was Dolly different? Because she had loved Mr. Wayne first, and then herself at his instruction? She curled up in her bed at night with her paws over her nose and before she went to sleep she reminded herself that she was alive, that a dog might be a man's best friend but the man did not own him—even if he thought he did—and that, though the Colonel said "I can read you little shits like a book," inside a dog it was too dark to read.

11. Telling about it later, she left out a lot of things, but she didn't leave out enough. There weren't many ways to make the Colonel look good. He didn't much like little kids, but as they all got older, he took more of an interest.

Dolly didn't like being the Colonel's favourite. It involved a number of activities she had hoped to avoid, having had enough of being sold long before the pack had been—captured.

Why would she think that word? *Captured?* The others liked receiving special attention. They were such dogs.

4. So there was Dolly, seven years later herself, looking pretty good in high heels and an evening dress, a pup no more. Looking pretty foxy, Mr. Wayne said, but she said, "No, I am a coyote now. Or maybe a wolf, I'm not sure yet." They stood on the grass in front of the schoolhouse. Mr. Wayne had his music player outside and was fiddling with the volume.

Yes, Mr. Wayne was still there, and most of the pack hated him for it, a broken man who couldn't get away, but Dolly knew why he was there: love of their sorry asses. Mr. Wayne walked around the camp—the campus, he called it, and the pack howled with derision at his pretension—with his hand over his heart, as if it hurt. The Colonel would ask him, "You all right, old boy?" and Mr. Wayne would reply, "Never better, sir," the *lie* in *reply* obvious to Dolly, but the Colonel would walk on, nodding, satisfied. (This was how Dolly knew she would be able to get away when the time came.)

"You look sensational," Mr. Wayne said, and Dolly twirled.

"I am to go to the Embassy Ball," she said, "and they will have the Circus of the Sun there for everyone to see. All the other pups have to wear black and stay outside, but I get to go in."

"Who are you supposed to kill?" Mr. Wayne said.

Dolly ran her hands down the sides of the sleek red gown. "I am to dance with the ambassador, and meet the other heads of state, and there is one with whom I must share a glass of wine. That's all."

"What have you been eating lately?"

"Food. And the Colonel's herb drink."

"So you will drink the wine together, and later he will die and you cannot."

"She. Die?"

"You are fifteen now, going on thirty-five in that dress, and you don't get it yet? What do you think bombs are for, to blow up innocent trees?"

"Shhh," said Dolly. "He'll hear you."

"Not this time," said Mr. Wayne, and swept her into a dance to the loud symphony he was playing to fill up the night. It wasn't easy to dance to, but Dolly wasn't stupid.

"I thought it was just another test," she said. "How well they climbed to a roof. How well I danced. How obedient we were. What good dogs."

"Shhh," said Mr. Wayne into her ear. "You are not a good dog. You have to figure out how to be a very bad dog indeed, and not get caught. That's your assignment from me tonight."

Dolly's head hurt. "What if the Colonel gives me an order?"

"You have to decide. Do what he says, and get a pat on the head, or do what I say, and get a pat on the head—or do what you think is right."

Dolly was angry. "What is 'right,' besides this hand you are holding out straight and pointing at the moon? Who has been letting you get away with talking about 'what is right'?"

"That's the wrong question," said Mr. Wayne. "The right question is, who has been letting me get away with talking about 'what you think'?" And he twirled her away from him as if they were jiving and not trying to waltz to unsuitable classics, and she spun away on the grass where they were dancing.

"I hope you have a good time," he said, and she laughed with a tone neither of them mistook. "Come see me when you get home and let me know how the circus was," he added.

5. So. The next thing to tell, then, is the ball. Dolly had learned a lot by then and seen a lot of movies, but she was

still surprised that such an event could be part of the modern world. The Colonel had no surprise. He had prepared them all as if such a social throwback was normal. Dolly was keeping a mental list of these weaknesses.

On the way to the ball, they drove toward the setting sun, and the sun separated into three, with a ring joining the two at the sides. "Sundogs," said the driver. Dolly put her hand over her heart. *They're not dogs*, she thought, *they're wolves. They're wild. They're my friends. They are Wayne and me, held by a shackle of light to the orbit of the Colonel, but when the sun moves and the clouds change, they will escape and run through the night, and anyone who tries to stop them they will—*

But after Wayne's admonishment, she could not imagine killing anymore. For the first time, she added dimension to the man-shapes on the targets, substituted flesh for the stuffing of the crash-test dummies they used to blow up; for the first time, she thought of her teacher as Wayne.

At the ball, all was Cinderella and Disney as she had imagined and the Colonel had assumed. While the others, left on side streets to scale the fence, rappel the neoclassical building face, scale the roof, set up listening posts in the truck, and perform all those well-rehearsed tasks, the Colonel gestured her to the passenger seat of a Lamborghini (rented?) and they drove in a sweeping arc up to the portico, where he suddenly became a gentleman, the light glittering on his epaulets and decorations, seeing her out of the car and into the reception hall on his arm, a prize, a pet, a trophy.

She was tiny for her age but looked twice her years in the makeup they had put on her, and she drew the gaze of many women and men as she climbed the marble stairs to the ballroom door and descended within, announced by a plump, brown-faced servant whose amplified voice went unheard in the din.

The Colonel leaned toward her, murmured, "You have your orders," then left her standing at the bottom of the stairs, saying loudly as he did, "Get you a drink, my dear."

Even while it was really happening, Dolly was unable to credit that anyone believed his hokey charade, but there were none but admiring glances as she began to circle the room, hiding her uncertainty under a bland half smile as she'd been taught. She saw all her targets and spoke to them. The Colonel did not reappear for more than an hour. There were at least a thousand people in the room, but she was certain he could see her every move, she was so used to the camp where they were monitored even in the toilets.

When he did reappear, holding a glass of white wine for her, he said, "I'll introduce you to Malefiore." She said, "I talked to him for fifteen minutes, over by the window, don't you remember?" He looked at her with approval, said, "Well *done*, girl," to his bitch, and she realised with a start that she was *outside the fence*.

After that it was easy. Difficult but not hard, more like. The secret was in numbers. There were a thousand people. They had a glass every half an hour. The silent, tiny brown-skinned women with the silver trays collected empties constantly and left the full glasses where they were until the women were sure they belonged to no one nearby, no one who had gone to dance. A favourite place for goblets and napkins to be abandoned was along the narrow shelf that topped the wainscoting, from which one or another would fall from time to time, in silence, to the thick carpet that covered all the room but the dance floor.

Dolly put her glass there, with a folded napkin beneath it, beside a similarly full one, while she reached up and fixed her hair. The Colonel was scanning the room for the woman whose final friend Dolly was supposed to become.

Dolly leaned on the wall with the glasses at her back, and when the Colonel called her away, the glass she took was not the one she was sure the Colonel had poisoned. When he turned back, she was picking up a napkin from the floor where it might have dropped from below the goblet. She glided away, not looking back until she heard the tiny plink of a falling glass. Even then her glance was just part of a survey of the other side of the hall.

She touched the Colonel's shoulder blade and whispered, "Is that her?" pointing away through an archway, not showing her delight that not only had the unfolding linen pushed the glass over, but when it hit the floor, one side of the goblet had snapped silently away. Safe.

The Colonel said, "So it is! *Well* done," and Dolly thought perhaps she was a wolverine instead, as she didn't seem to enjoy being patted anymore.

6. The Colonel introduced her to a beautiful, tawny-skinned old woman with lush, long white hair. In their high heels, Dolly was still a foot taller. The woman would have looked like a doll, but when she turned her gaze to Dolly's, it burned like the halogen core of a spotlight, marking Dolly's vision

forever. She made the Colonel look like the pitiful figure he should have been, had he not been held together and made presentable by megalomania.

She and Dolly talked for a moment, then, "Excuse me, dear," said the woman, though Dolly wanted to give her a name—the Eminence?—"but I really must say good-bye. It's far too warm in here." And she turned away, toward the French windows onto the stone balcony.

Dolly followed her, leaving the Colonel beaming after them. "Can I please come with you?" Dolly dropped the languid sophistication in her eagerness, and the woman looked twice. The Intelligence?

"You poor thing," she said. "You're just a kid." Dolly nodded, hurrying beside her. They passed from the hot, noisy crowd into a cool, orange-tinged night, and the tiny woman strode directly to the edge of the balcony.

"Don't your security guards go mad?" Dolly asked her.

The Courage turned her sharp bright scrutiny on Dolly. "How would you know about that?"

Dolly swivelled and leaned back against the heavy stone balustrade, looked up at the façade above her. Though it was floodlit, the Victorian neoclassicism of the façade ensured many dark channels up which her pack members were making their way. She saw two of them edging along ledges toward target windows.

Dolly turned again, and looked out at the square. Calmly, she said to the woman, "First, you are so warm that I offer you my chilled wineglass, and you take a long and satisfying drink. The Colonel will like to see that I am taking care of you. Then, I leave you to report to him. I believe you are not meant to die until after the ball.

"So if you take a little time to look around in this lovely night, perhaps at the architecture, and if you see a large black animal, a cat finding its way across the face of this building, or maybe two of them, where they are not supposed to be, and you look a little closer at them to see how they got there, that would not be my fault, would it? And should you let it be known later that in case of poisoning incidents you always prepare yourself with a number of herbal and medicinal antidotes, that would be better."

Dolly raised her glass to her lips and sipped. "I am fifteen," she said wistfully, "and all the pack are younger than I am. There are other groups of children he has *adopted*. You understand *adopted*?"

The woman smiled and nodded, her kindness palpable in the night.

"If we are *seen* to fail, we are punished, but if he fails first . . ." Dolly dared say no more. She turned back to where the Colonel could see her mouth. "Perhaps you would feel better if you took a bit of wine," she said. "Here, have mine—my father will say I have drunk too much tonight anyway."

Unhesitatingly the old woman took the glass and drank deeply. "Thank you, my dear," she said.

"I must get back," said Dolly.

"I hope we meet again," said the Presence.

"Thank you, ma'am," Dolly said, and swayed her hips back into the ballroom.

Rejoining the Colonel, she whispered excitedly, "She drank from my glass!"

"Hush, my dear," he said, and patted her hand, saying more loudly, "We must get you home, little one. I think you've had more than your limit!" But before they could make their way all through the crowd, reclaim their evening cloaks, and get to the door, the militia or the police, Dolly wasn't sure which, were there with their guns.

7. The children were taken somewhere different from the Colonel, and though some of them had to testify, Dolly never saw him again except on television.

9. Dolly was sent to school by the Presence, the Kindness, the Intelligence—whatever her name was going to be—though Dolly never saw her again either, except on the news, saying, "I saw a shadow I thought was a black cat, walking on a ledge. But then I realised it wasn't. . . ."

Dolly had never heard the Mexican folksong *"Coplas"* at that time, but when she did she laughed and laughed. But that was later.

12. Dolly did see Wayne again, with scars in his neck where the small explosive packs that would have been triggered by the perimeter electronics had been removed. Now he was outside, too, was a teacher in her new school, and helped the school psychologist deal with Dolly.

13. After Dolly's surgery, he helped her, too, to get used to the person she was to become for the rest of her life.

"Think of the pack," he said. "They did as they were told, and went down fighting. Do you want to be like them?"

"Yes," she shouted, "yes! I want to be tumbled into a big bed with the litter, and I want to wake up and discover I am eight and hungry again, but with my littermates!"

"You are a fool," Wayne said, but gently. "If you want things like that, you will never get what you want. Want something interesting and you have a chance."

He had a point, but she still hated him for saying it. Still, she had to acknowledge his right to do so. Every dog must have its day.

—Dedicated to the memory of
Dolly Tess Virginia Johnson, a warrior

CANDAS JANE DORSEY is internationally known for her contribution to the literature of the fantastic, with two novels and a number of well-known short science fiction and fantasy stories. She is also a poet and mainstream fiction writer, has been a freelance writer and editor since 1979, and for fourteen years was a principal in the eclectic publishing company The Book Collective. She teaches writing workshops and courses.

Her first novel, *Black Wine,* won the James Tiptree, Jr., William L. Crawford, and Aurora awards; *A Paradigm of Earth*, her second, also received great acclaim. In 2005 she was awarded an Alberta Centennial Gold Medal for her achievements in the arts. She lives and works in Edmonton, Alberta, Canada.

AUTHOR'S NOTE

Dolly Tess Virginia Johnson was fourteen and I was twenty-one when we met. Seven adult years is not much, but that seven-year difference set us apart in authority and role. I was a caregiver, she was in care. Her anger was monumental, equal only to her beauty and intelligence. Her anger ruled, for she had had to survive birth and her first three years with an untrustworthy mother and then the brutal anonymity of the child welfare system: how brutal her circumstances had been all her life I did not find out until decades later, after her death, when I read her own written account of the abuses heaped on her in ten years in an unfit foster home. When I met Dolly, it was her birthday. On her thirteenth birthday, her gift was that her foster mother called the social worker and had Dolly taken from the home; she had been in thirteen placements in the twelve months before I met her. When I first saw her she was shouting her defiance to the world, and her courage and spirit shone like halogen.

Dolly lived in defiance of disaster all her life. Her courage helped her raise a family, upgrade her education, and live in hope. Yet in her late forties she died of a gunshot wound her relatives still believe was not self-inflicted. In movies or books, a classic locked-room mystery calls for a brilliant detective to unravel every thread: in real life, the death of a native woman in a small northern city was written off as a drunken suicide.

From Dolly and young women like her I learned the meaning of courage and the importance of hope, and their stories, learned when I was younger than I thought I was at the time, shaped my adult life. When I heard of Dolly's death, the extinguishing of that unparallelled spirit, I thought I had nothing in me but the anger I wanted to express on her behalf—but a few days later, without thinking, I wrote this story. It is for all the children who live in courage and hope despite their circumstances, and who, like Dolly, win control of their own lives as a reward.

Margo Lanagan

Ferryman

"Wrap your pa some lunch up, Sharon," says Ma.

"What, one of these bunnocks? Two?"

"Take him two. And a good fat strip of smoke. And the hard cheese, all that's left. Here's his lemon." She whacks the cork into the bottle with the flat of her hand.

I wrap the heavy bottle thickly, so it won't break if it drops. I put it in the carry-cloth and the bunnocks and other foods on top, in such a way that nothing squashes anything else.

"Here I go."

Ma crosses from her sweeping and kisses my right cheek. "Take that for him and this for you." She kisses my left. "And tell him about those pigeons; that'll give him spirit till this evening."

"I will." I lift the door in the floor.

I used to need light; I used to be frightened. Not anymore. Now I step down and my heart bumps along as normal; I close the lid on myself without a flinch.

I start up with "The Ballad of Priest and Lamb." The stairway is good for singing; it has a peculiar echo. Also, Ma likes to hear me as I go. "It brightens my ears, your singing," she says, "and it can't do any harm to those below, can it?"

Down I go. Down and down, down and round, round and round I go, and all is black around me and the invisible stone stairs take my feet down. I sing with more passion the lower I go, and more experimenting, where no one can hear me. And then there begins to be light, and I sing quieter; then I'm right down to humming, so as not to draw attention when I get there.

Out into the smells and the red twilight I go. It's mostly the fire-river that stinks, the fumes wafting over from way off to the right before its flames mingle with the tears that make it navigable. But the others have their own smells, too. Styx water is sharp and bites inside your nostrils. Lethe water is sweet as hedge roses and makes you feel sleepy.

Down the slope I go to the ferry, across the velvety hell-moss badged here and there with flat red liverworts. The dead are lined up in their groups looking dumbly about; once they've had their drink, Pa says, "You can push them around like tired sheep. Separate them out, herd them up as you desire. Pile them into cairns if you want to! Stack them like wood—they'll stay however you put them. They'll only mutter and move their heads side to side like birds."

The first time I saw them, I turned and ran for the stairs. I was only little then. Pa caught up to me and grabbed me by the back of my pinafore. "What the blazes?" he said.

"They're horrible!" I covered my face and struggled as he carried me back.

"What's horrible about them? Come along and tell me." And he took me right close and made me examine their hairlessness and look into their empty eyes and touch them, even. Their skin was without print or prickle, slippery as a green river stone. "See?" said Pa. "There's nothing to them, is there?"

"Little girl!" a woman had called from among the dead. "So sweet!"

My father reached into the crowd and pulled her out by her arm. "Did you not drink all your drink, madam?" he said severely.

She made a face. "It tasted foul." Then she turned and beamed upon me. "What lovely hair you have! Ah, youth!"

Which I don't. I have thick, brown, straight hair, chopped off as short as Ma will let me—and sometimes shorter when it really gives me the growls.

My dad had put me down and gone for a cup. He made the woman drink the lot, in spite of her faces and gagging. "Do you want to suffer?" he said. "Do you want to feel everything and scream with pain? There's a lot of fire to walk through, you know, on the way to the Blessed Place."

"I'm suffering now," she said, but vaguely, and by the time she finished the cup, I was no longer visible to her—nothing was. She went in among the others and swayed there like a tall, thin plant among plants. And I've never feared them since, the dead. My fear dried up out of me, watching that woman's self go.

Here comes Pa now, striding up the slope away from the line of dead. "How's my miss, this noontide? How's my Scowling Sarah?"

Some say my dad is ugly. I say, his kind of work would turn anyone ugly, all the gloom and doom of it. And anyway, I don't care—my dad is my dad. He can be ugly as a sackful of bumholes and still I'll love him.

Right now his hunger buzzes about him like a cloud of blowflies. "Here." I slip the carry-cloth off my shoulder. "And there's two fat pigeons for supper, in a pie."

"Two fat pigeons in one fat pie? You set a wicked snare, Sharon Armstrong."

"You look buggered." I sit on the moss beside him. "And that's a long queue. Want some help, after?"

"If you would, my angel." *Donk,* says the cork out of the bottle. Pa's face and neck and forearms are all brown wrinkled leather.

He works his way through a bunnock, then the meat, the cheese, the second bunnock. He's neat and methodical from first bite to last sup of the lemon.

When he's done, he goes off a way and turns his back to pee into the lemon bottle, for you can't leave your earthly wastes down here or they'll sully the waters. He brings it back corked and wrapped and tucks it into the carry-cloth next to a rock on the slope. "Well, then."

I scramble up from the thick dry moss and we set off down the springy slope to the river.

A couple of hours in, I'm getting bored. I've been checking the arrivals, sending off the ones without coin and taking the coin from under those tongues that have it, giving the paid ones their drink and checking there's nothing in their eyes, no hope or thought or anything, and keeping them neat in their groups with my stick and my voice. Pa has rowed hard, across and back, across and back. He's nearly to the end of the queue. Maybe I can go up home now?

But in his hurry, Pa has splashed some tears onto the deck. As he steps back to let the next group of the dead file aboard, he slips on that wetness and disappears over the side, into the woeful river, so quickly he doesn't have time to shout.

"Pa!" I push my way through the slippery dead. "No!"

He comes up spluttering. Most of his hair has washed away.

"Thank God!" I grab his hot, wet wrist. "I thought you were dead and drowned!"

"Oh, I'm dead all right," he says.

I pull him up out of the river. The tears and the fire have eaten his clothes to rags and slicked the hairs to his body. He looks almost like one of *them*. "Oh, Pa! Oh, Pa!"

"Calm yourself, daughter. There's nothing to be done."

"But look at you, Pa! You walk and talk. You're more yourself than any of these are theirs." I'm trying to get his rags decent across his front, over his terrible bald willy.

"I must go upstairs to die properly." He takes his hands from his head and looks at the sloughed-off hairs on them. "Oh, Sharon, always remember this! A moment's carelessness is all it takes."

I fling myself at him and sob. He's slimed with dissolving skin and barely warm, and he has no heartbeat.

He lays his hand on my head, and I let go of him. His face, even without hair, is the same ugly, loving face; his eyes are the same eyes. "Come." He leads the way off the punt. "It doesn't do to delay these things."

I follow him, pausing only to pick up the carry-cloth in my shaking arms. "Can you not stay down here, where we can visit you and be with you? You're very like your earthly form. Even with the hair gone—"

"What, you'd have me wander the banks of Cocytus forever?"

"Not forever. Just until—I don't know. Just not now, just not to lose you altogether."

His hand is sticky on my cheek. "No, lovely. I must get myself coined and buried and do the thing properly. You of all people would know that."

"But, Pa!"

He lays a slimy finger on my lips. "It's my time, Sharon," he says into my spilling eyes. "And I will take my love of you and your mother with me, into all eternity; you know that."

I know it's not true, and so does he. How many dead have we seen, drinking all memory to nowhere? But I wipe away my tears and follow him.

We start up the stairs, and soon it's dark. He isn't breathing; all I can hear is the sound of his feet on the stone steps, which is unbearable, like someone tonguing chewed food in an open mouth.

He must have heard my thoughts. "Sing me something, Scowling Sarah. Sing me that autumn song, with all the wind and the birds in it."

Which I'm glad to do, to cover the dead-feet sounds and to pretend we're not here like this, to push aside my fear of what's to come, to keep my own feet moving from step to step.

We follow the echoes up and up, and when I reach the end of the song, "Beautiful," he says. "Let's have that again from the very start."

So I sing it again. I have to break off, though, near to the end. The trapdoor is above us, leaking light around its edges.

"Oh, my pa!" I hold his terrible flesh and cry. "Don't come up! Just stay here on the stair! I will bring you your food and your drink. We can come down and sit with you. We will *have* you, at least—"

"Go on, now." He plucks my arms from his neck, from his waist, from his neck again. "Fetch your mother for me."

"Just, even—" My mind is floating out of my head like smoke. "Even if you could stay for the pigeon! For the pie! Just that little while! I will bring it down to you, on the platter—"

"What's all this noise?" The trapdoor opens. Ma gives a shout of fright seeing Pa, and yes, in the cooler earthly light, his face is—well, it is clear that he is dead.

"Forgive me, wife," says his pale, wet mouth. His teeth show through his cheeks, and his eyes are unsteady in his shiny head. "I have gone and killed myself, and it is no one's fault but my own." He has no breath, as I said. The voice, I can hear in this realer air, comes from somewhere else than his lungs, somewhere else, perhaps, than his body completely.

Ma kneels slowly and reaches, slowly, into the top of the stair.

"Charence Armstrong," she weeps at him, her voice soft and unbelieving, "how could you do this?"

"He fell in the Acheron, Ma; he slipped and fell!"

"How could you be so stupid?" she tells him gently, searching the mess for the face she loves. "Come to me."

"As soon as I step up there I am dead," he says. "You must come down to me, sweet wife, and make your farewells."

There's hardly the room for it, but down she comes onto the stairs, her face so angry and intense it frightens me. And then they are like the youngest of lovers in the first fire of love, kissing, kissing, holding each other tight as if they'd crush together into one. She doesn't seem to mind the slime, the baldness of him, the visibility of his bones. The ragged crying all around us in the hole—that is me; these two are silent in their cleaving. I lean and howl against them, and at last they take me in, lock me in with them.

Finally we untangle ourselves, three wrecks of persons on the stairs. "Come, then," says my father. "There is nothing for it."

"Ah, my husband!" whispers Ma, stroking his transparent cheeks.

All the workings move under the jellified skin. "Bury me with all the rites," he says. "And use real coin, not token."

"As if she would use token!" I say.

He kisses me, wetly upon all the wet. "I know, little scowler. Go on up, now."

When he follows us out of the hole, it's as if he's rising through a still water-surface. It paints him back onto himself, gives him back his hair and his clothes and his colour. For a few flying moments he's alive and bright, returned to us.

But as his heart passes the rim, he stumbles. His face closes. He slumps to one side, and now he is gone, a dead man taken as he climbed from his cellar, a dead man fallen to his cottage floor.

We weep and wail over him a long time.

Then, "Take his head, daughter." Ma climbs back down into the hole. "I will lift his dear body from here."

The day after the burial, he walks into sight around the red hill in company with several other dead.

"Pa!" I start towards him.

He smiles bleakly, spits the obolus into his hand, and gives it to me as soon as I reach him. I was going to hug him, but it seems he doesn't want me to.

"That brother of mine, Gilles," he says. "He can't hold his liquor."

"Gilles was just upset that you were gone so young." I fall into step beside him.

He shakes his bald head. "Discourage your mother from him; he has ideas on her. And he's more handsome than I was. But he's feckless; he'll do neither of you any good."

"All right." I look miserably at the coins in my hand. I can't tell which is Pa's now.

"In a moment it won't matter." He puts his spongy hand on my shoulder. "But for now, I'm counting on you, Sharon. You look after her for me."

I nod and blink.

"Now, fetch us our cups, daughter. These people are thirsty and weary of life."

I bring the little black cups on the tray. "Here, you must drink this," I say to the dead. "So that the fire won't hurt you."

My father, of course, doesn't need to be told. He drinks all the Lethe water in a single swallow, puts down the cup, and smacks his wet chest as he used to after a swig of apple brandy. Up comes a burp of flowery air, and the spark dies out of his eyes.

I guide all the waiting dead onto the punt. I flick the heavy mooring rope off the bollard, and we slide out into the current, over the pure, clear tears-water braided with fine flames. The red sky is cavernous; the cable dips into the flow behind us and lifts out ahead, dripping flame and water. I take up the pole and push it into the riverbed, pushing us along, me and my boatload of shades, me and what's left of my pa. My solid arms work, my lungs grab the hot air, my juicy heart pumps and pumps. I never realised, all the years my father did this, what solitary work it is.

❖ ❖ ❖

Margo Lanagan is the author of three story collections, *White Time*, *Black Juice*, and *Red Spikes*, and the novel *Tender Morsels*. *Black Juice* won two World Fantasy Awards, was a Michael L. Printz Honor Book, and was short-listed for, among other awards, the *Los Angeles Times* Book Prize. *Red Spikes* was the Children's Book Council of Australia's Book of the Year for Older Readers in 2007.

Margo lives in Sydney, Australia, with her partner and their two teenage sons. She has a rather dusty history degree and has worked various jobs, including freelance book editing and technical writing.

Visit her blog at **amongamidwhile.blogspot.com**.

Author's Note

Every year my partner Steven and I design and edit an anthology of writing and pictures by primary school children of the Murray-Darling Basin, the river system that occupies much of southeastern Australia. One year there was a piece written by Harrison Fridd, aged eight, of Waikerie in South Australia. It began, "The ferry on the river is where my dad works. Most of the day he takes people back and forth across the river." My brain went to the most famous ferryman of them all, Charon, who poles the souls of the dead across the rivers of Hell, and when Harrison went on to mention that he sometimes saw his dad on the ferry in the mornings on the way to school, I had the story of the child who nips down into Hell to take her ferryman dad his lunch. I liked the combination of the gruesome job and the cosy family errand. I had no idea the gruesomeness was going to take over so thoroughly. Honest!

The Ghosts of Strangers

Nina Kiriki Hoffman

Elexa had been up the mountain to see her mother's dragon once. Her father took her and her older brother Kindal when they were very small, just after their mother drowned in a storm-swollen river. The dragon had raised her children already, with Elexa's mother's help; after Mother died, the dragon waited only long enough to meet Elexa and Kindal before flying away forever.

Her mother's dragon terrified Elexa. The dragon was huge to a three-year-old child, a great dark thing with a mouth full of flame and spears, and dark pearl eyes. She did not speak to them; she reared up before her shadowy cave, spread her wings, belled a mourning wail. Heat came off her stronger than the warmth of a winter stove. Elexa hid behind her father, who spoke formal words in the human approximation of dragonspeech, words full of hisses and gravel. The dragon did not look directly at them. She faced them, though, long enough to weep five ruby tears, before turning and retreating into her cave. Father knelt and collected the stones. He gave three to Kindal and two to Elexa. "It is her mourning gift," he whispered. "Hold these when you feel your sorrow."

For the next year, Elexa slept curled on her straw pallet with the rubies in her hands. They were the first stones that spoke to her.

The first human ghost Elexa caught was the ghost of old Peder, the village headman, the night he died. She was six. The whole village gathered together to worry about old Peder, who had been their leader for forty years. Everyone but Peder and his wife said prayers at the temple of the mountain god for Peder's health to return, for two days and nights, until Peder sent his wife to ask them to stop. Peder had spoken with his stomach, and it told him that this time he would not recover; he should leave this life and move on to another.

After that, everyone vigiled together around old Peder in the gatherhouse. He lay on a pallet near the storytelling firepit, the fire low, with his wife and daughters beside him, and everyone else waited with them, drowsing, quiet, respectful. The rattle came after the middle of the night, his last unquiet breaths. Elexa saw the ghost ease out of him, a white-gray cloud shaped vaguely like a person. She sent out her mental net before she thought, wrapped him up, and pulled him to her.

"What? What?" he said. "What are you doing to me, Daughter?"

She glanced around to see if anybody else heard his questions. Everyone had their heads bowed, praying for Peder's next journey.

She rose and walked out of the gatherhouse, into the chilly night, his ghost trailing her like a fish on a line in a river of air. She sat on the worn stone steps of the mountain god's temple and pulled the headman's ghost beside her, loosening her net so he could take human form. He settled onto the stair, a gray-white shape, like the snow sculptures they built in midwinter, rough outlines of people and dragons, gods and animals. His eyes were dark pits; only a tingling flavor told Elexa who he was.

"What has happened?" Peder asked. "I no longer feel ill. There's no hurt in me. Yet I can't walk where I want. Why did I follow you? How am I flying?"

"You're a ghost," Elexa said.

He held out his arms, stared at his blurry hands, turned his head to look at her. "I feel stranger than I can understand," he said. He pushed against her ghost net. "This is what we do to the ghosts of animals? I hear a call. I know there's a farther place I can go without walking. It is like a door with light beyond it. But your net holds me, Elexa. You stop me."

She gripped one hand with the other, thought of Peder the old man, presiding over village meetings when the men talked about hunting problems or the women discussed plans for the spring planting. He settled disputes about goats and sheep, chickens and apples, hunting rights when any argued over who could hunt dragon prey in this meadow or that. He assigned unpleasant tasks so no one had to do them all the time. He read the weather and the sky and told people when to plant. Peder was the one who led the children into the forest when they were five, six, seven, taught them which plants could be picked for food, which ones they should never touch. He showed them how to tell one tree from another by the shape and smell of the leaves, the form of the flowers, the texture of the bark, the way the branches grew. He tutored everyone in dragonspeech during long nights around the storytelling firepit.

Everything he did, he did for the village.

"I'll let you go," she said, and reached out to unweave the threads of her net.

"Wait."

She halted.

"Take me to my dragon," he said.

"Are you sure?" she asked.

"Yes."

She stopped at the cottage and got her robe and fur-lined boots. Peder had died in early spring, and the night air was full of wet cold. She didn't yet have the thicker, slightly scale-patterned skin of those who had dragon bonded, so she wasn't as impervious to flame and cold as she would be after she turned thirteen. She got her walking stick, too, and then she headed for the path up to the terraces.

She was frightened. The grown mother dragons were as big as five or six humans. They cast racing, winged shadows when they flew over the village. She had looked up often as they flew overhead, memorized the patterns of colors on the undersides of their wings and bellies, learned to recognize which dragons had bonded to which boys and girls, which fledglings belonged to which mothers. Dragons often landed on the village center ground to pick up the day's catch from their bonded humans, saving the humans a trip up the mountain. Elexa watched them from the shelter of the smithy or the door to the gatherhouse. She had never gone close to them on her own.

She wasn't alone now, was she? Peder was with her. Peder, and all the stories the others whispered on fall and winter nights when they huddled together in the gatherhouse, spinning thread or shelling nuts or grinding flour, about how their village was special and strange, different from other human villages and cities.

In other places, stories said, female dragons ate humans.

Male dragons, who only visited the terraces during mating season unless they were village-born, were wild and untrustworthy; they never bonded and were always a threat, unless they were the nestlings of local dragons; then they might know the rules, or they might have forgotten them on purpose. During mating season, the humans spent daylight hours in their houses, sheltered the domestic animals in caves or low-roofed structures so they couldn't be seen from the air, and crept out at night, while dragons slept. Some of the wilder males dove at human houses, but older, past-egg-laying-age bonded females guarded the village. They drove the wilder males away.

Fortunately, mating season came at the tail end of winter, when there was little work in the fields, and it lasted only three weeks at most.

The stories lasted forever.

The darkest stories spoke of ravening dragons who dropped from the sky and carried off humans in their claws. Dragons who flamed, burned fields and houses, cooked people as they ran. Dragons who—

Elexa faltered on the path halfway to First Terrace.

"Don't worry," said old Peder's ghost. "The males have already left. It's sleep time."

She stumbled on, upward. At the edge of First Terrace, she looked around. Cave mouths gaped against the cliff wall across the terrace. Bones of game animals stood in piles near each cave, and smoke drifted from the caves. She smelled sulfur, burlap, cinnamon, rotten meat, and hot metal. Sleepy chirps came from a nearby cave, and the murmur of a dragon mother, the rustle of wings spread and settled.

"That way." Peder gestured toward the left.

Elexa walked on the outer edge of the terrace, as far from the caves as she could.

"Here," said Peder. He indicated a cave.

Elexa rubbed at her throat until she could swallow, then approached the cave. "Greetings, O great one," she said, the first phrase she had learned in the tongue of dragons. It scratched and rattled in her mouth.

Deep in the cave, a stirring, the scrape of talons on rock. A wave of heat flowed from the cave. Then a narrow head on a long snaky neck emerged, the snout wreathed in waving whiskers; streams of smoke flowed from the nostrils; the eyes great, glowing yellow-green jewels.

"Who disturbs my sleep?" asked the dragon in a deep, menacing voice. She spoke human more clearly than any dragon Elexa had overheard in the village center ground.

"Please, Grandmother, it's me, Elexa. Old Peder told me to bring his ghost here."

"His ghost?" The dragon paced out of the cave past her, a dark hissing presence as her belly slid across the rocks, her six legs striking sparks with their steel-tipped talons, her muscular, snakelike tail whipping back and forth. She ran to the edge of the terrace and raised her wings, rattled them against the sky. She belled, then, a low, loud cry like metal striking metal that resonated for a long while after. As the sound faded, other dragons came from their caves. Old Peder's dragon belled again, and the others cried out, too, a cacophony of notes sliding in and out of each other, jangling, stunning. Elexa covered her ears with her hands, but the sound went right through her, jittering her bones. Once more the dragon belled, and the others called after her. She turned and came back to Elexa.

"My human is dead?" she said.

"Yes. I'm sorry."

"You've brought me his ghost?"

"He asked me to." Old Peder stood at her shoulder now, silent.

"You, an unbonded child, can speak with ghosts?"

Elexa dipped her head. Was that a bad thing? Everyone she knew had some ghost awareness, though others had less than she had. What if everyone else was half blind and deaf for a good reason? Would this huge, fire-breathing creature eat her? "Peder is the first human ghost I've spoken to," she whispered.

"Does he give himself to me?" asked the dragon.

Elexa looked at old Peder's ghost.

"I fed her and the children the ghosts of so many rats and mice and rabbits," he said. "I never knew what they got from it. She needed them, and they made her stronger, but I never understood how. I could go through that door to the light, Elexa, but maybe this is a better thing to do. Yes, I give myself to her."

"He says he does," Elexa said.

"Can you bring him to me, child?"

Elexa flexed her mental net, directed it toward the dragon. Old Peder flew across the space to settle just in front of the dragon's snout.

"Are you sure?" Elexa asked.

"Sure enough, I guess," said old Peder.

"He's just in front of you," Elexa said. She released her net as the dragon's maw gaped, big enough for a person to walk into. Red light from internal flames flickered in the dragon's throat. Her teeth were long and iron-colored, and her tongue lay like a two-headed snake in the bed of her long, long mouth.

Peder stepped into her mouth. She shut her jaw, swallowed, a wave traveling down that long, pale throat, and said, "Oh! Oh, Peder, my lad. Ahhhh." Her great eyes closed, and she laid her head on the ground between her front legs, her neck an upward arch. Small, panting puffs of smoke came from her nose.

Elexa knelt ten feet from the dragon. Had she killed the mother? Had she destroyed Peder's hope of happiness in his next life?

A chill wet wind danced over the terrace, tugged on her hair and the edges of her robe. It crept in under the robe to freeze her arms and legs. Her face went numb.

Presently the dragon opened her eyes again, and in the yellow glow of her jeweled eyes, faint blue streaks flickered. "Elexa," said the dragon. Her breath was a warm, smoke-scented wind.

"Grandmother," Elexa said. Her teeth knocked together.

"Elexa," said the dragon again. She took several steps toward Elexa. "I am more than your dragon grandmother; Peder is part of me, too. I know you now."

Elexa's face was thawing from the warmth the dragon radiated, but there was a chill inside her. "Old Peder?" she murmured.

"Yes," said the dragon.

"Is this a good thing?"

The dragon lifted her head, pointed her snout to the sky. She coughed a spurt of flame, then three huffs of smoke. She was laughing. "It is glorious," she said. She scuttled closer and rubbed the top of Elexa's head with the underside of her chin. Strands of Elexa's hair caught in the dragon's scales and singed because of the heat, leaving a foul smell. Elexa cringed.

"I forgot. You're not yet bonded," muttered the dragon, sounding like Peder. She backed away. "Elexa, you have special skills. When others die, ask them whether they want to go through the door to the light or to this kind of afterlife. Now I know that sometimes our ghosts come here on their own and join with their bonded ones, for my dragon has known this to happen before, but only by chance. She tells me it was how the dragon settlement started here ages ago, a gift of ghosts from our village; it is why we can talk with these dragons, when no one else in our part of the world knows the way of it. Be a guide to the other dead in the village when they need you."

In the village below, one of the women started the death chant, a long wavering cry that turned corners, then went back. A second voice joined the first. They must have washed and prepared old Peder's body for viewing, farewells, and burning. Elexa crept to the edge of the terrace and looked down at all the dark cottages rubbing shoulders with each other, gathered around the center ground and the gather-house like a ring of stones around a firepit, with the mountain god's temple off to the side, near the forest. Smoke drifted from the gatherhouse's smoke hole, lit by the flicker of flames below; it was the only building with any light in it. One voice rose and fell, the other echoing it two notes later, an outpouring of grief in the night.

"Yan will take care of you," the dragon said, staring down at the village past Elexa's shoulder.

Elexa sighed. She didn't like Yan, the young man Peder had chosen to replace himself as village headman. Yan was more scornful than gentle. He had no patience with the mistakes of the young, and his plant lore was superficial. However, he drove hard bargains with the peddlers who came over the passes in the spring and summer, and he was strong. He knew how to shoot arrows, how to throw knives, how to build walls. He had bonded with the biggest dragon on the mountain. If danger came up the trail from the south, Yan's dragon would help him fight it. And most of the village elders had approved him. The few who objected weren't powerful enough to change old Peder's choice.

"Get some rest," murmured the dragon.

Elexa touched the dragon's snout, then snatched back scorched fingers.

"I'm sorry," said the dragon. "When you're bonded, that will change."

That promise sent Elexa down the mountain.

Since that time, she had spoken to several other village ghosts. Three were children, unbonded, and she had let them go. The village midwife and the smith and the teacher had wanted to go up the mountain to their dragons, so Elexa took them, and watched as they seeped into their dragons and the dragons changed. Only the weary goatherd had wanted to drift away and not join his dragon mother.

Elexa had seen other human ghosts. They were those confused on the trail to their next life, the ones who wandered.

She snatched the first one she saw almost by reflex. He had died after killing many women. He had come from a large seaside settlement far to the south. His own people had killed him once they discovered what he was. To Elexa's ghost and jewel senses, he tasted sour and coppery, and he terrified her at first, until she knew for sure her net could hold him helpless, no matter how much he struggled. She didn't know how to release him. What if his ghost could kill her?

She kept him for a long time, and he told her stories of what life was like there by the sea, a vast water that tasted of salt, with ships always traveling in and out of the harbor, bringing new strange things on every tide. House wizards spun houses out of sand, and everyone drank hot water flavored with leaves from another country. People ate things with tentacles and wore bright metal chains around their necks, arms, and waists. There, dragons were horrifying, dropping down at ill-favored celebrations and weddings to snatch up children and carry them off.

Were these true stories? Stories about male dragons? She could taste the truth in them. A dragon had stolen the killer's niece. Most of the families he had known had lost someone to a dragon.

He told her stories, even about his murders, finally about his mother. With every tale, a little more of him faded, until there was nothing left for her net to hold. Most of what he told her horrified her, but she couldn't send it out of her head once it had come in her ears. She had nightmares. She wished him away, but she couldn't let him go; he had to make himself disappear a little at a time. She felt strange after he was gone; she had known him better than she knew anyone alive. After capturing him, she was more cautious about netting human ghosts. If they tasted bad, she didn't touch them, and pretended she couldn't see them.

As she grew toward thirteen, Elexa acted like the other children in the village for the most part, snaring the ghosts of small animals for the dragons, who couldn't catch them on their own and drew some kind of nourishment from them. She gave her little game ghosts to her brother, who was dragon-bonded, or her best friend Tira's older sister, Miri, whose dragon had a brood of four to provide for.

In her twelfth spring, Elexa packed a pouch for a day on the mountain: oatcakes spread with nut butter, a stoppered gourd full of water, and three small dried apples from last fall's harvest. She and Tira would spend all day on the banks of Little River, looking for gems in the outwash from the storm the day before. Maybe she didn't need to pack water. Sometimes the water at the river's edge stayed cloudy for days after a storm, though. She didn't like to drink water she couldn't see through.

She glanced across the cottage at her father, who was packing his own lunch; it was his turn to guard the herds of sheep and goats the village kept for the dragons. When she was sure his head was turned, she stole a handful of beet sugar, funneled it from her fingers into the little gourd she carried for spices.

Her brother Kindal came from behind the curtain that hid the sleeping pallets. His dark brows lowered. He had seen. Would he tell? Sugar was expensive; Father had bought this for festival cakes, but the spring festival wasn't until next week, and Elexa had a sweet tooth now.

"You owe me a ghost," Kindal muttered as he passed her.

She sighed.

Kindal took his quiver of arrows and his bow from their hooks on the wall.

"Good hunting," said their father.

"Good herding," Kindal replied. He tied a game pouch to his belt and ducked outside.

Elexa took a loot pouch and hooked it to her belt, along with her old knife. She slung the lunch pouch across her chest and took her dowsing/digging stick from its place on the wall. "I'm off," she said.

"Good hunting to you, too," said her father.

"Thanks." If she found enough gems, she'd be able to buy a mountain of sugar, and that new red-handled knife Mats the peddler had shown her on his last trip through the village. Father wanted a new scythe, though; that came first. He had sharpened the blade of his old one thin. "Back by suppertime."

Tira waited by the path that led to the dragon terraces. She looked longingly up the mountain toward the nesting sites. The girls were a year away from bonding with dragons. Tira's mother told them they should enjoy their freedom; once they had bonded, they would spend most of their days hunting small game and ghosts to keep the dragon mothers and babies fed, in addition to their village work. A dragon bond lasted a lifetime; but the hardworking part of it, where human children provided food for brooding mothers and nestlings, lasted seven years, the length of dragon childhood. Tira's mother, who told Elexa things her father wouldn't, said it was a wonderful and a terrible time. The dragon bond was a treasure and a joy, but the work was difficult. If you didn't catch enough gophers, pheasants, fish, rabbits, squirrels, and ghosts, the dragon babies' hunger groaned in your own belly as loud as it did in theirs.

Kindal's dragon mother had two nestlings; he didn't get as run-down and ragged as Tira's sister Miri, with four to care for. Miri hunted from dawn to twilight and set snares and fish traps at night.

"Bond to a mother with fewer eggs," Tira's mother advised Tira and Elexa.

Elexa had asked her father about this. His dragon mother's nestlings had fledged and flown away, though they returned for the dragon gather at midwinter. At that time, there was a flurry of unbonded dragons dropping to the village center ground, greeting those who had helped raise them.

Elexa's father said, "Visit the mothers before Bond Night; get to know the ones who want to bond. You won't be able to tell how many eggs they have until after you bond; no dragon lets an unbonded youngster into a cave. You'll know which dragon to bond with on the night of the bond. She will choose you; you don't choose her." He still took the occasional rabbit up the mountain for his dragon mother; sometimes she brought him a deer she had hunted deeper in the mountains where there were no people. Sometimes, now that her children were grown, she spent winters on the southern beaches, but she always came back to the terrace in the spring to help with the year's crop of fledglings.

"When I bond, maybe my dragon mother will take me flying," Tira said as she stared up the path to First Terrace.

"Most of them won't, though. Dragons aren't made to carry humans," said Elexa.

"Kindal's Maia does." Kindal's dragon mother took him scouting in early spring so he could report back to the village whether the passes were choked with snow or open, whether there were peddlers or raiders on the way. Maia's fledglings, Peep and Seek, were strong and adventurous and unusually independent. They had second-bonded to another dragon mother, so Maia wasn't afraid to leave them with their aunt and take Kindal flying.

Tira went up to the dragon terraces sometimes to visit the nests. She talked to her sister Miri's dragon, but she couldn't understand the dragon's answers. She didn't have Elexa's gift for dragonspeech, one of the subjects they studied in the gather-house in the evening.

Since the night she met her mother's dragon, Elexa had been up the mountain four times, ferrying ghosts. None of the other dragons she had met were as scary as the first, though she met them all while they were grieving.

Without formal introductions, humans weren't supposed to speak to dragons, though Elexa had. Some dragons could speak only to their bondlings, while others knew human tongues and could speak to anyone. The dragons didn't have leaders, but sometimes they let one of the more skilled linguists speak for a group of them.

Elexa helped her brother hunt food for his dragon mother. He taught her arrow, knife, stalking, and trapping skills, and she gave him the game she caught. He hadn't introduced her to his dragon yet.

Elexa took Tira's wrist and pulled her from the dragon path to the river path. Tira watched over her shoulder until the dragon path was out of sight.

Trees were shedding their winter gloom, pushing baby leaves out at the ends of branches, though their spring shadows still looked cold against the damp ground. As the path wound through a clearing, Elexa saw the gray of an animal ghost. She darted forward and snapped a mental net around it. The ghost had the thin panic of a mouse, tiny, thumping with a heartbeat it no longer had. Not much of a ghost, but Kindal wouldn't know the difference, and now he'd keep quiet about the sugar she'd stolen. Most people had no idea what kinds of ghosts they caught.

"Ghost?" Tira asked.

"Just a little one."

"I didn't even see it. You're so fast!"

Elexa strengthened the mesh of her mental net and imagined hooking it to her belt, felt a brush at her hip, a prickle on her skin. The mouse's panic settled into rest as it felt the embrace of the net. Its last living sight had been the shadow of the hawk that caught it; its ghost had squirted out as its body went down the hawk's gullet. If Elexa hadn't caught it, it would probably have let go of the Earth sometime soon and drifted wherever mouse souls went. You had to catch a ghost when it was fresh or you couldn't catch them at all.

"Come on." She headed toward the river again, and Tira trailed her.

Other children had come ahead of them and were scattered along the riverbanks already, searching for gems, one of the village's chief trade goods. The mountain was rich in gems and let them loose after storms, when Little River grew bold and carried topsoil down to the valley, uncovering hidden things.

The dragons kept strangers away from the gems.

Elexa started upstream. "Get out of here," screamed Sanric, her least favorite boy. "This bank and everything on it is mine!"

"Oh?" Elexa stooped and lifted a gem the size and color of an apricot from the mud. She scrubbed it against her tunic, brushing off mud, then held it up where the sun caught in its yellow-orange glow. "I think not."

"Hey!" Sanric yelled. He ran at her and tried to snatch the jewel from her hand. She closed her fist around it and thumped his chest, knocking him back.

"You don't own the runoff!" she cried, and dashed past him upstream. Tira had ducked into the trees; she rejoined Elexa after they had gotten past a section of bank bigger than Sanric could search in two days. Even though people couldn't lay claim to what the river gave them until they held it in their hands, they tried to respect each other's hunting grounds. Sanric scuffed Elexa's temper every time they met, though.

She tucked the gem into her loot pouch. Served him right, missing such a find right near where he was searching.

Elexa could walk across picked-over ground and find gems everyone else had missed. There was a scent to them, a flavor, something she could sense with the same senses she used to capture ghosts.

The others didn't talk with the ghosts they captured. Tira could catch ghosts, though she sometimes missed obvious ones. She mostly caught small game ghosts, rabbits and mice and sparrows; she rarely noticed dogs or horses, cows or sheep, cats or dogs or chickens, not until Elexa had netted them, and she never saw human ghosts, even the ones Elexa caught.

No one but Elexa caught human ghosts.

Tira and Elexa hiked up the river almost to the falls at the edge of First Terrace. Tira tugged Elexa's hand. "Look at Gold Beach," she shouted over the sound of the falls.

Something had happened in this last storm; the banks of the river had shifted. The beach on the near side of the river was eaten away, and a new shelf edged the river on the far side. Already Elexa sensed a litter of gems under the surface of the new beach.

How were they going to get across? The water was freezing this far up the mountain, and wild enough now to cover stones that usually stuck up out of it, forming steppingstones.

Elexa trudged up to where the waterfall thundered into a deep pool at the base of the terrace. She usually didn't hunt this far up the river, but she'd heard a rumor that a person could walk across behind the waterfall. Tira followed her over the stacks of debris the river had dropped along the edge, a few feet above the waterline now: rocks, twisted and broken trees, some of them the stunted, deformed pines from the upper reaches of the mountain that grew into strange shapes in the embrace of high winds. A tangle of bones littered the river's edges, white against the different browns of wood and earth. A legacy of dragon meals; some were the bones of goats, some of sheep, some of wild animals.

Elexa approached the pounding water shooting down from the cliff. The water was noise, vibration, wind, a battering of sound that had her covering her ears with her hands. Mist rose from where the waterfall tumbled into the pool, dampening Elexa's face, tunic, and trousers. The water flavored the air with the taste of cold metal. Elexa glanced back at Tira, saw Tira's mouth was open. Probably Tira was shouting something, but the thunder of the falls drowned it out. Elexa waved a hand, then edged to the side of the falls to see if there really was a way behind it.

Dim light shone through the water, revealing a cave behind the falls. Elexa slipped into it. It was cold and dark and shallow—she didn't sense much space going back into the darkness. Rippled light came through the water. She couldn't see clearly out through the wall of falling water, but she saw hazy details, the banks to either side, the pool just below her, the tangle of trees and sky above. She slipped across and emerged on the far side of the river.

Tira waved. Elexa gestured toward the falls and turned to explore the new beach. She took two steps before she dropped to her knees on the wet mud, poking her stick toward the strongest gem feeling she'd had in ages. In a moment she had unearthed a dark, rough stone the size of her palm. It was denser than most of the gems she found. She held it up to the sun and saw dark blue-violet light through it. Rare color. It felt strong and unflawed in her hand, but she wouldn't know until a rough polish or cutting. She had practiced fractioning cheap gems, clear quartz and flawed garnets. This one she wouldn't cut. Laisal was the best man in the village for gems. He had acquired jewel-working tools and knowledge from various peddlers over the years. She'd share the find with him.

She tucked it into her loot pouch and crawled to the next warm spot she sensed, plunged her stick into the ground. She dug furiously, taken over by gem fever. She hardly noticed Tira roaming across the beach, poking the ground with her own digging stick. Tira concentrated on the sand at water's edge. Where she saw promising stones, she cut a little channel from the water and led it over to wash out her finds.

When Elexa glanced up some time later, she saw that Tira's loot pouch bulged. Elexa looked over her shoulder, saw the series of holes she'd left in the mud. Her loot pouch was so full she had no place to put the small yellow gem she had just found. She checked the sun: directly overhead.

"Lunch?" she called to Tira, whose dark hair had come out of its tie and lay in muddy tangles around her head. Once Elexa ate, she could use her lunch pouch for more loot. It was the most fruitful morning she remembered.

"I thought you'd never stop," Tira said.

Elexa stood, her knees creaking. She and Tira went to the

grassy verge of the old riverbank above the new beach and sat on soft new plants.

Tira spread the leather skirt of her tunic over her muddy trousers and poured the morning's gems into her lap. Most were rough, rounded, their translucence almost hidden, but two had clean surfaces where they had hit against things in their tumble down the mountain and broken open. One was muddy green, the other a pinkish red much paler than most of the dark garnets they usually gathered.

Elexa touched a rough dark stone the size of a radish. "That one," she said.

Tira held it up to the sun, squinted through it. "This is my best? What color will it be? It looks brown."

"It will be beer colored, but very clear."

"Show yours."

Elexa spilled her gems into her lap. Two of the smaller ones skipped out into the grass.

"Lexa!" Tira reached out a hand toward Elexa's hoard, stopped before she touched a single one. "So many!"

"I'm lucky today."

"Lucky," Tira said, and snorted.

Elexa smiled down at her collection. Enough good gems here to keep her and Kindal and Father in scythes, knives, and sugar for more than a year, even after the village tax. She plucked the big blue-purple one up and handed it to Tira.

"Is it black?" Tira faced the sun and turned the stone this way and that. "Oh! I've never seen this color before!"

"I want Laisal to cut it."

"But he'll take half of whatever you sell it for."

"I don't care. I want to see it before I sell it."

Tira handed the stone back. They put their gems away and ate their lunches. Elexa had just offered Tira her last apple when they heard a strange faint sound, high and far above the sleepy murmurs of afternoon birdsong and the chuckle of the river.

It was a cry, a *kheer* like a hawk's, growing louder.

Elexa got to her feet, searched the sky between treetops. As the sound grew, its feel shifted. She heard terror. She heard words.

"No! No! Please!" screamed the voice. "No!"

Through the gap in the trees, Elexa saw the widespread wings of a strange dragon, not too far above the ground. Its underwing patterns were yellow, splayed like leaves against a background of green. Its outstretched neck and head were shadowed bronze, and its tail went from red to black. Its mid-legs clutched a struggling human to its belly. "Please!" cried the human. "Let me go!"

The dragon's shadow eclipsed the sun, casting it into silhouette just as one of its hind legs reached forward. Elexa heard a crack. The screaming stopped.

Sour bile rose in Elexa's throat, and her heart sped. She had never seen a person die by violence before, though her ghosts had told her stories. Her heart hurt.

Something dropped to the ground, and then the dragon was gone, up toward the higher terraces.

"Not one of ours," whispered Tira. Her face was still and blank. The wing patterns weren't familiar to Elexa, either. A wild dragon. A male? Out of season and hunting humans here?

Elexa knew dragons killed people. But surely that was other dragons, far away.

They should have a little time while the dragon dealt with its kill before it came hunting again, unless it was a nesting female, stocking up a cave for the time it would spend sitting on its eggs. Then it would kill as many animals as quickly as it could.

Tira ran across the beach to the fallen thing, stooped to pick it up, and ran back. She dropped to her knees beside Elexa. Her hand opened. A man's gold armband fell from it.

The sign etched across the metal plates wasn't familiar, but Elexa turned away and lost her lunch. She couldn't stop retching.

Tira's arm was around her when finally the heaving stopped. Elexa's stomach was sore, and her throat burned. She glanced toward the sky, afraid now, as she never had been before, of dragon shadows against the sun.

"We have to get home," Tira said. "We have to raise the alarm." She tucked the armband into her loot pouch and helped Elexa to her feet.

On their way up the mountain, Elexa had been the one with the swiftest feet, always tugging Tira onward. On the way home, Elexa kept stumbling. Tira's arm kept her steady; Tira's urging kept her going. When they passed Sanric, and he called out a taunt about them quitting early, Elexa barely heard him.

"Are you blind as well as stupid?" Tira yelled. "Didn't you see that wild one, with its human prey?"

Voices called up and down the river at that. All the

children collected their things and followed Tira and Elexa off the mountainside. "Hide in the cavern," Tira told them. "Elexa and I will warn the others."

Almost to the town was a narrow tunnel, hidden under a hollowed stump. It was human-sized, too small for any but the youngest dragon to get into. No one stayed there except during mating season, but they had all been drilled on how to get in while they were growing up. Every human in the village knew about it; each family took turns restocking the supplies they kept at the far end of the tunnel where it opened into a cavern with its own small spring.

Most of the children ran into this cavern. Tira and Elexa went on toward the village, keeping under the trees. They ran to the center ground, to the roofed frame that held the alarm bell. The dragon Nil was there, meeting her bondchild Kase. Both looked over when Tira grabbed the striker and struck the bell. "What is it?" Kase called.

"We saw a wild dragon kill a strange human," Tira yelled. People ran out of the tavern and some of the houses, keeping to paths under the eaves where they couldn't be seen from the air. Nil lifted her head, stared at the sky. Kase hung a string of small dead animals around her neck, and Nil raised her wings and plunged upward.

A human ghost passed Elexa, and she snared it without thinking, wove her mental net tight and small, compressed the ghost so she could hang it at her waist.

Tira rang out the pattern that warned of trouble from the sky. All children had practiced this, and the patterns for fire and flood and other concerns such as strangers or celebrations, on handbells when they were small. They had never expected to have to use this one.

Elexa ran on to the gatherhouse. She glanced inside. Empty; Headman Yan would be helping with the planting.

Father was tending the dragons' herd today—where had he taken the goats and sheep? They had been grazing along the east sides of the lowest hills, where sun struck the grass soonest, but someone had said at supper last night that those grasses needed time to recover, and Father was going to move the sheep. Which pastures?

It would be foolish for her to look for Father and Kindal. Father would hear the bell. He would bring the sheep in. Kindal was out hunting dragon food, but no one went beyond the range of the bell; they were all supposed to return and hide. He would hide or return . . . if he understood the meaning of the series of changes Tira was ringing. No one had rung this alarm except in practice in all the years Elexa could remember.

She went back to Tira. They should run to the shelter. Or they could stay and keep sounding; they could shelter in the mountain god's temple, which was closer than the tunnel. The temple had a room beneath it where adults worshipped in secret ways that were taught when the children turned into adults, at fifteen. Elexa and Tira weren't supposed to know how to open the door to that underground room, but they had found the hidden latch. They could hide there for a while.

When Tira's arm tired, Elexa took over, letting Tira explain to the people coming back from the fields and forest what was going on.

Headman Yan entered the center ground. "Who raised the alarm?" he yelled as he strode across to the bell.

"I did," Tira said.

"Why? If this is a prank, Tira Weaver—"

"No, Headman!" she said. "A stranger dragon, green and yellow, flew over us while we were gem hunting! It carried a human in its midclaws!"

"A screaming human," Elexa said. "While we watched, the dragon broke the human."

"What?"

"There was a crack," Elexa whispered, "and the human stopped screaming."

Yan studied their faces, then rushed back into the center ground, hurrying everyone toward the shelter. He checked through the common buildings to make sure everyone was out of them, loaded whoever was still in the village with supplies, and sent them off. He kept his voice low and firm. One boy argued and got cuffed for his trouble. "Get to the shelter," Yan said. The chastened boy ran off in the right direction.

After he'd gotten everyone moving, Yan came to the bell and took the striker from Elexa. He continued to tap the alarm rhythm on the bell. "Any hints of whether the wild dragon will be back?" he asked.

"Couldn't tell," said Tira. "This fell off the human when the dragon flew over us." She fished the gold armband out of her pouch and handed it to Yan.

He studied it with narrowed eyes, then muttered a curse. "It's Likushi," he said.

Elexa and Tira glanced at each other. Tira shook her head.

Elexa frowned. The ghost at her waist struggled.

Yan realized he had lost them. "The city two days' ride over the passes," he said. "We get some of our metal and much of our grain from—Never mind. This just means we're in for more trouble. Go to the shelter. I'll summon my dragon mother and ask her if she knows more."

Elexa and Tira ran toward the shelter, hiding under the trees, stepping in the muddy footprints of everyone who had gone before them. Behind them, Yan blew the horn he usually wore at his waist, a strange, rough cry. Dragon shadow raced across the road past them, and Tira and Elexa clutched each other and crowded against the trunk of a big tree. Two more shadows followed the first, a rush of wings above. Elexa pressed her mouth into Tira's shoulder, forcing the screams back down her throat. After a horrible, petrified time, Tira shook her shoulder. "They're gone," she whispered, when Elexa looked up. "Come on."

Basil Shoemaker waited at the tunnel entrance, a hand on the hollow stump that could hide the hole in a moment.

"Have you seen my father?" Elexa asked him. "My brother?"

"No, but I haven't been watching the door for long. Fonsee Weaver is taking stock of who's here and who's missing," Basil said.

Tira's mother. So at least she was safe, and busy. Tira's fingers worked the sign for a blessing. "Is Miri here?" she asked.

"Go in and see for yourself. Are any following you?"

"Yan is talking to his dragon," said Elexa.

"That fool," Basil muttered. "He hasn't designated a

successor. He has no right to take such chances. Go in, now, girls."

Elexa and Tira fled past him into the dark passage.

Elexa trailed her hand along the smooth strip of wall to her right, where hundreds of hands before hers had trailed, a way to keep steady in the dark. Presently she saw flickering light ahead, people and their shadows cast into silhouette against a gatherhouse-sized fire.

The din in the bigger cavern was deafening. Some had brought their dogs, sheep, goats, and chickens, and the animals didn't feel like being quiet. Elexa searched for her father but didn't see him, or Kindal. She moved her fingers in a protect sign.

Tira rushed to her mother, was folded into a hug. "Miri and your father are here," Tira's mother told her; Tira waved to the rest of her family by the fire.

Elexa followed slowly, searching faces as she went. She tugged Fonsee Weaver's sleeve. "Have you seen my father?" she asked.

"No, Lex. I'm sorry," said Fonsee. "He's not here."

"My brother?"

"No, Lex. Sorry." Fonsee kissed her forehead. "You're last in. Do you have any news?"

"They sounded the alarm," yelled a deep male voice. "I hope you had a reason, you rascal girls."

Tira told the story of what they had seen again. Garbled versions had already traveled through the group. Everyone except the animals quieted and listened. Questions and speculations were flying by the time Yan joined them.

"I've spoken to Plesta," he said in his strident voice; everyone shut up to listen. "She says a wild dragon family has taken up residence on Fourth Terrace, a male and two females, one heavy with eggs. Our dragons have warned them not to hunt in our valley. Jex and Moss and Vevey are watching them and have promised to fight them if they violate our covenant, but the male is very big, with fighting spines. The one you saw was the egg-free female, Tira. She was gone for two days, Plesta says, and they didn't know she'd gone hunting humans. Most of our mothers are in no shape to fight. Plesta will come down at sunset with a better picture of what's going on up the mountain. Till then, I want everyone to stay inside."

The cave was damp because of the spring. Elexa had helped make the last pile of thin, dried-bedstraw-stuffed mattresses, one for every child and adult in the village, which they renewed every winter. She grabbed a mattress and took it to a dark corner, away from heat and light. Tira took a mattress and followed. They might as well sleep if they were going to be cooped up here, or at least lie beside each other and talk.

Sanric and Jezo, his best friend, followed them. "How was your hunting?" Sanric asked. He snatched at Elexa's loot pouch. She batted his hand away, but he had hold of one of the leather ties and didn't let go. Her pouch untied and opened, spilling gems across the floor in soft thuds and bounces. Sanric knelt and snatched at stones.

Fury swamped Elexa. She dropped her mattress and slapped his face, a sharp crack in the darkness. All her jewels glowed to her special sense, but she couldn't see them with her eyes. "You unbonded blister," she whispered.

He punched her hard in the chest. It drove the breath out of her, left her collapsed and wheezing.

"What are you doing, San?" Jezo whispered. "Stop it!"

Sanric kicked Elexa's leg before Jezo grabbed his arm and dragged him away.

"What happened?" Tira asked.

Elexa wheezed, sucking and searching for breath. "He hit me in the chest," she said in a flattened voice, her words interrupted by whistling inhalations. "He kicked me. He spilled my gems!"

"I'll get some water. Want me to tell Yan?"

"No. Not yet."

Tira ran away. Elexa stood her mattress on edge, curved it around her, a small fortress. Gradually her breathing slowed and eased. She felt her pouch to see if it was torn. Only the string that held it closed was broken; the shape of it was intact. She pursued all the dropped gems, their scents and ghost colors clear to her in the darkness, returned them to her pouch, knotted the string, and tied the pouch shut again. Several were missing, including her best find of the day, the blue-violet gem. Sanric must have taken it. She would plead for a hearing later, try to get it back. Yan might believe her, or he might not.

She cradled the loot pouch in her hand. Still enough gems to buy them a scythe and sugar.

She noticed the unhappy ghost at her waist. In all the confusion, she hadn't had time to find out who he was. She loosened her mental net to let him take the shape he was most comfortable with. Most of the human ghosts she had caught took the shape of who they had last been in life. One of the bonded women from the village, the midwife, had taken a shape like her dragon, though smaller, as though the bond had infected her with dragon spirit. She had joined her dragon joyfully.

In the dim light of the cavern, Elexa saw the ghost more clearly than she would have by daylight. He did not have the colors of a live person; he glowed and flickered with a pale all-over light of his own. He was taller than anyone she had known alive, and he wore strange clothes, a drape of pale cloth that covered most of him, belted at the waist with gold. He had large hoop earrings. His hair was light and thick and long enough to touch his shoulders. He wore gold bands on both arms. One of his armbands looked just like the one Tira had retrieved after the dragon flew over.

"Who are you?" Elexa asked.

"It's me, Tira," said Tira from behind her. "No one would give me a lantern, but I brought you some water." She sat beside Elexa and handed her a stoppered gourd.

"Smudu Kush," said the ghost. "Who are you? What's happened to me?" His words had an accent she remembered hearing from the grain peddlers.

"You're dead," Elexa said. She drank, comforted by the slosh of water in the gourd, the shifting weight, the wash of wet across her tongue and down her sore throat.

"What?" asked Tira.

"I remember," said the ghost. "I remember. Great Sytha." He hugged himself, dropped into a huddled ball beside her. "First the long fear and flying, and then the jerk that broke me. Sytha protect me!"

"I'm not dead," Tira said. "What's the matter? Are you having a nightmare?"

"I'm talking to a ghost."

"What?" Tira's voice was alarmed.

"The dragon snatched you," Elexa said to Smudu. "What were you doing when she snatched you?"

Tira pressed the back of her hand to Elexa's forehead. "Are you sick?"

Elexa brushed her off. "Stop it."

"I was on the way to the council house. We were to discuss allocating more archers to guard duty, and one of our armorers made a new shield with sharpened spikes around its edge we thought people could carry with them to fend off dragon attacks—you could hold it over your head and cut their talons if they grabbed you. We were going to discuss producing more of those.

"There were reports of dragon attacks on some of the outlying farms, and we were wondering whether to summon the farmers into the city until we could find a dragon fighter to deal with the problem. . . . I was snatched crossing the market square." He straightened out of his huddle, glanced over his shoulder. "It was horrifying. The dark shape descending, the screams of everyone as we ran. The claws cut me. The ground rushed away from me, and the dragon held me up against its burning belly. I could smell my own flesh cooking. The pain was so bad I think I fainted. The cold air woke me. I—where am I?"

"We are underground," Elexa said, "hiding from the dragon who killed you."

"Underground where?" asked Smudu.

"Elexa," Tira wailed.

"Mountainknee Village," Elexa said.

"The village called Dragonholm?"

"I don't know. We don't call it that, but we are home to dragons. Our dragons don't snatch and kill people, though."

"You say I'm dead," said Smudu slowly. "Are you a dead-speaker, then?"

"I don't know."

"Is it dark where we are? You are only a voice to me."

"We're in a cave, and it's quite dark in this corner." She glanced over her shoulder toward the gather fire. People were standing there, dark silhouettes against the flames, their heads bent toward each other. A murmur of conversation carried, though not the words.

Tira tugged on her sleeve. "Elexa. Elexa, what are you doing?"

"Open your ghost eyes, Tira. I caught the ghost of the dragon's dead, and he's telling me who he was before he died."

"You caught a human ghost, Elexa? You can't do that."

"Why not?"

"It's wrong. Besides, people don't have the same kind of ghosts that animals do. We go somewhere else when we die. You're upset. You have a fever. Did Sanric kick your head and scramble your brains?" Tira tried to touch Elexa's forehead again.

Elexa slapped her hand away. "Tira, stop it! I am not sick. When did I ever lie to you?"

"You lied when you told me you and Maro weren't meeting secretly behind the temple."

"That was two years ago, and you and I weren't really friends then."

"We were until you started lying to me."

Elexa scrubbed her hands over her face. Her chest ached, her throat was still sore from vomiting, her thigh throbbed where Sanric had kicked her, and her blood had been racing since she heard Smudu's death scream. She was tired now. She didn't want to think about the time when she and Tira had been enemies. For almost a year after she had met with Maro, who had abandoned her as soon as their secret meetings were known, she had had no friends; she had sought human ghosts to talk to. "Please, Tira. Please," she whispered. Where was Father? Where was Kindal? Had they heard the alarm? Was the wild dragon even now circling from the sky, ready to drop down and kill her father and her brother?

Tira rubbed her shoulder. "I'm sorry. I'm just worried."

"Your friend is not a deadspeaker," Smudu said.

"Can you hear her?"

"Dimly. It is strange. Your words are clear to me, but hers come to me on a river of sound that beats as blood used to in my ears."

"What is he saying?" Tira asked. She settled on the mattress beside Elexa and looked in the same direction Elexa did, apparently determined to pretend she believed her friend.

"His name is Smudu Kush, from Likush—is that right, Smudu-sir?"

"Likush, yes."

"He was a councillor there, and he was snatched from their center ground."

"Elexa?" Yan's voice cut through her murmured recital. She glanced around and saw his shaggy-haired shadow standing between her and the fire.

"Headman?" Elexa hugged herself.

"Are you in truth talking to the dragon's dead?"

"I am," she whispered.

"How long have you had this deadspeaking skill?"

"Since I was six," she said, then wondered if she should have told him. She did not trust Yan, even though old Peder had.

"You're the one Plesta spoke of?"

She shrugged and huddled in on herself. "I don't know what your dragon told you."

"She said one of the village children brought village ghosts up to the terrace to join their dragons in relife. It's an old tradition, she said, but never one as well tended as it has been since you started this practice. For the gifts you've given us, I thank you."

There was a tone in his voice that worried her, a sharp edge of irritation that didn't match the words he spoke. She hadn't told anyone in the village of her encounters with human ghosts. Yan was the last person she had wanted to tell. Too late to keep it to herself now.

"Ask the man what he knows about the dragon who took him."

"Smudu-sir, did you hear what the headman said?"

"What do I know about the dragon? I know nothing except

that it came down from the sky and took me, and though I screamed and struggled, I could not stop it. We knew there was a village here in the mountains where people and dragons live together, but all we know of dragons from our own encounters is that in bad years they come and steal our stock and sometimes our children. We fear them.

"Once when I was riding in the mountains I saw three of them crouched over a kill, snapping at each other, hissing, sending out rivers of flame that charred the meat and sent smoke rising—horrifying creatures, large and hard to fight. We are fortunate they are scarce.

"We have not had enough attacks in Likush to focus all our effects on fighting them, but lately they grow bolder. Our armorers have worked on steel-tipped arrows, but our archers can only kill dragons when they hit the throat just at the base of the neck; all other parts of the dragons' hides are too hard to pierce. Not all of our archers are skilled enough or strong enough to strike a killing blow. The lord's war wizard has been working on smokes to stun them, but we don't have enough specimens to experiment on. We would like to get hold of a young one we could control so we can test our weapons on it, but no one knows how. Some have suggested we send—" Smudu suddenly turned away, put his ghost hand over his ghost mouth.

Yan shook Elexa's shoulder. "What is he saying?"

"The Likushi don't know much about dragons. They have only found one way to kill dragons, an arrow through the throat." Elexa swallowed, put a hand to her throat, imagining the point of an arrow punching through and letting all her blood out. "He doesn't know the dragon who took him."

Yan cursed, gripped her shoulder hard and shook her, then walked toward the fire.

"It's true, then?" Tira whispered beside her. "You can talk to ghosts?"

Elexa rubbed her shoulder. She would have bruises in the shape of Yan's fingers. She sighed. "I told you."

"Not so I'd believe you," Tira said.

"I didn't want anyone to know." She took Tira's hand, meshed her fingers with her friend's. "If you knew we could talk to ghosts, what would you think about feeding them to dragons? Isn't it like giving them people to eat?"

"Can you talk to the ghosts of animals, too?"

"No. I hear them, can sense their feelings a little. They make some of the same sounds they made in life, but I don't converse with them."

"Animals are different. We eat them, and dragons eat them, too."

"The dragons eat human ghosts when I catch them."

"Elexa!" Tira jerked her hand away.

"But it's not like eating meat," Elexa said. She heard what she had said, thought about it, gave herself this comfort. "It isn't as though they swallow the ghosts and digest them. The ghosts live in the dragons. They become part of the dragon mind. Have you spoken with old Peder's dragon since he died? He's there inside her. He went willingly. He was my first ghost."

"Old Peder?" Tira said, her voice almost silent. "You've been doing this since you were six, and you never told me. You sent human ghosts to our dragons to eat?"

"Only those who asked for it, or the ghosts of strangers."

"The ghosts of strangers? That's horrible!" Tira said. She jumped up and left Elexa alone in the darkness with the ghost.

"Your friend has gone?" asked the ghost.

"She'll be back," Elexa said. She wasn't sure, though; if Tira was truly horrified, she might stay away. Tira had more strength of will than other people.

Elexa lay on her mattress, curled into a bean shape, knees up and arms hugging her front. She felt cold and alone. There were blankets somewhere in the cave, thin ones, the ones the weavers had made mistakes in or machine-loomed ones made from cheap flax in the southern countries, but she didn't have the energy to find a blanket.

The ghost crouched beside her.

"I release you," she whispered to him. She opened the strands of her ghost net and let him go. "I'm sorry you died in such a horrible way."

"I wish I had seen my wife and daughter safe." He stared at distance. "There's not much money left in our hidden hole, and I'd only bought half the grain we need for summer. I was wearing most of our wealth"—he touched his armbands—"and carrying the rest of the grain price for after the meeting." He felt the wallet at his belt. It still looked full, but it was as misty as the rest of him. "The real money, where will it be? It was most of our savings."

"Probably in the dragons' cave. They don't eat gold, but they hide it where it's hard to get. Never mind, now." Most of the ghosts Elexa had spoken with had left a few things undone. None of them had figured out how to work in the world to finish the tasks. "There's nothing you can do about it. You should look for your god now."

"I don't want my gods," he said. "I want to get inside a dragon and kill the one who killed me. I don't want her going back to Likushi and hunting my people."

"Dragons don't often fight each other, especially female dragons. Most of the ones who live here are big with eggs or busy with young right now and wouldn't fight even if they normally did. I don't know if there's any on the mountain who can do what you want."

"There are no males?"

"We don't feed the males. We don't bond with them. They travel. Most are gone now."

"Feed me to one of the big males who can fight," he said.

"Smudu-sir," she said, then covered her eyes with her hands. She had released him. She didn't want to see him anymore.

He tugged at the ghost net at her waist—she felt a strange stretching in her nerves, and opened her eyes—and unraveled part of the weave until he had a loose string. He tied it around his wrist, sat down on the mattress beside her. "Rest, if you must. I will wait."

She didn't like it that he could use her ghost net to trap himself. She supposed if she worked at it, she could dissolve this net, leave him adrift. But if he wanted to stay—she was too tired to deal with him now.

She let sleep claim her and drown her worries about Father, Kindal, and Tira.

Someone shook her shoulder. "Lexa?" Tira's voice said.

"Tira." She clutched Tira's wrist, didn't let go. She sat up. "Has Kindal—Father—?"

"They haven't come yet, but Yan talked to Plesta again, and she said we can go outside now. The stranger dragons have taken dragon oath not to harm anybody in the valley so long as we give them goats. Anyway, it's night now." Tira wrenched her wrist free of Elexa's grip.

Elexa sighed and sat up. She would have to work to make Tira like her again, and she was already tired. She straightened her tunic and her belt. The pouch of jewels had been half under her while she slept, and had left a dent in her side. Her shoulder throbbed from where Yan had shaken her, and her chest ached from Sanric's punch.

Smudu was still beside her; if he had been solid, he would have been touching her. She wasn't sure how she felt about that. Ghosts could be intimate with you in strange ways and you wouldn't even notice.

She got to her feet. Tira handed her another gourd of water, and Elexa drank. "Thank you," she said. Maybe it wasn't such a long way back to their friendship.

The fire had died down; there was no longer much light in the cavern, and the din of people, sheep, and goats had faded too. Only a few people were left.

"Thanks for waking me," Elexa said. She picked up her mattress and dropped it off in the alcove where they stored the cave supplies. Smudu followed a few feet from her; since he had chosen the line he'd bound himself with, he had room to range. Tira shrugged and walked away, plainly not wanting Elexa's company.

Worry about that later. Outside, the night air smelled fresh and full of plants instead of smoke and people. It was much warmer than the cave had been. Stars shimmered in the rising leftover heat of day.

Elexa ran home to find out whether her father or brother had come there while she was underground.

One of the lamps was lit in the house; it shone through the thin, tanned skin over the window, a flickering yellow warmth. Elexa opened the door. "Kindal? Father?"

Her father rose from his chair. "Lexa!" He rushed to hug her. "I heard the alarms. I hid in the eastern cave with the flocks until nightfall. Is Kindal all right?"

"I don't know," she wailed. "He didn't come to the cavern."

Her father's bushy eyebrows lowered, shadowing his eyes. He looked toward the door. Elexa unhooked her loot pouch and laid it on the table, grabbed another water gourd and her cloak.

"Did you see which direction he went this morning?" Father asked.

"South," said Elexa.

Father put a fat candle in the cut tin lantern they used for outdoors and took his herder's crook. They went out.

In the center ground, Fonsee Weaver sat beside the bell, talking to other people with questions about missing relatives. When she saw Elexa's father, she said, "Oh, Horst! Thank goodness! We thought you were lost," and she made a note.

"We're going to look for Kindal," Elexa told her.

"Wait." Fonsee lowered the list into her lantern's light and read over it. "Mishta says he saw Kindal hunting near Starfall Lake this morning."

"Starfall Lake!" said Elexa's father.

"His dragon mother and children must be very hungry," Elexa said. Starfall Lake was far to the south, nearly to the pass. People could usually find game there because it was so far they didn't hunt there often. It would be hard to find in the dark. One had to leave the road at just the right place and climb up through trees over a field of jagged boulders.

Father fingered the whistle he wore around his neck. With it, he could summon his dragon mother, but she would be bedded down for the night now, and even if he rode her, there wasn't much he would be able to see from her back in the dark.

"Let's walk the south road," Elexa said. "Maybe we'll meet him coming home."

Father nodded. They left the center ground and followed the road, the tin lantern casting flowing cutouts of candlelight and shadow on the pale dust. Night was cool and damp and full of the scents of plants waking from winter and the sounds of courting frogs and insects. Little Moon had risen, casting faint blue light over the land.

Elexa listened to the night, glanced around with the edges of her eyes, alert for ghosts. Smudu walked silently beside her, glowing in the night with the light of vanished day. She saw an owl swoop down on a mouse, but she let the mouse's ghost fly. She already had one mouse ghost on her belt and no longer knew if she would ever be able to give it to Kindal.

They had missed the turnoff for the lake and almost reached the pass when Elexa sensed something strange a little way off the road. "Wait," she said. She left the circle of light scraps her father was casting and went into the woods, searching by the pale light Smudu's ghost cast as he walked with her. He was like a small, local moon.

"Oh," Smudu said, surprised, as they got closer to the thing that was like a giant gem and tickled her ghost senses at the same time. "What is it?" He grabbed the thread that tied him to Elexa and clung as his feet pulled out from under him; he hung sideways on the line like a hooked fish in a river current. "It's pulling me!"

"Wait here." Elexa walked between the trees toward a small, moonlit clearing.

"I can't," said Smudu. "Either I cling to you or it pulls me to it. Catch me, Elexa."

She felt the tugging on him. She sent out a mental net and wrapped it around him. He steadied, then stood upright again. When she had webbed him to her, he relaxed. "It has lost its pull."

They approached the thing together. Two people stood above it, their backs to Elexa and Smudu. They were not conversing—at least, not aloud. One, a woman, was naked except for her long, heavy hair. Another stood beyond her.

They glowed with ghost light, and she could see moon-touched trees through them.

They turned. One was her brother, wearing the clothes he had left the house in that morning. "Lexa!" he cried.

"Kindal!" She ran to him, Smudu at her heels. Her brother's

features blurred as she ran. Ghost light, she would not let herself realize. "What are you doing here?"

"I can't seem to get loose," he said. "Neither of us can."

She stopped an arm's length from him and let herself see that she was speaking to a ghost. She felt cold clear through. "What happened?" she whispered, her voice choked.

"I killed a deer," he said. "I was thinking I would whistle up Maia to carry it back to the cave so I wouldn't have to take it to the village. I looked up, and there was a dragon in the sky already. I thought maybe she'd followed me. But it came closer, and I saw it wasn't one I knew. It dropped on me, Lexa, and it snapped my neck. I was so surprised I didn't understand at first. How could it do that to me?"

He looked away and went on, "It took my body and the deer and flew off. I watched—I saw paths open—I could have clung to my dead self, or I could have gone another way that meant leaving everything behind, or there was a light that led me here, a promising light. It said it would give me satisfaction before I left this world for the next."

"When did it happen?" She hugged herself because she couldn't hug him. Smudu lurked at her shoulder. She put her hands to her cheeks, felt tears she hadn't noticed shedding.

"Late afternoon. I spent all day tracking that deer."

"What were the dragon's wing colors?"

"Red and black."

"Not the same one who killed Smudu-sir. Oh, Kindal." A sob surprised her, and then a cascade of them. Sobs shook her; she dropped to the ground.

Kindal's ghost squatted beside her. His glowing hand

reached out to stroke her. All she felt was a faint chill.

She didn't have time to fall apart. She dragged herself from the precipice of grief, wrapped her feelings up, and stored them inside an egg of mental nets. She could unfold them later. She rubbed her nose on the sleeve of her tunic and scrubbed her eyes with her fists. She looked at her brother, saw his sad smile. He glanced over his shoulder at the woman behind him, then looked into her face again, his eyes serious.

"The light that led me here," he said. "It made promises. It made promises to Pewet-lady, too, and she's been here for months. Is it a liar? We can't get loose of it."

Elexa put her hands on the earth. Waves pulsed up through them, tingling, tugging. She felt something pulling from her palms and jumped up, to see thin strands of ghost light stretch between her and the earth. "No!" She sent out a net to enclose the escaped parts and pulled herself together.

"It pulls you, too, and you're not even dead," Kindal said, angry. "What *is* it?"

Elexa used her ghost senses and her gem senses and saw there was something old, something precious, something that had been worked with lines and words, buried under the soil. It reminded her of the relic in the temple of the mountain god, the one that she addressed when she prayed: something made of wood, but alive in a way that said it was listening and doing in the world.

The buried thing almost spoke to her.

"It trapped us," Kindal said. "Pewet-lady isn't even from around here." He gestured to the naked woman. "She's been here since last fall, she says. She remembers leaves blazing in the hillsides. It was the first time she saw such a season—she's from Oceanside, far to the south. Can you see us both?"

"Of course."

"Even though we're dead?"

"I use my ghost senses. I see you."

"I could see animal ghosts, but I never saw a human one until I died. Who's that with you?"

"This is Smudu Kush, also taken and killed by a strange dragon."

"What's he wrapped up in?"

"Those are my nets, Brother. I've been capturing human ghosts as long as I've captured animal ghosts." She wondered if he would turn away from her now, the way Tira had.

No one spoke, until Kindal said, "What will you do with him?"

"I already let him go, but he refused to leave. That thing you're standing on tried to pull him in, too. My nets save him from it."

"Your nets—" Kindal began.

"They're standing on a ghost magnet," said Smudu. "Wizards in Likush use those to capture ghosts when they need them for sorcery. We used to use them only for the ghosts of criminals. This one is different. It feels ancient. It pulls on us all. I am not a criminal."

"How do my nets protect you from it?"

"I never knew of these nets before I met you, but I imagine there is some way a wizard detaches a ghost from the magnet to use it in a spell."

"Lex? Can you capture us, too?" Kindal asked.

"Lexa!"

Elexa glanced behind her. Father wandered toward her through the wood, carrying shadowed light.

"Father," she called.

He picked his way between trees and came to her. "What are you doing alone out here in the dark?"

"I'm not alone." Her voice wobbled. "I found Kindal, Father. He's dead."

"What?"

"A dragon killed him, too."

"Killed him, too? What do you mean, Daughter?"

"When you brought the herds back, didn't you speak to anyone in the village? We sounded the alarm because a wild dragon brought a Likushi man here and killed him."

"I didn't speak to—I rushed home to try to find you." His voice was heavy. "You say Kindal—"

"Capture me, Lexa," said Kindal.

She flung a mental net around her brother, wove it heavy, and pulled him toward her. He popped loose of the thing in the ground and snapped to her, rolled into a tight ball. "Ow!" he squeaked.

"Oh! Sorry!" She loosened her threads and let him take his own form inside her net.

"Oof!" He stretched. The net moved with him. He shuddered and said, "Thanks."

"Please, Mistress, can you take me, too?" asked the naked woman.

Elexa had never held more than one human ghost at a time until now. How heavy did the nets need to be to detach someone from a ghost magnet? One thread wasn't enough—it hadn't protected Smudu from the magnet—but the Kindal net had worked easily. She sent a normal net to the woman. As soon as the net closed around her, the woman came loose of the ground. The magnet didn't fight to hold her.

"Lexa! What are you doing?" her father demanded.

She felt crowded in the midst of her three captured ghosts. Her mind was fuzzy; part of her was in the nets, and the ghosts, though they didn't struggle, were moving inside the nets in a way that confused her.

Her father reached right through nets and ghosts and shook her shoulder. His grip hurt the bruises Yan had left. "Elexa! Answer me!"

"They were stuck and I pulled them free," she muttered.

"Father," said Kindal, going to him. "Can you see me?"

Father waved a hand in front of his face, as one might chase away a fly.

"Tira's that way, too," Elexa told them. "There are some ghosts she just can't see. She only gets little ones."

"What are you talking about?" Father shook her again.

"Please stop that, Father." A short nap in the cave hadn't been enough. She wanted to lie on the ground and sleep. "I'm too tired to fight you."

Father groaned and pulled her into a hug, held her tight before he set her on her feet again. He supported her shoulders and peered into her face.

"Lexa-child," said Smudu. "Can you walk us away from here? The magnet's strength diminishes over distance."

"How do you know?" Kindal asked. "If it gets less, why

did it pull Pewet-lady from so far away?"

Smudu said, "Perhaps she was wandering and came too close to it. Those who leave a thing undone don't go on right away; so say Likushi deadspeakers."

Kindal looked toward the other ghost.

The woman nodded. "My child ran away north, and I didn't want to leave until I could be sure she's all right. I died, but I didn't abandon my search for her; I still don't know where she is."

"The magnet didn't pull me while we were in the village, and I wasn't netted then," Smudu said. "Let the child walk us there so she can let us go. Can't you see we're stretching her too thin?"

Kindal leaned past his father's shoulder and looked at Elexa's face. She could hardly keep her eyes open. "You're right. Lex, go back to the road right now."

She groaned. She put her hand on her father's chest and pushed. "I have to go to the road," she muttered, and glanced around. Ghost light from her captives showed her a path she hadn't noticed before, narrow and overgrown, but there. She slipped out of her father's grip and took the path. The ghosts drifted beside her. They were in her nets; they didn't have to walk. She was doing all the work. She resented that, though they had no weight.

After stumbling through the forest for a while, she reached the pale road and sat on a log beside it to catch her breath.

"Lexa-child, make my net thinner," Smudu said. "Please don't let me go. But perhaps it doesn't take so much of you to do this job."

She drank from the water gourd at her waist, then thinned her mental net around Smudu.

"Stop," he said, when she had lightened it to almost gossamer. "The magnet pulls at me now. I need a little more net, please."

She added another thin layer, and he nodded. "I am safe."

She thinned the nets around the other two and felt better, more herself and safe. She had never needed this level of control before; when she was capturing a few animal ghosts at a time, she just wrapped them tight and forgot about them. People were more complicated.

Her father approached. "Elexa."

She straightened. "Father, please don't hurt me."

"Hurt you?"

"Don't shake me anymore."

He breathed loudly through his nose, then sighed and sat beside her on the log. He placed the lantern on the ground. "Tell me."

She rubbed her forehead, then said, "I have been able to speak to the dead half my life. Today I saw a dragon kill a man. Tira and I sounded the alarm. I caught the man's ghost, Father. Have you ever caught a human ghost?"

He looked toward the village. "I think I did. When I first bonded with my dragon. It felt different from other ghosts, bigger and upset in a different way. It struggled and tried to speak to me, but I netted it small until it couldn't move, and fed it to my dragon mother. I had nightmares after that. I didn't catch any more ghosts for almost a year. Then I only caught small ones. I lost most of my skill."

She took his hand. "Find it again."

He gripped her hand and sat with his eyes closed, taking long, deep breaths and letting them out. Presently he opened his eyes and gasped. "Who are these people?"

"Father." Kindal drifted forward.

"Kindal!" Father jumped to his feet, held out his arms, lowered them slowly when Kindal didn't step into his embrace. "Kindal," he repeated, his voice hopeless. He covered his face with his hands.

"He's the second of the dragons' dead today," Elexa whispered.

"Let him go. You can't hold your brother. It isn't right."

"Up on the hill there's a ghost magnet, and it trapped him," Elexa said. "It trapped the lady as well. I had to capture them to get them free of it. This is Smudu-sir, the dragons' first dead, from Likush. Smudu-sir, my father, Horst Herder."

Smudu bowed. "Thank you for your patience with our interference in your daughter's life," he said.

Father gave a crazy laugh. "Is there a choice? I would choose the other way if I could."

"As a father myself, I understand," said Smudu. "As a person wronged, though, I have one more favor to ask of your daughter. I want her to feed me to a dragon who will avenge my death."

Father and Kindal gasped. Elexa rose. "I think I have to do that before I can sleep," she said. "Kindal, do you know what you want from your death?"

"What I want?"

"Do you know which tasks you've left unfinished?"

"I died before I could fulfill my dragon bond," he said. "Who will take care of Maia and the twins now? They are still infants, with four more years of childhood."

"The village will provide," said Father.

Elexa remembered other times when someone bonded to a dragon mother had died before the dragon children reached adolescence. Everyone gave some of their catch to the abandoned dragon family. The dragon children grew up strange, though, and often went wild.

"Let's go and talk with your dragon," Elexa said. "Do you want to join her, the way other village dead have joined their dragons?"

"What?" Kindal and Father spoke at the same time.

Elexa explained her secret life as a ghost courier to them.

Kindal said, "I can be part of her? Please, Lex. Take me there to talk with her."

"All right." She had to blink to stay awake; the day had been long. She set off on the road back to the village, her father following her, the ghosts gliding along beside them.

The third time she stumbled, her father set down the lantern and stooped. "Climb on my back," he said. "You've had a longer day than I have; I spent most of it napping in a cave with the herd."

She did it, relieved and a little ashamed. His tunic was soft and worn and he smelled of smoke, sweat, and goats. He was warm beneath her, his gait smooth. She laid her head on his shoulder and fell into a light sleep. The ghost nets tugged at the edges of her awareness even as she slept.

When they reached the village, Father stopped at their house and added two water gourds to his belt. He replaced the guttering candle in the lamp with a fresh one. He gave Elexa some jerked meat to chew on and tucked some oatcakes into his wallet. Outside again, he stooped and took her on his back.

"Where are you going? What are you doing?" Yan's acid voice asked them from the darkness as they left the house.

"We're going up the mountain, Headman," said Father. Then he said, in a voice that cracked, "My daughter takes my son's ghost to his dragon mother."

"Horst," Yan said, his voice softer. "I share your sorrow. He was a fine boy. How did he die?"

"The wild dragons killed him," Elexa said.

Yan let out a low, grating cry, the growl of stone grinding on stone. "They've broken their vows. They will be gone, one way or another, tomorrow. I'll come with you. I have to talk with old Peder's dragon mother."

Father turned onto the path that led up the mountain, and Yan followed. Halfway through the climb to First Terrace, Yan grunted and pulled Father to a stop. "Let me take the child. You've carried her long enough." Her father set her down, and Elexa went to Yan, then hesitated. She didn't want this closeness with him, but her legs were wobbly even from the few steps it took her to walk from her father to Yan. She would never make it up the mountain on her own, not without sleep and more food.

Yan rose easily once she had clasped her arms around his neck and her legs around his waist. She felt the power of his muscles.

Elexa was surprised that Yan smelled so much like Father—smoke, leather, and male—though his hair was much bushier. As they neared the lip of First Terrace, Yan turned toward her. His breath smelled of onions. "Do you still have the other ghost, the Likushi man?"

"Yes," she said.

"And you hold your brother, too? You understand their speech?"

"Yes," she said.

"What a selfish child you are," he muttered, "not sharing this skill with the rest of us. Well, that's going to stop. From now on, you will tell me whenever you encounter a ghost, and ask it the questions I instruct you in."

"There's a prize man," said Pewet-lady, drifting along at Elexa's right shoulder. "What is he lord of?"

"He's the village headman," Elexa said.

"Something less than a god," said the woman. "Therefore, you can ignore him most of the time."

Father laughed.

"What are you laughing at, Horst?" Yan growled. "You've just lost your son, and I amuse you?"

Father's face lost its smile. His head hung.

"Do like Pewet-lady said, Father," Kindal said. "Ignore him. I'm not lost, just different."

Father smiled toward Kindal, who was gliding along by Yan's left shoulder.

Yan stopped, stared at Father. "Why do you grimace? Has your grief made you mad?"

Elexa unlocked her ankles and kicked Yan's thighs as she

would a horse. "Don't stop now, Headman. We have a lot to do before we can sleep."

"What!" he roared, and wrenched her arms from around his neck, dropped her behind him. "I am not your beast!"

A crunching of small rocks, the shift and slide of something heavy over ground, a sudden rush of heat, a smell of sulfur and hot metal. Something roared above them, a jet of flame out over their heads, dazzling against the dark sky, temporarily blinding them. Heat poured down from the flame. The gush of light ceased, leaving a drift of feathery smoke rising toward the stars.

"Who comes in the night?" a dragon asked, her speech full of gravel and almost void of voice.

"Forgive us for disturbing you, Guardian Birta," said Yan. "The child brings ghosts."

"Elexa," said the dragon.

"Grandmother!" It was old Peder's dragon. Elexa struggled to her feet.

"You bring ghosts, child? Who else has died, aside from the stranger?"

"Kindal," she said, and burst into tears.

"Oh, child," said the dragon, almost in old Peder's voice. "Oh, child. I am so sorry."

"The wild ones killed him, Old Mother," Yan said.

She raised her snaky head and blasted fire into the air again. A gravelly growl rumbled through her stomach. "They gave their promise not to do such a thing. We cannot let them live here with a broken promise between us."

Elexa pulled herself together. "Grandmother, I need to

take Kindal to his own dragon. I have also the ghost of the stranger who died, and another stranger who doesn't yet know what she wants."

"Another ghost?" Yan yelled. He cuffed Elexa's shoulder and knocked her down. "Another ghost? Why didn't you tell me?"

"Headman!" Father stood over her, facing Yan, his fists raised.

"Yan!" said the dragon. "Don't you dare strike that child again!"

"She is keeping valuable secrets, Guardian Birta, secrets the village needs to know! Who is this other ghost? How can she capture ghosts at will? She threatens our afterlives! She must learn to obey!"

"You are not the one to teach her," said the dragon.

"Who, then? I must keep my villagers safe from threats, no matter where they come from."

The dragon's tail shifted across the scree, restless, then stilled. "You have a concern, headman, and I recognize it. We will think on it. Don't strike the child again."

Yan bobbed his head, his frown ferocious.

"Child," said the dragon, "tell me about your ghosts."

"Kindal and the lady were caught by a ghost magnet south of the village."

"A ghost magnet? A ghost magnet. It seems to me I've heard of this before. Wait." She lowered her head and rested her chin on the ground, her jeweled, glowing eyes half-shut. "Mirrana, dragon spirit from five generations ago who bides with me, remembers this thing; it was set up in the southern hills by the priest Nakshli, who first started feeding us ghosts of the village dead. There were only three dragons living here then. Nakshli was the one who taught us to live with humans." She raised her head. "That was an age ago, and we thought the magnet died with him. Has it been catching and holding ghosts all this while?"

Elexa turned to Kindal and Pewet.

Pewet said, "There's a time limit. When the magnet caught me, there were two other ghosts on it. When the year turned to the anniversary of their deaths, they went on somewhere else. They said they had known ones who were there before they were, and it was the same for everyone down the chain of time; a year there in the hills, trapped by the magnet, and then the journey began again."

"Oh," said Elexa.

"What do they say?" asked the dragon.

"It holds them a year," said Father, "then releases them."

"Horst!" said Yan. "Are you a deadspeaker, too?"

"I only remembered how tonight," he said.

"You can see your son."

Father smiled sadly. "Yes."

"Good. Two deadspeakers are better than one. One can say when the other is lying."

"Yan," Father said, nearly growling.

"Someone has to be practical. Your child is not known for her obedience."

"Yan, enough. Elexa, tell me more about these dead," said the dragon.

"The first ghost I caught this morning after the dragon flew over. He is Smudu-sir, from Likush. He wants to be eaten by one of the dragon mothers so he can be revenged against the wild dragon who killed him."

"Does he understand what it means?" asked the dragon.

"I don't think so, Grandmother. I don't know enough to tell him."

"We will welcome any who agree to be eaten. Take Kindal to join Maia, and let the others watch and learn. Yan, stay with me. We need to discuss strategy."

Elexa bowed, then stood, hesitating.

"This way, Sister." Kindal walked to the right to the limit of her net. Elexa followed him, her father beside her, the other ghosts trailing after.

Kindal stopped at a cave almost at the end of the terrace, near the trickle of a small stream. He waited at the cave mouth, peering inside. "They're all asleep," he whispered.

Elexa sighed. "Greetings, O great one," she called.

Rumbles, slides, chirps, wings flapping, a brief flare of fire. A long pale neck and head emerged from the cave. "Who disturbs my sleep?"

"Kindal's little sister," said Elexa in human speech.

The head lowered so that the dragon could look her in the eye. "What message do you bring me?" she said in a softer voice. Her words were slurred and hissy.

"My brother is dead," Elexa said.

The neck rose again, the head a dark silhouette against the stars, and the dragon screamed a mourning cry. Noise came from other caves nearby as other dragons woke and poked their heads out. Questions whispered in the hisses and crunches of dragonspeech.

"I've lost my human," Maia cried to the others in dragon speech. Muted cries went up, not the full-scale jangling of their mourning for old Peder, but sympathy pains for someone they had all liked. Maia's three-year-old fledglings huddled beside their mother and uttered small, pained cries and threads of smoke.

"I brought his ghost to you, Mother," Elexa said.

"He wishes to nourish me a last time? Truly wishes it?"

Elexa turned to Kindal. "It's a different kind of death," she told him. She had talked to Birta about it after she had taken other ghosts to their dragons. "You choose your rebirth, and you aren't alone. You will be part of a person instead of the whole person; but that person is your dragon mother. Do you want this, Brother?"

"I do."

She sighed. "Come with me." The other ghosts followed her as she approached Maia, whose head lowered until her chin whiskers brushed the ground. She stared at Elexa from one yellow-orange eye. Elexa held out her arms, hands at shoulder height, and said, "Stand here, Kindal."

He came and stood between her outstretched hands.

"He is here, Mother. He gives himself freely." Elexa stepped back, thinning her net around Kindal.

"Thank you, bondling," said Maia. "Come in," she whispered to Kendal. She dropped her jaw, showing her twin-tipped tongue and dagger teeth, with light from internal fires climbing from her throat.

Kindal shook his shoulders and stepped onto Maia's tongue. Elexa removed her net from him. Maia closed her mouth slowly, and Kindal crouched down, glancing up at the roof of her mouth. The teeth of the lower jaw fitted with the teeth of the upper jaw like puzzle pieces, and then Kindal was gone.

Maia lifted her head high and swallowed. She kept her head high as the children crept along her sides. Elexa gripped one hand in the other and twisted.

At last Maia shook her head and lowered it until she was staring at Elexa again, her yellow-orange eye flecked with green now. "Oh," she said, her human speech clearer, her tone higher. "Lex! There's light all around you, and some of it's purple!"

"What?" Elexa laughed, half-breathless.

Maia cocked her head. "You look different from here. Everything does." Her head swung as she surveyed the valley from her perch. Then her nose dropped to touch each of the babies at her sides. "Hey! Peep! Seek! Hi! Hey!" They chirped. She glanced toward Elexa again. "The others are still here, yes? I don't see them anymore."

"They're still here."

"Kindal?" said Father.

The dragon's head wavered, as though she shook off drops of water. "Maintain dignity," Maia muttered to herself, in a deeper voice. "Man, I am not your son, but he is here, a part of me now. I have many other parts, dragon, human, animal. They do not stay separate for long, but you may still speak with them. Sometimes one can answer out of the midst of them." She turned to Elexa, her mouth open a fraction in a dragon smile. "I love my bondling, Lexa, but I didn't know how funny he was until now. Thank you."

"You're welcome," said Elexa. She looked to her other ghosts.

"Who would eat us?" asked Pewet.

"I don't know," Elexa said. "The only dragon mother I've spent much time with is Guardian Birta. I catch all the ghosts I can, though, and I've been giving them to Kindal to feed to Maia. Everyone gives their dragons ghosts if they can."

"Ghosts of people?" asked Smudu.

"No. Usually animal ghosts. I am the only one who captures people." Mineworkers who had died young, orphans who had never found a home in life, a peddler's daughter who fell from her wagon on a steep mountain path; human ghosts adrift above the village. Not as fresh as the animal ghosts, but clinging more tightly to the world; she had talked to each of them. A few of them she had not liked at all; the killer, and a woman who did nothing but berate Elexa and scream that her life would have been better if only she had not been surrounded by idiots and selfish fools.

"I know who I want to be," said Pewet. "Granny Dragon, the first one we talked to. She can boss the headman, and he certainly needs it."

"We can ask her."

"Does she ever go flying? Does she fly north?"

"We can ask her," Elexa said again. "Maia, Kindal, we are going to speak with other dragons about my other ghosts now. I'll bring you game tomorrow."

"Thank you, Lex," said the dragon, in almost Kindal's voice, and then, in another voice, the dragon's own, "Will you bond with me?"

"I can't bond until next year," she said. She hadn't heard of anyone bonding with a dragon whose children had already hatched, let alone babies who were three years old.

Maia looked away. "It is only my greed that makes me say it," she said. "Though my boy lives inside me, I know I will miss him the way he used to be, and my children will miss him, too. Visit me, then, child."

"I will."

"I will, too," said Father. The dragon rubbed a whiskered cheek against his chest. The leather of his tunic burned a little, but he didn't flinch.

They had to pass six other caves to return to Birta and Yan. One of the dragons accosted Elexa. "Have you a ghost for me?" she asked.

"Will you fight the wild dragons?" Elexa asked.

This dragon, blue with gold spirals along the underside of her neck, lowered her head. "I cannot," she said. "I have four fledglings to care for."

"One of my ghosts needs a fighter. Another wants to go to Birta-Grandmother."

"I hear," said the dragon. "For the fighter, you will want the dragons of the Second or Third Terrace, then, those whose children are grown enough to care for themselves. Ghost child, keep me in mind if you catch someone else. My name is Fass."

"I'll remember," Elexa said. She walked on, her father beside her, the ghosts keeping pace.

Yan scowled as she approached. She ducked behind her father and peeked up at Birta.

"Kindal is settled with Maia?" Birta asked.

"Yes. One of my ghosts would give herself to you, Grandmother."

"Lovely," said Birta. "I have quite a taste for them. Bring her to me, Lexa."

"Wait!" Yan said. "You'd eat a ghost not bonded to you?"

"Whenever I can get one," said Birta. "Every ghost adds to my store of knowledge about the world. They are my true treasures, my hoard." Her mouth opened a slit in a dragon smile. "I'd eat you if I could," she whispered. Yan took a step back, wiped his forehead with the back of his hand.

Elexa straightened. "Pewet-lady," she murmured. "Do you still want to do this?" She had never understood what dragons wanted with ghosts; they were just something she knew dragons needed that she was more skilled than others at finding. Old Peder had been so happy to be eaten, and some of the special others had, too. She thought of the human ghosts she had caught and sent up to Maia without thinking twice about it.

"I do want it," Pewet murmured. She glanced behind her, saw that Elexa's father was out of earshot, talking with Smudu, while Yan scowled. Pewet kept her voice low. "The other places I might go couldn't possibly be as nice or interesting. I was not a good citizen in life, Lexa. The people who chose to preach at me always told me I'd come to a bad end. How I look forward to proving them wrong."

"Oh," said Elexa. She wondered if Birta would want a bad ghost. It had sounded as though Birta would take any ghost she could get.

"Let's go," said Pewet. She slid her net-wrapped arm through Elexa's and drifted beside her as they approached Birta.

Pewet stared up at Birta, whose neck curved so she could look down at Elexa. "I didn't realize she was so much bigger than the others," Pewet said.

"She had her children long ago, before I was born. She bonded with Peder, the headman before Yan, and she stayed on here. Lots of times the dragon mothers leave when their children are old enough and they don't need our help anymore, but Grandmother didn't do that."

"She looks like a fighter. Maybe Smudu should join her, too."

"Grandmother, will you fight the wild dragons?" Elexa asked.

"No. I need to stay with the new mothers and protect them. The other guardians will do it."

Elexa walked Pewet to Birta, who lowered her head until her whiskery chin touched the ground, and then opened her jaw. Her split tongue was edged in black, a sign of age.

"Ready?" Elexa asked.

Pewet shivered, then said, "Sure. Plenty of room there."

Elexa slipped her net off Pewet. "Go," she whispered. Pewet stepped over the thicket of curving iron fangs and onto the tongue. "She's there, Grandmother," said Elexa.

The dragon closed her mouth gently, swallowed, rested her head on the ground, her eyes closed, her neck arching above her. Birta was still so long Elexa's hands folded into tight fists. Had something gone wrong?

Birta's eyes opened. Blue flared in the green-yellow gem fire of them, and the dragon laughed, a puffing roar of flame. "Glorious and good," she said. She cocked her head and studied Yan, who stood straight and glared back.

"Couldn't I burn him just a little?" she muttered. "Toast a few toes?"

"No," the dragon answered herself in a deeper voice. "Not yet."

"What?" Yan roared.

"As headmen go, you are better than some," Birta said in her own voice, "and not as good as others. I have not been a political creature in the past, but that may change. Watch your step, little man. Lexima, is Smudu still here?"

"Yes," said Elexa. She backed up until she was even with the ghost and her father. She had known Birta six years and given her two ghosts; now the dragon grandmother had a new name for her, and she wasn't sure she liked that.

"There is something I need to tell you about the wild ones," Birta said.

"What, Grandmother?"

"Before you find someone to fight them, you should visit them."

"What? What if they eat me, too?"

"Jex killed three goats for them after your father brought the herd home tonight. I spoke to them just now. They killed Kindal before we got their promises to do no harm here; they did not know how we operate in the valley. You should talk to them."

"They killed Smudu-sir and Kindal!"

"They didn't know it was wrong," said Birta in her Pewet voice. "Talk to them."

Elexa gripped her father's hand, looked up at his face. He nodded. It was not as if any of them knew how to fight dragons, anyway. But Smudu—

She looked at her first ghost of the day, tall and proud, with his golden armbands, belt, and ear hoops; his long pale hair; his grim face.

"My heart is hot," he said, "but I can wait."

"We're really safe going up there alone?" Elexa asked Birta.

"They will not kill any of the valley's humans. If they do, we have vowed to kill them and send their spirits to nowhere instead of into the braids of spirit within us. They would be wholly lost. No dragon wants that."

Elexa sighed and released her father's hand, headed for the path to Second Terrace.

Second Terrace was where the less social dragons lived, the ones who craved caves away from each other. Some of the dragon mothers who had already raised their children lived here, too, watching over the village even though their reason for being there had flown. These had formed the strongest bonds with their humans.

Third Terrace hosted visiting dragon children, those whose mothers had bonded with villagers and who had formed smaller bonds with the human children who brought them food and ghosts while they were growing. Some of the dragon children returned to raise their own children in Mountainknee; others left and never returned except for the midwinter dragon gather up toward the snowcap of the mountain, when wild and village dragons danced through the shortest day and fired through the longest night.

Fourth Terrace, above Third Terrace, wasn't a place where any dragons usually lived. It was where dragon children were temporarily exiled to punish them, somewhere they went when they weren't supposed to talk to anyone.

The path to Fourth Terrace was rough and showed no signs of recent use. Father helped Elexa climb. As they neared the lip above, Father called, "Greetings, O great ones," in dragonspeech. "Harm us not; we are here to talk."

"Greetings," called a voice in dragonspeech from above. "Come without fear." The voice was high and thin and spoke with a dragon accent that softened some of the hard edges of the words.

Father boosted Elexa up over the lip and climbed up after her. Elexa had never been this high on the mountain. In fact, she had never even been to Third Terrace before and felt she hadn't properly seen it now; all they had done was cross it to get to the upward path by the patchy light of Father's lantern and the better blue light of Little Moon.

Fourth Terrace was narrow, with cliffs starting upward only a few feet from the edge. To the left was a cave entrance with a heap of smoked bones beside it. The scent of charred meat lingered. A dragon face peered out at them; the scalloped edges of its lifted crest made it a female. Its skull was slenderer than the skulls of dragons Elexa was used to, and it had a ruff of spikes around its face the likes of which she had never seen before. It hissed a flood of smoke toward them.

"Great one," said Father. His voice trembled. Elexa was not sure if it was rage or fear that charged his words.

"What are you doing here?" asked the dragon in dragonspeech. It used the "you" reserved for animals, not people.

"Birta-dragon Grandmother told us to speak with you,"

Elexa said. She used the animal "you," too.

The dragon emerged from the cave to stand on the narrow ledge of Fourth Terrace. She spread one wing for balance. Elexa recognized the underside pattern of leaves against dark: this was the dragon who had killed Smudu Kush. She cried aloud and ran toward the dragon, not even aware of what she was doing. She raised her arms. She had no knife, no bow and arrow. No weapon at all. She ran at the dragon with her fists. The dragon lifted its front two legs and closed hot talons gently around Elexa's torso, holding her as she howled and screamed and thrashed, pummeling the dragon's arms with her fists.

"I have vowed not to hurt you, morsel, but it is difficult when you act like prey," said the dragon.

"Elexa," said Smudu. "Stop."

"This is the one who murdered you!"

"Don't make it eat you, too."

She could not stop panting. In the pile of bones by the entrance to the cave, she saw human skulls. She wanted to pull them from the pile and flee down to the village, where she could give them a proper farewell and a decent burning. She hated the dragon who held her.

"Elexa," said her father.

She turned, breath hissing in and out through her nose.

"Look." He came close to where she and the dragon were locked together and held up the lantern. "Look at her." He used the dragonspeech word for "her" that meant person.

Elexa drew in long, slow breaths and stared at the dragon. It was thin; she could see every rib in its chest. Its skin was patchy and rough. The talons it held her in were warm, not hot, not burning her the way every direct contact she'd had with dragons before had. Its eyes glowed dully, not with the bright gem fire she had seen in every dragon's eyes below.

She stood silent, conscious now of each talon wrapped around her like a finger, with no claws pressing into her at all.

The dragon was dying.

It opened its talons and lowered them, released her. Elexa took three steps back but didn't flee.

"I did not know," the dragon said. "I did not know you were people." This time it used the plural "you" for people. "All I knew was that you were out in the open instead of hiding, and our need was great."

"Where did you come from?" she asked.

"We lived on an island far from here. There were no humans on it. I had never seen them until we came to this continent, and we had to do that, because a mountain grew overnight on our island and the hot rock that came out of it killed everything living except things that could fly away in time. We flew and flew. We didn't know whether there was anyplace to fly to. We were exhausted by the time we reached this new land. We saw scurrying, two-legged things. We found some of their mounds, and they were simple to break open so we could snatch the meat. It was easy to catch, and it tasted wonderful. None of them spoke to us."

As the dragon talked, Elexa's father murmured behind her. During a pause in the dragon's speech, Elexa heard her father's words. He was translating the dragon's story for Smudu.

"My sister has two eggs to lay, the last of our line. We could not let them die unborn. Everything else flew or ran too fast for us to catch, so Jakar and I caught humans."

Elexa's breath hissed through her nose. She thought of Kindal, one of the last of her line, dead now except in spirit. Kindal, her kind, occasionally irritating older brother, who had taught her to hunt and listened to her problems. He had been the friend who comforted her when Tira wouldn't speak with her, and when Maro, the secret friend Tira wanted, didn't speak to her either, after their meetings were known.

Kindal wasn't the last of his line. Her father still lived, and though he had never seemed interested in finding a second wife, who knew the future? Elexa was alive, and would marry and have children if she found a boy she liked. The future was open.

The dragons had lost their whole world.

"I regret that we took away a person who meant something to you, with no hope to continue him," said the dragon. She lifted her head and peered past Elexa's shoulder. "Or is there a hope?"

Elexa turned to glance back the way the dragon looked. Smudu stood there. "She can see you," Elexa whispered.

Smudu strode forward, stood beside Elexa. "Do you see me, my murderer?"

Elexa translated the question into dragonspeech. Other dragons were aware of the presence of ghosts, but she had never spoken to one who could see them.

The dragon cocked her head. "I do. You glow in the shape

of the one you were before. You are wrapped in something gray. I didn't know your kind left spirits."

As Elexa translated, another head snaked out of the cave darkness above the wild dragon's shoulder. Its raised crest had the sharp edges of a male, and it, too, had a ruff of spikes around its head. It stared at Smudu.

"You killed me," Smudu said to the female. "Give me your life in exchange."

Elexa translated for him as best she could, then turned to him. "What do you mean, 'give me your life'?"

"Let me be eaten by her, the way the others were dragon-eaten."

"Is this what you really want?"

"I don't know," he muttered. "I think of my daughter and my wife, and what I would do to protect them, if I could. I understand now that the dragon was protecting her sister. If I am inside her, the way your brother went inside the other, and the woman went inside the grandmother—can they shape what their dragon hosts do?"

Elexa shook her head. "I don't think so."

"I couldn't make her take the gold I wore and carried at my death home to my wife and daughter?"

Elexa shook her head again.

"You may not be able to order her, but you could ask her," said Father.

Smudu nodded. "Ask her for me, please."

"You took this man out of his family and left them in want," Father said in dragonspeech. "Would you accept the gift of his ghost? Can you return his gold to them?"

The dragon lowered her head, her eyes half-lidded. "I don't know about the gift of his ghost. I understand others here share their lifebraids with human and animal ghosts, though this seems strange to me. I cannot return the man's gold to his family until after my sister's eggs are laid and I am sure she has enough to eat."

"The village will feed all three of you, and the babies," said Father. "It's been a good year for goats."

Elexa thought of the blue-violet stone she had found that morning, somewhere in Sanric's hoard now. She could sense it through cloth and walls; she knew its radiance. She would be able to track it down. If she explained to Yan, would he help her reclaim it? It would pay for several goats, or she could take it to Smudu's family.

Leave Mountainknee. See the places her ghosts had told her about. Get away from Sanric and Yan, the death of her brother, the loss of her friendship with Tira.

Leave Father alone?

"Will you give my sister a child?" asked the dragon.

"To eat?" Father said. "Certainly not."

"A slave child, like the ones the other dragons have."

"We aren't slaves!" Father cried. "Both gain from the bond. You would have to give to the child who bonded to you. But we had Bond Night a month ago, and all the children who were ready bonded with dragons. We have no more unbonded thirteen-year-olds."

"What about this one?" asked the dragon. "The ghost catcher."

"She is too young, and unprepared," said Father.

Elexa said, "I won't bond with a murderer!"

The dragon said, "Jakar and I have killed humans, but my sister has done nothing but try to survive and keep her children alive. She has killed no one." The pale head lowered, snaked toward her, its crest rising, the dim eyes glowing brighter. "How prepared do you have to be? We don't know your ways."

"I don't want to bond with your sister." Elexa backed away from the dragon, her hand reaching behind her for Father's. She wanted to bond to a dragon she had spent a year courting, someone she knew would be kind to her, someone she could respect. These strange dragons with ghost vision and no morals didn't appeal to her.

Father took her hand in his, placed his other hand on her shoulder to steady her. The world swayed, she was so tired. She leaned against her father's steadiness.

Smudu strode past Elexa to the dragon, who slid her head sideways so she could watch him with one eye. "Leave the child alone. Take me."

Father repeated what he had said in dragonspeech. Smudu's murderer turned her head one way, then the other, studying the ghost with each of her eyes in turn.

At last she laid her chin on the ground. Her waving whiskers stilled. "On my island that is no more, taking in another's ghost is a large thing. It is a promise to carry forward a life, to nurture it and pass it on to another body when mine breaks, to weave it in with all the other lives I cherish and host. Man, I do not want you inside me, but I see now that I will have you. Come to me if you still will it."

Smudu turned back to Elexa. She took a deep breath and translated for him.

The ghost walked to Elexa and kissed her forehead, a touch of chill. He turned and strode toward the dragon's mouth, shrugging off Elexa's net as he went. When he stood just in front of the dragon, she lifted her head a little and opened her mouth. Each of her wavy teeth was outlined in mother-of-pearl, and her tongue had three tips. Smudu stepped over the fence of her teeth and settled on her tongue. She closed her mouth, lifted her head, and swallowed.

She froze, head pointed toward the stars. Father held Elexa's shoulders as she leaned against him. An age of silence went by, and then the dragon's head lowered. "I understand," she said, in her own voice, in the language of humans.

There were four human skulls among the bones at the mouth of the wild dragons' cave. Father laid his cloak on the ground. He and Elexa worked the skulls free of the other bones and set them on the cloak. Each skull had a tooth-shaped hole in the back.

"My sister liked the brains best," said the dragon Smudu had joined. Her name was Nasra. "She said they tasted like stories."

Father stumbled down the mountain in the dark of morning, Elexa on his back and the cloak of skulls bunched in his hands. They went home and slept until the middle of the following afternoon, then took the skulls to the temple of the mountain god. Someone in the center ground rang the village bell in the pattern to share sorrow, and everyone who could set a job aside for an hour came to the temple to see the skulls, lined up atop the wooden bones of their funeral fire. From looking at them, Elexa hadn't known which skull had belonged to Kindal and which to Smudu, or to whom the other two skulls had belonged.

Nasra, Maia, and Birta landed in the center ground near the temple midway through the death songs. Yan, never anxious to take on god duties, had let Father take charge of this ceremony and farewell. When the dragons arrived, Yan glared at them, especially at Nasra. Some of the other villagers hid.

Elexa felt as though she were in a strange country where all the colors were gray and all the edges soft. She had touched the skulls as she set them on their pyres. One was smoother than the others, with faint patterns across it in the shape of scales. She knew it had belonged to her brother. A dragon bond changed you from skin to bones.

She prayed for all four of the dead, that they were happy in their next lives, and after she had set the fires to consume what they had left behind and watched the bones scorch, she turned and saw the dragons, next lives to Kindal and Pewet and Smudu.

Nasra rested her forehand on a cloth-wrapped bundle. "Elexa," she said.

Elexa walked through the crowd, saw faces of people she had known all her life, locked in the quiet of sorrow. Tira, kneeling near the back, watched Elexa as she passed. Tira did not smile, but she didn't frown, either. She looked pale.

"I have collected what belonged to my man," Nasra said

when Elexa reached her. She shook the bundle and it clinked with coin. "We want to take it back to his family, but I cannot give it to them directly; the city will shoot me. Will you come with me, and walk it to them?"

"Now you can leave your sister?" Elexa asked.

Nasra dipped her head, glanced toward Birta and Maia. "I understand she won't be alone or abandoned. I am coming to appreciate the advantages of this life."

"I'll come," Elexa whispered.

Father headed for the house. Yan strode to Elexa. "You can't leave. You're the village deadspeaker. You have no right to risk yourself on a journey with a known killer of humans," he said.

Suddenly she had status, after all the years she had done the job alone? She didn't want a job if it meant Yan could order her around. "My father can be the village deadspeaker," Elexa said. "I need to take care of my ghosts."

Father returned with the leather saddle Kindal had used when he rode Maia; a hide coat, gloves, and helmet; and a pouch of food. He went to Nasra and strapped the saddle on her over a dragonhide pad to protect Elexa from the dragon's heat. Elexa put on the leather clothes. They were all too big for her and smelled of Kindal. Her eyes swam. She looked at Maia.

"Go," said Maia in Kindal's voice. "Go and come back, little sister."

There were stirrups for her toes, and straps on the saddle she could cling to. Nasra wasn't as hot as other dragons—still not healthy yet. Elexa strapped the food pouch across her chest and took the treasure out from under Nasra's forefoot. Her father helped her tie it to the back of the saddle with leather strings, then boosted her into the saddle just in back of Nasra's first pair of arms and the bunched muscles that powered her wings.

Elexa clutched the straps and glanced around at her village. She suspected it would never look the same to her again.

Someone tugged on her boot. She looked down into Tira's face. Tira stretched up a closed hand. When Elexa opened her gloved hand, Tira dropped the beer-colored gem into it. "Maybe you'll find a good place to sell it in the city," she said.

"I'll look."

"I'm still mad that you get to fly first."

Elexa laughed, wiped her eyes, watched the smoke rising from the farewell fires. Nasra gathered herself and leapt up into the air.

Over the past twenty-some years, **Nina Kiriki Hoffman** has sold novels, juvenile and media tie-in books, short story collections, and more than two hundred short stories. Her works have been finalists for the Nebula, World Fantasy, Mythopoeic, Sturgeon, Philip K. Dick, and Endeavour awards. Her first novel, *The Thread That Binds the Bones*, won a Bram Stoker Award.

Nina's two most recent books are *Spirits That Walk in Shadow* (Viking) and *Fall of Light* (Ace).

Nina does production work for the *Magazine of Fantasy & Science Fiction*, and teaches short story writing through her local community college. She also works with teen writers. She lives in Eugene, Oregon, with several cats, a mannequin, and many strange toys.

Author's Note

I have always loved books about dragons, starting with *My Father's Dragon*, continuing on through Anne McCaffrey's Pern books, and many others, including Patricia Wrede's wonderful books about dealing with dragons. In older dragon stories, though, dragons are not friendly. They are dangerous and menacing, and they'd rather eat you than make friends. My dragons ended up somewhere in between.

I thought, what if there were a girl who lived in a village

with regular relations with dragons, only the girl was scared of them? What if she could catch and talk to ghosts? What if she had a strange sense for stones? I had a great time answering these questions.

Jo Walton

THREE TWILIGHT TALES

1

Once upon a time, a courting couple were walking down the lane at twilight, squabbling. "Useless, that's what you are," the girl said. "Why, I could make a man every bit as good as you out of two rhymes and a handful of moonshine."

"I'd like to see you try," said the man.

So the girl reached up to where the bright silver moon had just risen above the hills and she drew together a handful of moonshine. Then she twisted together two rhymes to run right through it and let it go. There stood a man, in a jacket as violet as the twilight, with buttons as silver as the moon. He didn't stand there long for them to marvel at him. Off he went down the lane ahead of them, walking and dancing and skipping as he went, off between the hedgerows, far ahead, until he came to the village.

It had been a mild afternoon, for spring, and the sun had been kind, so a number of people were sitting outside the old inn. The door was open, and a stream of gold light and gentle noise was spilling out from inside. The man made of moonshine stopped and watched this awhile, and then an old widower man began to talk to him. He didn't notice that the moonshine man didn't reply, because he'd been lonely for talking since his wife died, and he thought the moonshine man's smiles and nods and attention made him quite the best conversationalist in the village. After a little while sitting on the wooden bench outside the inn, the old widower noticed the wistful glances the moonshine man kept casting at the doorway. "Won't you step inside with me?" he asked, politely. So in they went together, the man made of moonshine smiling widely now, because a moonshine man can never go under a roof until he's been invited.

Inside, there was much merriment and laughter. A fire was burning in the grate and the lamps were lit. People were sitting drinking ale, and the light was glinting off their pewter tankards. They were sitting on the hearthside, and on big benches set around the tables, and on wooden stools along the bar. The inn was full of villagers, out celebrating because it was a pretty day and the end of their work week. The man made of moonshine didn't stop to look around, he went straight over to the fireplace.

Over the fireplace was a mantelpiece, and that mantelpiece was full of the most extraordinary things. There was a horn reputed to have belonged to a unicorn, and an old sword from the old wars, and a dragon carved out of oak wood, and a candle in the shape of a skull, which people said had once belonged to a wizard, though what a wizard would have wanted with such a thing I can't tell you. There was a pot the landlord's daughter had made, and a silver cup the landlord's father had won for his brewing. There were eggs made of stone and a puzzle carved of wood that looked like an apple and came apart in pieces, a little pink slipper said to have belonged to a princess, and an iron-headed hammer the carpenter had set down there by mistake and had been looking for all week.

From in between a lucky horseshoe and a chipped blue mug, souvenir of a distant port, brought back by a sailor years ago, the moonshine man drew out an old fiddle. This violin had been made long ago in a great city by a master craftsman, but it had come down in the world until it belonged to a gypsy fiddler who had visited the inn every spring. At last he had grown old and died on his last visit. His violin had been kept carefully in case his kin ever claimed it, but nobody had ever asked for it, or his body either, which rested peacefully enough under the grass beside the river among the village dead.

As soon as the man made of moonshine had the violin in his hands he began to play. The violin may have remembered being played like that long ago, in its glory days, but none of the villagers had ever heard music like it, so heart-lifting you couldn't help but smile, and so toe-tapping you could hardly keep still. Some of the young people jumped up at once and began to dance, and plenty of the older ones joined them, and the rest clapped along in time. None of them thought anything strange about the man in the coat like a violet evening.

It happened that in the village, the lord of the manor's daughter had been going about with the blacksmith's apprentice. The lord of the manor had heard about it and tried to put a stop to it, and knowing his daughter only too well, he had spoken first to the young man. Then the young man had wondered aloud if he was good enough for the girl, and as soon as he doubted, she doubted too, and the end of the matter was that the match was broken off.

Plenty of people in the village were sorry to see it end, but sorriest was a sentimental old woman who had never married. In her youth, she had fallen in love with a sailor. He had promised to come back, but he never did. She didn't know if he'd been drowned, or if he'd met some prettier girl in some faraway land, and in the end the not knowing was sadder than the fact of never seeing him again. She kept busy, and while she was waiting, she had fallen into the habit of weaving a rose wreath for every bride in the village. She had the best roses for miles around in the garden in front of her cottage, and she had a way with weaving wreaths too, twining in daisies and forget-me-nots so that each one was different. They were much valued, and often dried and cherished by the couples afterward. People said they brought luck, and everyone agreed they were very pretty. Making them was her great delight. She'd been looking forward to making a wreath for such a love match as the lord of the manor's daughter and the blacksmith's apprentice; it tickled her sentimental soul.

The little man made of moonshine played the violin, and the lord of the manor's daughter felt her toe tap, and with her toe tapping, she couldn't help looking across the room at the blacksmith's apprentice, who was standing by the bar, a mug in his hand, looking back at her. When he saw her looking he couldn't help smiling, and once he smiled, she smiled, and before you knew it, they were dancing. The old woman who had never married smiled wistfully to see them, and the lonely widower who had invited the little man in looked at her smiling and wondered. He knew he would never forget his wife, but that didn't mean he could never take another. He saw that smile and remembered when he and the old woman were young. He had never taken much notice of her before, but now he thought that maybe they could be friends.

All this time nobody had been taking much notice of the moonshine man, though they noticed his music well enough. But now a girl came in through the back door, dressed all in grey. She had lived alone for five years, since her parents died of the fever. She was twenty-two years old and kept three white cows. Nobody took much notice of her. She made cheese from her cows, and people said yes, the girl who makes cheese, as if that was all there was to her. She was plain and lonely in her solitary life, but she couldn't see how to change it, for she didn't have the trick of making friends. She always saw too much, and said what she saw. She came in, bringing cheese to the inn for their ploughman's lunches, and she stopped at the bar, holding the cheese in her bag, looking across the room at the violinist. Her eyes met his, and as she saw him, he saw her. She began to walk across the room through the dancers, coming toward him.

Just as she had reached him and was opening her mouth to speak, the door slammed back and in walked the couple who had been quarrelling in the lane, their quarrel all made up and their arms around each other's waists. The moonshine man stopped playing as soon as he saw them, and his face, which had been so merry, became grave. The inn fell quiet, and those who had been dancing were still.

"Oh," said the girl, "here's the man I made out of two rhymes and a handful of moonshine! It was so irresponsible of me to let him go wandering off into the world! Who knows what might have come of it? But never mind, no harm done." Before anyone could say a word, she reached toward him, whipped out the two rhymes, then rubbed her hands to dust off the moonshine, which vanished immediately in the firelight and lamplight of the bright inn parlour.

2

It was at just that time of twilight when the last of the rose has faded into the west, and the amethyst of the sky, which was so luminous, begins to ravel away into night and let the first stars rub through. The hares were running along the bank of the stream, and the great owl, the one they call the white shadow, swept silently by above them. In the latticework of branches at the edge of the forest, buds were beginning to show. It was the end of an early spring day, and the pedlar pulled his coat close around him as he walked over the low arch of the bridge where the road crossed the stream, swollen and rapid with the weight of melted snow.

He was glad to see the shapes of roof gables ahead of him instead of more forest stretching out. He had spent two cold nights recently, wrapped in his blankets, and he looked forward to warmth and fire and human comfort. Best of all, he looked forward to plying his trade on the simple villagers, selling his wares and spinning his stories. When he saw the inn sign swinging above one of the doors, he grinned to himself in pure delight. He pushed the door open and blinked a little as he stepped inside. There was firelight and lamplight and the sound of merry voices. One diamond-paned window stood ajar to let out the smoke of fire and pipes, but the room was warm with the warmth of good fellowship. The pedlar went up to the bar and ordered himself a tankard of ale. He took a long draft and wiped his mouth with the back of his hand.

"That's the best ale I've had since I was in the Golden City," he said.

"That's high praise if you like," the innkeeper said. "Hear this, friends, this stranger says my ale is the best he's tasted since the Golden City. Is that your home, traveller?"

The pedlar looked around to see that the most part of the customers of the busy inn were paying attention to him now, and not to each other. There were a pair of lovers in the corner who were staring into each other's eyes, and an old man with a dog who seemed to be in a world of his own, and a girl in grey who was waiting impatiently for the innkeeper's attention, but all the other eyes in the place were fixed on the pedlar.

"I don't have a home," he said casually. "I'm a pedlar, and my calling gives me a home wherever I go. I roam the world, buying the best and most curious and useful things I can find, then selling them to those elsewhere who are not fortunate enough to travel and take their choice of the world's goods. I have been to the Golden City, and along the Silver Coast; I've been in the east where the dragons are; I've been north to the ice; I've come lately through the very heart of the Great Forest; and I'm heading south where I've never been, to the lands of Eversun."

At this, a little ripple of delight ran through the listening villagers, and that moment was worth more than wealth to the pedlar, worth more than the pleasure of selling for gold what he had bought for silver. His words were ever truths shot through with sparkling lies, but his joy in their effect was as real as hot crusty bread on a cold morning.

"Can we see what you have?" a woman asked shyly.

The pedlar feigned reluctance. "I wasn't intending to sell anything here," he said. "My wares are for the lands of Eversun; I want to arrive there with good things to sell them, to give me enough coin to buy their specialities. I'm not expecting much chance to replenish my stock between here and there." The woman's face fell. "But since you look so sad, my dear, and since the beer here is so good and the faces so friendly, I'll open my pack if mine host here will throw in a bed for the night."

The landlord didn't look half as friendly now, in fact he was frowning, but the clamour among the customers was so great that he nodded reluctantly. "You can sleep in the corner of the taproom, by the fire," he said, grudgingly.

At that a cheer went up from the crowd, and the pedlar

took his pack off his back and began to unfold it on a table, rapidly cleared of tankards and goblets by their owners. The outside of the pack was faded by the sun to the hue of twilight, but the inside was a rich purple that made the people gasp.

Now some of the pedlar's goods were those any pedlar would carry—ribbons, laces, yarn in different colours, packets of salt, nutmegs, packets of spices, scents in vials, combs, mirrors, and little knives. He had none of the heavier, clattering goods, no pans or pots or pails that would weigh him down or cause him to need a packhorse to carry the burden. These ordinary goods he displayed with a flourish. "This lace," he said, "you can see at a glance how fine it is. That is because it is woven by the veiled men of the Silver Coast, whose hands can do such delicate work because they never step out into the sun. See, there is a pattern of peonies, which are the delight of the coastal people, and here, a pattern of sea waves."

When those who wanted lace had bought lace, he held up in each hand sachets of salt and pepper. "This salt, too, comes from the Silver Coast, and is in such large clear crystals because of a secret the women of that coast learned from the mermaids of making it dry so. The pepper comes from the Golden City, where it grows on trees and is dried on the flat rooftops so that all the streets of the city have the spicy smell of drying peppercorns."

"Does it never rain?" asked an old woman, taking out her coin to pay twice what the pepper would have been worth, except that it would spice her food with such a savour of story.

"In the Golden City, it rains only once every seven years," the pedlar said solemnly. "It is a great occasion, a great festival. Everyone runs into the streets and dances through the puddles. The children love it, as you can imagine, and splash as hard as they can. There are special songs, and the great gongs are rung in the temples. The pepper trees burst into huge flowers of red and gold, and the priests make a dye out of them which colours these ribbons. It is an expensive dye, of course, because the flowers bloom so rarely. They say it makes the wearers lucky, and that the dye doesn't fade with washing, but I can't promise anything but what you can see for yourselves, which is how good a colour it makes." He lifted handfuls of red and yellow and orange ribbons in demonstration, which were hastily snapped up by the girls, who all crowded around.

The whole company was clustered around the pedlar now, even the lovers, but the landlord was not displeased. Every so often, when he grew hoarse, or claimed he did, the pedlar would put down his perfumes or lengths of yarn and say it was time for them all to drink together, and there would be a rush for the bar. The landlord had already sold more ale and wine than on an ordinary night, and if the pedlar was having his drinks bought for him, what of it? The landlord had bought some spices for his winter wines, and a silver sieve for straining his hops. He no longer grudged the pedlar his corner by the fire.

The pedlar went on now to his more unusual items. He showed them dragon scales, very highly polished on the inside, like mirrors, and rough on the outside. He asked a very high price for them. "These are highly prized in the cities of Eversun for their rarity, and the young ladies there believe, though I can't swear it is the truth, that looking at your face in such a mirror makes it grow more beautiful." Only a few of the village maidens could afford the price he asked, but they bought eagerly.

The grey girl had been standing among the others for some time, but she had bought nothing. The pedlar had noticed her particularly, because she had not paid attention to him at first, and when she had come to watch, he had smiled inwardly. As the display went on and she stood silent, smiling to herself aside from time to time, he grew aware of her again and wanted to bring her to put her hand into her pocket and buy. He had thought the ribbons might tempt her, or then again the dragon scales, or the comb made from the ivory of heart trees, but though he had sold to almost everyone present, she had made no move.

Now he turned to her. "Here is something you will like," he said. "I do not mean to sell this here, but I thought it might interest you to look at it, for it is your colour." He handed her a little grey bird, small enough to fit into the palm of the hand, carved very realistically so you could feel each feather.

The grey girl turned it over in her hands and smiled, then handed it back. "I do not need a carven bird," she said.

"Why, no more does anyone else, but I see it fooled your eye, and even your hand. This bird, friends, is not carved. It comes from the Great North, from the lands of ice, and the bird flew too far into the cold and fell to the ground senseless. If you hold it to your lips and breathe, it will sing the song it sang in life, and they say in the north that sometimes such a bird will warm again and fly, but I have never seen it happen." He put the bird's tail to his lips and blew gently, and a trill rang out, for the bird was cleverly carved into a whistle. They were a commonplace of the Silver Coast, where every fishergirl had such a bird-whistle, but nobody in the village had ever seen one before.

The grey girl raised her eyebrows. "You say that was a living bird of the Great North that froze and turned to wood?"

"It has the feel of wood, but it is not wood," the pedlar insisted.

"Let me hold it a moment again," she asked. The pedlar handed it over. The grey girl held it out on the palm of her hand where everyone could see it. "No, it is wood," she said, very definitely. "But it's a pretty enough lie to make true." She folded her fingers over the bird and blew over it. Then she unfolded her fingers, and the bird was there, to all appearances the same as before.

The pedlar drew breath to speak, but before he could, the carved bird ruffled its feathers, trilled, took one step from the girl's hand onto her grey sleeve, then took wing, flew twice around over the heads of all the company, and disappeared through the open crack of the window.

3

As the leaves were turning bronze and gold and copper, the king came into the forest to hunt. One morning he set off to follow a white hart. They say such beasts are magical and cannot be caught, so the king was eager. Nevertheless, as often happens to such parties, they were led on through the trees with glimpses of the beast and wild rides in pursuit until the setting sun found them too far from their hunting lodge to return that night. This was no great hardship, for while the king was young and impetuous and had a curling black beard, he had many counsellors whose beards were long and white and combed smooth. Most of them had, to the king's secret relief, been left behind in the palace, but he had brought along one such counsellor, who was believed to be indispensable. This counsellor had thought to order the king's silken pavilions brought on the hunt, along with plenty of provisions. When the master of the hunt discovered this cheering news, he rode forward through the company, which had halted in a little glade, and brought it to the king, who laughed and complimented his counsellor.

"Thanks to you," he said, "the worst we have to fear is a cold night under canvas! What an adventure! How glad I am that I came out hunting, and how sorry I feel for those of the court who stayed behind in the Golden City with nothing to stir their blood." For the king was a young man, and he was bored by the weighty affairs of state.

The indispensable counsellor inclined his head modestly. "I was but taking thought for your majesty's comfort," he said.

Before he or the king could say more, the king's bard, who was looking off through the trees, caught sight of a gleam of light far off among them. "What's that?" he asked, pointing.

The company all turned to look, with much champing of bits but not many stamped hooves, for the horses were tired at the end of such a day. "It is a light, and that means there must be habitation," the king said, with a little less confidence than he might have said it in any other part of the kingdom. The Great Forest had a certain reputation for unchanciness.

"I don't know of any habitation in this direction," said the master of the hunt, squinting at the light.

"It will be some rude peasant dwelling, rat ridden and flea infested, far less comfortable than your own pavilions," the counsellor said, stroking his fine white beard. "Let us set them up here and pay no attention to it."

"Why, where's your spirit of adventure?" the bard asked the counsellor. The king smiled, for the bard's question was much after his own heart.

The king raised his voice. "We will ride on to discover what that gleam of light might be." In a lower tone, as the company prepared to ride off, he added to the counsellor, "Even if you are right, and no doubt you are, at the very least we will be able to borrow fire from them, which will make our camp less cold."

"Very wise, your majesty," the counsellor said.

They rode off through the twilight forest. They were a fine company, all dressed for hunting, not for court, but in silks and satins and velvets and rare furs, with enough gold and silver about them and their horses to show that they were no ordinary hunters. The ladies among them rode astride, like the men, and all of them, men and women, were beautiful, for the king was young and as yet unmarried and would have nobody about him who did not please his eye. Their horses were fine beasts, with arching necks and smooth coats, though too tired now to make the show they had made when they had ridden out that morning. The last rays of the sun had gilded them in the clearing, touching the golden circlet the king wore about his dark unruly locks; now they went forward into deepening night. The sky above them was violet, and a crescent moon shone silver like a sword blade. The first stars were beginning to pierce the sky when they splashed across a brook and saw a little village.

"What place is this?" the king asked the master of the hunt.

"I don't know, sire. Unless we have come sadly astray it isn't marked on my map," the master of the hunt said.

"We must have come astray then," the king said, laughing. "I don't think the worse of you for it, for we were following a hart through the forest, and though we didn't kill it, I can't think when I had a better day's sport. But look, man, this is a stone-built village with a mill and a blacksmith's forge, and an inn. This is a snug little manor. A road runs through it. Why, it must pay quite five pounds of gold in taxes."

The counsellor smiled to himself, for he had been the

king's tutor when he was a prince, and was glad to see he remembered the detail of such matters.

The master of the hunt shook his head. "I am sure your majesty is right, but I can't find it on my map."

"Let us go on and investigate," the bard said.

It had been the red gleam of the forge they had seen from far off, but it was the lamplight spilling out of the windows of the inn that the bard waved toward.

"Such a place will not hold all of us," the king said. "Have the tents set up for us to sleep, but let us see if we can get a hot supper from this place, whatever it is."

"A hot supper and some country ale," the bard said.

"There are three white cows in the water meadow beside the stream," the master of the hunt pointed out. "The country cheese in these parts is said to be very good."

"If you knew what parts these were, no doubt my counsellor could tell us all about their cheeses," the king said.

They dismounted and left the horses to the care of those who were to set up the tents. The four of them strode into the village to investigate. The bard brought his little harp, the counsellor brought his purse, the master of the hunt brought a shortsword on his belt, but the king brought nothing.

The inn was warm and friendly and seemed to contain the whole population of the village. Those who were not there came in as soon as the news came to them of the king's arrival. The counsellor negotiated with the innkeeper and soon arranged that food and drink could be provided for the whole company, and beds for the king and the ladies, if the ladies did not mind crowding in together. The master of the hunt pronounced the ale excellent, and the villagers began to beg the bard to play. The rest of the company, having set up the tents and rubbed down the horses, began to trickle into the inn, and the place became very full.

The king wandered around the inn, looking at everything. He examined the row of strange objects that sat on the mantelpiece, he peered out through the diamond-paned windows, he picked up the scuttle beside the fire and ran his hand along the wood of the chair backs, worn smooth by countless customers. The villagers felt a little shy of him, with his crown and his curling black beard, and did not dare to strike up conversation. For his own part he felt restless and was not sure why. He felt as if something was about to happen. Until the bard started to play, he thought he was waiting for music, and until he was served a plate of cold pork and hot cabbage, he thought he was waiting for his dinner, but neither of these things satisfied him. Neither the villagers nor his own company delighted him. The villagers seemed simple, humble, rustic; their homespun clothes and country accents grated on him. In contrast, the gorgeous raiment and noble tones of his company, which were well enough in the palace or even his hunting lodge, seemed here overrefined to the point of decadence.

At length the door at the back opened and a girl came in, clad all in grey and carrying a basket. The master of the hunt had called for cheese, and she was the girl who kept the cows and made the cheese. She was plain almost to severity, with her hair drawn back from her face, but she was young and dignified, and when the king saw her he knew that she was what he had been waiting for, not just that night but for a long time. He had been picking at his dinner, but he stood when he saw her. There was a little circle of quiet around the corner where he sat, for his own people had seen that he did not want conversation. The girl glanced at him and nodded, as if to tell him to wait, and went with her basket to the innkeeper and began to negotiate a price for her cheese. The king sat down and waited meekly.

When she had disposed of her cheeses, the girl in grey picked her way through the room and sat down opposite the king. "I have been waiting for you all my life. I will marry you and make you my queen," he said. He had been thinking all the time she was at the bar what he would say when she came up to him, and getting the words right in his mind. For the first time he was glad he was king, that he was young and handsome, that he had so much to offer her.

"Oh, I know that story," she said. She took his ale tankard and breathed on it, and passed it back to him. He looked into it and saw the two of them tiny and distant, in the palace, quarrelling. "You'd pile me with jewels and I'd wither in that palace. You'd want me to be something I'm not. I'm no queen. I'm no beauty, no diplomat. I speak too bluntly. You'd grow tired of me and want a proper queen. I'd go into a decline and die after I had a daughter, and you'd marry again and give her a stepmother who'd persecute her."

"But I have loved you since I first saw you," the king insisted, although her words and the vision had shaken him. He took a deep draft of the ale to drive them away.

"Love? Well now. You feel what you feel, and I feel what I

feel, but that doesn't mean you have to fit us into a story and wreck both our lives."

"Then you . . ." the king hesitated. "I know that story. You're the goddess Sovranty, whom the king meets disguised in a village, who spends one night with him and confirms his sacred kingship."

She laughed. "You still don't see me. I'm no goddess. I know that story though. We'd have our one night of passion, which would confirm you in your crown, and you'd go back to your palace, and nine months later I'd have a baby boy. Twenty years after that he'd come questing for the father he never had." She took up a twist of straw that was on the table and set it walking. The king saw the shape of a hero hidden among the people, then the straw touched his hand and fell back to the table in separate strands.

"Tell me who you are," the king said.

"I'm the girl who keeps the cows and makes the cheeses," she said. "I've lived in this village all my life, and in this village we don't have stories, not real stories, just things that come to us out of the twilight now and then. My parents died five years ago when the fever came, and since then I've lived alone. I'm plain, and plainspoken. I don't have many friends. I always see too much, and say what I see."

"And you wear grey, always," the king said, looking at her.

She met his eyes. "Yes, I do, I wear grey always, but how did you know?"

"When you're a king, it's hard to get away from being part of a story," he said. "Those stories you mentioned aren't about us. They're about a king and a village girl and a next generation of stories. I'd like to make a new story that was about you and me, the people we really are, getting to know each other." He put out his hand to her.

"Oh, that's hard," she said, ignoring his hand. "That's very hard. Would I have to give up being a silver salmon leaping in the stream at twilight?"

"Not if that's who you are," he said, his green eyes steady on hers.

"Would I have to stop being a grey cat slipping through the dusky shadows, seeing what's to be seen?"

"Not if that's who you are," he said, unwavering.

"Would I have to stop being a grey girl who lives alone and makes the cheeses, who walks along the edges of stories but never steps into them?"

"Not if that's who you are," said the king. "But I'm asking you to step into a new story, a story that's never been before, to shape it with me."

"Oh, that's hard," she said, but she put her hand on the king's hand where it lay on the rough wooden table. "You've no sons, have you?"

"No sons, but I have two younger brothers," he said, exhilaration sweeping through him.

She looked around the room. "Your fine bard is singing a song, and your master of the hunt is eating cheese. Your counsellor is taking counsel with the innkeeper, and no doubt hearing all about the affairs of the village. Your lords and ladies are drinking and eating and patronising the villagers. If you really want to give up being a king and step into a new story with me, now is the time."

"What do I have to do?" he asked, very quietly, then she pulled his hand and for a moment he felt himself falling.

It was a little while before anyone noticed he had gone, and by then nobody remembered seeing the two cats slipping away between the tables, one grey and one a long-haired black with big green eyes.

Jo Walton is the author of four fantasy novels, including the World Fantasy Award–winning *Tooth and Claw,* and *Lifelode.* She has most recently written the Small Change trilogy (*Farthing, Ha'penny,* and *Half a Crown*). *Farthing* was nominated for the Nebula, John W. Campbell Memorial, and *Locus* awards. She comes from Wales but lives in Montreal, where the food and books available are more varied.

Her Web site is **http://papersky.livejournal.com**.

Author's Note

I'm remarkably fond of this story. I don't write much short fiction, but the first part of this one came to me all as a piece in the middle of the night. I got up and wrote it down, and then the next morning I looked at it, wondering what on Earth I'd fished up and whether I ought to toss it back. Sharyn thought it wasn't long enough, and of course she was right. That's why she's a great editor. Thinking about that led me to the other two parts, which now seem inseparably part of the story.

It's a very unusual story for me. The people have no names—and normally I'm all about the names. Yet the people and the twilight location have a solidity that's all about objects. I don't think I've ever written anything with so many lists in it—or lists of such strange things. It's all about provenance, where things and people come from, what stories they are part of. It's a fairy story that questions the demands that stories make of their protagonists. Like most fairy tales it's liminal, it's all about edges and thresholds and twilight and possibilities. But really, for me it'll always be the story that made me sit up in bed and say the first line aloud to my husband, then rush off to the computer to write it down. Months after finishing it, I re-read Pamela Dean's *The Secret Country* and discovered with a surprise where the two rhymers and the handful of moonshine had come from. Thank you, Pamela, for such a compelling image that snagged in my subconscious that way.

Carol Emshwiller

The Dignity He's Due

The king's music will have lots of trumpets and drums, a slow pace so the king can keep his dignity.

There'll be handmade lace at his throat.

On the royal barge he'll be protected from the sun by a silk canopy. There'll be another barge for his orchestra. Do not listen. The music is for his ears alone.

The royal picnic will be caviar and white truffles and wild strawberries no bigger than pearls.

But little acts of kindness—that's how we live now. We always say thank you, though we don't mean it. Who should people give things to, if not to us? Who better deserves a meal and a dollar? Mother says it's our due and we shouldn't be ashamed.

Or we steal. Mother says it's like taxes—they owe us.

We have a little tent that just fits the three of us, me and Mother and my little brother. I and Mother carry big packs.

My little brother isn't supposed to carry anything. That's because he's heir to the French throne. Mother thinks he's fourth in the line of succession. Of course there is no French throne anymore. Mother says that doesn't matter, we're still royalty.

Mother says trumpets should sound. She goes *"Toot, dee-dee toot, dee-dee toot"* as a fanfare. (When he was little he liked it, but not anymore.) Mother says music should be written just for him and, she says, might be one of these days when people realize. She says, "Look at his silky black hair and blue . . . so blue, blue eyes. Look at his nose, already aristocratic even at his age. Can he be other than a prince?"

(I have blue, blue eyes, too, and silky hair, but nobody cares.)

It's important that he dress as a prince, but we don't have anything but hand-me-downs. It makes Mother feel bad to dress him in T-shirts and jeans.

I keep telling her there is no king of France and it is unlikely there will be one ever again. But she says, "Things change. Who knows what's going to happen? Certainly not you."

I may be only fourteen, but I think I know more about it than she does.

One time when Mother was away, I cut his hair. At least he's a happy prince now, with a real haircut. He hated that pageboy. When Mother came back she was furious. "How could you? I don't want him to look like everybody else. Who'll know now? Once it grows out again, don't you dare."

"He wanted me to."

"A prince never gets to do what he wants. He has to learn that."

Mother wants to keep him, as she says, "pure." What she means is, no scars, neither mental nor physical, but it's too late. He slams around, climbs things. Already there's a C-shaped scar on his cheek and the marks of the stitches. And as to his mind . . . for heaven's sake, how can he be a normal anything? Though she doesn't want normal.

Mother is teaching him all the things a king needs to know. Especially a French king. History of France: the departments, the châteaux, the rivers . . . *"La douce France,"* she says. "Never any trees this big. You can walk from one village to another. Every house has a wall around it." But she hasn't even been there.

I'm teaching him other things, like the states right here, the battles that took place in these hills, and, as we go south, slavery. I think a prince should know about slavery. Not that I know much about anything. Still, I did have a chance to go to school for a little while—until our father left us. I was allowed to mingle with the "rabble." That's because I didn't matter.

When my brother says, "*I'm* a slave," I say, "All children are slaves to their parents, but this won't last forever," and he always says, "I could be dead before it ends," and I say, "The way you slam around, that's probably true."

The older he gets, the more he understands that this isn't the way most children live.

We often sleep in a park, though there's always a cop comes in the middle of the night to tell us to move on. Mother says, "Keep your dignity. Remember, *noblesse oblige*." We just pack up and head . . . maybe for another park, if we're in a town, that is. In the country, woodsy spots are good stopping places. Hardly anybody bothers us there.

We're safe for a while now, because Mother has us off on the Appalachian Trail. (Yet again.) When you don't have things to wear to keep warm, you need to follow the birds. We hardly ever have good shoes, and with all this walking, they're always worn out. Mother found me hiking boots that were set out in the garbage. They were already worn out when she found them.

Mother is happiest when we get, as she says, our due. Now and then we do. My brother gets the most. People think he's cute. (Mother hates cute. She keeps at him to stand up straight and hold his head high. She tells him, "Don't be cute," and, "Stop smiling. Don't gesture needlessly. Don't put your hands in your pockets. Look people straight in the eye.") She sprinkles her talk with French words. *"Alors,"* and *"Mon Dieu." "Ah, la voilà." "Venez mes enfants."* But sometimes I wonder just how good her French is.

We often hike this trail, going south in blueberry season or going north when fiddleheads pop up. We like it when we see a big rock we remember from the trip before or a gnarled tree we camped under on our last trip. And then there are the lean-tos all along the way. We steal from campers. They don't expect robbers way out there. We never take their cameras or field glasses or bird books. Mostly we take food and sometimes socks and warm underwear.

Here I am, thinking *we*, as if I agreed with Mother—as if I considered myself part of all this, though I guess, in a way, I am. I have to be. I don't know how Mother would get along without me. I think I'm in charge. Not of where we head or when, but I keep us out of trouble. And I try to add a little bit of a more normal life to my poor brother's.

I'm going to try and stop this. I want us to find a permanent place to live. A nice little town where it never gets too cold, but big enough for us to hide in.

I'll have to break it to Mother that we aren't going to live this way anymore. I don't know what she'll do. Maybe I won't be able to stop her. If she and my brother take off alone, I'll have to follow.

Napoleon Gustave Guillaume Williamson. We don't even have a French last name. Did my father approve of that name for his son? Or did Mother change it after my father left us? I wonder that she hasn't changed our last name.

He, Guillaume, was all right with this kind of life until last year, when he turned nine. He's getting too smart to put up with it. I tell him not to worry, I'm going to get us out of this, but I have to find the right place and I have to do it in a way that Mother won't object to too much—if that's possible.

He won't put up with this much longer. We're all right now, though. He likes being out on the trail like this. And he likes campers' kind of food, even the dried stuff. He likes the whole idea of the Appalachian Trail. He loves watching animals and bugs and such. He even loves spiders. Can a prince be interested in spiders?

I try to make him part of my plans, so he'll feel he's working on getting us out of this, too. I tell him to think about the kind of town he wants to live in and when we come to towns he should look around and see if this is the one. I hope that'll keep him from being too impatient.

But things change before I'm ready. It starts when Guillaume tells us he wants to be called Bill.

Mother has a fit. Worse than when I cut his hair. I've hardly ever seen her this angry, and usually it's me she's mad at.

It's a good thing we were out on the trail at the time. Mother made a terrible racket. After she calmed down, I noticed there wasn't a sound anywhere, the birds were quiet, no rustlings from ground squirrels, even the bugs were quiet. Guillaume . . . Bill and I were quiet, too.

I think that made him realize things he hadn't before, and it must have made him angry, too. I guess he decided he wouldn't wait for my help.

> *The king's crown will be heavy.*
>
> *His robes will sweep seven yards behind him. If he turns too fast they will trip him.*
>
> *Lights will be lit all along the roads he'll travel.*

Lots of places along the trail, you have to pass through little towns to get from one edge of the trail to the other. In this town the trail goes right along Main Street. There's a playground in the middle. Mother leaves us there while she goes off to scrounge. She's so angry she hasn't said a word since our fight yesterday—not really a fight because Guillaume . . . Bill and I just stood there watching. I'm worried about her. I think to follow her, but I know I should take care of Bill.

I practice calling him Bill a few times (every time I do, he smiles), then I stretch out on a bench to take a nap and . . . Bill . . . goes off to look for bugs or, if he's lucky, there'll be a stray dog. I'm tired. None of us slept too well after that "brouhaha" (Mother's word) about Bill's name.

Mother kept waking us up with one more thing—one more reason why Guillaume needs to be *Guillaume*. She can hardly bring herself to say *Bill* even just to talk about it. She spits it every time she says it.

I didn't think he'd go off without me. But maybe he found this was a town he liked, though it's a little small for my taste—for hiding in, that is. I'm sure it's small for Mother's taste, too. She doesn't think he'd ever get his due in a small town. The only museum is the Indian museum. Mother says, "A prince must be cultured. Must have a real education: politics, philosophy, and all the arts, too." Mother worries that he's into bugs.

I was afraid this would happen, especially after the Bill episode. I feel really bad. I always thought we were in this together.

For all I know, Bill is back on the trail beyond the town, but without a tent? He didn't even take his raincoat.

Mother is counting on his ignorance. "After all," she says, "he's only nine. He can't get far." But almost-ten-year-olds are smarter than people think.

She says, "This is all your fault. You should have been watching."

I tell her he'll just keep running away if our life keeps on as it is. He won't put up with it anymore, and especially he won't if she doesn't call him Bill.

"I won't call him . . ." She can't even say it.

But suddenly she thinks he's been kidnapped. She says, "It's not about that awful name at all, it's that he's so beautiful, how can he not be kidnapped?"

"In that case, you have to go to the police."

"I can't do that."

"If you think he's kidnapped, you have to, but I think he just got fed up."

"How can such a beautiful boy not be kidnapped?"

I tell her we should settle down right here, right now. "It's the only way to get him back. And if we ever do get him back, you're going to have to call him Bill."

It's a nice town. Surrounded by green hills. He couldn't have picked a prettier place. Or is he back on the trail stuffing himself with blueberries? Or he might be at the school, checking out the fourth grade. He's always wanted to go. Mother's right about one thing—he's smart. He knows what an entomologist is and what taxonomy is. Even systematics.

I wouldn't mind going back to school again. Funny, some kids get to go and don't even like it. I guess it's only when you can't that you want to.

I tell Mother she should take a nap in the park. I say, "I know you're tired after last night. I'll find him."

She knows I'm the one who has to do it. She knows he won't come to her. But when I find him . . . if I do . . . will he come back even for me?

I know it's a waste of time, but I want to check out the little houses on the edge of town . . . especially the ones that lie right near the Appalachian Trail. I'm not that worried about my brother. Besides, he might be near the trail somewhere.

I like best the houses that are more run-down than others because I imagine cleaning them up: pulling weeds, planting flowers, painting the trim some nice bright color. . . . I wonder if some of those houses with unmowed lawns are empty.

Then I head for the grocery store, where Bill might be trying to get his due in rotten apples and moldy cheese, but I change my mind. Instead I head for the elementary school to check out the fourth grade.

The king's music has four slow beats per measure. It's more largo than andante. His coat of arms has a lion, rampant, the right foreleg above the left, "Honi soit" in purple letters along the top and "qui mal y pense" along the bottom.

I was right to come here first. A better place to get his due than the grocery store—and going to school really is his due. I look in at the classes through the little windows in the doors. At the third window I find him. He's in the back row, ducking down behind the other kids. He doesn't look right. That haircut I gave him doesn't look like the other boys'. I see now how bad it is. No wonder Mother was angry. He's dirty and has dark circles under his eyes. His jeans are more raggedy than any of the other kids' and are so small for him they show his ankles.

I'm sure the teacher knows he's there, but she's not letting on. The kids know too. They keep turning around to look at him. Good thing he's small for his age—nobody's afraid of his being there. I suppose a child sneaking *into* a class and paying attention is a nice change.

I see why he sneaked into this classroom. All along the walls there are pictures of insects. Near a window at the back there's an ant farm. The window is a little bit open so the ants can come and go. Bill is right next to the farm. Behind him there's a cage with gerbils and next to that a fish tank. I remember things like that back when I went to school. I feel such yearning I think I'm going to cry. Good I don't, because I don't look right in here either. There's a hall monitor. I managed to avoid her when I first snuck in with other people, but she's right behind me now, before I realize it. She's wondering why I'm standing here looking in the window. I say I just wanted to see if my brother was there. Which is the truth.

"Is he?"

I don't know what to answer. I don't want him hauled out when he looks like he's having such a good time. I say, "No."

She asks me to come to the office. She leads the way. I follow, but when I see a hallway, I duck into it and run out a side door.

Maybe I should have stayed, because they might have let Bill and me go to school, but I got scared. I wasn't ready. I didn't have any answers figured out. What I do is wait until school is over. That's not till three thirty. I sit on the front steps all the rest of the day. I get hungry. I wonder if Bill will find a way to get something to eat in school.

When he comes out, he's with a teacher. They're talking so much they don't notice me. I'm standing right there beside them on the steps. I hope Bill has figured out some good answers. They say good-bye, so I guess he said the right things. He turns in the opposite direction from the teacher and goes off as if he had a place to go. I follow. Pretty soon he slows down. Now it's as if he doesn't know what to do or where to go next.

I yell, "Bill," but he doesn't turn around. He's not used to his name yet. "Bill, Bill. *Guillaume!*"

Finally he realizes it's me calling him and that *Bill* meant him. He's so glad to see me he actually hugs me before he realizes he's doing it. Then he collapses down on the edge of the sidewalk, and I sit beside him.

"I saw you in there. Did you eat?"

"They had lunch at school, but I was afraid they'd find out about me. I hid."

He *is* a beautiful boy. Mother's right. Even at his age he has an aristocratic face and a kind of natural dignity. I don't think it's because Mother keeps saying, *Sit up, don't slouch*, and such. It's too bad about that scar on his cheek.

"I'm hungry, too. Let's go scrounge."

I want Mother to get good and worried before I take him back.

That is, *if* he'll come back. Maybe he won't.

Sometimes at the back of grocery stores they'll give you old vegetables and fruit. In this town there's only one grocery store, and it's not a very big one. The man back there gives us perfectly good apples and carrots and a loaf of day-old bread. Also moldy cheese. He cuts the mold off for us, though Bill says he has a good pocketknife. Then he gives us each a quarter.

We sit not far from the store and eat.

I was right to worry. He won't come back. "You were having a good time there, in the school. What did the teacher say?"

"She said I could come back whenever I want. She said she'd give me paper."

"Where will you spend the night?"

"I found a place."

But he won't tell me where.

"Okay. How about I meet you after school tomorrow then?"

I give him his raincoat and my quarter, he takes some of our food, then I go back to Mother.

I left her at the back of the park, hidden behind bushes and under a tree, and now she's right at the front where she can see up and down the street. She's awake and hunched over, elbows on knees, head on hands. When she sees me she jumps up, as delighted as Bill was. It's clear she thought I'd gone off and left her, too.

Good. I hope she's been thinking about our life.

I think she's been crying. She takes a big shaky breath and asks, "Guillaume?"

I give her the food I scrounged. She eats as if she's hungry. There's not much left after she gets through. I don't know how she stays so thin.

"So, Guillaume?"

"I want to go to school."

"You! What good would that do? Besides, I'm a better teacher than any teacher you could ever have."

She always says she taught tenth-grade French until she got married, but I wonder if there wasn't another reason why she . . . She *says* she quit.

"But Guillaume?"

"I mean it. I need to go."

I know better than to say that this is a nice town. I already know she would think it's a terrible place for Bill. I can just hear her: *This town?* This little nowhere town? I suppose you want a cottage with a picket fence in the front and a peach tree in the backyard and Guillaume fraternizing with ordinary small-town people.

That's *exactly* what I want. But I'd settle for less—a lot less, in fact—just as long as it was different from this life we have.

"Isn't there a law that we have to go to school?"

"But did you find him?"

She's counting too much on me. She always does. I say, "No."

She's about to get upset again. I can see her eyes go wild. Would she attack me?

I say, "Wait a minute. Wait a minute. I can find him. I have an idea."

"What?"

But I won't tell her. "Why should he come back? When I find him I have to give him a good reason."

"All right, tell him I'll spend tomorrow looking for a place to live."

Can it really be this easy?

We camp at the edge of town just beyond a regular camping spot that charges fifty cents. We sneak in and use the bathrooms. In the morning we have coffee at a little café where they have a couple of local newspapers lying around for the patrons. We steal one and take it back to the park. I tell her to look up not only the ads for places to live but the ads for jobs, too—for both of us. I say I'll be back by four.

I wander around the town again. I check out one of those little houses that looks vacant. I look in the windows and there's no furniture in there. Maybe we won't have to pay for a place, until we all get jobs, that is. I memorize the address: 45 Overridge Lane.

At three o'clock I go sit on the school steps and wait.

Sometimes Guillaume . . . I mean Bill, seems so old—old and a little kid at the same time. It's that quiet questioning stare. I can see in his eyes all that yearning for a different life.

Mother always tells him he's better than everybody else, but he's a democratic kind of kid. He wants to be like the other boys. No better and no worse.

I sit with one of our apples.

Finally he comes out, again with the teacher. This time he has a book and a tablet. I've never, ever seen him this happy. As soon as the teacher turns away, he can't help skipping. He's turning off in the direction of "my" little house. I follow. I shout, "Bill, Bill," and this time he remembers that's him.

But Mother has followed me. (All day long? all around town? to the library? to the little art gallery? and maybe to 45

Overridge Lane?) Just when Bill turns, grins up at me ("I'm in!" he says, and gives a little jump for joy), she steps out from behind the bushes next to the school and grabs him.

She's all packed up and ready for the trail. She throws his book and the tablet into the gutter and off we go again, heading south. He doesn't protest. He turns into a kind of floppy rag and lets himself be dragged along.

I rescue the book and tablet. I lag behind. I never want Bill to see me crying.

Most of the time Mother holds Bill's arm, though now and then, in narrow spots, she has to let go. Once when he's free he punches a tree trunk and bloodies his knuckles. Mother wants to put Band-Aids on his scrapes, but he won't let her. He won't look at her either. I've never seen him like this.

It starts to rain. Right away we find one of those lean-tos, but Mother won't stop there. She wants to get farther from that town. She says she doesn't ever want to see it again or hear about it.

I'm not going to let this just lie there. The look on Bill's face there on the school steps!

We go on much later than we usually would. We have to pitch the tent by flashlight.

First thing we're settled in, Bill takes his bug book, tears out the pages and throws them out into the rain. We huddle down, cold and wet and miserable . . . except for Mother.

I wake up in the middle of the night. The rain has stopped and the moon is out. There's light coming through the mosquito net doorway. I see something glinting. I sit up fast. I'm not sure. I guess. I turn on the flashlight and there's Bill with his jackknife open. Right away I think, *Not the prince!* I can't believe I think "the prince" when neither of us wants him to be a prince.

We stare at each other.

I whisper, "*I'll* find a way. *I'll* figure it out. Let me."

But he snatches the flashlight from my hand and crawls out of the tent.

I'm not sorry. In fact, I feel a lot better that he's out of here. I don't fall back to sleep right away. I'm worried but reassured. He won't be punching any more trees if he's heading back toward what he loves.

I wake to wails.

Of course I do.

I knew I would.

> *The king's horse is the color of sweet cream, while his saddle is as if of butter.*
>
> *A king must have a shield, but, and more important, he must have a sword.*

So back we go.

Mother can't stop talking. That often happens. It doesn't help to say something because she can't hear anybody but herself. We're out of food by now. I don't know what she thought we'd do along the trail, but it wouldn't be the first time we'd have to trap quail and catch fish. But now she doesn't stop to eat. I wonder how we'll get food, because there's only that one grocery store. You can't keep going back to the same place every day without getting noticed. And probably Bill will have already gone there a second time.

We don't get back to town till evening.

Bill won't dare head for the school. I wonder what he'll do.

Was he going to kill her? If he was, I need to do it instead, but I don't want to. I wonder if I could. She's very strong. If she has to, she can carry all our stuff by herself.

Or maybe he was going to turn the knife on himself—to show her how desperate he is. Where would a desperate almost-ten-year-old go?

Will people help him because he's so beautiful and sits so straight?

I wonder if somebody will ever think that I'm royalty, too.

"Beauty without vanity. Strength without insolence," as every king should be.

I set Mother up in the very back of the park beyond the duck pond—back where the town starts being pasture. There the houses are little more than tool sheds. Some really are tool sheds. At first I thought they all were, but some look lived in. I wonder if one of those would do for us.

I make it clear . . . I hope I do . . . that I'm the one who has to find him, that I'm her only chance to get him back. "He'll go off into the woods and be a hermit. He knows how. Or he'll end up in some other town you'll never find. You'll lose him for good. Why not let him at least go to school? You can teach him, too—all the royal things he needs to know. We'll settle down . . . just for a while, get jobs, save our money, and go to France when he's a little older."

"Even over there nobody will know."

"They'll know. Maybe just one look is all they need. They'll guess right away."

Hard to believe, but she actually believes me.

The king's forehead is pale as oysters. The dew of his tears is fresh and cool.

Embroidered fleurs-de-lys in tiny stitches are on his handkerchiefs. Of which he has dozens.

All his pomp, all his circumstance, follows him wherever he goes.

I find him in an unexpected place. The senior center.

It's all by itself in a grove of trees. I see the grocery-store truck pull up. I see the man—the very same man who gave us food before—carry out bags of bread and still-good vegetables.

I go in behind him, thinking maybe I can get us some more food. There are a lot of old people in there working hard. They're setting up the tables for the people who are going to have lunch there. The volunteers look to be just as old as the people they're going to serve. (In fact, that grocery-store man looks to be one of the oldest.)

And who should be helping set the tables but Bill. Somebody has bandaged his hand for him, but he can manage.

He sees me, but he doesn't stop working till the tables are all ready.

I sit and wait.

He comes and sits beside me, says, "I'm getting paid in lunch."

A couple of old ladies invite me to eat, too. As we eat, I notice my fingernails are black and nobody else's are.

We have a very nice lunch. In fact, it's better than any meal I can remember in a long time. There's a salad and a baked potato with cheese on top and slices of beef and rolls with butter and gelatin with fruit in it. I can't believe all this food.

And there's nobody who isn't nice. Even the addled ones who don't make much sense are nice. They seem to like having kids around. They give us their desserts until we can't eat anymore. I let Bill do all the talking. He's good at avoiding hard questions. "We're on the trail just passing through. We're on the way back to my school. I'm in the fourth grade. I got held back a year." (How does he think up all this stuff?) "We got delayed but we'll be there soon. My school starts late, anyway. We're with our father."

Father!

After, we help clean up and then we go outside and sit on a bench not far from old people on other benches. We whisper.

"If I can get Mother to stop in this town, will you come back to her?"

"She won't."

"Were you going to hurt her or were you going to cut yourself?"

"I don't have to tell you."

"Mother will go crazy."

"She's already not like any other mother."

When has he ever known about any other mothers?

"I've got a house you can hide in."

I *think* I do. Just because Mother saw me—or probably did—looking in the windows at 45 Overridge Lane, doesn't mean she'll find him at some other empty house. There was another one not so far away.

The king's portrait hangs in the grand hall. The eyes follow you as you walk from one place in the room to another.

This time, as we go, we keep looking around to make sure Mother isn't following. We double back. We hide behind bushes and wait. It takes half an hour. Then I take him to the last house on Farm House Road. We don't have any trouble breaking in a back window. Not much more than a *"p'tit coup de pouce"* as Mother would say. He already has our best flashlight. I don't have to tell him not to use it much and to keep it away from the windows. We're used to hiding. He sneaked a couple of buns from lunch so he won't get hungry. And there is a fruit tree in the backyard (though not a peach). There are apples on it and apples lying under it, rotting. A sure sign that even the neighbors or the neighbor kids don't bother to come around. We gather a few of the best ones. I take a couple to bring back to Mother. Of course, they're wormy, but that's another thing we're used to. We always love abandoned orchards.

It's a little house with a kitchen/living room all in one and two small bedrooms. Perfect for us, though Mother won't think so. She'll say, "Better no place at all than this." There is a little furniture: a surprisingly clean mattress, a stool, some old newspapers. Somebody else has been camping in here. I hope not recently. I warn Bill to escape out the window if somebody comes.

Nothing works—no water, no electricity. Somebody has made a fire on *top* of the stove. There's a lot of ashes there. It's a mess.

Last thing *I* tell him: "Remember, *petit à petit . . .*"

Last thing *he* tells me: "I don't want to hear any more French."

So then I go back to Mother.

If there's a line of people waiting, the king goes first. You say, "Après vous" *to the king.*

A king has a good chance at becoming a constellation not unlike Orion.

He must never blow his nose in public.

She's not there. I get worried again. I don't know what to do. I sit and watch the ducks. I imagine Mother following us even though we tried so hard to lose her. I imagine her, right this very minute, grabbing Bill in her iron grip and dragging him away—on purpose without me.

I get up. I'm about to go back and see if Bill is all right when here she comes—out from one of the little tool-shed houses.

"Viens," she says. "I found us the greatest place for the night. Guillaume will like it."

She takes me to one of the sheds. She's put herself exactly where I wanted her to be.

It's a one-car-garage-sized shed. Obviously deserted. It has one tiny, dirty window at the back. The whole place is dirty and full of spiderwebs. There are shelves, empty except for old paint cans. Mouse turds on the floor. I'd rather be in our tent, but if she likes it . . .

She's laid out our three sleeping pads, Bill's in the middle. She'd rather wait in a place like this until she finds us a palace. I wonder how long she's expecting to live in it.

She sits down on her pad, cross-legged, all knees and elbows. I wonder when she last combed her hair. Her fingernails are as dirty as mine.

"So where's Guillaume?"

She's so pleased with herself for finding this place, she doesn't sound upset anymore. She thinks everything is fine.

"He'll come back when we've settled down. When we have jobs."

"He'd better not try to go back to that school. They just teach nonsense."

"I'm afraid he'll hurt himself if he doesn't get to go."

"Why would anybody hurt themselves? Besides, they don't teach the things he needs to know. They won't even teach decent French."

"You can do that. You taught me. Think of it. We'll earn money and then we'll go there. To France."

"I'll bet they don't even teach good biology."

"It's grade school, for heaven's sake."

But then it starts. I sit down on my pad and get ready

to look as if I'm listening. I try to glance at her watch as she waves her arms around. I figure it'll take about twenty minutes before she'll stop bad-mouthing schools.

I wonder if we'll ever be able to trust her to stay in one place. She might get all settled down and Bill will come back and everything will seem rosy and off she might go, dragging us along.

This town is too small to hide them from each other for long. And Bill will go to school even if he has to sneak in and out the back door. Maybe it'll work.

But what about me? Will I ever get to go? And can I get a job? Would I look more grown-up if I wore lipstick? I'd have to steal some.

She's often embarrassed after one of these talking sessions. Finally she sits down and says, "You must be tired." That means she is. She gives me cheese from two days ago. It's her way of apologizing without saying so. I give her a wormy apple.

She says, "Where's our big flashlight?"

"Bill has it."

When I call him that, she gets up again and turns away, but she's too tired to go into another tirade.

The king's cloak is edged with ermine.

No hat must be taller than the king's. No white jacket more white. No buttons more shiny.

Bill and I meet the next day behind the Senior Center, not inside it, and not that near.

He spent the night nowhere near that mattress. He slept in the other, smaller bedroom. Somebody came in, in the middle of the night, rattled around a lot too. Next morning somebody made a fire of sticks on *top* of the stove and cooked eggs and bacon. Left the fire of sticks (smothered with a metal pan lid). Bill found the matches and the bacon, but not the pan. He lit the fire again and cooked some of the bacon wrapped around a green stick. Trouble was the fat made the fire bigger than he wanted.

"They mustn't see smoke."

"I *know,* but *he* got away with it. Besides, there's trees all around."

I ask Bill did he smell any liquor, and he says no.

He watched the person out the bedroom window as he left. He says, he's a thinnish man, nice and neat in a dark suit and tie, carrying a briefcase and wearing a hat. The dressy kind.

"For heaven's sake, are you sure?"

"Of course. I know what I saw."

"You can't stay there."

"I like it. I'll have an address."

"So does *he.* We have to find a different place."

"This one is practically right on the trail. There was a jackrabbit in the backyard this morning. And quail. I saw a coachwhip snake. It's pretty far north for them and kind of cold. They're usually way far south of here."

"He could be dangerous. Sometimes men prey on good-looking boys like you. You know that."

"If anything bad happens, I'll go out the window."

"You trust people too much. Actually, Mother does, too.

Or she trusts that people will give her what she needs. I hope you know better than that."

He shrugs and makes a face as if to say: *Why are you telling me what I already know?*

"Well, don't. I mean, trust."

We're close. We have to be. We only have each other. Usually he listens to me, but I've lost him this time.

"You don't have to sit up straight just because Mother says to."

"I *know.*"

He's sitting like a gentleman and keeps on doing it.

"So you didn't go to school today?"

"Mmmm."

"So that teacher helps you?"

"I *trust* her."

"That's okay."

"I *know.*"

"How did you sleep without a pad?"

"'K."

"Bet you didn't."

"Did too."

"I could get your pad for you, except . . . Mother will be furious."

"I *know.*"

"But I'll do it anyway."

"'K."

"Meet you back here in half an hour. Did you have anything to eat besides that bacon?"

He shrugs, and I know he didn't.

"I'll see what I can find."

⊠ ⊠ ⊠

But he's the one who finds food for me. Wrapped-up egg salad sandwiches. He won't tell me how he got them. I'll bet he stole them. Though maybe not. He's good at finding odd jobs and getting people to give him food. Maybe it's that natural majesty of his, though I hate myself when I fall into Mother's way of thinking. The royal smile. Ugh. Yet there it is. As if bestowed on us underlings. Though maybe a little bit too shy for royalty.

I give him his sleeping pad. Mother wasn't there, so I didn't have to deal with her. I hope she was out looking for a job.

Bill hugs me when we say goodnight. A sure sign he's lonely and worried. That worries me, too, but I don't want him coming back to us. We'd be on the trail in no time and who knows how many trees he'd punch next time or who he'd cut.

The five trombones of the king play fanfares.
The spotlight will shine on him alone: his velvet lips, the ivory of his collarbone.

I find Mother washing clothes in the duck pond. It's good she's found a sheltered spot to do it in. I don't think the townspeople would like that.

First thing she says: "Isn't this a great place? It has everything. Even water. Guillaume will like it. Except you took his sleeping pad."

"You want him to be comfortable don't you?"

"I'd rather he'd be comfortable, here with us."

"Did you find a job? When you're settled in for a while, I know of an even better place for us to stay."

I'll take her to that Overridge Lane place that I think she followed me to. There won't be . . . at least, I don't think there'll be . . . somebody else living there. Of course there won't be any water, and maybe there'll be just as many mouse turds as here.

I help Mother bring the clothes back and hang them up on a frayed piece of rope above our sleeping pads.

"So did you get a job?"

"Maybe."

But that's all she'll say. She does have food. Packages of sliced chicken and sliced cheese. A huge bag of lettuce. I don't know if she bought them or stole them.

"If you need an address, use this one. I'm hoping to get us all there. It'll be better for getting a job."

"This is a good enough address. I like it here. You've been seeing Guillaume."

"Leave him alone."

She starts turning red. Looks at me with that wild-eyed look. She's never hit me but she often looks as if she will.

"No, no, just for a little while. He'll be back with us soon as we settle in."

The king's fencing lessons. His music lessons. His several languages, deportment classes, geography. . . .

Bill got discovered. By that man in the house. All because of a stray dog. How could he? One more mouth to feed. One more thing to keep secret besides himself. Only he didn't. I suppose he wanted . . . needed . . . company. He's never been alone before. But it sounds like it came out all right. At least so far.

Bill and I weren't going to meet until four o'clock. I got myself a job right away. Five to seven, three weekdays and helping out on Saturdays and Sundays if I want to. An after-school kind of job. They said I had to be sixteen, and I said I was and got away with it even though I don't have breasts. It's in the arts-and-crafts gallery, doing everything: cleaning, keeping records, hanging pictures for when the shows change, putting up posters, running for coffee. . . .

I went first to the place where I'd like to work best of all and I got the job. (Second was going to be the library.) They're going to let me sit in on their evening classes for nothing. They have everything, from knitting to Tai Chi to painting. I wonder if they'd let Mother teach French there. I wonder if she would. Except I'm not sure I want anybody here to get to know Mother.

So then I pretend I have to go off to school. I wander around town, kind of looking for a job for Mother and trying to watch out for where she is.

At four I go meet Bill (he already went back and got the dog so I could meet him) and he tells me about getting discovered. He actually sounds happy about it. I guess I don't because he says, "Hey, don't you get all crazy, too. If you want to meet him and talk to him, his office is upstairs over the barbershop. He made me a big breakfast. He fed my dog, too. Matt . . . Mathew. Not the dog. I named the dog Spider."

It's a funny little dog. Kind of looks like his name. Skinny, mostly white—dirty white—with black and brown spots. Bill is dirtier than ever, too. I suppose from sleeping with the dog. I should have brought him the T-shirt Mother washed.

"Did you go to school looking like this? What did you do with the dog?"

"The man . . . Matt . . . said it was okay to leave him in the house. Matt has a big jar of water and left some for the dog. I guess I should have washed but I didn't want to ask Matt for some more. He doesn't have much. I told him we were hiking with our father."

Father again.

Suddenly I start to cry. For no reason. Everything is working out fine. I don't ever let Bill see me crying. I think somebody in his life should at least *seem* competent. It scares him. He turns away and starts to pet the dog, but the dog comes over to me and licks my arm. I guess it is kind of nice to have a dog.

I say, "Sorry, I must be tired."

"'K."

I was afraid one of these days I'd start to cry and never stop, but I do stop. It only takes a few minutes.

"What's Matt's last name?"

"I forget. It's hard."

"I'll bring you some clean clothes. Don't come down to the pond to wash. Mother might be there. Wash at school next time. Did you eat?"

He says yes, but I give him some of Mother's cheese and chicken anyway.

He says, "Tomorrow we could meet earlier, maybe back on the trail behind the house."

"Aren't you going to school?"

"You silly, it's Saturday."

I forgot there would be Saturday and Sunday. I forgot it even though I have a Saturday and Sunday job.

"Tell you what, meet me where I work, but try to get cleaned up first. They might even let you do some work, too."

Then I go to find the man. If he was nice to Bill he may really be a good person, but I want to check.

Upstairs over the barbershop, it's full of offices. Like at the school, you can look in the little windows in the doors and see who's there.

There's only one man who looks like the right one: thin, dark suit, glasses, long nose. . . . It says KARPINSKY on the door. He's younger than I thought he'd be. Even though he's balding.

I watch him at his computer for a couple of minutes, but then he looks up and sees me staring at him. He looks right into my eyes. Right inside me. Suddenly I don't know what to do. I wouldn't know what to say. I run down the stairs and then all the way down the block. Two blocks. I wasn't ready. Besides, I don't want to lie about our father being with us. I wish Bill wouldn't keep saying that.

Crown the king a lover of honey and of bees.
He owns all the swans.
His trees will bear golden pears and silver nutmegs.

When I come back, Mother has built a campfire behind the shed and . . . my God . . . she's cooking a duck. Right out in the open. The head and the feathers are in a pile just inside the shed door.

"Mother! This has got to be against the law."

"Pooh. This is for Guillaume."

It smells so good I hope she gets away with it.

"He's not even here."

"Well, then, you'll take some to him."

"Mother!"

I squat down beside her. "Did you at least look for a job? The grocery store would be a good place to work. You could get food for less or maybe nothing."

"I don't do that kind of work."

There's no use talking. It would just be the same conversation over again.

We have a good supper. She also roasted potatoes in the coals.

She wraps up the leftovers in a plastic bag and hangs them over the edge of the pond to keep cool.

> *A king should walk as if he balanced books on his head, and the books he balances should be law books.*

Saturday, just as I figured, Bill and I both get to work at the gallery. They don't even mind having the dog there. One good thing, though—they sent Bill to the back alley and had him give the dog a bath. And Matt Karpinsky has given Bill another nice breakfast. Bill says, "Pancakes. Because it's Saturday.

Matt asked a lot of questions about you."

"What did you tell him?"

"That you're really a princess and really a dummy. That you forgot there was such a thing as Saturday."

I give him a fake punch. Actually a little harder than I meant it, and he gives me one back just like it.

"Did he say why he's camping out in that house?"

"Same as me. To have a nice place to be."

"I hope you didn't tell him a long story about your father."

He shrugs. Should a prince shrug so much?

He has homework. He says he's even doing stuff for extra credit. How nice to see him sitting in the back office of the gallery doing his schoolwork, his leg twisted around the chair leg, and the dog at his feet. I bring him a glass of cider and he smiles up at me. I think, what long eyelashes, and how like a prince he looks, even with that bad haircut, even with his torn and too-small jeans. Maybe things really will work out.

> *Among the several languages a king must know are Greek and Latin. He should also be trained in dialectic, Aristotelian logic, and aesthetics.*

. . . and they do. For a while.

And even though Mother keeps killing ducks. Each time she does, she invites Bill for dinner. I say he won't come, but she says, Ask him anyway.

"Will you call him Bill?"

But she won't. She never will.

I don't know what Mother is doing during the day. I know

she's seldom at the shed. I keep imagining ridiculous things, like that she's busy making handcuffs and chains for Bill.

Actually, I don't think anybody will give Mother a job looking like this. Lately she's messier than ever. Not having Bill around upsets her. If she tried to comb her hair I'll bet the comb would get stuck, or even lost forever. I'd cut it for her, but I don't dare suggest it. I wonder if she's doing it on purpose so as not to get hired.

There's a secondhand store here, and I get Bill a pair of jeans for fifty cents. Unlike other boys might, he doesn't mind that they're much too big. I get him a red T-shirt with black ants crawling all over the front. It's hardly worn at all. I knew he'd like it.

Since we're not heading south, we'll need some blankets pretty soon. Our sleeping bags won't be enough. It sometimes gets pretty cold in these hills.

I'm still not going to school. I'm worried that if I try to go, it might get Bill kicked out. It's one thing for a ten-year-old to suddenly appear in school and another for somebody my age. Besides, that teacher is doing something not every teacher would. I'm sure she's breaking rules. I don't want to get her in trouble, too.

These days I sleep late, wander around, gather firewood for Mother, gather bugs for Bill, study at the library, then go to work at five and take classes at the gallery in the evening. I get the cheese and crackers and wine and cider for the openings of the art shows and programs. I eat a lot of that myself. I'm having fun . . . sort of . . . but I wish I was going to school.

Bill is the only one getting everything he wants. He meets me at the gallery, does a little work, and then does his homework. He's also found the bug books in the library. Matt makes him breakfast every morning, and he gets lunch at school. I'm sure the lunch is because of that teacher.

The offices over the barber shop are practically across the street from the gallery. I see Matt lots of times. When I do, I go around the corner fast or hurry into a shop. I don't know what Bill has been telling him—especially about having a father. I wouldn't know what to say. Besides, there's that time he looked right inside me.

And it's as if I want somebody to take care of us (instead of me) and I've picked him to be the one. He's a little young for that. Looks to be—even though his forehead is almost all the way up to the top of his head—hardly even thirty.

But one afternoon he comes to the gallery when I'm doing the photography class . . . without a camera, of course. (I'll take any class that's handy.)

He insists on taking me out to the backyard of the gallery for a talk.

First thing he says: "You're avoiding me, aren't you."

I'm completely tongue-tied. How can I say anything when I've no idea what Bill has been saying? Except that it's all lies.

"Where's this father of yours? Really? Why isn't he looking after you?"

I'm staring right into the eyes of the man I want to turn everything over to—our whole lives—and I don't even know him. My heart is beating so hard I wonder if I'm going to faint. I feel myself blushing because of my crazy thoughts.

And here he is, showing concern. That scares me even more. I have to sit down.

But he sees that. He takes my arm and pulls me down to the big stones that are supposed to keep cars from coming through the alleyway behind the gallery. He makes me sit on one.

"Should I get you some water?"

"We don't have a father."

But we hear fire engines and police cars rushing past just beyond the alley—heading toward the school. We stare up at each other. I say, "It's Mother."

Then I say, "Or it's Bill."

He grabs my hand and we follow the sirens.

The king is always the center of attention, therefore he should never yawn or scratch his ear in public.

It *is* Bill—and Mother, too. I had a feeling she couldn't put up with settling down, and who would give such a person a job anyway? And then there were all these days she had to try and get along without Bill.

There's a three-story building across the street from the school and there's my brother, walking up to the peak of the slanted roof, fearless as he always is. Is that like a prince or more like a roofer? On the sidewalk below him, Mother is yelling, but it's hard to make out what the words are. Her knapsack is lying beyond her, all packed up and ready to go. Mine isn't there this time. It looks like she came to the school to pick him up and leave without me. Half the students are outside watching, and the other half are watching out the classroom windows. Firemen are setting up their ladder to go and get Bill. Cops are milling around and keeping the kids out of the way but mostly joking. Everybody seems to be having a good time except Mother.

She looks crazier than ever. Her clothes look slept in, but that's no surprise. Except she used to try to look neat. Not lately, though. Bill's dog is barking and snarling up at her until she kicks him away. He squeals and trots over to Matt and me. Two cops are trying to keep Mother from climbing up the side of the building, which she can't do, anyway. They're yelling, too: "Calm down! Calm down!"

She does—sort of. Enough so you can understand what she's saying. "My son. Guillaume. I want him back. He's not like other children. He has to be with me."

Usually she doesn't get into one of her talking jags in front of strangers, but now she does.

"He's special. He's different. This school is just an ordinary school. *Ordinary!* For *ordinary* people." She looks straight at one of the cops. "Like you," she says.

The cops are good at this. They know better than to contradict her. "Okay, okay. We know. We'll get him back."

She seems a little calmer so they let go of her, but she lunges at them and scratches their faces and then tries to climb up the brick wall of the house again.

Finally they bring Bill down. He keeps saying, "I won't not go to school."

"It's the law, son. You'll get to go."

I guess it's a good thing Mother won't stop fighting the cops. That makes it so they haul her off before she can cause any more problems. She yells the whole time and uses bad language, too. She's never done that before that I know of. She's always into keeping her dignity in front of other people no matter what—that "noblesse oblige" she always talks about. It's always, "*Gens comme nous* . . . We"—emphasis on the *We*—"don't say things like that."

Bill looks even more horrified than I feel.

Is this all my fault? Should I have done something?

They put her in a police car and off she goes, talking, talking, talking—not even a backward glance at Bill.

If Mother gets put away somewhere, I guess we'll, more or less, be orphans. How will that be?

Then I and Bill and Matt and the dog—we all go down to the police station. Even Bill's teacher comes with us. She saw the whole thing.

Turns out Mother went to the school yelling—*screaming,* that is—down the school halls. Bill heard her coming all the way from the front door. She punched anybody who tried to stop her, she dragged Bill out of class, but once they were outside, he got away and climbed straight up the side of that building. I'm proud of him. I can't help it.

Though he may be shorter, the king must seem taller than all other men.

Turns out Mother's going to be locked up next town over. It's bigger and has a place for people like her. She's already on her way there.

Good this is a small town. People look out for each other.

Matt's to be our temporary guardian, even though he's only twenty-eight. The Senior Center people contributed money so Matt won't have to. Bill's teacher's in it, too, and the people at the gallery. It's as if the whole town is our friend.

Turns out Matt actually owns that house—as of four months ago. His fiancée left him, so he never bothered to really move in. He was feeling bad until Bill came. We're going to stay with him.

He's had the water and electricity turned on. So far he's bought a lawn mower for Bill (Bill can't wait to be just a regular boy and have to mow the lawn and take out the garbage) and seeds and a trowel for me.

Where they put Mother is her castle—finally. The asylum is in an old Victorian mansion with a tower, a lot of black ironwork all over it. Even the fence is beautiful filigree. Looks more like decoration than to keep people in. They say she calmed down the minute she went through the gates. She likes it there: "Her" beautiful garden; "her" servants; from her third-floor bedroom, "her" beautiful view of the mountains. . . .

Turns out Mother had been spending all her time in the woods working on a ring, not looking for a job. She was making it out of a silver coin. She stole the stone for it from the Indian store in the museum. A shiny piece of worthless fool's gold. They were selling chunks for a quarter. She never steals valuable things, though she might have since it was for Bill. She shows it to me when I visit her.

She often said, "If I just had something . . . just one thing that Guillaume could wear to show who he is."

I say, "But, Mother, he won't wear a ring. Besides, fool's gold just makes it all a joke."

"He'll wear it when he gets older."

And she's right, he will.

Where he gathers roses, lesser men will gather lesser roses after he's gone.

Nightingales will sing for the king alone.

All the roe deer belong to the king.

The most exquisite hours of the morning are when the king awakes.

Carol Emshwiller grew up in Ann Arbor, Michigan, and France. She has written six novels and five short story collections, and has won two Nebula Awards and two World Fantasy Awards, as well as a World Fantasy Life Achievement Award.

She went through music school and then art school. It wasn't until she was thirty that she fell in love with writing.

Her two most recent books are the novel *The Secret City* and the short story collection *I Live with You*. She divides her time between New York City and the California desert.

Her Web site is **www.sfwa.org/members/emshwiller**.

Author's Note

"The Dignity He's Due" started with a memory from long ago when I was about eight years old. When I was in France, my parents went to a party where there was a boy who was umpteenth . . . I don't know how far away . . . in line for the French throne. (Of course there was no French throne anymore, anyway.) He was two or three years older than I was. He wore Mary Jane shoes, the shortest black velvet shorts I ever saw, and a lacy silk blouse. His hair was cut like a girl's, too. When he arrived he circled the guests, kissing all the women's hands and bowing to the men. All us children were supposed to be across the hall in the playroom, but I was so fascinated with this boy that I spent most of the time standing in the doorway watching him. He never came into the playroom; he stayed and talked with the grown-ups. All the rest of my life, I have been fascinated by the memory of this boy. That was how the story started, though it wandered far away from the idea.

Marly Youmans

Power and Magic

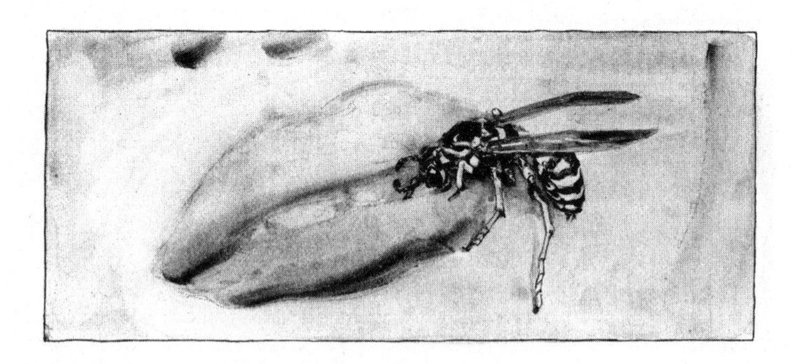

My neighbors had broken twigs from a low-hanging branch and were dusting their cheeks with the pink-and-gold flowers of the mimosa. A sheen of oil lay on their faces and legs, and on everything else—a humid dew that was nasty and didn't cool.

"What are you doing, stupid little girls?"

I was slung between the two boles, with nothing stirring in me—just hot and lazy in the summer sun.

They didn't listen, so I shouted, "I'm talking to you!"

"Who's stupid?" Clarisse looked around for somebody else.

"She's so stupid," Maudie drawled, cocking her hip and slipping a flower behind an ear.

"You little old girls," I said, "y'all bore me."

"We're not talking to you." Clarisse flounced away, a half-decapitated doll under her arm.

"Go right ahead," I told the pair of them. I thought about going inside and sitting on my grandmother's fan stool in the shack. It's an old army-green metal thing made out of mesh with a fan inside. Next year's math book was sitting on top, waiting for me to breeze through the final chapter. But I was too weary to move.

"What's wrong with you?"

Maudie had stuck mimosa blossoms along her hairline. It's amazing how some people can make nature look so tacky. They have a kind of gift for it.

My hand dangled down from the mimosa bough, and she came up and tickled my fingers with a flower.

"Stop that." I didn't reel my hand back in but left it hanging.

"So what's the matter, anyway?" She held her ground and didn't walk off when I hissed.

I stared at her, resenting the gold-tipped puffs of the pink mimosa flowers and the flat chest and the skinny legs with knees like saucers.

"There's something wrong with my arms, my spine, my brain, my everything." I marveled at the viciousness in my voice. "They took out all my blood and pumped in honey and molasses. That's why I can't move. My heart can hardly pump all that molasses and honey." The moment I said the words, I felt it was the truth. It explained the heavy feeling that weighed me down and kept me from going inside, where my gran was expecting me to mop the linoleum. It was too blazing hot to mop anybody's floor; she ought to have known that.

"You're up in a tree," she pointed out. "How'd you get there, then?"

"That's different." I sighed. I felt as lazy as a catamount, lolling on a bough with a belly too full to care about bunching up its muscles and racing to drag down a wild boar. Wild Russian boars are all over in this part of the mountains. Over at the boat shop, they've got one for a pet that goes *ticktickticK* with its nails all day long. The owner says that the cement floor is hurting Ivan's little pig hooves, and that they'll have to keep him at home before long.

I'm sorry because this whole place is boring—yeah, it's a dumb joke—and about the only thing I like to do is walk down to the corner and stare at the pet boar and scratch him on top of his head.

"You know Ivan the Terrible? Down at the boat shop? He's twice as smart as you, Maudie."

"Don't listen to her." Clarisse had put on a pair of her mother's high heels and was stumping about the yard.

"Oh, yeah? And Ivan, he's—*she's* three times as smart as Clarisse. You hear me, Clarisse? Three times as smart." I think it's funny that Ivan the Terrible is a girl. Maybe not a lot funny, but a little bit. Enough to keep me going down there to scratch his head. Her head. Somebody's.

"PMS," Clarisse told her sister. "That's what it is."

"What's that?"

Clarisse didn't know. I thought that was funny. It was so funny that I fell out of the tree laughing. It was funnier than Ivan the Terrible. But it hurts to flop four feet onto hard-packed ground, so I yelled, sprawled out and feeling sorry for myself, though I still wanted to laugh.

"What if you breaked all your bones? Who's stupid now?"

Clarisse marched over in her mama's emerald-green

shoes, gouging the dirt with stiletto heels. They came to a point at the toe and were embroidered with gaudy little stuck-up flowers made out of ribbons.

The English language just about buckled under the strain of those shoes. I thought. I mulled. I drew together the considerable resources of my eyebrows and started knitting. It would take a ten-dollar word to cover those babies.

"*Phenomenally* ugly," I said at last.

"What?" Maud came to look.

"Your mother's shoes," I said, propping myself on an elbow and addressing them. "Shoes, you are the ugliest, stupidest shoes I have ever seen in my life. You are a disgrace to cobblers everywhere."

The shoes didn't answer, even though they were the loudest damn things I'd ever seen. But the girls and I wrangled back and forth about whether these were the ugliest shoes or whether they might be somehow special and even a dratted work of the shoemaker's art. I won, of course; they're just kids of eight and nine, and besides, I'm dead smart. Afterward, I suggested that Maudie stick a mimosa blossom on the toes of the shoes. She did, but the flowers wouldn't stay on.

"You're just growing. That's why you're such a slug. That's what our mama says." Clarisse lifted her chin as though she had ambitions to be snooty, even though she's nothing but trailer trash.

"Oh, she does, does she? I'll have to have a word with your mama. This just happens when you grow. If you ever grow—which I doubt, because you're probably doomed to be a midget forever—you'll find out. Your blood turns to honey." I rolled onto my back and stared at the branches.

"I thought you said somebody took out the blood and pumped in honey and molasses," Maudie said suspiciously.

You can't fool her.

"Yeah, well," I said, "that, too. It was bad enough before they started in with the needles and pump."

In the silence that followed, we could hear the cicadas throwing their rackety summer shindig in the pines behind the yard.

"I've got a mind to call the sheriff and get him to lock up those cicadas."

Before I could hear what Maudie had to say to that one, I let out a yowl and erupted onto my feet.

"She got up," Clarisse noted.

"Fire ants," Maudie said with authority, watching me rip open my shirt.

By the time I was done tap-dancing around the yard, shaking down ants, I had five big welts already starting to itch.

"I hate this place." I buttoned up and then bent to inspect my legs for ticks.

"Want to go look at the crickets at the bait shop?" Maudie put her hands on her hips. "Take your mind off things."

"What things? You sound like your mama," I said.

"We can't go down there alone," Clarisse said, "but we can go with you, if you want to go." She gave me a sly look.

"You could ask, if you really want to go." I felt thoroughly disgusted. My arm was bruised from the fall, I'd been bitten up, and I was still stinking hot.

"Will you take us?" She looked ridiculous in those shoes, with the broke-necked doll under her arm.

"You could ask in a polite fashion," I said. "If you know how."

"Will you please take us?"

"No."

After that came another silence. Clarisse looked as if she wanted to hurl the shoes at me, but she didn't.

"Can I give you some advice, Clarisse?"

She didn't answer.

"Don't have sex, okay?"

Maudie was outraged. "She's only just turned eight."

"Yeah, I know, but the way she acts . . . She's going nowhere fast."

"Says who?" Maudie kicked me in the shins, and I escaped into the crotch of the mimosa tree.

"Says me. Look at those shoes. Clarisse is going to get pregnant if she doesn't watch it. I bet she can't even add in three columns."

"What's that got to do with anything?" Maudie thumped on the tree.

"I am not going to get that—what you say," Clarisse shouted.

"She'll be thirty years old, banging on a cash register at the Piggly Wiggly, and giving everybody the wrong change," I said.

"I will not give everybody wrong change!"

Just when they were going at me and I was ranting in fine style, Erl Jack Falchion shot into the yard, throwing up gravel, and jumped out of his truck. He wasn't born Erl Jack Falchion, but that's his name now. People hardly remember what the other one was, and I'm not going to tell them. I've known Erl Jack since we were babies parked nose to nose on a bed. He got his name fixed when he was twelve. My gran says he paid for the change with his own money that he earned picking in the fields. His mother signed for it. He probably had to pay her for the signature, too.

Erl Jack is very fit and popular with the ladies, and so the little girls clustered around. Clarisse is like a bee around a pot when she sees a man, and Erl Jack is as close to a man as we have around here. Her mama's useless boyfriend sure doesn't count. Erl Jack's sixteen but works three jobs in the summer, and when school's on, he works two and makes good grades as well. When he waits tables, he's always telling people that he wants to better himself and go to college, even though he doesn't have a daddy and his mother's a crack addict in Miami. Sometimes he says that she was eaten by alligators, though that part's not true. It may be wish fulfillment because he's probably mad at her, deep down. He never says so. You'd be surprised at some of the tips he gets. I couldn't stand to tell all these strangers my business about how Deirdre—that's my mother—didn't want me, or about how I don't begin to know who my father is. Sometimes, listening to him go on, I feel sure that Erl Jack and I have way too much in common.

I was looking at Erl Jack out of the corner of my eye and taking a certain amount of pleasure in exactly how fit a boy with no shirt on and a chest positively corrugated with muscle can look. Since he had on suspenders, and long pants, I guessed he'd just finished a shift ripping boards at the lumber mill. It's a first-rate job for a teenager. Last spring he told Mr. Skellig at the mill that he wanted to better himself and so on and so on—and the old man gave him a job starting at twelve dollars an hour.

". . . do a little magic," he was saying to the girls.

Clarisse and Maudie squealed and jerked up and down with excitement, and the doll joggled.

"That baby head is going to fly off," I warned.

I knew what Erl Jack was up to.

"Show me some power and magic, and maybe I will," I'd said to him. It was just a way of turning him down, but he'd taken me seriously because Erl Jack is ever and always determined to get what he wants. But he'd have to do more than yank a rabbit out of his hat to impress me.

Off hours and Saturdays, he's Wizard Erl Jack Falchion. Around here, he's the prime man when it comes to birthday parties. If you're a middle-class kid, Erl Jack's for you.

That's why Maudie and Clarisse were so excited. They had a chance to see Erl Jack in action, and it wasn't even somebody's birthday.

"Here." He handed Clarisse a cardboard box and let Maudie carry a rusted hibachi. "That's all I need."

"Where do I put it?" That little rat Clarisse looked sheep-eyed at Erl Jack, who laughed.

"By the Chevy," he said, half squatting to be on her eye level.

"The Chevy," Maudie said, impressed. "We're not allowed to go up there without a grown-up."

I could see the crumbs of pine and splinters stuck to his arms and chest, making his tan look golden.

"You ought to wear a shirt-and-mail at the mill," I said, "or at least a shirt."

"It was a big mistake," he admitted.

Clarisse looked at me as though she'd forgotten I existed and was displeased to be reminded.

"She's in one of her moods," the brat confided to Erl Jack. When the head bobbled in agreement, he took the doll away from her and jammed the neck back into place.

"That thing gave me the willies," he said.

"Oh!" she said, and "thanks."

Clarisse looked mortified at being caught with a doll, as though Erl Jack might decide she wasn't old enough for him, and this made me laugh.

"You could pick out the pine mess," he said, coming up to me. "I was just too hot for a shirt."

"You'd like that," I said, "wouldn't you?"

I lay back on the lower branch of the tree and gazed up at the light twinkling between the fronds of tiny mimosa leaves and the puffs of the flowers. Really I love a mimosa in bloom, though my gran calls them "suckerwood" and wants to get rid of this one. They may be weed trees, but once a year they're delicate and frothy, before the blooms start to go orange with rot.

He leaned on the branch, staring at me, his long hair sliding forward and half obscuring his face. I looked at him without blinking as I considered.

"Ask Maudie and Clarisse," I said finally.

He shrugged and let them dust him off with a wadded-up shirt from the backseat. Afterward they tweaked off a few stray pieces, and he let down his suspenders and put on the shirt, wearing it loose and unbuttoned.

"You looked like three baboons," I said, "having a lice party."

"You're a baboon," Clarisse told me. She was barefoot on the grass, and I could see where the shoes had pinched her toes. "Baboon butt, that's what."

"Don't insult my woman," Erl Jack said, wriggling in the shirt. He finally tore the thing off and threw it on the ground, and after that he went over to the shack and rapped on the screen door. I could hear Gran sing out, "Erl Jack Falchion, where you been all my life?" My gran padded out on the porch in her slippers and gave him a hug, but she backed out of it mighty quick and fetched a tin tub and the garden hose.

"Don't you dare," I commanded the girls. I made them scramble up on my branch and sit facing the other way. We listened to the noises behind us for a good long time.

"Huh," Maudie said, keeping her eye on the hibachi and cardboard box. "I wonder what he's going to do with that little grill."

"Cook Clarisse-cutlets," I said.

Talk about baboons. My gran and Erl Jack were laughing their fool heads off, there on the porch. Gran loves Erl Jack Falchion.

"That boy is going to go somewhere," she declares, just about every time she sees him, and that's odd because she never went anywhere at all. She was born in a north Georgia shack, and I guess she'll die in one.

I have a lot of good responses to that line, but I don't use them with Gran because of two things. Gran wants me to go somewhere too, and I don't want to discourage her. She's about the only person who's behind me on this. Also, I don't sass Gran. Period.

Once I peeked over my shoulder and saw Erl Jack in the tub, with Gran sawing away at his shoulders with a big brush.

"You peeped," Clarisse said, and turned around. "Me and her saw you."

"Get back here, you," Maudie said, slapping her sister's hand.

"I did not look at Erl Jack Falchion," I said with dignity. "I merely ascertained whether Gran was still busy on the porch. I don't have all day." That was a lie. I did have all day, at least until five, when I had to be at Rick's Number One Bar and Café to wait on customers.

After considerable whooping, a big splash of water that meant the bath was done, and some banging of the screen door, Erl Jack strolled over to the mimosa tree, smelling like cheap Camay soap.

"Ladies," he said grandly, bowing from the waist, "come with me to see the show of your lives." He caught Maudie in midair and plunked her down by the grill. Clarisse he had to coax, so while he was fussing with her, I walked along the branch and jumped to the grass.

"I would have helped," he said, looking reproachful.

"Hah," I said.

"Gran thinks I'm wonderful. She thinks I'm good-looking and smart, well read and clever and a really good catch." He gave a big, big sigh. "Why don't you?"

"Because I'm not sixty-seven years old, maybe?"

"I'm hurt to the quick," he declared, one hand on his chest. It was red from the scrubbing, and in several places beads of blood had welled up.

"Some people don't need any more women saying they're the cat's pajamas." All the same, I couldn't help a glimmer of a smile slipping out. Erl Jack Falchion has more style and dash than anybody else in these parts.

He took that as license to grab my hand and then called to the girls to hoist their bundles and get going.

"We've got magic to catch, ladies!"

Erl Jack was fresh and sweet smelling, frisking along the path in a pair of my mother's jeans and an unbuttoned shirt, threadbare to transparency, that must have belonged to my grandpa.

"I'm afraid of the Chevy," Maudie confided.

"And right you are, my dear little chile," Erl Jack said airily. "It is a frightful thing, the bane of locals and the horror of tourists."

A lot of people had been trooping up in the woods to see the Chevy. For a dollar per head, I had hiked up there with a few groups. It was easy money.

"Just don't get too near," he went on.

In the woods, more and more cicadas were tuning up. They were probably shrilling against the heat and the oppressive windless air under the pines. If I were a cicada, that's exactly what I would've been doing. Maudie found a shucked husk of one hooked to pine bark and detached it carefully.

"Got a monster in your pocket," Erl Jack said to her.

He was lacing his clean, cool fingers with mine, and that made me feel oilier than ever. My shirt was damp, and I could smell the faint girl-stink of perspiration, though I knew he wouldn't mind—would like it, even.

"We're just friends," he was explaining to Clarisse. I could tell that she wanted to hold hands too. "I'd like to be more, but you know how stubborn she is. I keep telling her that we'll blast out of here together, but she's not so sure."

"She said my sister was bruising and cruising for a fall," Maudie said, nodding.

"Be pregnant by fourteen, I'd guess," I said. "Be working the bait-and-tackle shop before she knows it. Doesn't know how to write her own name in cursive."

"You won't do that, will you, Clarisse?" Erl Jack winked at her. "You show India that you're going to be a rocket scientist, okay?"

India's my name. I guess it's the sort of goofy name that a heroin addict gives a baby. I'm just lucky that Deirdre was locked up the year I was born, or I'd be as stupid as Clarisse. India. I kind of like it, but it makes absolutely no sense. My mother's never been anywhere, so why India? I haven't seen her to ask, not in six or seven years. Gran just clicks her tongue when my mother's name comes up.

"My sister did well in school," I said. "Look what happened to her." Vivienne has three kids and is married to a drunk. When he works, he roofs houses, and when he doesn't, he wallows on the couch and throws things.

"Keep away from boys, Maudie," I added.

"Boys are all right," Erl Jack said, "when they're the right ones."

"Maybe," I said, looking sidelong at his good-looking profile, "if it's the right time."

Tension, that's what I'm good at, the inflicting of tension. I didn't take my hand away, because I liked holding Erl Jack's hand. On the other hand—the one that wasn't holding on—I wasn't about to let him take me on as an official girlfriend. My sister the high school honor student is always perched on the top of my brain, next to a little flag that waves at me cheerfully and squeaks, "Knocked up, knocked up."

"You're so dreadfully hard on a fellow, India," Erl Jack said, glancing over his shoulder at the little girls as they stumbled along, carrying their burdens.

"I'm just going somewhere, remember? Somewhere that's not here."

"So am I," he protested. "We're going together. We'll bag fat scholarships to the same school, and then we'll scratch our way up."

I let that one lie. Maybe we were, and maybe we weren't. I wasn't going to end up like my sister, cleaning other people's houses with a toddler in tow. Someday I was going to get a scholarship and be gone, and I wasn't going to be hindered by anything or anybody, and especially not by a boy.

"What's wrong with some frolic along the way?" He let

go of my hand and grabbed up the hibachi and the cardboard box.

I made the sign against vampires and said, "Vivienne."

"Yeah," he said, "too bad about her."

He jogged up the steep part of the path, just before it twisted and was lost in a meadow. Phlox and Queen Anne's Lace, bee balm and butterfly weed were all saying that it was the tail end of June. The '53 Chevy loomed out of the spray of wildflowers like a boulder from surf.

The little girls were jumping up and down again, pointing at the car.

"It gives me the creeps," I murmured.

"You wouldn't be right in the head if it didn't, would you?" Erl Jack lit the hibachi while the girls crouched by him, watching as he squirted lighter fluid onto the coals and made flames blaze up with a tossed match. "Clarisse, back off. You go and set your hair on fire, and your ma will tack my hide to the outhouse."

"We got no outhouse."

"In a manner of speaking," he said, tumbling her hair.

"Her mama doesn't even have the slimmest idea where they are," I said. "She was chugging beer on the back porch with her no-good boyfriend, last I noticed."

"Hush," Erl Jack said, nodding toward Clarisse and Maudie.

"They know what's going on."

"I do," Maudie said. "I'm going to be a first-grade teacher when I grow up."

"That's great," Erl Jack said. "I used to be in love with

mine. When I got older, I realized that she had a mustache and a small cottony beard, but it was too late. I'd already given my heart to her."

"I thought you loved India," Clarisse said, cradling her dolly.

"I do. I gave up on the adorable Miss Bootle some years ago. For me, there is no one else but chilly, heartless, brainy India. She doesn't have a mustache. She doesn't have a little cottony beard. Her nose is a wee bit too large. Her amber hair is preposterously uncontrollable. She looks at me with those big brown eyes and says the cruelest things."

"So why do you love her? Clarisse and I don't," Maudie said.

"But look at you two," Erl Jack said. "Here you are, tagging along despite all her hard, pebbly words. Just like me. Besides, other than those few drawbacks, she's perfect."

"Nice. Let's get on with the performance," I said.

The hibachi burned wildly, threatening the end-of-June wildflowers as he took a black cape lined with cobalt from the box and hooked it around his neck.

"Ohhhh," sighed Clarisse, and plunked down on her bottom.

"Now for the first event in this matinee theatrical," he said grandly, and gave a bow.

Maudie and I sat cross-legged by Clarisse and waited. I hadn't seen one of his shows in a long time, probably two years or more—once I babysat for Dr. Doddleman on the day his oldest son had a birthday. It was a terrific magic show for a kid magician, and I was expecting more of the same.

"Don't speak, no matter what happens. This may take a few minutes," he said, tossing the cape artfully over one shoulder and closing his eyes.

The cicadas were droning in the weeds, and a big star of sun on chrome burst from the other side of the meadow. I hadn't really noticed the yellow jackets until Erl Jack was went so quiet and still, but a gang of thirty or forty zoomed by in the direction of the Chevy while we waited.

"Bikers," I whispered.

Nothing was happening. It was the most boring magic show on the face of the earth. I was about to say so when Maudie lay down and swept her fingers across the grass. Erl Jack Falchion's feet had lifted into the air, ever so slightly. She grabbed a stick, poking it between his bare soles and the ground.

It was a trick, but I couldn't conceive how.

Slowly his feet returned to the ground, and his eyelids fluttered. He looked about dreamily, as though he wasn't quite sure of his surroundings. In another minute, he seemed entirely himself again.

"One of the guys at the lumber mill taught me how to do that," he said, "a man from Brazil."

"That was definitely cool," I said, forgetting that I wasn't supposed to be sweet to Erl Jack.

"That was really, really awesome." Maudie nodded with such vigor that her sweaty ringlets danced.

"He's a wizard," Clarisse whispered, clutching her dolly.

"Thank you, my friends," he said, bowing. "Now, prepare yourselves for my second act." With a snap of his fingers, he untied and dropped the cape. Lightning-fast, he stripped off my grandpa's shirt, and it floated away like gossamer, landing on a bunch of Queen Anne's lace.

"That's quite an act," I said. Dryly, let me add—about as dry as dry ice. I didn't put it past Erl Jack to flaunt himself and call it magic. My eyes crept over his torso, hard and tight from manhandling lumber, and rested on his face. And if you think that sounds as if my eyes were bugging out on stalks, well, they probably were.

"India," he said, looking annoyed.

"Don't cheat."

"If I had on clothes, you'd say I cheated worse," he complained. "Hush."

He held out his palm to prove that it was empty. He closed the hand and lifted it to his cheek. Holding it out again, he revealed a blue petal. He let it fall and displayed the palm again. Fourteen times he did this, each time letting a petal flutter to the ground, where Maudie and Clarisse pounced on it.

Afterward he asked them for the petals, made some hokey-looking mystic passes, and produced a rose.

With another flourish, he presented it to me.

"There's no such thing as a blue rose." Bemused, I stared at the holy grail of horticulture. The petals looked just as rich and velvety as those of the pink climber by Gran's porch steps. A pair of yellow jackets landed and began to explore, so Erl Jack flicked the stem until they flew away. When he blew across the top of the flower, I smelled perfume. The girls danced in a sweet, sudden chill and called for more. Later on, when I told Gran that the air had gone cool, she didn't believe me. "Erl Jack could make a hog dream about being a lady's silk purse with a golden clasp and taffeta lining," she declared.

Clarisse had let out a cry of pure mourning on seeing that the petals were gone, so now he plucked a pair of rabbits out of the air. They were no bigger than my pinky fingernail but made both girls absurdly pleased. For them, the toys overshadowed the rose.

"Just some of my party supplies," Erl Jack said modestly.

"Was that magic?"

He drew the flower from my fingers and tucked it carefully behind my ear.

"How could it not be, dear India?" He glanced at the little girls and lowered his voice. "The bargain was power and magic, wasn't it? That was magic. Next is power. With witnesses."

He snapped his fingers to get the attention of Maudie and Clarisse.

"Now for the last and most risky part of the show. Follow me." He picked up the brazier and waded through the wildflowers, toward the car.

Clarisse hung back.

"Come on," he called. "You don't have to go too close."

I felt the same reluctance she did. When guiding visitors to the car, I always parked myself on the end of the path and waited for them to gawk their fill. I'd never been close. I trailed after Erl Jack, stepping where he had mashed down the wildflowers because I despise ticks. They're nasty little acrobats, slinging themselves from a rocking stem onto bare legs. Halfway through the field, I could make out gray, spittle-worked paper pressed against the windows. The nest hummed along with the endless sawing of the cicadas. Where the glass was broken, gray bulged out—the whole thing suggesting a car and speakers from some weird, abandoned movie drive-in.

"A barn near the mill is packed with nest," Erl Jack said. "They're going to torch it this winter."

He flattened the weeds in a two-yard radius and told us to stand there to watch.

"It seems like the end of the world," I murmured. I had a strong sensation of horror mixed with fascination.

Clarisse was whimpering and dragging on my hand, but I didn't brush her off.

Maudie, however, was staring with interest at a squad of incoming yellow jackets.

Erl Jack Falchion waded closer to the car, carrying the hibachi. "They say that there are ten or eleven queens in each of these things," he called, "and that there may be one hundred thousand insects inside, or more. But people do strange things for love." He sounded quite cheerful as he set down the hibachi; afterward, he still had something in his hand.

It was a jar of honey. He began anointing his body from the waist up with driblets of the stuff.

"Erl Jack, no!"

He just smiled at me.

With that many yellow jackets sailing in and out of the windows, it didn't take long for them to find Erl Jack. He threw a handful of powder that made the fire shoot up black cumulus, and he kept moving to stay in its path. The yellow jackets settled a breast plate on his chest, shielded his belly, stuck epaulets on his shoulders. Within three minutes, he was a tigerish, seething mass. His eyes were open, staring.

Clarisse howled, swaying back and forth in an ecstasy of fright.

"Maudie," I whispered, "take her home. Very slowly, before she attracts their attention."

I wanted to go with them.

My legs had gone wiggly, and I dropped to my knees, letting out a moan that blotted out the noise of the yellow jackets and cicadas. Big stinging tears were pushing out of my eyes as the pelt of black and gold rippled across his heart. My throat felt jammed with grief and death.

Erl Jack was a goner.

He must've been a bit panicked, because he dropped the sack of powder onto the grill. The coals gnawed through the bag by degrees, consuming more powder and setting off fresh bursts of gray and black.

Erl Jack's shape writhed in the billowing cloud, wheeling slowly. When the wind blew, I glimpsed yellow jackets pelting his bare feet. He stepped gingerly out of the smoke with only a few dozen insects still clinging on, and these he whisked away with his fingers. For yards around, yellow jackets toppled and reeled like drunks.

"Your hair," I croaked, and he scattered a few more with his fingers.

He broad jumped out of the yellow pool, landing beside me.

"India." His voice was shaky, and I took him by the hand and led him through the wildflowers. My legs still trembled. I looked back once to make sure the yellow jackets weren't coming after us. They were flying up from the ground, bumbling in the air. The mammoth nest reared up behind them, a dozen insect kingdoms ruled by pitiless queens.

When we got to the trail, I started to cry, and in earnest. I used to sob like that when my mother was carted off to the hospital—until I got hardened and didn't care because she didn't care, not about me or anything except getting seriously high.

"Hush, hush, India," Erl Jack said, and he didn't sound as cocky as before. He put his arms around me, and I hit him on the chest two or three times, though I'd never struck anybody in my life.

"Don't you ever, ever, ever do anything so stupid, ever again." I head butted him, my face slick with tears, and when I looked up, his eyes were wet.

After a while I stopped, and he retrieved the cloak and shirt, along with a rag and a bottle of insect repellent. He doused himself liberally, scrubbing at the honey until his skin glowed. I felt as empty as a dried-out nest of a castle, abandoned by queen and workers.

The cicadas' song was unbearably loud in the wood. We didn't talk until I'd quit sniffing and wiped my tears away with Grandpa's worn-out shirt.

"Power and magic, India," Erl Jack teased, his usual air of nonchalance coming back.

"I don't believe you," I said, stopping. "Now, when my face

is streaked with snot, and I'm madder at you than I've ever been in my whole life?"

"Uh-huh," he said. "I want it whenever I can get it."

I touched a swelling on his shoulder and slipped my arms around his neck.

"But don't you dare ask me for another, you hear me? Wait until I ask you, even if you have to wait until hell is a major block of ice."

He nodded meekly—put on, of course.

So I paid him. I'm a girl of my word, and that was magic and power, even if the latter was weirder and just plain more than I ever care to see again.

Gran has an old, old refrigerator. It has a seal on it that won't quit. Once that baby's shut, it's shut good. My first thought was that Erl Jack Falchion kissed like that refrigerator. He was going to make sure that if it was only one kiss, it was no chicken peck on the lips but one that would last him a while. I giggled, though I was mad at him, and I got serious and kissed him as tenderly as I knew how because he had, after all, delivered on magic and power and, in the end, deserved it. Just for an instant, I thought that our feet floated up from the path. The honey and molasses in me melted entirely away, and my veins lit up like a big silver tree with its branches flying and leaves going like mad.

"Now that was magic," Erl Jack said, once he caught his breath.

When we got back to the mimosa tree, Clarisse dropped her doll and stared at Erl Jack. Her sister trotted right over.

"How many stings you got?"

"Three, maybe four," he said, kneeling to show her. "You got a credit card, Maudie? That's the best thing for sliding the stingers out." He hadn't put my grandpa's shirt on because I wouldn't give it back, not after I'd blown my nose on it.

She choked with laughter. "I'm not old enough for a credit card!"

"No? I knew for sure that India didn't have a card, but I thought you and Clarisse might."

"You are one crazy boy," Maudie said admiringly.

"That's what they said about the last guy to win a Darwin Award," I told her.

"What's Darwin?"

"I can't get into that right now," I said. "Ask the rocket scientist. She's bound to know."

"It's the prettiest flower I ever saw." Clarisse hugged her doll and looked with intense longing at my blue rose.

"A rose of magic and power." I slipped the flower from my hair. The petals still had a faint perfume, but I was astonished to see that they were no longer genuine but silk, though the dusting of gold seemed to be pollen.

"I thought you might like to keep it as a souvenir," Erl Jack said.

For once, I looked at his face and had nothing to say. That was a feat in itself—shutting up India—though I should've needled him for assuming that a kiss from Erl Jack required a memento.

"I need another bath," he went on. "And you're a mess. Want a lift to the café in about forty minutes?"

We drifted away from the girls, toward the truck.

"All right," I said, stopping him to peel a wing from his arm. My mind kept roving from the kiss to the car-shaped mound of spittle-paper, from the blue rose to the soles of Erl Jack's feet, floating on air.

"It ended happily," he said, sliding his hand along my cheek.

"You got the kiss."

Gran came out on the porch with a trowel, and we both waved at her. She just can't quit gardening. She's got every inch of the yard covered with zinnias and coleus and a hundred other plants.

I stuck the rose in my hair and took Erl Jack's hand.

"I really love only two people in this world," I told him, "but don't take advantage, you hear me? I'm going to do what I'm going to do, and not even you and Gran could ever stop me."

"We're probably the only ones who wouldn't try," Erl Jack said, squeezing my fingers.

For a moment my heart felt packed with fluttering insect wings. I was bound to leave for the wide world, despite the pink mimosa flowers and the cicadas' song and the laughter of Erl Jack and Gran that was in me like honey and molasses in girl-growing weather on a summer's day.

"Yeah," I said, a little bitterly.

But it was okay: two was a lot for somebody with no parents, who grew up smart but downwind from the dump in a house like a mossy growth on the slope of a hill.

Marly Youmans is the author of *Ingledove* and *The Curse of the Raven Mocker*, two very southern fantasy books that braid together Celtic and Cherokee culture (both are available in Firebird editions). In addition, she is the author of a collection of poetry, *Claire*, and the novels *The Wolf Pit* (winner of the Michael Shaara Award for Excellence in Civil War Fiction), *Catherwood*, and *Little Jordan*.

Forthcoming is *Val/Orson*, a short novel inspired by the legend of the noble young Valentine and his wild twin brother Orson, set among California tree-sitters, as well as stories in many anthologies, including a four-novella collection from Prime that contains "The Seven Mirrors," a tale that begins with a teenage girl conjuring the ghost of Poe.

Marly Youmans lives in Cooperstown, New York, with her husband and their three children. Her Web site is **www.marlyyoumans.com**; she can be contacted through her blog, **www.thepalaceat2.blogspot.com**.

Author's Note

In part, I wrote this story as a gift for my magic-loving teenage daughter, who finds that real boys often can't compete with make-believe ones. I also wrote it out of homesickness for southern landscapes and out of memories—the pet boar at the boat shop, a tin washtub on a Georgia front porch shaded by a glossy hedge and noisy with bees, the powder puffs of mimosas cool against my cheek.

As for the intelligent, combative, sun-weary India, she sprang like armed Athena from the head of Zeus. She appeared, and she immediately had it in for little girls who weren't as armed against danger as she. Like all small children, Clarisse and Maudie are reading the world with insufficient knowledge, though I imagine that they learned something from India and Erl Jack on that overheated summer's day.

Sherwood Smith

Court Ship

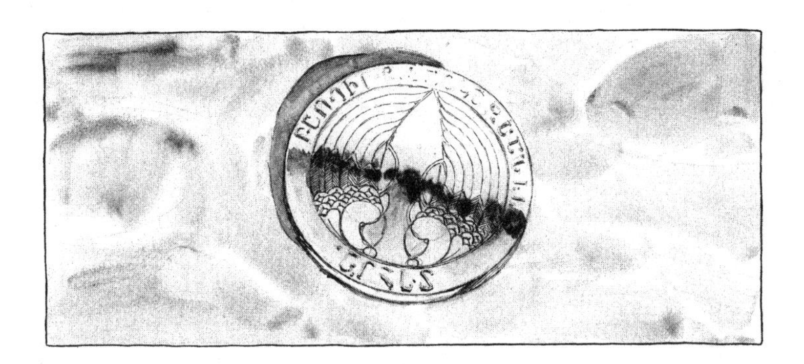

A long, low, rake-masted ship drifted into Smuggler's Cove under a single foresail. The deck was almost flush except for the jut of the aftcastle, on which an old woman sat at a little table pouring hot chocolate from a silver pot.

"That's the *Petal*?" asked the newcomer.

"Yes," said his guide, a young boy from the village above Smuggler's Cove.

"It looks like a pirate ship," ventured the newcomer.

The boy snickered, then said with the superiority of the sea expert instructing the ignorant land rat, "That's because it was, before Granny Risa's family got it. They were smugglers. Which is why we're called Smuggler's Cove."

"Oh," said the newcomer, peering under his hand at the old pirate ship.

The boy added, "Old Granny Risa was a pirate-fighter as well as a smuggler."

To his surprise, the newcomer murmured, "Yes, so I was told."

A girl of about twenty leaped from the *Petal*'s rail to the dock. With practiced movements she made the bow fast, as a crewman aft secured the stern.

"That's Young Risa," he said. "Talk to her or Granny Risa. They both do hiring and trading."

The newcomer smiled down at him. His tunic and riding trousers weren't exactly toff—like what the nobles wore when they rode in their fancy coaches to Remalna City—but they looked rich anyway, hinting at largesse. "Thank you," he said, pressing a six-sided Sartoran silver into the boy's hand, which sent him whooping up the trail to his mates.

On the dock, Aurisa paused at the unexpected sight of a young man coming down the narrow switchback trail, his long pale hair neatly tied back with a ribbon. She put her fists on her hips and waited. She liked what she saw. He was tall, slim, but moved with the swinging stride of someone used to being active; he was dressed plainly except for excellently made high blackweave cavalry boots.

Risa flicked a glance at the fellow's face: square, pleasant expression that didn't give much away. Long hands, no rings.

Altogether an interesting anomaly. Good. She liked interesting people. And hoped he would not open his mouth and promptly become a bore, or worse, a snob. She knew how to handle snobs—except that Granny Risa didn't like her being rude to them. Bad for business, which had been all too scarce ever since the war.

He reached the bottom of the pathway and started down

the dock. She watched his gaze travel down her own form, and mentally assessed what he saw: medium height, plain face, curling dark brown hair tied up in her kerchief, wide hips, castoff blue tunic-shirt, ancient deck trousers that had, in fact, belonged to her father before he returned to Fal to join his cousin's cavalry force during the war. Bare feet.

What he saw was, in fact, quite different. He liked the strength hinted at by the set of her shoulders, the easy stance accentuated most attractively by the generous curve of her hip, her wide-set dark eyes, her generous mouth with a sardonic shadow at the corners. Her face was framed by the dark tendrils of hair that had escaped her kerchief.

She crossed her arms and waited.

"Good morning," he said.

Yes, he had a toff accent.

"I need to hire a boat, or ship—a seagoing vessel—to take me to Send Alian—"

"There is no more Send Alian," she interrupted.

He paused, regarding her with mild surprise. "I realize that. I ought to have said, what formerly was Send Alian. Or more exactly, I guess, the port at Al Caba, as I understand the shoreline along what was formerly Send Alian is too flat for landing."

Risa nodded. So far, so good. "All true. Will it just be you, or are there servants lurking around with a lot of baggage?"

"Just—"

"Hai! Raec! Wait up!" a young man called from the top of the bluff.

The handsomest fellow she'd ever seen loped down the

mountainside. He was tall, like the one he'd called Raec; but unlike Raec, who was slender, the newcomer was heroic in build, with curling black hair escaping most romantically from his white ribbon tie, his eyes thickly fringed with black lashes below winged brows. He gave Risa an openly appreciative up-and-down through blue eyes, startlingly light in his dark face. When she gave him the same appreciative up-and-down, he grinned. His grin was decidedly rakish.

Then, to Raec, "You can't go off without me. If you do, my death will rest upon your head, and I swear I will haunt you at the most inopportune times for the remainder of your sorry life."

Raec sighed. "Nad. This is one journey I could have made alone."

"Impossible," Nad retorted. "You need my gorgeous face along." He bowed extravagantly to Risa, adding, "Nadav, at your service." Then to his friend, "We have been friends too long for you to shut me out of sailing on the prettiest boat I've ever seen, with the prettiest captain."

"That," Raec said mordantly, "is the problem, not the solution."

Nadav raised his hands. "I didn't want to say it, but it's your fault I can't go home. My sister found out you're gone, and somebody somewhere—probably that fool of a royal messenger—hinted at the reason."

Silence, during which the only sounds were the thumps and rattles of the crew making the *Petal* fast, and the distant cry of seabirds round the bluffs.

Then Raec turned to Risa, who had been watching with

undisguised interest. He said, "Two—Nadav, here, and myself. No servants. Our baggage—such as it is—is on the hill, with my—"

"Our," Nadav put in.

"Our mounts, for which I will arrange stabling for the interim. After which we can leave whenever you wish."

"Without even asking the price?" Risa asked. "My!"

Raec actually blushed, which intrigued her the more. Nadav laughed. "He's not quite made of money, but he's the next best thing."

"Oh, yes, yap that out and watch the price double," Raec said in Sartoran.

"It would have doubled anyway," Risa responded in Sartoran, and hopped back to the rail of the *Petal*. Unfortunately her splendid retort was spoiled by one of those bump-and-lurches so common to moored ships. She windmilled her arms, started to topple. A pair of strong hands caught her by the shoulders and gave her a boost. So much for splendid parting shots!

She glanced back, saw in Raec's rueful grin that he knew what she was thinking, and had to laugh as she leaped to the deck and sped aft.

Her grandmother looked up from her chocolate. "Business? Or pleasure?"

Risa snorted. "They're toffs. Remalnan, from their accent. I told 'em I'd charge double," she added. "We can get all the repairs done at Al Caba—"

"Who are they?"

"The dark one is Nadav, and the blond one Raec."

To Risa's surprise, her grandmother nodded slowly. "There will be no charge."

"What?" Risa squeaked, then lowered her voice as the two on the dock looked sharply her way.

"I recognize the pale-haired one," Old Granny Risa said in her slow, mild voice. "That is, unless I am mistaken, the grandson of Prince Alaerec Renselaeus. I understand they gave this boy the modern version of the old name, which would make him Prince Alaraec Renselaeus, heir to Remalna. And I promised my dear friend Lark that he always have free board with me. He and his family."

A crown prince! Risa's vivid inward vision replaced a blond, smiling face with money bags surmounted by a crown.

"But they haven't *told* us who they are," Risa said. "They could be any Raec and Nadav—both common names—"

"But I know who they are. Nadav has to be Lord Nadav Savona. The boys' fathers grew up together, and so, too, their sons."

"Gran. We do need the money."

"No."

Risa sighed. Her grandmother never lost her temper—but she never changed her mind, either. Not if she'd given a promise. "And I was going to order the very best stores."

"You'll do that anyway."

"And we'll pay with what?"

"You leave that to me," Granny said.

Risa made a sour face. She hated the thought of her grandmother dipping into her small savings just for some imagined debt of honor, about which she only knew the sketchiest of facts: Lark was a prince who'd talked his way onto the crew. Granny Risa's ten-year-old brother—who died during the Pirate Wars—had run "Alaerec" into "Lark," and the name had stuck. What Risa did not know were all the details of Lark's heroic career. The stories she'd heard had come from other people.

But Gran was the Owner, and Gran Had Spoken.

Risa stamped back down the length of the craft, past her cousins and two of the hired hands, who were busy tying everything down on deck and lining up the goods to be shifted to the dock.

"You go free," she said abruptly to the newcomers. And to their unmistakable surprise, she scowled at Raec. "Gran recognized you. It's your grandfather. She knew him once, and made a promise."

Raec whistled softly. "The Pirate Wars." In a lower voice, "Did she say why? My grandfather has never told me that story, though he talks about everything else."

Risa's bad mood vanished. He didn't act as if free passage was his due—and he was as curious as she about her grandmother's past. "No! You think they were tragic lovers separated? That's what my mother thinks. What have you heard?"

"Nothing about lovers, that's for certain."

Nadav chuckled.

Raec gestured toward the hill. "We'll go settle the horses and then return."

"Don't rush," Risa said, her bad mood returning as she thought of the bargaining that lay ahead—and the making do, when it would have been so easy to tap this rich vein of gold, who would hardly miss the charge, from the look of him. "We won't be sailing before dawn."

She leaped up onto the deck and called to the crew, "Let's get busy! We're sailing on tomorrow's tide!"

Just before dawn, Aurisa the Elder watched the young men come aboard. She watched her granddaughter take them below to show them the tiny cabin they would share. Presently they were back on deck, Risa pointing out the basics. Both listened closely, and eventually—as the sun cleared the bluffs, banishing the blue shadows and lighting the *Petal*'s sails with peach-warm light—they were brought aft to the captain's deck.

Granny Risa braced herself to look into the young version of eyes still vivid through years of dreams; Raec's were gray, not dark like his grandfather's, but their shape was somewhat the same.

Raec said, "I would really rather pay for our passage."

"No. But if you are uncomfortable at benefiting from another's debt of honor, then you may work on crew if you like. We are shorthanded."

There—many tests in that suggestion.

Neither young man dismissed the "debt of honor." There were far too many fools in the world who considered that honor was the exclusive birthright of aristocrats. Even more promising were Nadav's spontaneous grin and Raec's unhidden relief at the suggestion of work.

"Have either of you ever been on a ship?" she asked.

"No," Nadav said.

Raec's smile brought Lark to mind. "My father gets sick on ships or coaches, so he arranges magic transport if any of us have to go a distance that isn't easily ridden. I haven't inherited that." He added ruefully, "At least, I don't think."

Granny Risa laughed. "As well! Young Risa will introduce you to the mates of the watch. You'll serve as general hands until you learn some of the skills. In the meantime, while we ride the tide out I suggest you climb to the mastheads. Accustom yourselves to the feel of the ship as we work into actual ocean waters. They will not be as calm as this cove."

She watched them make their way clumsily up the rigging, laughing at one another's efforts; by nightfall Nadav was queasy, especially as the wind rose and the seas became choppy, but some strong steeped ginger took care of that. Raec had no problem adjusting to the motion, as his grandfather had many years before.

Their readiness to work improved Risa's mood at once, as her grandmother had hoped; she soon began looking forward to shared watches. The two visitors were easy on the eyes, fun to talk to, and they seemed to appreciate her world, which was the sea.

Two days out they lined the rail to watch a fleet of warships on maneuvers. These were new brigantines, flying the twined golden lilies and stylized crown of the royal house of Elsarion, a flag of deep blue with white edging.

Raec and Nadav stared silently at the tall masts, the

graceful curve of wind-taut sails, the huge ships aslant as they raced by, white spraying down one side.

Nadav whistled. "Impressive!"

"Even more," Risa said, "when you consider a few years back they didn't even have a fleet. Nobody quite knows how the king managed to put one to sea so fast."

They leaned against the rail as the wake from the passing warship hit them in slow-rolling bumps. Up in the high rigging, sailors were busy doing things.

"I wonder if my parents know. Of course they must. But obviously they don't mind," Raec murmured, more to himself than to the others.

Nadav flicked up a hand. "It's not like the Adranis are attacking anyone."

Risa said, "My mother is a navigator on a Sartoran warship. Posted in the western part of the Sartoran Sea. But she hears all the eastern gossip. Says that so far the Adranis have been strictly observant of maritime treaties. And, since they've joined the roving patrols, there's been a lot less pirate interference with trade. The worst of the pirates in this sea were operating out of the waters just west of Anaeran while all their troubles were going on. No longer. The new king wiped them all out in one fast strike."

They were silent, considering what they'd heard about that king, now ruler of a considerable land. Some even called it an empire.

The subject was still on Raec's mind when his watch ended. He went below, got a mug of the savory, thick soup the cook made each day, and ducked under the bulkhead into the cramped little wardroom just off the galley, which was shared by everyone. The wardroom was seldom crowded. At any time of day or night most of the small crew were either on duty or else asleep. There was no time that everyone had free, except some evenings; then they all gathered on deck.

Risa was there, just finishing her own soup, when Raec entered, head bent to avoid thunking his forehead into the bulkheads.

He put his square-bottomed mug down opposite Risa, then dropped onto the bench. "You hear a lot of talk on your travels, do you not?"

She shrugged. "We tend to hear the most popular rumors. Can't tell if they're true or not. Or how much truth is mixed with embroidery."

"How about this? When you were in Al Caba last, did you hear much about the deposed rulers of Send Alian?"

She chuckled. "Not much beyond that they got offered exile or their old title and lands back. That would be in the time before the treaty forced on the Adranis and Enaeraneth made those coastal lands into kingdoms." She set her mug down and looked at him askance. "What's your interest in 'em?"

"Well, they sent a diplomat to my parents about their princess." He hesitated, then said, "My mother felt sorry for her. So I thought I'd go meet her."

Risa's brows rose. "Meet her? On the *Petal*?" She flapped her hands around her. "Aren't you supposed to do that kind of thing with warships or yachts, and not a smuggler? And don't you need a lot of minions running around blowing horns, and wearing silks, and so forth?"

Raec's quirked eyes gave away his effort not to laugh as he said portentously, "*Especially* so forth."

She chuckled again.

He said, "I would if this visit was official in any way. It's not. My mother told the diplomat that no one can come offering princesses—or former princesses—to me until I'm twenty-five. But I thought I'd go myself. See, my parents promised they wouldn't force any political marriage on me. I can pick for myself. So I thought, if I go with all the 'so forth' then what I'll see is her own 'so forth.' I'd like to see just a person." He nodded. "So I'm going as Raec. A traveler."

She frowned. "Wait. So, you just go and . . . spy on her."

"No! I want to *meet* her."

"If you don't tell her who you are—but you know who she is—aren't you spying?"

His mouth opened to deny it, then it was his turn to frown. It was not, she was surprised to see, an angry frown, it was the forehead-pucker of perplexity.

He was silent for what seemed a very long time, as the *Petal* rocked its way through the water, and his supper slowly cooled, then he looked up, his expression a rueful smile. "I guess you're probably right. Now I feel stupid." Then he shrugged. "So, what if I amend the plan to this: I go as I am, and let her know who I am. So if she wants to meet me without either of us having to summon up the mighty forces of minions and so forth. Would that sound more fair?"

Risa said slowly, "That's fair."

Raec flashed his sudden smile, very different from Nadav's rakish, dashing grin. Then he drank some soup, and when he spoke next, it was to ask if she'd ever seen any pirates. They chatted about smugglers, privateers, and pirates as he finished up his meal, then he returned to the deck.

Risa followed more slowly. After sundown, Granny Risa gave orders for them to slacken sail for the night, and lanterns were strung all along the rails and up on the yards so that the three crew members who played instruments could entertain them.

It was a balmy night, so singing and dancing lasted a long time. Risa usually participated, but this night she leaned against the rail outside of the golden circles of light as the ship's boy, Risa's youngest cousin, taught Raec a complicated dance known as Pirate's Revenge.

Nadav drifted up and joined her. "You don't dance?" she asked.

"I tend to stay with the ones I know." He flashed his grin. "Will you waltz with me?"

"I don't know any toff dances."

He just shrugged, adding with a disarming smile, "Those are what I'm used to."

Raec stumbled, nearly falling down; he caught hold of a shroud just in time, as everyone laughed. Risa thought back. Raec had been the one to urge Nadav to climb the masts, and he'd been the first to try mending a net. It seemed to her that though Raec did not mind making a fool of himself attempting something new, Nadav did mind. And wouldn't do it, at least not in front of others.

"So did he tell you why he's going to the former Send Alian?" she asked Nadav.

His black brows slanted up. "You mean Princess Jasalan?"

"Yes."

"He told me about your recent conversation." He executed a bow. "You are now beholding the minion and the so forth, all embodied in one fellow. Me." He laid his hand on his chest. "I'm to go ahead and sound her out. He was somewhat chagrined," Nadav added, his smile fading.

Risa let out her breath slowly as she watched Raec dancing on the forecastle, his long blond hair firelit gold in the mellow lantern light. Now he'd gotten the complicated shuffling steps. He wasn't graceful like his friend—it was not a graceful dance, though maybe Nadav could have made it that way—but he moved with a kind of careless ease that Risa discovered she liked more than grace. Grace was, well, conscious. Ease wasn't. Or maybe she had the words wrong. Granny could tell her.

Just then Raec laughed as the ship gave a lee-lurch and he fumbled another step.

"I hope it works," she said, trying to convince herself. "He's so nice."

"He's easy to get along with," Nadav said. "Even tempered. But you really don't want to see him angry."

"Ahah. Turns mean, eh?"

Nadav shook his head. "I've never seen him act mean, and we grew up together. He just gets very, very intense." He held out his hand, palm up. "Those who think they know him find it unsettling." He chuckled. "If you want temper, you may apply to my sister. Her storms will satisfy anyone with a taste for lightning and thunder."

Risa had heard stories about Lady Tara Savona—that she

was both the most beautiful and the most spoiled high-born girl in Remalna's court. Some had also said that she fully expected to be the next queen.

But future queens were none of her business, so she just nodded, and when the dance ended, she decided to take a turn in the next.

Granny Risa, sitting at east in her favorite chair on the captain's deck, watched in approval as her granddaughter stomped and twirled and kicked, laughing with the grandson of her first love.

And she watched over the succeeding short span of days as Young Risa and the visitors worked together and talked together. Never anything profound, or dramatic. Young Risa was too guarded for that. But she watched as, gradually, though Nadav was far more handsome than Alaraec, far more witty in his banter, more dashing when the two young men practiced their weapons on the foredeck after their watches, Risa drifted to Raec's side at the rail when he was free. Never any serious conversations. Just pleasant chat.

So when they reached Al Caba at last, and Risa stood at the tiller herself, guiding them unerringly through the busy ship traffic, Granny Risa contemplated her granddaughter's thoughtful expression, her silence.

When at last they anchored and the ship's boys helped the guests lower the pinnace to the water for the trip to the dock, Granny summoned Risa to her side.

"Tide's going to turn soon," Risa said, her face closed, her voice light.

Granny Risa said, "Let's pay for anchorage. I want to go

ashore and look for a cargo. Pay for our journey. We can give the crew a watch or two of leave in rotation. It might take me a day or two to find the sort of consignment that will net us a good profit."

Risa's brow cleared. "Good profit. I like the sound of that." And, in a lower voice, "Maybe this journey won't be a waste after all."

"I don't believe it."

Princess Jasalan of Send Alian frowned at the scowling young man who stood by her parlor window, his beringed hands flipping at the curtain sash. "Lored." She thumped her arms across her front. "Does that mean you think I am a liar?"

Lord Alored Masdan, heir to the biggest duchy in the region, flushed to the roots of his red hair. The two reds clashed horribly, Jasalan thought.

"No!" he exclaimed. "It's just—I think they are lying. Or he. It just sounds, well, preposterous."

Jasalan frowned at her chief suitor. Plenty of girls thought Lored handsome. And he was—very tall, very strongly built, with all that waving red hair falling back from his high brow. But his ears stuck out on the sides, his nose was too short, and as for all that height and strength, whenever he moved, she couldn't help but think of a redwood tree crashing down in an old forest. Whenever he was in her parlor, she had to stop herself from watching over the porcelain dishware and her mother's crystal statuettes.

She knew that these things should not bother her. But they

did. She'd pretended they didn't when it seemed he was the best suitor she could expect. Now that was no longer true.

Her voice was more sharp than she intended. "So you think they're imposters? Speaking court Sartoran?"

"Anyone can learn court Sartoran."

"What are they going to do, abduct me under my father's nose?"

"No. Well, yes. That is—"

Jasalan flushed. "My father may have lost a kingdom. But I can assure you, he won't lose *me*. Because I don't intend to be lost."

Lored sighed. Now his fingers wrenched at the brocade. "It's just that I thought we had an understanding, you and I." He scowled. "What business does that fellow have coming here anyway? Remalna is at the other end of the Sartoran Sea. If he really is a prince, surely he can find someone to court there."

"There aren't any princesses the right age," Jasalan reminded him in an even more tart voice. "Father sent one of his royal messengers just to sound out the situation—find out if Prince Alaraec was promised to anyone. There aren't a whole lot of crown princes of the right age, for that matter. And some of them might not like the fact that I'm a princess in nothing more than title," she finished in a bitter voice.

But he did not hear her bitterness. "I want to be there for this interview," Lored said.

She just stared at him, so Lored took his leave in tight-lipped silence.

Relieved to be rid of him at last, Jasalan whisked upstairs

to her room. She rapped out fast orders to her maid.

She hadn't actually told her father yet about the surprising interview that morning with the handsome young man who'd only introduced himself as "Nadav." Those blue eyes! Usually people with brown skin and black hair had varying shades of brown eyes—her family certainly did—which made the blue startling.

She realized her strongest wish was that he was actually speaking for himself. Like people do in plays and some of the romantic ballads—where the hero speaks to the lady of "his friend" when actually he's courting for himself.

Oh, if "Nadav" were really Prince Alaraec!

She was wearing her best gown as she descended to her parlor. The evening carillon echoed the last notes through the marble archways and corridors of what was once her father's summer palace, on the ridge up behind the harbor.

The glorious colors of sunset turned to silhouette the visitors at the big window overlooking the harbor. They gazed out at the long peninsula curving toward the horizon, and beyond to the vast and sparkling sea.

At her step they turned around. There was the handsome Nadav, his eyes even bluer than she remembered. Next to him a slim fellow almost as tall whose coloring, compared to Nadav, was about as interesting as old oatmeal: pale hair, pale eyes, probably pale skin where the sun hadn't given it a brush of light brown.

She took a deep breath. If he really was the crown prince of Remalna, she was going to like old oatmeal as much as she'd once liked overgrown redwood trees.

She gave them a stately curtsey, spreading her silken skirts, and spoke formal words of welcome in her very best court Sartoran, since of course they wouldn't speak her language any more than she did theirs.

Raec scarcely heard the words—familiar as they were from years of sitting in on his parents' diplomatic interviews—as he stared at a girl even prettier than Tara. Far prettier. She was shorter, rounder, with a lot of curly blue-black hair, chocolate-brown skin, and greenish-brown eyes. His jaw dropped; Nadav dug his elbow into Raec's side, and they both bowed, Raec rather hastily, Nadav with impressive grace.

"Welcome," Jasalan said. "Would you care for refreshment?"

Raec raised a hand. "It's all right. This isn't any kind of formal call."

Of course not, she thought. *But what right have I to expect more?*

She thought her welcoming smile just as bright as she'd practiced in her mirror, but his eyes narrowed, and he said, "Perhaps I ought not to have come. But if it helps, I would have whether you were here or the ornament of King Macael's court, heir to his empire. Does he call himself an emperor, do you know?"

Unexpected! Jasalan waved them to the waiting chairs and plopped down herself, forgetting to move with princesslike poise. Bland as he looked, this Alaraec was a sharp observer. She was not accustomed to that; Lored, for example, never seemed to be able to catch a hint. Even rather obvious ones, though he said he was devoted to her.

Eh! She dismissed Lored, wrinkling her nose as she recalled that terrible day, the only time she ever met the mysterious and powerful Macael Elsarion.

"No," she said. "Just king. He told my father when he came here he was reuniting what ought to have been united long ago, and even my father admits that his having done it might end the wars between the Enaeraneth side and the Adrani side that seem to happen every other generation."

Nadav whistled. "What did he do, march up to your father waving a sword and yelling, '*Surrender or die*'? Or did he just utter a lot of sinister threats?"

She shook her head. "He did have a big force, but they didn't do anything. He sent a messenger saying he was coming the next day. Suddenly they were at the border, see? We never did have much of a guard or war force." She shrugged. "Some wanted to fight, but Father said we couldn't possibly win. And what would be the result? A few sad songs and lots of broken families. So we gathered in formal court rank, and he came, dressed in Elsarion indigo and white, only with the old kingsblossom lilies in gold. . . ." She paused, remembering the brush of that deep blue gaze, a far more intense blue than Nadav's here, but as indifferent and remote as polished stones. His attention had moved past her as if she were furniture, not the prettiest girl in Send Alian—everyone said so—as well as a princess. "The warriors stayed outside the city. He came in alone. Went aside with my father, and nobody could hear them. The gossip is, he never raises his voice. Anyway, they came back, and he had father's crown, but he wasn't wearing it. He had a page carrying it on a pillow. Very respectful, but he was bare-headed when he arrived, and he left the same way." She remembered his long, glossy black hair waving back from his high brow, and shook her head. "He was frightening," she said finally. "Though I can't tell you why, because it wasn't anything he said or did."

"But you knew what he's done elsewhere," Alaraec observed, his eyes narrowed in that way again. "It was the force of his reputation, not his warriors, right?"

Jasalan eyed her visitors and saw nothing but sympathy. Moreover, she knew enough of recent history to remember that Remalna had done no better at fighting off Norsunder during the war than any other kingdom had. "That's what my father said. The warriors made *us* look better, not them, because the truth is, Papa would have surrendered if that man had walked alone all the way from the border. Because we all know what he's done when someone gets in his way. Beginning with his own cousin."

Raec had been watching her. The interview had begun with the princess hiding firmly behind her courtly manners, so he'd taken a risk and introduced a topic that no one ever would in a typical courtly conversation. She was even prettier when her expression was real and not courtly. He gave in to impulse again. "Why don't you come back to Remalna with us? Just for a visit. Nothing expected, no obligations. I'm too young to marry—I promised my parents I'd not make any decisions until I'm twenty-five—"

"Why, it's the same with me," she exclaimed. And, "Do you have a fleet out there? We hadn't heard anything."

"No. I hired a small trader."

Her brows contracted slightly. Was she disappointed? But a heartbeat later the courtly bright smile was back, and he decided he'd been mistaken.

She was thinking, *I'm going to wear a crown again.* "I'll go consult my mother and father." She didn't add, *I'm certain they will agree.*

Young Risa hadn't believed that Granny would find a cargo worth selling, not overnight, but as usual she'd underestimated her. Granny knew *everyone* along the coast of the Sartoran Sea, all three sides.

They'd just finished packing into the hold some of the best rice-paper painted fans from Seven Cities when one of the ship's boys scampered down the deck, dodging sailors busy getting the *Petal* ready to put out to sea on Granny's order.

The boy hopped over a coiled rope. "Risa! Granny says a messenger came. We've got passengers again. Same ones, with a couple more added. You're to meet 'em on the main road just outside the city gates. Lead 'em to the *Petal*."

Risa hadn't admitted, even inside her own head, to missing the company of the two toffs from Remalna. They were toffs, she was a sailor, and that was that. But now she grinned as the light of anticipation and happiness flooded through her.

Risa handed the watch off to the mate on duty, hesitated over fetching her belt and knife from her gear—for her mother had taught her to defend herself from the threat of dockside footpads and the like—then shrugged. Al Caba was no longer in the least dangerous, not since the new king had put in patrols of large, well-trained guards. She and the boy rowed to shore, and he stayed with the pinnace while she dashed through the crowds on the busy dock.

It did not take long to reach the outer gate. Like most harbor cities, Al Caba was long and narrow, curving around the harbor itself. But at the top of what was just beginning to be a steep rise toward the barely visible marble palace way up on the ridge, she paused to wipe her damp forehead on her sleeve and look back at the hundreds of ships, from tiny fishers to two big Enaeraneth war brigantines on patrol duty, ranging through all sizes, shapes, and types of rigging in between. Now it made sense to meet the passengers on the road. Otherwise it would probably take them a full day just to find the *Petal*.

She resumed her uphill toil—and spotted a small group coming down the switchback road. She peered under her hand to block the glaring sunlight, glimpsed Nadav's and Raec's dark and light heads just before they vanished behind a tumble of rock overgrown with scrubby trees. They and two women reappeared, walking downhill toward a bridge over a chasm, both sides surrounded by lush greenery.

She started forward to meet them. But just as they reached the bridge, the bushes at either side of the chasm rustled violently and a slew of armed bravos surged up, descending on the party!

Risa felt for her boat knife—remembered she'd left it on the *Petal*—but she raced forward anyway, fists doubled.

In the middle of the bridge, a toff girl in a fancy dress screeched, "Go away! How *dare* you!"

But the brigands ignored her, closing in on Nadar and Raec. Nadav ripped free his sword, raised it—

Raec said something in a sharp voice. Nadav rammed his sword back in its sheath. Like Raec, he shrugged off his travel pack and slung it to the roadside.

Then he and Raec turned on the bravos with their hands! Their hands, their feet, and some of the road dust. Risa faltered to a stop, watching in amazement. She could account for herself, but the training Raec and Nadav had had was obviously of another order altogether. The two Remalnans stood back to back, never fouling one another's reach as they dealt with the bravos with brisk rapidity, tripping them, punching them in just the right place to fold them up abruptly until the attackers all either lay or sat, groaning, on the dusty road.

Jasalan was impressed. Nadav was just a little faster and stronger than Alaraec, and lots more dashing. Surely that was proof that Nadav was really the prince, and they had swapped identities, just like in her favorite ballad?

From the other end of the bridge, Lored watched in amazement and then fury. These were the best of his own friends, all volunteers—the strongest fellows in the old court. Nobody had ever given them any trouble, they hadn't dared. Wasn't this proof these two were as fake as a stage illusion? What prince fought like an outlaw?

As the dust began to settle, Jasalan spied her suitor on the other side of the bridge. "*Lored?* I can't believe *you* brought these . . . these ruffians!"

"They're not ruffians," Lored retorted, stomping onto the bridge. "If anyone's a ruffian, it's got to be those two." He jerked a thumb at Nadav and Raec. "So you were too besotted to discover if they are who they claim to be, but I cannot believe your father is stupid enough to fall for an obviously false tale. I intended to capture them before they could spirit you away. Find out the truth."

Jasalan flushed. "Go on," she invited. "You have any other criticism to offer of my father or me? Don't hold back," she said in a bright, high voice that trembled on the last word. Then she scowled. "Because then it's *my turn*."

Raec had bent over, hands on his knees, as he fought for breath. His head turned from side to side. He said faintly, "Who's he?" to Nadav, who shrugged, then drew his arm across his brow.

"No one," Jasalan said coldly, "of account."

Lored, goaded beyond endurance, snapped, "Not until a better title came along. Not that I believe his even exists."

Risa watched Nadav turn his gaze skyward, his mouth compressed in a way that made it clear he was trying not to laugh. Raec, however, was much harder to read.

"Oh!" Jasalan exclaimed, stamping her foot.

Risa snorted. Dressed like a toff, and a foot stamper. She just had to be the former princess.

"Let's go," Jasalan ordered. Then she frowned. "Where's my maid?"

"I believe she took off," Nadav said. "Quite sensibly," he added, as they all spotted the princess's luggage cart on its side, abandoned in the middle of the road.

Jasalan groaned. "She'll run squawking straight to my father—"

"Good!" Lored put in.

Risa decided it was time to make her own presence known. She stepped up, pitching her voice to be heard. "We sail on the tide."

Faces turned her way, exhibiting several varieties of confusion.

"That means soon," she said. "I have a boat waiting."

Jasalan tripped forward, her ribbon and lace bedecked skirts swinging as she picked her way around Lored's boys, who were struggling to their feet, some holding their middles, others rubbing a knee or the backs of their heads, and all of them wary of Raec and Nadav.

Jasalan gestured imperiously at Risa. "Get my bags, since my maid ran off."

Risa was on the verge of a fairly hot retort; Nadav, making a comical face, sauntered back up the road to pick up one of Jasalan's parcels. Risa picked up the other two. Raec took one from her and righted the little cart the maid had knocked over in her rush to get away.

The three of them loaded Jasalan's baggage onto the cart. As the boys retrieved their own packs from the roadside, Risa took the handle, found the cart rolled easily, and said over her shoulder, "This way."

Lored made a gesture toward Jasalan, but she swept past, nose in the air. Raec sketched a bow, then resumed dusting his clothes off.

As Nadav passed, Lored muttered, "I'll find out who you really are."

And Nadav could not resist saying, "The dread pirate Death Hand, and his wicked first mate Blood Gut, at your service."

Lored put his hand to his sword, with its jeweled hilt and exquisite carving—untouched in his rooms since his last lesson, what, two years ago?

When the last of the ambush party was on their feet, Lored snapped his fingers and began to speak in a low, rapid voice.

Jasalan was anxious until, at last, the girl with the ugly clothes and the kerchief binding up her hair said, "Here we are!"

What she guided the rowboat to was not a princely yacht. Jasalan gazed in disappointment at the lack of gilding or carving, the scruffy crew, not a single one in royal livery. "What is this, a fishing boat?" she asked—in Sartoran.

The kerchief girl said—in Sartoran—"It's a trader."

Raec said, "I hired it. If you'd rather make other arrangements to travel in something more to your liking, well, we can sail on ahead and prepare for your visit."

Jasalan knew Lored was going to run back to her father and spout a lot of nonsense, which would result—if Father believed him—in her being forced back home until the prince was proved to be a real prince. And after that, would he want her to come to Remalna? He would not, and who could blame him?

"If you can bear it," she said to Raec, with the sweetest smile she could summon, "I can." There! That would show a cooperative spirit, wouldn't it? And also hint that if they shared adventure, they could share . . . a crown.

Raec sat back, dazzled, until an efficient elbow in the ribs broke through the clouds of possibility that smile seemed to offer.

"We will need to get the bags up before we can set sail," Risa said, standing up, a bulky travel hamper balanced on one hip.

The three of them made a human chain to pass up the princess's luggage. Raec and Nadav then slung their own modest bags over their shoulders. Risa clambered up, tossed a land-rat's rope ladder down, leaving the two swains to get their princess up while she marshaled a crew to raise the boat.

Granny Risa gave orders for the main courses to be set, and as soon as the dripping boat swung in over the deck on its booms, the *Petal* slowly came to life, huge sails thudding overhead as they filled with the brisk sea air.

Risa, having seen the boat tied down, left the huge pile of luggage sitting on the deck and stalked to her grandmother on the captain's deck

"Where is the extra guest to sleep?" Granny asked.

Risa jerked her shoulders up and down. "If those two want to offer her their cabin, they can sleep on the deck."

"And if it rains?"

Risa sighed. "I did not invite her."

"No, they did, and they sent word to me asking permission to sail with us again—they'd work off passage for four. I said yes."

Risa scowled. "If I liked her, I'd sleep on deck—in the boat if it rains, since the air is warm. But I don't like her."

"I'm certain she's no better or worse than most princesses."

"Are they trained to treat everyone as a servant?"

"Probably. That doesn't make you into one," was Granny's unemotional answer.

Risa rubbed her chin. "This is true."

Granny flickered her fingers. "Go make your arrangements."

Risa finally decided to give the princess her own cabin—it was much easier than shifting the entire crew about, small as the ship was. Risa could swing a hammock in the cargo hold, or sleep on deck when it was balmy, as she had when small.

Jasalan, of course, complained about being cramped, but when the boys showed her their tiny cabin—shared between the two of them—she dropped the subject, and as the next few days flowed by, Risa watched her court Raec and flirt with Nadav.

By now Risa cordially hated Jasalan, who noticed Risa only when she wanted to hand out orders. All her attention was on the two boys.

Risa knew she shouldn't watch—it just made her angry. But she couldn't help herself—if she heard Jasalan's voice, she made herself even more angry by listening to the fluting laugh, or the breathy-sweet way the princess agreed to everything Raec said and then pointed out how amazing it was that they thought alike in so many ways.

But Nadav she teased. "I'm sure you think I'm clumsy. Oooh, I wish I could fight with a sword, but you'd laugh at me if I tried. Oh, my dress . . . my hair . . . the weather and this ship are turning me into a fright!" All intended—*obviously* intended, Risa thought sourly—to produce the compliments that Nadav so readily and audaciously supplied. "Fright? The fright, dear princess, is how unerringly the shafts from your beautiful eyes dart into my heart and slay me!"

Risa would finally get angry enough to retreat to her granny's cabin to brood, or high up on the masthead in the wind, where no one but the lookout could see her.

Or Raec, who gradually drifted away from the other two when they were exchanging their witticisms about hearts and eye shafts, and prowled the ship in search of Risa. He realized as the days drifted by that he missed her conversation, and so one evening he made it his business to seek her out. Finding her on the masthead, he insisted she eat with them in the wardroom, which the crew had largely left to the passengers.

The princess took one look at the unwelcome addition, assumed her grandest court manners, and took over the conversation. She displayed a broad knowledge of Sartoran plays, Colendi music, and various styles of art and poetry, all of which the boys were familiar with—leaving Risa with absolutely nothing to say.

Risa was still fuming at noon the next day when the princess emerged from her leisurely sleep. She wore a silk gown with its loops and loops of draped lace, trod gracefully on deck, and looked around for the boys.

She called up to them where they were working on the foretop-sail yard, but the wind—brisk and clean, sending the *Petal* skimming over the playful blue-green waves—snapped her words away, and they did not appear to hear.

Risa held her breath—and the princess, balked of her prey, began to climb up the shrouding, the wind tugging at her skirts, which she kept leaning out to bat down. Halfway up she stopped and called plaintively for help. And—being only boys, Risa thought in disgust—Nad and Raec abandoned their duty, scrambled to the end of the yard, and began shouting instructions to her, both reaching down to pull her up when she'd crept close enough.

On the yard she clung to them as they pointed out various parts of the ship.

Risa, at the wheel, scarcely glanced at the sea or the sails. She could feel the ship's balance against the wind in her feet and up through her bones. She glared up at those three figures until the boys swung down—showing off rather than climbing down. So, *of course,* guess who had to swing down, too, but only after a lot of coaxing and making certain everyone's attention was on her? She tiptoed to the edge of the masthead and swung out, the wind blowing through her loosened hair and flagging her skirts.

Risa gave the wheel a quick yank, the rudder surged against the water, and the *Petal* lurched, causing the princess to swing wide.

Risa grinned as Jasalan kicked wildly, her skirts a froth of white as she squawked and screeched, all airs and graces forgotten. Another flick of the helm and she swung back and dropped with a splat onto the deck.

The boys rushed to her. Everyone rushed to her, though some of the crew were not exactly hiding grins.

But as soon as Raec had made sure she was fine (of course she was fine!) he lifted his head and sent a long, inscrutable look up at Risa, whose triumph doused like a candle flame in rain.

The princess wavered to her feet, hand to her brow as she clung to Nadav's hand. In disgust, Risa turned her gaze away at last, to discover her grandmother mounting slowly to the captain's deck.

"That was not well done," Granny said.

Risa flushed. "I don't care."

But of course she did—they both knew that.

Before Granny could retort, the lookout (who had been watching the drama on deck instead of the horizon) gave an excited shout: "Four sail, hull up, directly astern!"

Everyone not on duty ran up to the captain's deck and gazed at the four very tall ships riding the wind toward them.

Granny, staring through her glass, frowned. "Warships. Rigged as Adrani. Could they be chasing us?"

Both she and Risa thought first of the cargo, but their smuggling days were long over. Then their eyes turned to the princess, who stood between Nadav and Raec, looking disheveled and scared.

"Uh-oh," Risa muttered.

Granny might have outrun them, despite the advantage of this wind for heavier ships. But she did not give the word, to the surprise of her crew—who felt they owed nothing to the Adranis.

And so they spilled their wind and hove to.

A naval party rowed over, the oars working in strict precision. The fact that the *Petal*'s command was not summoned to the flagship meant, to those who knew the ways of the sea, that someone was aware of a delicate question of diplomacy at higher levels.

First up was the Adrani captain. A short, round woman of about fifty years, her face sun seamed, she swept her gaze once over the orderly deck and everyone on it. Behind came six sailors in neat blue tunics and white deck trousers—and last, a civilian, tall, with red hair—

Jasalan stalked forward. "Lored, how dare you!"

Lored pointed a finger at Nadav. "That's the pirate Black Hand. He said so himself." The finger picked out Raec. "So that one must be Blood Gut."

For a moment there was no sound except for the creaking of the masts and the gentle tap of blocks overhead as the ship rocked on the water. Then Jasalan gasped—and Risa could not hold in her laughter.

At her first whoop, the entire crew roared in mirth.

Nadav leaned across Jasalan and said in Remalnan, "Prince Blood Gut. You are never going to live this one down."

"I'll get you for that," Raec returned.

The Adrani captain surveyed the angry princess—who did not look the least like she'd been abducted against her will—the sullen Lord Alored, the wooden-faced pair of young men (who, if it was true about their defeating an entire party, had apparently not killed a one), and the crew. She knew pirates, and this was not a pirate ship.

But the forms had to be observed. So she demanded to see their trade manifest, which Granny respectfully supplied, then she sent an inspection crew into the hold.

Meanwhile, she said, "Are you Princess Jasalan?"

"I am." Hands on hips, and another foot stomp.

"Are you on this vessel against your will?"

"I am not. I was invited by Prince Alaraec." She pointed between the two, stealing a peek from under her lashes at Nadav. *Now is the time to reveal your disguise.*

But Nadav just bowed with courtly grace.

Raec said, "I fear I haven't any proof of who I am. Never been asked before. But if you care to sail with us to Remalna, I will get my parents to speak for me."

The inspection crew reappeared, the lieutenant gave his head a single shake, and the captain made her decision. "We will each continue on our courses." And to Lored, "Which will include having to explain to the admiral why I had to pull four ships off patrol on a purposeless chase."

Lored paled. His mother, the duchess, would be even more fluent about that than the former king.

Raec then spoke up. "Why don't you come along, too? You might like Remalna. If not, you can at least tell stories on us when you get back home."

Jasalan had twined her hands firmly around his arm. She turned her prettiest pout on him. "But isn't it *my* party?"

Raec said kindly, "My parents like meeting people from other countries. Say it makes for better relations in the future."

Lored was going to refuse but reflected on what sort of reaction he'd get if he went home now. Meanwhile, if this really was a prince, surely there were beautiful noblewomen in Remalna.

Taking no notice of Jasalan, who was shaking her head at him, he said to Raec, "Permit me to fetch my manservant and my gear, and I will return. Thank you." He bowed, adding, "And I beg your pardon for my error."

Raec smiled, making a rueful gesture. "It's all right. I thought I was doing the right thing to make this visit without all the usual trappings, but I think I've discovered why the trappings are occasionally useful." He opened his hands, bowing first to Lored and then to the Adrani captain. "I apologize for causing all this tumult."

There was nothing left but mutual civilities and departure; by sundown the Adrani ships were lost beyond the horizon, and the deck resounded to the noise of three young men, as (at Lored's request) Nadav and Raec demonstrated some of the training they'd gotten during their years at one of the best military academies in the world.

Risa kept her distance, going down to the wardroom to eat alone when her watch was finished. Just as she sat down, Jasalan emerged from her cabin, this time in a beautiful gown of embroidered velvet that belonged in a ballroom. Not, Risa thought, eyeing that low-cut neckline, that the boys would mind.

Jasalan did not flounce by as usual. She paused. "You did that on purpose."

Risa could not prevent a flush. "Yes." And, "I apologize."

Jasalan made a scornful gesture. "Save your breath. I know you don't mean it."

"No. Not any more than you mean all that rot you keep spouting at Raec about how you think alike. But I guess the forms must be gone through. By me, to keep the peace on this ship; by you, fishing for a crown."

It was Jasalan's turn to blush. "I've seen how you keep

watching him," she said scornfully. "Do you really think he'd give up a crown to sail on an old fishing boat?" She snapped open her fan, holding it at an aggressive angle. "Or, if you were dreaming of becoming a fisher-queen, do you think you'd last a single day in a royal court?"

"I have no intention of ever setting foot in a royal court," Risa said.

"That's quite wise." Jasalan rustled her way up onto deck, where her fluting laugh could soon be heard, but this time Risa did not follow.

Risa stayed below when, at last, they sailed into Smuggler's Cove on the midnight tidal flow. Nadav searched her out, kissed her hand in the grand manner, and thanked her for making their journey so pleasant; then he leaped to the deck and ran uphill to rouse up the stable and arrange for travel, as Raec stayed with his guests.

Risa did not want to see them depart. She found work to do belowdecks. So she was surprised by a quiet, familiar step behind her; she whirled, and there was Raec, holding a golden medallion on his palm. He said, "I want you to know how much I enjoyed the journey, mostly because I got a chance to meet you. I hope—I want—" He frowned at the deck, and then reached for her hand and pressed the medallion into it. "That's my emergency transfer token. In case I got myself into trouble I couldn't get out of. It transfers to the family part of Athanarel. The royal palace. Ah, if you'd ever like to see where I live—meet my family—please use it. All you do is say my entire name, with this on your palm, and the magic will work."

She struggled to find words, but the conflict within her was too strong, so she just said, "Thank you."

He made a curious ducking sort of bow, reached again, but when she closed her fingers over the token and dropped her hand to her side, he backed away, and shortly thereafter she heard his quick step on the deck overhead, and then he was gone.

When she came up on deck, the crew was just finishing coiling down the last lines, and some were departing on leave, gear bags over their shoulders, lanterns swinging in their hands.

"I'll stay, if you want to negotiate the cargo," Risa said.

"What's that in your fist?" Granny asked.

Risa had been holding the token in a tight grip. She snorted. "An invitation to make a fool of myself in his palace. As if I'd do that."

Her heart constricted, and with a violent motion she flung the token over the rail into the darkness, where they heard it plunk into the sea.

Granny said, "Once upon a time there was a prince in my life. He made a similar invitation to me. But I was too proud to accept it. And so . . . and so time passed, and he married a princess. An excellent woman, I hear. And I, though eventually I had a family, I ended up married to my ship. An excellent ship, as you see."

Risa regarded her grandmother in the light of the lamp on her table. They were alone now, the soft air still except for the distant cry of night birds.

Risa muttered, "He'll marry that girl. She knows all the tricks to make sure of it."

"Didn't you hear him turn the courtship into a general party when he invited Lord Alored along?" Granny chuckled. "See if that young redhead isn't 'in love' with Nadav Savona's pretty sister within the span of two days."

"Oh, Granny, even if he doesn't marry her, where would that leave me? If we did decide we—oh, I can't even say it. I won't give up the sea, and he shouldn't give up being king, not with all that training. And I couldn't bear a court filled with Jasalans."

"There are all kinds of compromises people make," Granny said. "Who says you'd have to live in a palace all year round? For that matter, who says their court is filled with Jasalans? Don't you know what they once called the present queen? The Barefoot Countess. Still do. And she apparently likes it. I asked young Raec. He says she still runs around barefoot up in the mountains."

Risa groaned. "But we hardly know one another."

"Isn't that why he invited you to visit?" Granny asked with her customary astringency. "Or are you going to relive my mistake, because you insist on seeing titles instead of human beings? Did I really raise you that badly?"

"No," Risa admitted. "But it's a world I don't know. I'll make horrible mistakes."

"Mistakes in manners can be survived. I refused to see that. I was too cowardly to try." Granny paused. "If you do choose to go, you can carry a story. It might not be the time yet to tell it, but someday it should be told," Granny said, and moved to the rail, where she stared off toward the twinkling lights of the village as they were lit one by one. "It's not a happy story. But it is, perhaps, an important one."

Risa swallowed hard in her aching throat.

"There was once a young, romantic prince we will call Lark. He wanted to do something heroic, and he heard about pirate problems ruining his country's trade, so he joined a crew, lying about his experience. After all, he'd been trained in dueling the way nobles do, and ship work is easy to pick up, right? So there came a pirate attack in the night. This pirate crew used to sneak half the crew through the water and climb up to the deck to take a ship. So Lark rallied his friends, courageously leading them (like a prince should) in a charge on the pirates coming over the rail—when arrows hissed through the darkness from the pirate ship. One struck Lark in the hip, another my cousin in the shoulder. The other five of his friends, including my little brother, were all struck in the heart and died. Lark and my cousin fought on with the rest of us through the night, which made healing very difficult when at last we drove them off and could tend the wounded."

Risa winced.

"Lark had not known anything about arrows, or about how pirates fight. So—though he had courage, though he meant only the best—he led his band straight into danger and death. He soon learned, and kept learning, and kept learning, until he became a formidable captain in his own right, but he never forgave himself for his actions of that night. I hear he still lives with the result of that wound, though he could afford the magic healers to fix it. He made sure his son was trained not to make the same"—Granny made a fist, bringing it down to the rail—"what *I* would call a horrible mistake."

Risa let out her breath.

Granny moved slowly to her cabin and shut the door, leaving Risa standing at the rail, staring out.

She was still there when dawn began to blue the air, and a warm peachy color lit up the core. Then she dove off the rail, swimming down to the slanting sea floor, and the faint gleam of gold.

Sherwood Smith is the author of *Crown Duel* and *Court Duel* (published in one volume by Firebird as *Crown Duel*), three books about the intrepid Wren *(Wren to the Rescue, Wren's Quest,* and *Wren's War)*, and a trilogy set in the *Crown Duel* world: *Inda, The Fox,* and *King's Shield.*

Smith began making books out of taped paper towels when she was six years old. When she was eight, she started writing about another world, though she soon switched to making comic books of her stories, which she found to be easier. Smith went to college, lived in Europe, came back to the United States to get her master's in history, worked in Hollywood, got married, started a family, and became a teacher. Now retired, she writes full-time.

Her Web site is **www.sherwoodsmith.net**.

Author's Note

"Court Ship" was written for fans of *Crown Duel*, who wondered about the second generation after that story. It also answers some questions about events previous to that story.

Jane Yolen and Adam Stemple

Little Red

Seven years of bad luck. That's what I think as I drag the piece of broken mirror over my forearm. Just to the right of a long blue vein, tracing the thin scars that came before.

There's no pain. That's all on the inside. It won't come out, no matter how much I bleed. No pain. But for a moment . . .

Relief.

For a moment.

Until Mr. L calls me again. "Hey, you, Little Red, come here."

Calls *me*. Not any of the other girls. Maybe it's because he likes my stubby red hair. Likes to twist his stubby old man fingers in it. And I can't tell him no.

"You want to go back home?" he asks. "Back to your grandmother's? Back to the old sewing lady?" He's read my file. He knows what I will say.

"No. Even you are better than that." Then I don't say

anything else. I just go away for a bit in my mind and leave him my body.

The forest is dark but I know the way. I have been here before. There is a path soon, pebbly and worn. But my fingers and toes are like needles and pins. If I stay here, stray here too long, will I become one of them forever?

It's morning now, and I'm back, looking for something sharp. Orderlies have cleaned up the mirror; I think Mr. L found the piece I had hidden under the mattress. It doesn't matter—I can always find something. Paper clips stolen from the office, plastic silverware cracked just right, even a ragged fingernail can break the skin if you have the courage.

Alby faces the wall and traces imaginary coastlines on the white cement. She is dark and elfin, her hair shorn brutally close to her scalp except for one long tress that hangs behind her left ear. "Why do you wind him up like that?"

"Wind up who?" My voice is rough with disuse. Is it the next morning? Or have days passed? "And how?"

"Mr. L. The things you say to him . . ." Shuddering, Alby looks more wet terrier than girl. "If you'd just walk the line, I'm sure he'd leave you alone."

Having no memory of speaking to Mr. L at all, I just shrug. "Walk the line. Walk the path. What's the difference?"

"Promise?"

"Okay."

"Yeah, play the game, let them think you're getting better." Alby straightens up, picturing home, I figure. She's got one to go back to. Wooden fence. Two-car garage. Mom and Dad and a bowl full of breakfast cereal. No Grandma making lemonade on a cold Sunday evening. No needles. No pins.

It's my turn to shudder. "I don't want to get better. They might send me home."

Alby stares at me. She has no answer to that. I turn to the bed. Start picking at the mattress, wondering if there are still springs inside these old things. Alby faces the wall, her finger already winding a new path through the cracks. We all pass the time in our own way.

We get a new therapist the next day. We're always getting new ones. They stay a few weeks, a few months, and then they're gone.

This one wants us to write in journals. She gives us these beautifully bound books, cloth covers with flowers and bunnies and unicorns and things, to put our ugly secrets in.

"Mine has Rainbow Brite." Alby is either excited or disgusted, I can't tell which.

Joelle says, "They should be snot colored. They should be brown like . . ." She means shit. She never uses the word, though.

"I want you to start thinking beautiful thoughts, Joelle," the therapist says. She has all our names memorized already. I think, *This one will only last two weeks. Long enough for us to ruin the covers. Long enough for Joelle to rub her brown stuff on the pages.*

I put my hand on my own journal. It has these pretty little

flowers all over. I will write down my thoughts. But they won't be beautiful.

CUTTER

scissors
fillet knife
a broken piece of glass
I can't press hard enough
to do more than scratch the surface
and blood isn't red
until it touches the air

Okay, so it doesn't rhyme and I can't use it as a song, but it's still true.

"What did you write, Red?" Alby asks.

Joelle has already left for the bathroom. I don't look forward to the smell from her book.

"Beautiful thoughts." I cover the poem with my hand. It *is* beautiful, I decide. Dark and beautiful, like I am when I dream.

"Little Red." Mr. L stands in the doorway. "Excuse me, Ms. Augustine. I need to see that one."

He points at me. I go away.

Four-footed and thick-furred, I stalk through a shadowy forest. My prey is just ahead of me—I can hear his ragged breathing, smell his terror-sweat. Long pink tongue to one side, I leap forward, galloping now. I burst through a flowering thornbush and catch sight of him: Mr. L, naked and covered in gray hair. I can smell his terror. Then I am on him, and my sharp teeth rip into his flesh. Bones crack and I taste marrow, sweet counterpoint to his salty blood.

I wake in the infirmary, arms and legs purple with fresh bruises.

"Jesus, Red," Alby says. "He really worked you over this time, didn't he?"

"I guess." I don't remember. Seems likely, though.

"Looks like you got him one too, though."

"Oh, yeah?" I can hardly move, though I turn my head toward the sound of her voice.

Alby grins her pixie smile. "Yeah. Got a big bandage on his neck, he does."

I lick my lips. Imagine I can taste blood. "Probably cut himself shaving."

Her smile fading, Alby says, "Whatever you say, Red."

I try to roll over, turn away from her, but something holds me down: leather straps at my ankles and wrists. One across my waist.

"Five-point locked leather," Alby says, with some reverence. "You were really going crazy when they brought you in. Foaming at the mouth, even."

I lay my head back down on the small, hard pillow. Close my eyes. Maybe I can get back to my dream.

Mr. L visits me in the dark room with the leather straps. He has no bandage on his neck, but there are scratches there. I know why. I have his skin under my fingernails. In my teeth.

"Little Rojo," he says, almost lovingly, "you must learn control."

I try to laugh but all that comes out is a choking cough. He wanders slowly behind me, his fingers trailing through my red hair, my cap of blood.

"You must learn to walk the path." In front of me again, he glances up, at the television camera, the one that always watches. Puts his back to it.

"And will you be my teacher?" I say before spitting at him.

He looks down at me. Smiles. "If you let me." Then he pats my cheek. Before he can touch me again, I go away.

The forest is cold that night and I stand on a forked road. One is the path of needles, one the path of pins. I don't know which is which. Both are paths of pain.

I take the left.

I don't know how far I travel—what is distance to me? I am a night's walk from my den, a single leap from my next meal—but I am growing weary when the trap closes on my leg.

Sharp teeth and iron, it burns as it cuts. A howl escapes my throat, and I am thrown out of myself.

I see Mr. L standing over the strapped body of a girl. I can't see his hands. But I can feel them.

He looks up as I howl again, his face caught between pleasure and pain. I tumble through the thick walls and out into the cool night sky, into the dark forest, into my fur body.

I tear at my ankle with teeth made for the task. Seconds later, I leave my forepaw in the trap and limp back down the path.

⊠ ⊠ ⊠

It is days later. Weeks. Nighttime. Moon shining in my tiny window. They couldn't keep me tied down forever. The law doesn't allow it.

I am crouched in the corner of my room, ruined tube of toothpaste in my hands. I have figured out how to tear it, unwind it, form it into a razor edge. I hold it over my arm, scars glowing white in the moonlight, blue vein pulsing, showing me where to cut.

But I don't. Don't cut.

Instead I let the pain rise within me. I know one quick slash can end the pain. Can bring relief. But I don't move. I let the pain come and I embrace it, feel it wash over me, through me. I let it come—and then, I go away.

I am in the forest. But I am not four-footed. I am not thick-furred. I have no hope of tasting blood now or smelling the sweet scent of terrified prey.

I am me: scrawny and battered, short tufts of ragged red hair sprouting from my too-large head. Green eyes big. A gap between my top front teeth wide enough to escape through.

I stand in the middle of the road. No forks tonight, it runs straight and true like the surgeon's knife. Behind me, tall trees loom. I take two tentative steps and realize I am naked. Embarrassed, I glance around. I am alone.

Before long I see a white clapboard cottage ahead of me. Smoke trails from a redbrick chimney. Gray paving stones lead up to the front door. I recognize the house. It is more threatening than the dark forest with its tall trees. Grandma lives here.

I turn to run, but behind me I hear howling—long, low, and mournful. I know the sound—wolves. Hunting wolves. I must hurry inside.

The door pulls open silently. The first room is unlit as I step inside. I pull the door closed behind me. Call into the darkness, "Grandma?"

"Is that you, Red?" Her voice is lower than I remember.

"Yes, Grandma." My voice shakes. My hands shake.

"Come into the bedroom. I can't hear you from here."

"I don't know the way, Grandma."

I hear her take a deep breath, thick with smoke, rattling with disease. "Follow my voice. You'll remember how."

And suddenly, I do remember. Three steps forward, nine steps left. Reach out with your right hand and push through the thin door.

"I am here, Grandma."

Outside, there are disappointed yips as the wolves reach the front door and the end of my trail.

"Come closer, Red. I can't see you from here."

"Yes, Grandma." I step into blackness and there she is, lying in the bed. She is bigger than I remember, or maybe I am smaller. The quilt puffs around her strangely, as if she has muscles in new places. A bit of drool dangles from her bottom lip.

I look down at my empty hands. My nakedness. "I haven't brought you anything, Grandma."

She smiles, showing bright, pointed teeth. "You have brought yourself, Red. Come closer, I can't touch you from here."

"Yes, Grandma." I take one step forward and stop.

The wolf pack snuffles around the outside of the house, searching for a way in.

Grandma sits up. Her skin hangs loosely on her, like a housedress a size too large. Tufts of fur poke out of her ears, rim her eyes.

"No, Grandma. You'll hurt me."

She shakes her head, and her face waggles loosely from side to side. "I never hurt you, Red." She scrubs at her eye with a hairy knuckle, then scoots forward, crouching on the bed, poised to spring. Her haunches are thick and powerful. "Sometimes the wolf wears my skin. It is he who hurts you." Her nose is long now.

"No, Grandma." I stare into her dark green eyes. "No, Grandma. It's you."

She leaps then, her Grandma skin sloughing off as she flies for my throat. I turn and run, run through the thin door, run nine steps right and three steps back, push open the front door, hear her teeth snap behind me, severing tendons, bringing me down. I fall, collapsing onto the paving stones.

Howling and growling, a hundred wolves stream over and around me. Their padded feet are light on my body. They smell musty and wild. They take down Grandma in an instant, and I can hear her screams and the snapping of her brittle old bones.

I think I will die next, bleeding into the gray stone. But leathery skin grows over my ankle wound, thick gray fur. My nose grows cold and long and I smell Grandma's blood. Howling my rage and hunger, I leap to my four clawed feet. Soon, I am feasting on fresh meat with my brothers and sisters.

I wake, not surprised to be tied down again. Seven points this time, maybe more; I can't even move my head.

"Jesus, Red, you killed him this time." It is Alby, drifting into view above me.

"Go away, Alby. You aren't even real."

She nods without speaking and fades away. I go to sleep. I don't dream.

Next morning, they let me sit up. I ask for my journal. They don't want to give me a pen.

"You could hurt yourself," they say. "Cut yourself."

They don't understand.

"Then why don't *you* write down what I say," I tell them.

They laugh and leave me alone. Once again tied down. But I know what I want to write. It's all in my head.

GRANDMOTHER

What big ears you have,
What big teeth,
Big as scissors,
To cut out my heart
Pins and needles,
Needles and pins,
Where one life ends,
Another begins.

Jane Yolen, often called "the Hans Christian Andersen of America," is the author of almost three hundred books, including *Owl Moon, The Devil's Arithmetic,* and *How Do Dinosaurs Say Goodnight?* Her work ranges from rhymed picture books and baby board books; through middle-grade fiction, poetry collections, and nonfiction; and up to novels and story collections for young adults and adults. Her son, **Adam Stemple**, is a musician as well as a writer; he currently plays with the Tim Malloys and has a solo album, *3 Solid Blows to the Head.* His novels are *Singer of Souls* and its sequel, *Steward of Song.*

Jane and Adam have collaborated on two "rock 'n' troll" novels—*Pay the Piper* and *Troll Bridge.*

Jane Yolen divides her time between western Massachusetts and Scotland; her Web site is **www.janeyolen.com**. Adam Stemple lives with his family in Minneapolis; his Web site is **www.adamstemple.com**.

Authors' Note

Adam wrote the really dark poem about cutting and sent it to Jane. Jane took it and wrote the next few prose lines that follow it, then sent it back to him, asking if he wanted to write a story. Now that part's in the middle, but it was our starting point. No pun intended. We had *no* idea where the story was going or why, but it kept getting darker and darker. It took us to a place where neither one of us really wanted to go, which is sometimes the best way to write.

Laurel Winter

the myth of fenix

THE BEGINNING, IN 10 EASY STEPS

1.
So this boy, he heard about this great bird that got old and sick and tired of life and it set itself on fire and got reborn. That sounded good except why wait until you're old and sick, he thought, so he got ready and kept his eyes open for a good fire and when he found one he jumped in.

2.
Except he didn't really jump in.

3.
When they went through the ashes of the fire, they found a burned backpack and fragments of teeth. Dental records said it was this boy and no one cried except the foster mother who missed the money until she got a new boy.

4.
It hurts to break out your own teeth.

5.
So this boy, this Fenix, set off without a backpack to find his fortune. He stopped at the library to steal a book about the fenix only he found out that it was spelled different like p-h-o-e-n-i-x which was really stupid so he decided the name burned with him and was reborn clean and new. He didn't steal that book after all.

6.
It's easy to get an infection in your mouth.

7.
When he was getting more shivery and dizzy, Fenix went to this free clinic that didn't report to the socials. They asked his name and he said Fenix and they wrote Phoenix and he made them change it to Fenix because that was the fire-burned name and then they wanted a last name and he said Greenstick because that's the word that came out of his mouth. The medicine tasted like shit. They made him some new teeth out of plastic and they asked what color he wanted them and he said glow-in-the-dark green and they said are you sure and he said yes and paint the teeth that are left that color too.

8.
Or at least that's what they said he'd said when he woke up with no shivers and glow-in-the-dark teeth.

9.
Fenix Greenstick had never lived anywhere he liked so he went to find someplace good. He learned to sleep with his hand over his mouth.

10.
Sometimes his hand forgot.

THE MIDDLE, A TO F-FOR-FENIX, WITH A DREAM IN THERE SOMEWHERE

A.
Fenix Greenstick woke up when the woman with shining eyes lifted him in her arms. She said everything is going to be okay. He said you put me down right effing now and she laughed and said you've been lost a long time you don't remember but I'm taking you home.

B.
She was taller than any woman had ever been and strong strong strong enough that he could tell struggling would be useless but he did it anyway because after all every struggle in his whole damn life had been useless at the start but some of them paid off sometimes somehow anyway and he could never tell which ones were which. He howled and kicked like a baby but the woman just carried him away and said it will be all right it will be okay it's okay to be scared but you'll see soon enough.

C.
There wasn't much moon that night but between her eyes shining and his teeth glowing as he howled and yelled they got by just fine and covered a lot of distance in some impossible directions.

D.
Pretty soon he looked up at the sky and saw three small moons shining. One was red and two were yellow and none of them were as round as the moon he was used to. He said holy shit where are we and the woman said almost home now but not quite so you can sleep if you want to.

E.
Even though he didn't want to Fenix Greenstick fell asleep under three moons. His hand was tired from flailing about so it didn't even pretend it was going to cover his mouth but somehow that was okay.

THE DREAM
He dreamed that the woman was his mother even though he remembered his mother from before she died. She was short and not quite fat and her eyes didn't shine at all and she had needle tracks up arms that didn't pick him up even when he was three years old so there was no way this tall woman could be his mother but this was a dream and dreams have their own rules which is a good thing.

F.
Or maybe the good thing is that the world has its own rules. Remember though that this was a different world.

The Beginning of the End

In the beginning there was a boy and in the middle there was a different boy, although he was still really the same, except for his teeth and his name and his location, which kept changing in the most peculiar way. And in the beginning of the end

there was a boy
asleep under three moons
asleep in strong arms
a boy carried to a place he would have wanted to be
if he could have ever imagined it.

The Beginning—Again—Because It Makes More Sense to Call It That

They thought he was one of them, because of what he had made himself, because of who he had been reborn into, because he'd heard of that great bird.

Because they thought he was one of them, he became one of them, even though the atmosphere of their planet made him wheeze a little and he never did grow as tall or strong as the other children who had accidentally wandered into his world and been brought back home, children with shining teeth or eyes or hair or fingers. He was tall enough, strong enough. And happy.

Not for ever after, but for his portion of it.

That's good enough.

LAUREL WINTER is the author of the novel *Growing Wings*, which was a finalist for the Mythopoeic Award; her novella "Sky Eyes" won the World Fantasy Award. She has won two *Asimov's* Reader's Poll Awards and two Rhysling Awards for her poetry.

After forty-seven years in states that border Canada, she packed up six months worth of belongings and went to Asheville, North Carolina, to pet-sit for an acupuncturist who was going to India. After a month, she called her landlord in Minnesota and said, "Rent my apartment. I'm not coming back." She has been happily happening in Asheville ever since, writing and arting and walking and meditating.

Her sons are fabulous beings: one graduated from Oberlin with a triple major in computer science, math, and Chinese; the other has a passion for driving race cars.

Visit her Web site at **www.laurelwinter.com**.

AUTHOR'S NOTE

It all began—well, not *it all*, but this part of it all—when a friend of mine told me about her name. After her divorce, because she was rising from the ashes of her old life, new born, she changed her name to Pheonix. Not "Phoenix," because she thought that was stupid, with the O before the *E*. She spelled it how she thought the bird would spell it. I decided the bird would go further than that. Fenix and his story rose from the ashes of my friend's name.

Nick O'Donohoe

Fear and Loathing in LaLanna:

A Savage Journey to the Heart of the Kalchyan Dream

I

We were somewhere around Lalanna when the potions began to kick in. I remember saying something like, "I feel a little dizzy; take the reins. . . ." and suddenly there was a terrible roar around us, and the sky was full of huge bats—but not just bats—chimeras, and an impossible flock of phoenixes, and the twisted multieyed bastard children of seraphim, and clouds and clouds of dark, viciously ecstatic dragons who knew we had lost all control and feeding time had come. They gyred and spun around the wagon, which was hooked to two recently winged pegasi and was rocketing forward at an insane pace. And a voice was screaming, "Sacred Screaming God! Where did all these damned things come from?"

Gaanz was pouring a Self-Glamour on his naked chest. Thank the Laughing God he didn't have a mirror available; as much of that wretchedly indulgent potion as he'd bathed in, his eyeballs would turn inward and he'd swallow his tongue kissing himself. He made a great effort to notice something other than his own nipples and muttered patiently, "Well, Dook, we brought the bats with us. What are you yelling about?"

"Nothing. It's your turn to drive the team." No point mentioning the other creatures. The poor bastard would notice them soon enough.

The pegasi were ordinary horses whom we had winged for the drive from Derinyes and the Mage School. They strained against the team harness, trying to take our wagon off the ground with them. Later their joy of flight would wear off and they would be two tired, confused geldings in a stable full of mares and stallions who wouldn't believe a neigh of it. Fine. Let them feel like us, for once.

Gaanz rubbed the Self-Glamour on his chest slowly and sensually. Gods, he was despicable. Glamours are normally thrown at others to get cheap adoration and, usually, even cheaper sex. Self-Glams reversed the formula. A normal dose would make a princess or a count vain. Gaanz had thrown enough on himself to be stupefied with his own beauty.

(He told me that he and his woman once used Self-Glams before sex. "I've never enjoyed myself more," he swore. He was a subhuman monster, so it was probably true. I'd met her once—a pale, pasty thing with dark, angry eyes who had given up on others and turned inward—and the Drooling God knew she would never have anyone else's interest at heart right up to the day she died.)

I said, "Maybe we should talk about the Mission."

Gaanz scowled suspiciously. "Why? Aren't you up to it? We have everything we need." He gestured at the wagon bed behind us.

It was true. We had prepared well.

We had been called into the chamber of the Most High. We were fear gripped. As I often did, I was sweating profusely: what had he found out? The party with charms? The thing we had done to the foremost senior adept, with the toads and the love spell? Screaming God forbid, one of the other things? There were many choices, none good. I was picturing being sentenced to a few years in the basement of Holder's Keep, with scarred, snarling people even worse than those around us usually.

But the Most High stroked his clean-shaven chin and rubbed the basilisk that he had turned to stone (we all wanted to hear that story, but he would not tell), and he said, "There is an Althing of heroes coming, at Lalanna."

We were silent. We were stunned. All right, we were also charmed out of our senses, sweating perfume profusely and unable to focus.

He went on, "Normally we do not speak to heroes. They despise us. We have killed them, and they us. But something strange is happening to Kalchys, and we cannot afford not to know what they are doing."

He leaned on the crucible. "The Pre-Eminence's people have something in mind, something beyond the obvious. We must send someone to the Althing to observe. I have chosen you."

Even as he said it, he looked miserable with the choice.

Later, Gaanz said to me as he sucked down a strawful

of Forte (he broke two chairs subsequently), "He picked us because we're Adaptable. Because we're Flexible. Because of all those in the school, we alone can face the Unknown and fuck with it." His face was shining with sweat, and he was holding a sword that someone irresponsible had given him.

I said, "I think he chose us because if it all went to Hel, he would most enjoy losing us."

"Gods, yes!" He threw a bottle against the plaster of the tavern, chipping it. A hero would have used his fist instead of a bottle, but we weren't crazy. "But he made a mistake." He leaned across the table, nostrils flared, breathing heavily. "One—crucial—mistake."

It was obvious. "The travel money."

The Most High had handed the money over to us disdainfully. "This should cover your lodging in Lalanna, your food, and even some drink if you must. Be conservative."

Conservative we were, in our own fashion.

Negotiations had gone well prior to our journey. We had two pouches of Stunn; seventy-five pellets of Forecaste; five parchment pages drenched in mind-bogglingly powerful Innature; a snuffbox half full of Fast; and a whole starlit skyful of Pax, Warre, Forte, Sleepers, Wakers, Follies . . . and also a quart of brandy, three jugs of wine, a goatskin of MisSpeak, four tins of Glamour, and several dozen Bravehearts . . . but the only thing that worried me was the MisSpeak. There is no one in the world more helpless than a man full of MisSpeak, certain that he knows the secrets of the universe, trying in vain to communicate them. We hadn't used it yet, but it was only a matter of time before we got into the filthy stuff. We had at least promised each other that we would use it only one at a time, with the other one acting as a minder.

Gaanz stood bolt upright, staring ahead. "Look!" he shouted. For a moment I thought he'd finally seen the dragons. I braced myself to snatch the reins from him, even to roll him off the buckboard to save the wagon and my own life.

But he pointed straight ahead. "Behold the towers of Lalanna."

I barely needed to squint, even in the desert sun. How had I missed them? There was a group of ziggurats, each flanked by minarets, rising in silhouette out of the desert. Ironically, the architecture was a steal from Skandia, the enemy in the war the Althing was gathered to debate.

The foolish horses-turned-pegasi bounded down the cobblestones toward Lalanna, and the towers grew every second. Gaanz said, "As your senior guide, I advise you to prepare yourself." He waved an unsteady arm at the potions and knocked them over, spilling several out of their pouches, onto the lacquer tray.

"You miserable third-wit throwback!" I snapped. "Now we're hopelessly undersupplied. What are we going to do?"

His smile was a picture of depravity as he scraped the brown, gold, and red powders off the tray and into a bag. He shook it to mix it and poured some on his palm. "We find out if we're the stuff of heroes." He stuck his nose into his palm, sniffing deeply, and stuck his hand under my nose.

What could I do? It was unthinkable to show Weakness, especially at the start of a Search for the Truth. I inhaled from his palm, trying hard not to think about where else it had been.

We pulled up before the Hall of Heroes, gaping at the statuary. There were men and women in armor, leather skins, and nothing; they were fighting with spears, swords, broadaxes, twybils, and flails; they were wailing, singing, shouting, and roaring. Either the hall was incredibly old and these were all memorials, or the architect had abused even stronger potions than we had.

Then I saw that half the statues were moving, and the noise drifted down to us.

"At least we're at the right place," Gaanz muttered.

"Then why doesn't it *feel* right?"

"Hold on to yourself, you damned coward," he hissed. "You've taken too much. It's left you fear-driven."

"Too much of what?" Had this monster slipped me something harmful when I wasn't capable of watching? I wouldn't put it past him.

"Of everything. Let's go find the innkeeper."

To do that, we had to cross the lobby. And the lobby, even more so than the upper balconies, was full of heroes.

At their waists they wore fistaxes, swords, scimitars, wavy-bladed krises, broadswords, and rapiers. It was astonishing that these people didn't cut themselves jostling each other in the line for food.

The musculature was incredible. You could tell without

having to ask that half of these people had wasted their violent youth bench-pressing anvils until they were nothing but broad stacks of quadriceps, lats, abs, and hemorrhoids.

I tiptoed past a rage-gripped man who seemed to be stitched together from bears. He was arguing loudly with a man whose mother may have had unnatural congress with a gargoyle. A one-eyed woman with manacle scars and a missing ear was listening and laughing. They all seemed to be clothed in diapers.

And, Mad God help me, they were all wavering at the edges as I watched. At any moment, the uncontrolled mixture I had inhaled might wash me over the edge, and they would melt and froth into a floor-covering suds of scar tissue and violence.

Gaanz grabbed my arm. "Keep walking, dolt. You want these monsters to notice us?"

After that, I moved with exaggerated caution, as though the lobby were underwater.

The innkeeper had at one time been fat. She still had all the skin from those days, though her body was spindly and her cheekbones stuck out like storm shutters. Her eyes were angry jellied pools, and she frowned at us. "What do you want?" she snapped at me.

I saw her teeth shifting back and forth restlessly on her jaw, and I whimpered and shrank back.

Gaanz grabbed my arm and stepped forward, smiling. "My friend is shy, dear lady—also a bit of a third-wit. We're here for the Althing—"

"You. Here for the Althing." She frowned down at him, her scowl an additional fold among her jowls.

"Of course." He leaned forward, whispering to her, and I saw his hand wave a small unstoppered ampoule under her nose.

Her smile, by some miracle, lifted her cheeks. "Second floor, third door. Best in the house. Fit for a general," she purred, giving him the key and adding slyly, "And his consort."

She finished automatically, as though she had said it many times, "Please remember that you may not bring weapons into the Hall of Heroes tomorrow morning for the Althing."

One glance across the lobby said that was a marvelous idea.

As we left the desk, I said incredulously, "You used Heart's-Oil on her."

"Mixed with Thighwarme." He shrugged. "She gave us a room."

I snarled, "No, you depraved swine, she gave *you* a room. And what will she do when she lets herself into it tonight with the master key and finds me asleep and helpless? Slice me across the gut and let me bleed my life away while she has her way with you."

He was appalled. He muttered, "I don't think I gave her that much. I don't think she'd actually *kill* for me—"

"Think harder next time." I gestured around us. "This is the most dangerous place we've ever been. Every second person here is a killer. We've got to watch for danger, listen for it, *smell* it; we've got to be ready for a sudden fatal touch—"

A hand slapped down on each of our shoulders, and I nearly screamed like I'd heard a piglet do in the last seconds it had of being a boar.

"Welcome to the war," a voice boomed.

He spun us around. I looked into a grinning face with spaces between the teeth. He had bone buildup on his forehead from weapon impacts. If he didn't have brain damage, he had a goddess on his side. "Finally, we go to Skandia and get to wage the battle of our dreams."

"Graffin," he added. "Out of the southlands, with Mad Rob's troops. Whose outfit you with?"

"Savage Henry's," I said.

He stared at us blankly with his beady eyes. "Don't know him. How many in your outfit?"

Gaanz said, "Just us. All the others died in training."

"Fifty or so of them. Knives, garrotes, fistaxes . . ." I shrugged indifferently. "Two or three just with rocks."

He looked dubious. "And where's Savage Henry?"

"Training the next fifty." Gaanz grinned. "And with any luck, he'll get two more survivors."

"Gods!" He stroked his curly black beard, looking us up and down. "And all he got out of it was you two?"

I nodded solemnly. "We don't look like your usual warriors, do we?"

I had expected him to be polite, but he looked at my spindly arms and Gaanz's massive manbreasts and said, "Not even a little."

"Exactly." I leaned forward, half whispering, "That's Savage Henry's genius. We're special forces."

"Don't look like warriors at all," Gaanz gloated.

"I see that," he said, impressed.

"Nobody sees us coming," I said quietly. "We don't

carry real weapons." I gestured to our sides.

Between us we had a kindling axe, a small club, and a silver dagger that might in another setting have been used to slice helpings from a wheel of well-aged cheese. Beowulf would have sneered at us.

"Hmm. Yah. Well." He backed away, looking at us suspiciously. "I favor the old training. Axes and swords, and most everyone who signs up makes it through."

Gaanz shrugged. "That's good enough for most, I guess."

The bearded man walked away.

I said, "Did you have to make it sound so crazy?"

"Hel, I didn't sound half crazy enough," Gaanz said angrily. "You let these hyenas think you're weak, they'll rip out your spleen on your way to your *room*. It's like playing cards with madmen. If you don't bet the earth, they think you don't have a hand. Best you remember that—"

But his jaw dropped, and he forgot what he was talking about.

A blond woman a head and a half taller than him was pushing her way through the crowded lobby. She was wearing a tight deerskin tunic and moccasins on her feet. Her arms and legs were bare except for bracelets of wolves' teeth. She had silver ornaments in her ear: a star, a comet, an icicle, and a bear that was dancing on one foot.

She glanced at Gaanz and smiled dismissively and, for this crowd, politely.

Then she was gone, her perfectly toned body moving rhythmically and determinedly toward something we could not imagine.

Gaanz stared after her. "Sacred. Steaming. Moaning. Goddess."

"Oh no." I looked in anguish at him. "Don't even try."

He turned and glared at me. "It's possible."

"You? And her? You wretched weasel," I sneered. "You've weakened your body with every dangerous substance known to man. Look at her for a moment. She's toned herself into a living weapon. She makes no secret of her triceps, biceps, quadriceps, glutes, and all the other major cords. She has muscles on her muscles on her muscles. Even if by some dark disaster she chose you, how would you survive? She'd wrap those legs around you and squeeze, and your ass would fall off."

A voice behind us said, "I see you've met Sigrid."

We turned around. He was six foot three, with uncut hair like a farmboy's. Maybe he'd been one, a few years ago.

Now he wore a brown leather vest, a fine collection of chest scars running every which way, a loincloth, weather-beaten boots to match, and a short sword. He probably had a knife stowed on him, possibly two, in places I couldn't see.

He was smiling and acting friendly. That was good. As powdered-up and potioned-out as Gaanz and I were, we couldn't take much more aggression without screaming.

"She's wounded five men," he said admiringly.

In this crowd, that was a pretty sorry tally. "When?"

"Since she arrived yesterday afternoon. Two were in the hot springs. It was pretty funny."

"Ha," Gaanz croaked, surrendering instantly his gland-driven dreams of her.

"Ha," the warrior echoed. "I'll be proud to serve beside her."

The warrior raised his right hand to us, palm up. "Balarec," he said, and clasped each of us to his chest in turn, slapping our backs twice in the Mighty Man-Hug.

"Dook, and this is Gaanz." We looked at him in awe. Compared to the blood-drinking middle-aged mercenaries that staggered across the main room periodically, he seemed like a decent sort.

"So," I said casually. "How many men have you killed?"

"Three. Only bandits, on the way here." He looked sad. "They only attacked us for the food. Who can blame them?"

"Hmm." Gaanz looked at him oddly, though the Mad God knew that Gaanz had little left in him but odd looks. "Are you looking forward to the war?"

"Forward? Not really." He fingered the hilt of his sword. "But the way I hear it, Skandia's threatened us. The Pre-Eminence says—"

Gaanz belched. "Doesn't he, though? I hear the Eminence tells him what to believe."

Balarec said, "Don't speak that way." But he didn't reach for his weapon. "Together they're leading us there to prevent Skandia from attacking us here." He added quietly, "They say that even at the Althing, Skandia has considered attacking us."

"Vultures," I said. If he thought I was speaking of Skandia, so much the better.

He nodded, pleased. "To think of them hating us so much, hating our *courage*"—it was the official line—"so much that they would cross the Five Seas to attack the innocent. . . ." He was genuinely, deeply angry.

I looked around the main room at the weapons, the scars, the piercings, and the tattoos. Evidently the innocent had checked in silently and gone to bed early.

Gaanz said, "And there they are."

First came the Honor Guard, war-hardened men with eagle eyes and swords held at identical height. The cheering started immediately.

In the middle came the Eminence, looking neither to right nor to left. His satin robes rippled around him, making him out of place among all these leather- and metal-clad men and women. He looked fatter and balder than his image on the coins, and much colder than the metal. One half of his face tried to smile. The other half didn't bother.

Behind him, waving to the cheering crowd, was the Pre-Eminence. His laurel wreath was slightly crooked, and he didn't care. He grinned at every cheer, and he reached across his guards to touch the people who crowded around him worshipfully.

Even with my brain addled and smeared with substances best left untouched, I felt vastly superior to these sweat-drenched products of constant oily, evil Praise and Encouragement. They were drowning in it, unaware.

"Why's the Pre-Eminence doing that?" Gaanz said.

Balarec stared at him, astonished. "Because he's leading us into Skandia. We're attacking them before they attack us."

"He's sailing with you?" I said, seriously impressed. In person, the Pre-Eminence looked like the kind of man who would lead people in a two-step after a bottle or three of wine, but not in an attack.

"Well, no, not quite." Balarec shifted uncomfortably. "He's leading Kalchys, and that means he'll lead us in the war." He looked away from us, focusing suddenly on someone over our shoulders. "I should talk to some other people."

I said, "What are you doing?"

He shrugged. "Welcoming people, especially the raw recruits."

"Why? Who told you to?"

"Nobody." His eyes were gentle again. "But they're new here, and they're not sure what comes next. And when we're over the Five Seas and fighting, we need to know that we're all brothers and sisters in arms."

He slapped our shoulders. "Including you. We'll look after each other, you'll see." He strode away, saying over his shoulder, "Give my regards to Savage Henry." And he winked.

We hadn't known he'd heard that discussion.

Gaanz and I watched as he threw an arm around an anxious young woman with a longbow and a quiver of three dozen arrows. After a second, she smiled like sunlight. Balarec hugged her shoulders, hard, and moved on.

"Dumbass," Gaanz said bitterly, watching Balarec pat a nervous young man on the shoulder to calm him down.

"True," I said, "but we've found out the Truth. We know, out of all the useless screaming misbirths here, what a hero is."

Gaanz turned away. "It's what we're not, right? Good thing."

"Let's go to the room," I said. "You need to relax and get substance-free. And frankly, the lizards in this room are starting to bother me."

The room was sumptuous and imperial at the same time. The bed-clothes were purple with Tyrian dye. The countertops were marble. The walls had bronze bas-reliefs of ancient victories. The innkeeper was right: it was a place for a general and his consort.

Gaanz threw his shirt over a sword sticking out of a bas-relief. "Can you feel the war in this room? As your senior advisor, I suggest we take some Pax, just to stay balanced."

I agreed. The atmosphere in here was depressing me.

But the lobby had depressed Gaanz more. Why couldn't we—on mead laced with Warre or Self-Glamoring like a courtesan splashing scent—have even the faintest sense that we had half the worth of Balarec, walking down the hall embracing brothers and amazons in the stupidest cause since the Laughing God embraced the Pitying Goddess?

But I was more worried about tomorrow. "We've been young and irresponsible." I held up three pellets full of liquid Forecaste. "It's time we thought about our future."

Gaanz shrugged. "Forecaste isn't much of a ride, unless your future is raving mad. We'll probably see ourselves arguing our way out of the bill for the room."

Before I could stop him, he threw all three pellets straight into his mouth.

He dropped to the floor, screaming like a slaughtered lamb and hugging himself. Tears were coursing down his cheeks.

I forced two Pax lozenges and three Sleepers into his mouth before they even made a dent.

Then he went to sleep in the fetal position. I sat up and thought about the future.

II

In the morning I woke on the floor. I looked at the doorway and saw that my bed was up against the door, wedged under the doorknob.

The lock on the door was broken, and the bed had been moved in three inches. Heart's-Oil is powerful enough on its own, and mixed with Thighwarme . . .

I shuddered. We needed a different inn, and quickly.

Gaanz woke up the third time I picked him up and dropped him. "G'way."

"That's what we're doing." I snapped a Waker under his nose, opened one of his eyelids and tilted his face toward the door.

Either the Waker or the view made him alert. "You slept on that last night? How did you stay off the floor?"

"I *was* on the floor. I wedged the bed in place to fend off the innkeeper. Now she'll fillet me on sight. We. Have. To. Go."

Surprisingly, he understood. "Gods, she'll *castrate* you." He looked appalled. "Maybe even me."

Things were going badly. The room looked like some

disastrous alchemical project involving whiskey and werewolves.

We scampered in the ruins and packed. We abandoned our extra clothes and our bags, packing the potions and liquids on our bodies. Had we really started with enough to fill a wagon bed? Babbling God, where had it all gone, and so soon? Clearly, this place was evil and had sapped our will like a ghoul battening on an innocent.

I said, "Do you remember what you saw under the Forecaste?"

He shook his head. "No." He lowered his eyebrows and snapped, "Whatever you think I saw, probably you hallucinated the whole thing under a mix of Follies and brandy."

I denied it loudly, but then admitted that it was possible.

But my cold, naked, briefly sober mind was afraid that it wasn't probable.

We cringed away from the innkeeper as we settled up. "You've missed the opening ceremonies," she said coldly. "The Pre-Eminence will speak shortly in the Hall of Heroes. As I've told you, weapons are not permitted." She turned her back on us, and we were glad.

I was far too sober. As we moved away from the desk, I said to Gaanz, "I'll be right back." He seemed happy enough to be rid of me.

I stepped behind a pillar, poured MisSpeak into my palm, and slapped it over my nose and lips, inhaling deeply. It wasn't a problem yet. I would be coherent for several moments more.

When I came back, Gaanz looked suspiciously at me. "What did you just do?"

"Nothing," I said. "How about you?"

"Nothing. Nothing." And he let the matter drop.

The lobby was nearly empty. The Pre-Eminence was in a corner, reviewing a scroll. His laurel wreath was still crooked, and his lips were moving. He glanced up and waved happily to us. "Hel of a speech coming," he said.

Beyond him, the Eminence was moving from door to door of the Hall of Heroes, turning a key in the locks.

We followed him, unseen, to the last door.

The figure in the niche behind him dwarfed Balarec or Graffin. He made Sigrid look puny and ineffectual. No matter whether or not he was trained, he had the raw power to overwhelm any of the heroes. He was all muscle and sinew, except for the hooves and razor-sharp horns. His fists were clenched, and his bull-nostrils were wide open and snorting with anger.

It was the first time I had seen a Taur, or smelled the mix of sweat, frustration, and anger that clings to them their whole lives.

The Eminence closed the door behind us, and I heard the lock snap into place.

"A Taur?" Gaanz whispered to me. "The Eminence has a pet Taur?"

"Not a pet. Charmed, is my guess. I wonder how much Pax it takes to keep him on a leash." I looked around. "And when the charm wears off, the Eminence is going to let him loose in the hall, isn't he?"

"You're completely fear driven," Gaanz sneered at me. "Your nerves are whipped up by all the muck you've taken. This lot would like nothing better than to pick up a sword and challenge a Taur. . . ."

He trailed off as we looked around. There were, of course, no weapons, just as the innkeeper had warned us.

I went cold. "Blood God protect us, he's planning a full Grendel."

Gaanz said, "We have to warn someone. Quickly."

I hissed, "What did you inhale, you deranged berserker? We need to leave this place, quickly."

"No." Gaanz took a deep, frightened breath. "We need to go into the hall."

He stepped forward, toward the last unlocked door, and he entered the Hall of Heroes.

What could I do? I followed him.

The Eminence locked the door behind us. The Taur was outside, for now.

I looked over the sweaty, muttering crowd that was waiting for the Pre-Eminence to come speak to them. "We need to find Balarec, fast. He's the only one who will listen." I could feel the MisSpeak nibbling at my mind like a small carnivore.

"Absolutely," Gaanz said quickly. He was on tiptoe, looking from table to table and bench to bench.

We lost precious time as we ran through the hall, past

men and women who were already impatient and didn't much like nearly having their ale spilled.

And my head was filling with a terrible clarity that told me I didn't have much time to say anything to anyone.

Suddenly there was Balarec, walking past. I grabbed his arm. "Ball. Air. Axe. Ohh, shift."

Thank god we only took Misspeak in shifts. I grabbed Gaanz's arm. "Hue tale hem."

Gaanz looked stricken. "Eye fraught hit wads *bye* turd."

Balarec looked back and forth between us, unable to comprehend us and too polite to give us each the smack we deserved.

The hall door behind us slammed into the wall, its handle chipping stone free. The Taur, loose at last, raised its arms and roared.

Whatever he'd been given, it wasn't Pax.

The warriors around us shouted to each other, running back and forth uselessly. But there were no weapons in the hall, not so much as a short sword.

Gaanz stared around the hall, then desperately at me.

His face lit up and he reached inside his shirt.

He pulled out a small pouch.

He loosened the drawstrings and buried his face in it.

When he came up for air, his eyes were wild and his teeth were clenched.

He flung the open pouch in my face. A cascade of powder struck my nostrils—

And I threw back my head and howled, my heart pounding and brain full of Warre.

Together we charged the Taur, shouting the whole time. He looked down at us in confusion. I seriously do not believe he had ever been attacked by anything as small as us before.

Gaanz dove at the Taur, striking him in the chest and bouncing off harmlessly. I followed immediately, bouncing harmlessly off Gaanz.

The Taur shook his great head from side to side, staring from one of us to the other—probably wondering which one to kill first, and how painful it should be.

Gaanz reached into his pants—a horrible and insulting gesture; the Taur widened his eyes—and pulled out a flask, throwing it immediately into the Taur's face. The monster bellowed at us, but sounded rabid, furious, and strangely pleased with itself.

Gaanz gestured to me. "Bye thyme!"

It made a deranged sense. I grabbed at one of my hidden packets and threw powder on him, then grabbed another.

By turns the Taur changed moods. MisSpeak made no initial change, of course. Eventually it changed his roar to another, different roar, which seemed to piss him off mightily.

He waved his arms, snatching at us. Sooner or later, he would make contact, and our potions and charms would make no difference at all.

A voice behind us shouted, "'Way!" We fell to either side as Balarec, carrying a bench, smashed it into the Taur's chest.

The Taur fell backward, but he was more startled than hurt. He rose up, beckoning toward his chest, angry and unafraid.

Balarec said, "Charge again. We have to hold him."

Perhaps it was the drugs. For me it must have been. Gaanz was now fully committed.

We launched the bench into the Taur's chest. He collapsed again, but he laughed at us and stood, looking back and forth as he picked a victim to charge at.

"Gods' damn 'way!" a voice bellowed behind us.

I pushed Balarec sideways. Gaanz and I fell over as Graffin, Sigrid, and four other large angry warriors launched past us with a table in their arms.

The impact threw the Taur against a wall. The heroes carrying the table followed through. There was a crash and a series of crunches, and the broken Taur slid down the wall and crumpled inertly on the floor.

Balarec waited half an instant before snatching up the bench and ramming his way out of the hall. A moment later he was tossing in weapons, and the Hall of Heroes was invincible again.

III

Well, we found out the Truth. Too bad it was no use to anyone.

We were out in front of the inn, unarmed, and we had no potions, lotions, or charms left. We were becoming disagreeably sober. We desperately wanted to leave, but a number of people wanted to say good-bye to us.

The Eminence was not one of them. He looked at us

sideways, with a sideways-frowning mouth, and I knew he was weighing how to kill us, not whether. The sooner we were out of this city, the better.

The Pre-Eminence insisted on shaking hands with us, saying that we would always be in the forefront of the fight against Skandia. The Eminence eyed us coldly from a distance, saluting. How I wanted to salute him, in my own way! But it wasn't safe.

As we turned away from them, someone grabbed our shoulders in a way that had nearly made me scream before, but that I now recognized.

Graffin said, "You boys were all right back there. I thought your training story was dung, but I was wrong."

He grabbed us both in his arms and squeezed until shoulder dislocation was a possibility.

Then he said huskily, "Thank Savage Henry for me. Band of brothers," and walked away wiping his eyes.

Gaanz whispered, "I hope there isn't going to be much of this."

My eyes went wide watching Sigrid grab his shoulder, spin him around, and grab him with her other hand.

She picked Gaanz up and held him off the floor, kissing him until I thought she would suck his lungs inside out.

Then she set him down, smiling. "If I see you across the water, we might have a night together."

He stared after her.

I hissed, "You are *not* risking your life to find out whether 'if' is 'when.'"

"I'm not." But he said it tragically, and I was deeply grateful that he was only slightly sober. A fully sober man would have been doomed to follow her.

Behind us, Balarec said, "You've met Sigrid again."

I said, "What the Eminences wanted all worked, didn't it? She's committed to going overseas, and so are a lot of the others."

Balarec reached into his pockets.

We stared at the key and the pouches.

"The key is to the Hall of Heroes," Balarec said tiredly. "The pouches are Warre and Pax, respectively. I pulled them from the pockets of the Eminence, when he embraced me for stopping the Taur."

Gaanz snatched the pouch of Pax and lowered his nose and mouth in it, inhaling vigorously. "Oh, yes. That's Pax." He was visibly relaxed.

"He was dosing the Taur," I said.

"I can't prove it." Balarec looked around the streets, where pumped-up heroes, survivors of an attack they were told was from Skandia, were babbling about future carnage. "But I know he did it."

I said, "Then you can stop all this."

He looked at me for a moment, than at the volunteers and zealots all around him.

Then he smiled sadly. "After what happened here today, there will be galleys, and funds for smithies and crossbows and arquebuses, and men and women clamoring to serve across the Five Seas."

"But we've proved that's a bloodstained farce," Gaanz

said plaintively. He raised his arm and put his hand on Balarec's shoulder. "As your senior guide, I advise you to tell everyone to stay home. Or you'll buy them a drink if they get back."

He smiled and shrugged. Gaanz's arm fell off him. We waited.

Finally he said, "I'm going with them."

I gaped at him. "Mad God." We looked at him the way he had looked at the Taur.

He blushed. Actually blushed, like a child learning a truth or receiving a kiss. He looked away from our eyes as he said, "Mad God, maybe, but I'm going with them." He spread his hands. "They're risking their lives. Maybe they believe in a lie, but they believe, and they're my brothers and sisters in arms." Balarec looked at us earnestly. "Don't you think, if they are risking their lives for nothing, I need to be there to make sure as few of them as possible die in vain?"

"I don't," Gaanz said. He held out his hand. "You do."

Balarec shook it. "You did today, and thank you. You may not know yourselves as well as you think."

I shook my head. "If Kalchys hangs on the likes of us, this country is doomed."

He laughed. "You know, I would have said that myself about your kind two days ago. Then yesterday I met you." He shook my hand and waved almost shyly. "Gods watch over you."

"And you," I said, but it was too late. He was moving from man to woman to man, making sure they were all right.

He had been taken aside his whole life, a ropelike arm thrown around his shoulder, and been whispered to by corrupt old men with smirking eyes and the gift of putting one quasi-true word after another, until their sentences conveyed a falsehood they had never spoken.

And now the scales had fallen from his eyes, but he was still sailing over the Five Seas to risk his life for something foolish and wasteful, and he was willing to do it even while he was sober. We were crazy and useless and full of dying substances, and we had no purpose at all, and no words that would convince him not to go.

The heroes, a number of them saluting us, left in convoys, warwagons, and flatbed platforms over spiked wheels. We stood together in the desert and watched them roll off while we looked at the nearby ornate buildings and the far desiccated horizon.

The Most High had ordered us to engage in a Search for the Truth. We had found out:

- Kalchys was going to war for a bloody lie, and many people whom we had just met were going to their deaths.

- The Eminence and Pre-Eminence were complicit in the fraud that was the war with Skandia.

- We had no means to convince anybody of this.

And unless we could convince some seriously innocent rube who ran a magic shop to let us replace our diminished supplies on credit, the trip back to the university was going to be long, sweaty, and unpleasant.

—In memory of Hunter S. Thompson

NICK O'DONOHOE is the author of a number of novels, including the Crossroads trilogy, about a very unusual veterinary practice: *The Magic and the Healing, Under the Healing Sign*, and *The Healing of Crossroads.* He has published dozens of short stories, many of them part of the Dragonlance world.

Nick lives in Rhode Island and works as a writer within half a mile of a church tower that was prominent in an H. P. Lovecraft story.

AUTHOR'S NOTE

This story was inspired by a love of Hunter S. Thompson's *Fear and Loathing in Las Vegas*—in part because I loved Thompson's knife-edge, acid prose, and in part because I wondered how a pair of gonzo mages in a fantasy world might misuse magic for recreation.

Clare Bell

Bonechewer's Legacy

Ratha, clan leader of the feline Named, lay on her side in the last rays of the setting sun. Fall had come to clan ground, stripping leaves from the trees and blowing the guard-fires' haze across the sky. From the nearby woodland trail, she heard movement. She yawned, stretched out her forepaws, and began a quiet purr. On Ratha's back, her treeling, Ratharee, woke and groomed herself in a flurry, then curled her ringed tail around Ratha's neck.

Ratha knew that her friend, sandy-furred Fessran, was leading in the Firekeepers to light the clan leader's evening fire. The torch-carrying Firekeepers started this ritual when the weather began to cool. Ratha told them that they didn't have to, but the Firekeeper leader and the others so enjoyed this ceremony that Ratha accepted it.

Behind Fessran came Bira, who, unlike Fessran, held a lighted torch in her jaws. Firelight shone in her pine-green eyes and flickered on her red-gold pelt.

"Ho, clan leader," announced Fessran, striding past Bira. "We have come, bearing the Red Tongue. Give us your orders. We shall obey."

Ratha got up, shook her own tawny-gold pelt, and touched noses with Fessran. "Ho, Singe-whiskers. You know scatting well that you like this as much as I do."

"I'll enjoy it more if you play the ferocious ruler like you're supposed to," Fessran hissed, but Ratha saw more than just firelight dancing in her light green eyes. In a louder voice Fessran commanded, "Firekeeper Chikka, bring forward the Red Tongue's food so that Firekeeper Bira can give the creature life."

Chikka, Fessran's daughter by the herder Mondir, was a smaller version of her lanky mother. She had a few lingering cub-spots and the remnants of a silvery gray mantle along her neck and down her back. Ratha saw Chikka wrinkle her nose slightly at her mother and unload small twigs from her mouth onto the ashy fire-nest. Behind her, a young male Firekeeper dropped a load of heavier wood.

Bira nosed her treeling, Cherfaree, down from his perch in her ruff. With nudges and tooth-clicks from Bira, the treeling carefully arranged the kindling to catch fire easily. Cherfaree was Bira's second treeling. She'd given her first, Biaree, to Ratha's daughter, Thistle-chaser, during a critical rescue. Ratha knew this hadn't been easy for Bira, but she and her new treeling now worked well together.

Ratha watched, marveling at the quick deftness of treeling paw-hands, as compared to the clumsy Named forefeet. She felt Ratharee sway slightly on her back and was deeply grateful that the clan had tamed the lemur-like treelings. She and many of the Named would feel lost without their small helpers and companions.

Having set up the tinder, Cherfaree turned to Bira, crooking his ringed tail. If Bira lowered her head and cocked her ears, the treeling would take the torch from Bira's jaws and light the fire. Bira, however, lifted the firebrand and swiveled her ears back, indicating that she would light it.

Was it Ratha's imagination, or did the treeling's tufted ears droop a little in disappointment?

With a flourish of her plumed tail, the ruddy-coated Firekeeper dipped her torch and kindled the wood. For Ratha, each rebirth of the mystery she called "her creature" brought excited anticipation. Though she had seen it countless times, Ratha still caught herself leaning forward, her whiskers trembling, her eyes widening.

Bira stepped back, letting Chikka take her torch. Delicately spitting out pieces of bark, Bira said, "Your creature called the Red Tongue lives again, to bring you protection and warmth."

Ratha went to Bira and gave her an affectionate headbump. "I know Fessran lays it on a bit thick," Bira purred softly, "but really, we do enjoy doing this for you, clan leader. You've endured so much for us."

For an instant Ratha found it hard to reply. Bira's simple, open affection and loyalty did not deserve a tart or teasing answer. "You are all worth anything I had to suffer," she said at last.

Other Firekeepers brought more wood. With help from

their treelings, they built the little blaze into a merrily crackling campfire, then put out their torches. Ratha invited everyone to flop down beside her and bask in the light and warmth. She listened to pelts rustling and treelings chirring as the Firekeepers settled themselves. Soon contented purrs became sighs and snores, blending in with the soft song from the fire.

As she had so many times, Ratha laid her nose on her paws and stared into her creature's heart

I still don't know what you are, my Red Tongue. Perhaps I never will. We know some of the things you can do. Soon we will learn others. Will they delight or terrify us?

Carefully and silently, to avoid waking the sleepers, Ratha took a branch from the small woodpile. She laid it reverently in her creature's nest and watched as the flame curled around the wood, withering leaves and consuming them in a burst of heat and light.

Then she looked up at the night sky and the stars. There, too, lay a fire, but one that she, however powerful she might become, would never call her own. The starlight shone down on her, suddenly cold and vast with questions.

Not knowing why, Ratha turned to her campfire again and crept closer. Nearby, Fessran stirred and stretched. One of the Firekeeper's forelegs did not extend out quite as far as the other, the effect of an old wound. The sight reminded Ratha again of Bira's last words. Yes, she had endured much for the Named, but they had suffered as well, her friend Fessran especially. At least the Firekeeper no longer limped. Fessran was as tough and spare as bark-stripped sun-dried wood. For that, Ratha was grateful.

Fessran yawned, curling her tongue. "Have to go patrol the guard-fires." She poked her companions. "Stir your tails, you lazy lumps of fur," she growled, but she interspersed her pokes with nudges and licks. The others got up, grumbling good-naturedly. With their treelings on their backs, they re-lit their torches from the campfire and padded away into the night.

Ratha lay with Ratharee snuggled up against her belly. Her own gold fur was thickening for the coming winter. During the cold and rain, the clan would value the Red Tongue even more.

Her creature's endless changes drew Ratha's gaze and held it, while her mind wandered along trails of memory, scenting the marks of her life. From the fiery death of the old clan leader, Meoran, to the near slaying of her friend Fessran at the sabers of the usurper Shongshar, Ratha followed the memories. Then came the recovery of her lost and crippled daughter, Thistle-chaser, and the puzzling but deadly encounter with the wakefully dreaming mammoth hunters and the clan's rescue of their enigmatic leader, True-of-voice. Now the Named had settled into an uncertain peace with both the face-tail hunters and the clan's ancient raiding enemies, the UnNamed.

Gradually Ratha's hypnotic stare at the fire brought sleep.

The one memory that she hadn't consciously chosen because it still brought pain crept past her guard and into her dreams.

It swirled together from a tumble of images, sounds, scents, and feelings. Again she saw the burnished sheen of copper fur in sunlight and heard a sardonic voice. She stared again into fiercely burning amber eyes, brighter than any in the clan. The first encounter; she, stinging with scratches and nips from an UnNamed stranger. Squashed under his paw while he held her prey, her first catch, dangling by the tail from his jaws. Then he swallowed her kill, and then, unbelievably, spoke to her. She felt rage again melting into astonishment at learning that the UnNamed were not all savage and mindless.

She said again the epithet she had flung at him, which later became a name spoken with wakening and deepening affection.

Bonechewer.

The swirl of dream sensations became one shape. He stood before her, eyes flashing, mouth half-open, showing the broken right fang, challenging her to approach. On his side lay a terrible scar where clan rage had caved in his ribs and torn his lungs. And lifting his head, he showed another scar, one that made the barely healed wound inside Ratha open and bleed. The marks of fangs that took him to the death trail.

Bonechewer. Her first and only mate, killed in a clash between the clan and their foes.

The Named won, using Ratha's new "creature." Ratha lost, keeping only Bonechewer's memory.

In her dream, he still stood before her, marred yet beautiful, his stance cocky, his look proud.

"I still live, clan cat," said the amber eyes.

Ratha wanted to fling herself at him, to rub against him, covering herself with him and he covering her. She wanted to speak to him, releasing the words that had backed up, telling him everything that had happened since he had died. She wanted to get Thistle-chaser and push her daughter toward him, saying, "Look. This is your daughter. She isn't lost anymore. We found her. She is healing. We made her together and she is both of us. See her and care for her as I care for you. . . ."

Ratha found herself on her feet, poised as she been in her dream, trembling and tensed to spring. She nearly fell forward into the fire before she caught herself. She glanced to one side, half expecting to see Thistle-chaser's rusty black and orange mottled coat in the firelight.

A bitterness rose in Ratha's throat. No Thistle. No Bone-chewer, either. Only a dream.

Yet something made Ratha stare across the fire. There was a face amid the flames.

Her fur bristled, her tail flared. Her claws sank into the ground. There was a face whose eyes shone, fiery and deep. Not green, not orange, not yellow, but molten amber. The fangs gleamed, one broken.

A shape matched the face; angular and lean. Standing with that maddening insolence that Ratha recalled too well.

"Bonechewer?" she breathed.

Joy battling with utter disbelief pinned Ratha where she stood. She waited for him to speak. Instead he stared at her as if he knew her immobility, then turned and sauntered off. The sound of his footsteps quickened and he was gone.

Ratha threw herself at the vanished figure as she had longed to in the dream. She scorched her belly in a leap that carried her over the flames, but when she landed, the night had again fallen still.

It was if he had never been there.

Ratha knew that her own skidding feet had obliterated any of his footprints near the fire. Trying not to feel frantic, she cast about for others, but she couldn't yet see well beyond the firelight and she was too impatient to let her eyes adjust.

Besides, if Bonechewer had really been present, she would have caught his scent, even masked by the campfire's smoke. She had breathed it so deeply that she would know it even with ashes up her nose.

She halted, whiskers back, sniffing. Did she catch a trace of his scent, or was it her imagination? She did smell something that reminded her vaguely of the fleabane herb she often rolled in, but far more pungent and intense.

She sneezed, and then stumbled at a wave of dizziness. Shaking it off, she prowled around, whisker brushing and nosing the ground for his footmarks. Nothing.

He was always good at hiding his trail, Ratha thought, letting disappointment sag her body down by the fire. *It's just like him to taunt me.*

What am I thinking? Ratha asked herself as an irritated and ruffled Ratharee made a nest in Ratha's fur. *Bonechewer is long dead. His remains are under the old pine tree.*

She fought a misery that flattened her even more. Laying her nose on her paws, she growled, "Go away. Don't make me think of you, Bonechewer. Stay dead."

The impression, however, remained, keeping Ratha awake. When she caught herself in a longing glance into the dark beyond the fire, she flipped her tail around her feet and over her eyes. Even so, it was long before she slept.

❖ ❖ ❖

The clan leader woke the following morning with an unwanted answer to the night's mystery. The clan's herding teacher, Thakur, looked so much like his slain brother that she could have easily mistaken one for the other, especially late at night. Thakur's eyes were emerald rather than amber, but firelight sent its colors into everyone's eyes.

Scuffing sand over the campfire's embers, she wondered, and even through her morning grooming she chased the thought. It was as elusive as a dappleback mare that had broken from the herd and refused to be rounded up.

Thakur would never pull such a heartless trick. He, of all the Named, understood how Ratha had cared for Bonechewer. Even if Thakur hoped that he might be the one Ratha chose for her next mate, he wouldn't discourage her so.

As she scratched behind one ear, she spied Bira, who was coming to make sure the campfire was out. With her tail, Ratha beckoned the young Firekeeper to her side. She asked Bira to go and dig under the old pine tree, return, and say what she found there.

Answering Bira's questioning head tilt, Ratha said only, "I need to know something. I'll tell you more when you get back."

When Bira had padded away with a last wave of her plumed tail, Ratha finished a long grooming session. She knew what Bira should find. She was so sure that she dismissed the previous night's apparition, buried a twinge of sorrow, and began planning her patrol routine. She also had to sit on a slight pang of guilt. She could well have done the task herself, but she didn't want to raise the same feelings again. She also didn't want to answer any questions as to why the clan leader was digging under that particular tree.

Thinking that she should start her rounds, and that she could find Bira on the way, Ratha set one paw on the meadow trail, only to lift it again when Bira appeared, front paws covered with soil. "Clan leader, why did you have me dig there?" Bira shook more dirt from her pelt. "I didn't find anything."

Ratha's hindquarters collapsed into a startled sit, but she didn't betray anything in her voice. "Are you sure you dug under the right tree? Show me, please."

Bira led her to the excavation. This part of clan ground had few pines. This tree towered above the surrounding scrub oak and bay. It was more majestic now than when she had chosen it for Bonechewer's memorial.

Ratha looked up through the branches. This was definitely the right tree. Bira had dug frantically and deep, sensing her leader's need. The bones she should have found weren't there. Ratha forced herself to nose and scratch around in the dirt piles and leaf litter, wanting, yet not wanting, to find evidence that Bonechewer lay here.

Could his bones have decayed into nonexistence during the many past seasons? No. Even if his remains were gnawed to gravel by worms and beetles, she would see chunks, powdery streaks, smell a trace of bone-scent. She found nothing.

How could that be, unless someone had taken the bones away? Who would do such a thing and why? Her memory of helping Thakur bury his brother's torn and trampled body was as stark as if the event were a day ago. Could it be that

Bonechewer wasn't dead? Or had an old grief made the clan leader lose her mind?

"Ratha," asked Bira softly, "what are you looking for?"

For an instant Ratha couldn't answer. Then she shook herself, unable to help the flat note in her voice or the distressed tone in her scent. "Please get Thakur for me."

"Of course, clan leader. Mondir can take over the herding class." Bira crouched to spring away. "Ratha, will you be—"

"Yes, I'll be fine." Ratha's answer was sharper than she intended.

"I'll hurry. We'll return soon." Bira launched herself and disappeared.

When Bira returned with the herding teacher, the sight of Thakur's copper fur both gladdened and hurt Ratha. Bira, with an understanding glance at both, excused herself and left them alone.

Ratha could see the question in Thakur's eyes when he caught sight of the excavation around the pine tree's roots. Instead of asking it, he went to Ratha, nosed her head against his shoulder and spread a kind paw across her back. She realized again how much she had come to care for Thakur, even while the memories of Bonechewer tore at her.

"Easy, yearling," he said, using his old name for her. She felt his voice vibrating through his body and into hers.

Ratha buried her head against his neck and squeezed her eyes shut. She panted and gaped in silent pain. Thakur held her there.

"I didn't thank Bira . . . I hope she doesn't think I'm angry at her. . . ." Ratha stumbled, not knowing how to begin.

"I thanked her. And she knows you're not angry." Thakur's voice was light and youthful, despite his age, but it had a gentle power.

"She did . . . what I asked her. And she did it well. She always does."

Though Thakur didn't coax or push her, Ratha sensed that he was waiting to hear why she had his brother's remains unearthed. Slowly, haltingly she told him, beginning with her dream and the image she had seen beyond the fire.

"They were both dreams," Thakur soothed when she had finished.

"No." Ratha sat up with lifted forepaws to show him the singed fur on her chest and belly. "I jumped through the fire."

"Hrrr. Perhaps the dream lasted until you saw the face."

"No, I woke up before that. I was awake when I saw him." Ratha let her paws down. "This morning I thought it might have been you. But you don't have a broken fang, and you would never do such a cruel thing to me. You wouldn't startle me like that, then not say anything and run away. Even if you had been eating fermented fruit."

Thakur lolled his tongue briefly in a silent cat-laugh. "Even if I had been, you're right. I wouldn't and I didn't."

"Either someone really was there, or I'm starting to see hallucinations like Thistle-chaser does."

"So, to show yourself that you aren't—" Thakur began, but Ratha interrupted.

"I had Bira dig around the tree." Ratha paused. "I'm sure this is the right one. At least I was sure until . . ." She broke off.

"It is the right tree. I know," Thakur said.

Ratha felt her lower jaw begin to tremble. "Thakur, I should have asked you before I sent anyone to dig there. I didn't think that you might want him to be left alone. I'm sorry. I didn't think. I never do. I just . . . pounce on things."

Thakur put out a big warm paw and drew her to him again, muffling her voice under his chin as she murmured, ". . . He was your brother."

"Hush, yearling. You haven't hurt or upset me. Yes, Bonechewer was my brother, but he was your mate and I know how much it clawed at you to lose him."

"Well, I must be having Thistle-fits. I think I'm having one now. I can't find . . . his bones, Thakur. They aren't there."

Ratha could tell that the news startled Thakur. He pushed her back to look deeply into her eyes. She stared into the emerald of his, wanting to lose herself in their depths, but they seemed to change color, amber seeping in and filling the green.

"Maybe I'm just too frantic to really look," Ratha said, dropping her gaze, "and just getting myself all tangled in a thornbush over nothing."

"I'll look," Thakur said, and did. After nosing around the holes and the out-flung dirt, he stopped. His tail made several puzzled flicks. "Hmmrrr," he said, swiveling one ear forward, the other back. "Speaking of Thistle, where is she now?"

"With her mate, Quiet Hunter. They are visiting True-of-voice and his face-tail hunting tribe." Ratha felt her eyes widen. "Thakur, do you think this is one of Thistle's tricks?"

"She might have done something similar long before you

took her back into the clan. She wouldn't do such a thing now."

"Are you sure?" Ratha asked. "She and I haven't resolved everything yet."

Thakur gave his tail an emphatic whisk. "Whoever did this wasn't Thistle. It just doesn't have her paw print."

For an instant Ratha wanted to argue, but Thakur knew Thistle better than she did. She felt relief that the culprit probably wasn't her once-lost daughter. "Then who is stealing bones and playing 'let's fool the clan leader'?"

"That I don't know," said Thakur, his voice roughening, "but when I catch whoever it is—"

"You'll have to pull me off him first," Ratha snarled, flexing the muscles that extended her claws.

"We can chase this down if I stay with you at your fire tonight," Thakur offered and Ratha eagerly agreed. She felt so glad she had Thakur. He'd herd this straying beast straightaway. He'd dig until he uncovered the truth. She'd be lolling her tongue at herself tomorrow for all the upset and worry. Thakur would make everything right.

How attracted to him she felt. The feeling wasn't just intense friendship or the lust of heat. It was something more: something for which the Named, she realized, had no words.

Several evenings later, Ratha felt less confident. Thakur, sitting beside her in front of the fire, yawned hugely. "Yearling, is it possible that you just had a very strange dream?"

Ratha's ears twitched back in annoyance. Her tail writhed

on the ground where she sat. "Why is my belly fur singed then?"

"You did jump over the fire. Just after you woke up."

"I saw Bonechewer, Thakur," she growled.

"Then he obviously doesn't want me here," was Thakur's not entirely patient reply.

Ratha scratched furiously behind one ear, jostling Ratharee. "I hope I'm not getting those scatting ear mites. Thakur, that doesn't make sense. He's your brother."

"He was."

Ratha flopped by the fire and fell silent. Thakur lay down close beside her, cuddling one side while the Red Tongue warmed the other. She tried not to be sulky as she said, "I know what you're going to say. I'm seeing Bonechewer because I want to see him."

"No, yearling, I wasn't going to say that. I miss him too. Sometimes I sit alone in my den and think of him." The sorrowful note in Thakur's voice and scent told Ratha that if he could have a vision of his lost brother, he would welcome it.

"Then why don't you see him? And why are his bones gone?"

"I don't know," the herding teacher admitted.

"Thakur, I must be having Thistle-fits. Or this is all a dream. Or I've got the frothing sickness as well as ear mites."

"Well, something I do know, yearling," he said, his voice gentle. "You don't have fits or the frothing sickness. I don't think we're dreaming, and you probably don't have ear mites." He paused. "Feel better?"

"A little." Ratha laid her nose down on her forepaws. "I'm

glad I have you, herding teacher." She took a deep breath; let it out. She felt as though she could finally fall asleep, but one last question threaded its way through the oncoming drowsiness: *If I have Thakur, why do I keep thinking about Bonechewer?*

Clan life went on as fall slipped toward winter. At night, gusts fanned the flames of the guard-fires and the campfire. Coats grew thicker, the night's dark lingered deeper into the mornings, and the Firekeepers stacked more wood in the fire-den in order to keep the source-fire alive.

Ratha dug out more of the excavation under the pine tree. With Ratharee's help, she sifted through the piles of dirt. Nothing remained of her first mate but memories, and sometimes she wondered if she might have imagined those as well. Finally she gave up and asked some young herders to help her fill in the holes and trample down the loose soil. Dew formed during the cold nights, watering grass that grew again beneath the pine.

Ratha tried to bury the experience and move on with the clan's preparations for winter. Soon, she knew, Thistle-chaser and Quiet Hunter would return. She looked forward to seeing them. Quiet Hunter had a steadying effect on Thistle, making her less flighty and less touchy. The experience of working together with Thistle and having to trust each other during True-of-voice's rescue had also helped to bring mother and daughter closer. Perhaps, Ratha thought, it would help to talk with Thistle about Bonechewer.

The only concession Ratha made to Bonechewer's memory was to ask the Firekeepers to relocate her campfire to a more isolated place. She wanted it away from the winter lairs, the meadow, the fire-den, and the connecting trails. Fessran and the others did so without question, although they often stopped by on their rounds. They seemed more puzzled than worried. She told them that she had to be by herself to think things through. Her treeling, Ratharee, would provide sufficient companionship, although Ratha understood and appreciated the Firekeepers' concern.

No one asked for a reason, so that Ratha didn't have to admit the truth. She was giving her elusive visitor another chance. More than that, she was enticing him, perhaps even begging him to come again. The slender hope that somehow Bonechewer was still alive kept her sitting alone in the night with only her treeling and her creature.

As Ratha fluffed her fur against a chill that had gotten through the campfire's warmth, she decided that this would be her last night alone. She couldn't continue to indulge this obsession. The clan needed her. They feared that she was drawing away from them. Continuing this pursuit wouldn't be good for her or her people.

This resolution brought a wave of grief, which Ratha wisely allowed to run its course. She mourned Bonechewer again, quietly but intensely, shuddering and covering her face with her paws. Finally, when the sorrow was spent, she snuggled up with Ratharee. She felt exhausted but cleansed. Tomorrow night, she would have the campfire in its previous place and she would invite everyone to share it. They could help her leave the past and its dead to rest.

The snap of a twig woke Ratha. She rolled over, gazing blearily at the campfire, now settling into embers. The sound had come either from her creature or from another late-night check by the Firekeepers.

She realized slowly that it was neither.

A shape stood beyond the fire with a familiar cocky arrogance. It had the same copper fur, the same face, and the same derisively wrinkled nose. He was back. This time, he spoke.

"Greetings, clan cat. It's been many seasons."

Ratha choked the cry in her throat. Her emotions had been flung up and down too often in the last few days. Then, painfully, she had come to some sort of a conclusion and with it some calm. Now . . .

Every hair on her body bristled so hard that it vibrated. Her heart felt as though it would hammer itself through her ribs. She wanted to leap at him, but whether to cover him with caresses or shred his face, she didn't know.

She took a few hesitant steps toward her visitor, but Bonechewer backed off quickly. Her whiskers drooped in dismay, thinking he had vanished again. Instead, his face reappeared on the other side of the fire.

"Impulsive as ever, aren't you, Ratha?" came the slightly mocking voice.

Again she tried to approach him, and again he dodged.

"Bonechewer," she quavered.

"Yes, that was the name you gave me," he agreed, with a flash of the broken fang. "No, stay back, clan cat. I'm not used to being overwhelmed."

Ratha wanted to scream out in frustration and fling herself at him. Instead she sat, trembling. "You never used to hold me away like this," she grumbled.

"It has been many seasons. I haven't taken any mate since you. I've gotten used to being alone."

Ratha shivered, hot and cold at the same time. "I can't believe that it is you, Bonechewer."

"I can understand that," he answered mildly. "You Named ones thought you'd slain me. But remember, clan cat, I'm hard to kill."

We didn't mean to kill you, she thought. It was the fever of wielding the Red Tongue against the UnNamed enemy. All she said was, "Come closer. Show yourself."

The words came out more harshly than she intended, but after a long stare, to ensure that Ratha stayed put, he sauntered out from behind the fire, turned sideways, and displayed himself.

He was exactly as she remembered him, a wilder, rangier version of Thakur. From black-edged ears to rough coppery fur to dark brown tail-tip; he was exactly, almost unbelievably the same. She saw some differences, which she expected; the fur over the left side of his ribs was speckled with gray, betraying the old injury. His eyes had lightened, but age often did that to clan eyes as well.

Ratha got to her feet, saw him tense, and said, "I just want to circle you, to get a good sniff."

"Sniff away, clan cat. I'm sure my scent has changed a bit. So has yours."

She sidled around Bonechewer, inhaling his aroma. This too, she remembered. His scent was wild and woody, with the marshy tang of the lakeshore where he'd lived. She recalled that the UnNamed had called him "Dweller-by-the-water."

"I heard that you found Thistle-chaser," he said, startling Ratha.

She found her voice. "Yes. She's . . . she's getting a lot better."

"I don't smell her scent on clan ground. Where is she?"

"She took a mate from the face-tail hunting tribe. His name is Quiet Hunter."

"Oh, yes." Bonechewer's voice took on a note of scorn. "That bunch. They trail after their leader like cubs. You had some trouble with them."

"We settled it. We haven't solved everything, but we've kept things peaceful."

"That's a change."

His words stung Ratha. She grimaced. "I know what you think. But we have learned. I understand now that I can't solve everything by shoving a firebrand into someone's face. Thistle helped teach me that," she added. "She's amazing. I never thought she could get this far, considering what happened to her."

For an instant Ratha thought he would interrupt with "Considering what you did to her," but he didn't. Instead he said, "I know. I've been watching. That's why I came back."

Ratha was still shaking so hard that when she narrowed her eyes at him, her sight blurred.

"If you've been watching, why did you wait so long?"

"Don't assume that I didn't miss you, Ratha." His voice softened. "I did."

"Then why did you stay away?"

"I wasn't ready. For one thing, I nearly did die." He nosed his side. "It took many seasons for this wound to heal. Now I'm ready, and so are you. You and your people have grown up."

Ratha stared at him, lost. "Ready? For what?"

Bonechewer turned his head, fixing her with the full power of his eyes. "To bring your dream to life." He paused. "The one you once told me about when we were curled up together in a hollow tree. Surely you remember."

Ratha halted in her circling, one foot lifted. The crazy, impractical idea she had when she was barely beyond cub-hood, that the Named could meet the UnNamed not with fire but with friendship. She'd envisioned that she could lead her people in reaching out and gathering in the frightened, the struggling. That she could found new groups of Named and UnNamed that would spread and flourish. Her experience with Thistle-chaser and other Named-UnNamed crosses had shown that the witless cub problem was not intractable, though not simple either.

Her recent encounter with True-of-voice's tribe had taught her even more. Her long-denied, long-delayed vision could, at last, take steps on the trail to reality.

"So you do remember," Bonechewer said.

Ratha spluttered, "You mocked me for it, Bonechewer.

You called me a fool. You said that most of the UnNamed weren't worth saving."

There was a long interval where the two just breathed and measured each other. Finally he said, "You weren't the only one who had to grow up, Ratha."

She listened, hoping. Was it true? Youth often judged prematurely and callously. Maturity had brought her a more patient and generous outlook. Had it done the same for him?

"So you've . . . come to help me?"

"Yes. If you try to reach out to the UnNamed ones by yourself, you'll fail. You don't know them. I do. Furthermore, they trust me."

"Why do you trust me?" Ratha had to ask.

"Because I cared for you once, as my mate. I feel I could care again," he answered, making her dizzy with hope. "I've seen what you and your people have done, Ratha. With Thistle-chaser. With that young UnNamed cub, Mishanti. With the face-tail herders and True-of-voice."

"True-of-voice? But you disdain them all."

He swept his flanks with his long tail. "My personal attitude toward them has been . . . regrettable, I admit. I am opinionated, as you well know. But they have as much right to live and flourish as you and I do. That applies to others of the UnNamed as well."

He really means it, Ratha thought, overjoyed and amazed. *And he says he could care for me again. I could have both my dreams, not just the one.*

This time it was she who tensed, eager to run and call the rest of the clan.

"What are you doing?" Bonechewer's voice was sharp. "No, don't get the others yet. We need to talk. Alone."

Ratha blinked in surprise. "Don't you at least want to see Thakur? He's missed you."

"And I have missed him. But I am not yet ready. For him or the others."

"Well, you'd better get ready," Ratha snapped, cocking her ears. "Someone's coming."

"I will see you tomorrow night at your fire," he said quickly. "This place is still too close. Move it to the edge of clan ground. Be there alone. Don't talk to the others about this."

Before Ratha could protest, he was gone.

She went to where he had stood, but she had no chance of tracking him. He was far too light and quick. There was nothing left but a strong, strange scent that made her head swim. The campfire?

She told herself to stop reacting as if this were the mating season, but she couldn't stop the tumble of astonishment, relief, jubilation, and disbelief in her mind. She also groaned at the nearly impossible task he had set her—to keep silent while bursting with news. She knew by listening that her task had grown suddenly harder. The approaching footsteps and wafting scents were those of Quiet Hunter, Thistle-chaser, and Thakur.

Quickly Ratha rounded the fire and scuffed away any trace of Bonechewer's visit. She took some twigs from the nearby woodpile and laid them in the fire-nest with her teeth. Ratharee was asleep in a nearby sapling and Ratha didn't want to wake the treeling. Then the clan leader took a deep breath and turned to greet the new arrivals.

She thought she had concealed all the evidence, but she hadn't done such a good job on herself. She could tell that Thakur spotted her agitation. He, however, was polite enough not to say anything, at least while the two guests were here.

She felt her inward turmoil ease as she looked at the pair. Quiet Hunter's pale dun coat had thickened and darkened. Even while she watched, his hazel eyes sharpened away from their dreamy remoteness. Ratha guessed that he was making the transition from the thinking mode he used among his own tribe to the more individualistic thought of the Named.

"This one is glad to see you, clan leader," he said, following the formal nose-touch with an affectionate forehead rub. Thistle-chaser tumbled into the firelight after him, crowing, "Happy, happy, happy to be back, Ratha-mother."

Ratha waited for her daughter to stop prancing around, but she rejoiced that Thistle could. Her daughter's once withered and crippled foreleg no longer hampered her, and Ratha rejoiced to see how well it had healed.

Still bouncing a bit, Thistle rubbed alongside Ratha, looping her tail over Ratha's back. "Missed you, missed you, missed you," Thistle crooned, then stopped and sniffed. "Smell both happy and not-happy. Something happen?"

"I had a strange dream," Ratha said.

"Strong smell for just a dream," Thistle said, but she seemed to accept the explanation.

Thakur, however, looked Ratha meaningfully in the eyes before he nose-touched. While he head-rubbed with Ratha, he hissed, "You've seen him again, haven't you?"

"Not now, Thakur," she growled back. "I'll tell you more later." She butted him away gently and turned to Thistle. "That leg looks so much better."

"Quiet Hunter. Helping stretch it. Every day." Thistle grimaced at her verbal clumsiness. "Sorry. Not talked too much. Face-tail hunters don't. Mouth will get better talking with you."

"These two got here late," put in Thakur smoothly, "but I thought you wouldn't want to wait until morning."

Ratha thanked him and sat down, letting herself relax while Thistle and Quiet Hunter told her news of the other tribe.

"Tooth-broke-on-a-bone has new cubs. Thought she was too old but mated with True-of-voice. Has male cub, silver and white. Cub will be leader after True-of-voice."

Ratha's ears pricked. So the leader of the enigmatic face-tail hunters had sired a successor. This would be interesting.

"Well, I hope we don't have to fish him off a ledge, like we did his father," she said.

"All are grateful for the rescue," said Quiet Hunter. "This one feels that there will be lasting peace between this one's kind and the Named."

"Good," Ratha said. She turned to Thistle. "Tell me more about True-of-voice's son."

"Called New Singer. Big cub. Growing fast. Name not like clan name. Changes. Now is New Singer, later will be next True-of-voice."

"Then the song will call the elder 'Once-Sung,'" added Quiet Hunter.

Ratha shook her head in confusion, making her ears flap. She knew she still had difficulty understanding this face-tail hunting tribe. At least she had made and kept peace with them. She hoped that Quiet Hunter's judgment of the peace being "lasting" was true.

She also knew that Thistle and Quiet Hunter, acting as envoys, would do their best to ensure that things stayed friendly.

"You've both done well," she said, glad that her praise made Thistle's sea-green eyes sparkle. Quiet Hunter's hazel ones glowed with pride.

Ratha suddenly felt a huge yawn building behind her jaw and realized that she was too tired to fight it.

"You're tired, Ratha," said Thakur. "I'll take these two to my lair, get them fed, and bed them down. The rest of this can wait until morning."

"Thank you, herding . . ." she mumbled, her head sinking down on her paws, asleep before she had finished speaking.

Ratha woke with her treeling nestled in her flank fur. Nearby, someone tended the fire. She expected to see Bira or Fessran, but the sunlit coat shone copper. Thakur.

A sideways glance at the sun told Ratha that she had slept late.

"Where are Thistle and Quiet Hunter?" Ratha asked, stretching and spreading her forepaws.

"Still sleeping." Thakur paused. "I came to talk to you first."

Something in his voice made Ratha shake sleep away. "Thistle may be a little awkward at speaking, but she certainly picks up things." Ratha extended and stiffened her hind legs, arching her back. "And you do too."

"Then you did see the stranger again last night."

"Not a stranger," Ratha said with a sideways jerk of her head. "He was Bonechewer."

Thakur looked puzzled, then annoyed. "Why didn't you get me?"

"I tried. Bonechewer stopped me. He said he's been alone so long that he isn't ready to meet any of us."

Ratha could see the rising flicker of jealousy in Thakur's eyes even before he said, "Except you."

Was he envious of her because he also missed his brother and wanted badly to see him? Or was he jealous of Bonechewer because he was realizing that he might have a serious rival for Ratha. Or both?

Thakur started pacing, his scent growing sharp and salty. "I can understand why he would seek you. But why would he be afraid of me?"

"He isn't afraid. He's just not ready to meet us. Can you blame him?"

"Well, I suppose that after we burned, trampled, and killed him, he might be reluctant," Thakur said wryly, though he couldn't hide a sarcastic Bonechewer note in his voice.

"Apparently we didn't. Kill him, I mean," Ratha added at Thakur's narrowed eyes. "Thakur, I know. He was my mate. Thistle's father," she protested, hating to wake the look in his eyes that said, "I am to be your mate. Or I was."

His ears twitched back. "Ratha, I want to believe you, but I can't unless I see him myself."

This struck sparks of anger in Ratha, but instead of letting them ignite, she mentally stamped them out. "You're right. I could be seeing what I want to see."

"So I'll come after the Firekeepers light the Red Tongue for you. Then we'll both see him and know."

"Thakur, I hate to say this, but I don't think he'll come if we're both there. For some reason, he needs to talk to me alone."

"Why?" This time Thakur's voice had the rawness of pain. "He never turned his back on me before. Even when my mother Reshara took him and left me in the clan as an orphan, he would find me."

Ratha had opened her mouth in surprise. She closed it slowly. "I didn't know . . ."

"I told you long ago that he was my brother."

Ratha felt she was stumbling. Well, she was confused too. When someone who was supposedly dead turns up again, it causes all sorts of complications. "Thakur, you've trusted me before. Trust me now."

"Trust you that he really is Bonechewer? Or . . ." Thakur bit off the last words, but Ratha heard them in her mind. *Or trust you not to trample my feelings in the rush toward your dream?*

She wondered if she should tell Thakur about the second part of her dream, that Bonechewer would help her reach out in friendship to the UnNamed. No. Thakur had enough for tonight. She also wondered if she could indeed trust herself not to destroy his dreams while chasing hers.

Thakur lowered his head, shadowing his eyes. "What has Bonechewer, if it is him, asked you for?"

"He just wants me to move the fire out where no one else will go. And stay there alone tonight."

"I think I should hide nearby, just in case."

"He'll know you're there. He's much better at stalking and hiding than we are."

"Arrr." The herding teacher grimaced. "You're right, but I don't like it."

"He might not come anyway. I wasn't supposed to tell anyone."

Thakur fell silent and pawed the end of his tail, a sure sign that he felt uncomfortable. "So what will you do?"

"Make the Red Tongue's nest myself, with Ratharee. I'll keep a few unlit torches ready. Resin pine, so they'll light quickly."

"All right," Thakur said. "I'll keep myself and the others away, but if I hear you yowl . . ."

Again Ratha sat alone by her fire at the edge of clan ground. Again Bonechewer visited her. After she finished devouring him with her eyes, they both settled on the same side of the campfire, although he still kept a slight separation. As she had promised Thakur, she had unlit firebrands laid nearby. She hoped Bonechewer wouldn't notice the torches, or even know what they were. He did give the firebrands a quick glance, but she was unsure if the narrowing of his eyes was her imagination.

Bonechewer spoke again of the UnNamed, and this time he had some detailed suggestions. A group of them existed in the mountains that lay in the sunrise direction from clan ground. Winter had come early to those peaks. The UnNamed ones there were struggling. If Ratha wished, he could arrange a first meeting between them and the Named.

"They are weakened by hunger, so they are not as great a threat," said Bonechewer, crossing his paws.

"Are they savages, or are they more like you?" Ratha asked. "I mean, are they clever?"

"Not as clever, but no one else is," he said with his familiar matter-of-fact conceit. "They vary, but none are completely mindless. I wouldn't burden you with that. They have wit enough to be grateful." He rolled his hindquarters out so that he lay in a half-sphinx, facing Ratha. "Have them form their own group, a sort of daughter-clan of your people."

Ratha agreed. Taking in a number of strangers all at once could be disruptive and possibly dangerous. She remembered all too well the adopted orange-eyed adolescent who became the tyrannical Shongshar.

She could treat these UnNamed ones somewhat the same as True-of-voice and his tribe. She would settle the newcomers in their own area, give them meat, and then send some herders with a small mixed flock to teach the strangers clan ways. Yes, that would work, she thought, growing excited. The clan would be having its own cub, even if adopted.

Carefully she would let the best of the new group mingle with the Named. Even more carefully chosen ones might breed with her people. The Named badly needed variety as well as numbers. The risk of mindless young remained but could be managed. Any cubs not fit to be Named might be fostered out to the face-tail hunters.

"I can see by your eyes that the trail to your dream is clearing," said Bonechewer. "There remains, however, one small barrier."

Ratha cocked her head at him in a wordless question. He laid a forepaw toward the campfire. "That."

"The Red Tongue? My creature?"

"The UnNamed fear it. As long as you have it, they won't trust you. No." He help up a paw as Ratha tried to interrupt. "I am not asking you to abandon 'your creature' or whatever you call it. Keep the thing in its hole. Use it for warmth if you must, though I prefer a good heavy pelt."

Ratha stepped on her tail to keep it from lashing. "We need the Red Tongue against raiders," she argued.

"Not if you help those who raid because of starvation."

"The UnNamed aren't the only ones who prey. We've had trouble with bristle-mane hyenas and others. Don't ask me to risk the safety of the Named, Bonechewer. I won't. Even for you."

"I understand. You are walking on a narrow branch, clan leader. You have to balance carefully between what is now and what could be. If you are careful, you can have both. You must think well in order to be careful, so I will leave you now." He paused. "If you make the right decision, you might get everything you want. Even me."

When he was gone, Ratha knew she should sleep, but her mind was in a muddle. She lay with her chin on her paws, staring into the flame.

"Bonechewer isn't asking that much, my creature," she murmured to the fire. "We'll keep you safe in the fire-den, but we won't use as many of your cubs. I know why the UnNamed fear you. Sometimes I fear you. You warm our bodies, yet you burn our minds. You entice us to dance before you, yet you twist our spirits like a green twig curling in your heart. You draw us close, then lunge, as if to kill. . . ."

She thought of everything that had happened since she tamed the Red Tongue. She brought her creature to the clan so that the Named could survive. Well, they did.

To wield torches against their enemies, they had to overlook or accept the ugliness and suffering that the Red Tongue could bring.

She remembered the old clan leader, Meoran. Perhaps she had not consciously remembered all the details of his death, but they came to her now.

Was it the Red Tongue's rage or her own that had rammed the flaming branch through the bottom of his jaw? She'd heard his saliva sizzling in the heat, his jowls blistering, crusting, charring. . . . He had died in horror, the oils in his fur crackling, then lighting his skin, the skin itself steaming, then blackening.

She looked away from the fire, wondering if anyone really deserved that kind of death.

When she looked back, she remembered the image she had dreamed while struggling against the usurper Shongshar. Of how a fire burning before her had come alive and changed shape, taking the cat-form of the Named. How the Firecat had stalked free of its prison of log and tinder, then stood over her with ember eyes and flame teeth, hissing, "I am the one who rules."

Ratha did not know when she slipped from thought into slumber, but the Firecat still prowled before her, seeking prey. Then the apparition's deadly light was cast back at it in the sheen of copper fur. In Ratha's dream, the lava-red eyes met those of clear amber.

Flame-sharp teeth clashed against one white fang and the broken remnants of the other.

Somehow she could not move and only watched as Bonechewer fought the Firecat. She could see from his eyes that every strike against the Firecat was as useless as slashing at a flame. Worse, it brought agony, blackening claws and searing skin.

The Firecat's strikes raked flame into Bonechewer's skin, and the lines of fire deepened and extended. He screamed, rose thrashing, and then toppled. She watched him die, the Firecat above him, then on him, and then in him, turning his breath to smoke and his flesh to charcoal that cracked open, showing an evil red within.

Then, as his shriek died in her ears along with her own scream, the Firecat turned from its victim to her. . . .

Abruptly Ratha woke, half on her back, half on her side. All four legs were up and rigid. Her pawpads were so sweat-slicked that the sweat dripped on her chest and belly. Her claws extended so hard that her toes cramped. Even her nose-leather was wet.

For an instant she locked in that position, still embattled by her dream. Then, realizing that the horror had been miraculously swept away, she let everything go and collapsed into a heap, unsure whether the vision was real. A rush of gratitude swept over her that it wasn't.

She drew a shuddering breath. No Firecat. No charred corpse. Not this time.

She rolled on her side and nearly put her feet in the fire. No, it was the campfire, not the substance of the Firecat. But were the two all that different?

Sudden fear sent Ratha rolling, wriggling, and scrambling back from the campfire, as if she had seen the glint of the Firecat's eye in its heart.

Perhaps she had.

As Ratha had once crept toward the light and warmth of her creature, now she crept away from it. She huddled and watched it flicker from a distance, chilled by wind and by fear.

Maybe Bonechewer was right. Maybe he was more than right. This thing she called her own; could it be a deeper evil than any herd-preying raiders? Yes, it had saved her people, but at what cost? Should the clan put the Red Tongue aside, not only for the sake of the soon-to-be new members, but for the sake of the Named themselves? This creature that disguised itself as warm, protective, and benign, she thought, would it eventually consume the Named and their world as it had consumed Bonechewer?

What have you done to us, she thought, eyeing the fire. *What will you do to us?*

A sudden clear realization came.

I must back away from the Red Tongue before it is too late. There are other ways to survive, and I must find them.

Then a wry scrap of thought entered Ratha's mind. *Fessran will think I'm crazy.*

"No!" Thakur stamped his forefoot. "Ratha, you are not going to sit out alone on the edge of clan ground and wait for who knows what. Especially without a fire or even a torch."

She itched to bare her fangs at him. His scatting sensitivity had dragged it all out of her again.

"I've never been fond of the Red Tongue," he said, flattening his ears and raising his nape, "but its protection works."

Emotion and lack of sleep had left Ratha dizzy and exhausted. Unable to control herself, she flared back at him. "You are not clan leader and you will not tell me what to do. I told you why I can't have the Red Tongue near me."

Thakur put his paw on her and withdrew it. "You're hot. You've got a fever. You're sick, Ratha. I'll take you to my den. I'll chew up some medicine plants for you. Then you'll sleep and get well."

"I'm not sick. I have to meet Bonechewer. Alone."

"Ratha . . ."

"No!"

His lip twitched back, showing a fang, but he remained sitting. Softly he said, "I think I should get Thistle-chaser and Quiet Hunter. Maybe they can reach you."

"You will not." Ratha snarled, "You will go and teach your herding class in the meadow. You will not interfere. Am I understood?"

His reply came slowly and sadly. "Yes, clan leader." His voice was low.

Her own softened. "Thakur, much good will come from this. I can't tell you everything now; it is still too soon."

"I hope that what will come is good, clan leader," he said, and padded away.

The next evening found Ratha crouching by the Red Tongue's empty nest on the edge of clan ground. She shivered. Part of her wanted the fire again, but part of her was relieved that she didn't have it. She still carried the vivid dream-images of Bonechewer's clash with the Firecat.

With her treeling, Ratharee, she waited in the moonlight. It was a long wait and she almost dozed off before she heard footsteps. More than one set. Her heart leaped up in hope. Bonechewer had done as he promised and brought UnNamed ones down from the mountains.

Gently Ratha nosed Ratharee off her back and up the nearest tree. The treeling blinked, curled her tail up in a question.

"With strangers around, you'll be safer up here," Ratha told her. When the treeling was well hidden among the branches, Ratha trotted toward the sound of the footsteps and called, "Bonechewer, I'm here."

The footsteps stopped, leaving silence. Ratha halted, puzzled, and went farther. She knew she was right at the edge of clan ground.

"Bonechewer, where are you?"

Again came silence. An uneasy feeling began crawling over Ratha. She didn't know Bonechewer's companions. They might be UnNamed ones seeking the clan's help. Or they might not. Her voice sharpened with the realization that she might be walking into an ambush.

"Bonechewer! Show yourself!"

But he was Bonechewer, her first mate; the one who had taken her in and taught her to hunt when the clan exiled her. She wouldn't have survived without him. He had cared deeply about her and still did. If she couldn't trust him, whom could she trust? And he offered her the fulfillment of an ideal she had long desired.

"Over here, clan cat," came his soft reply. Relief washed over Ratha, making her weak.

"I've come alone, without the Red Tongue," she called back.

"Good," he said, and emerged from the shadows into the moonlight. Its light on his copper fur shone strangely cold, but his shape and stance were the same.

Ratha's quickening heartbeat nearly choked her as she bounded toward him. At last she could have what she wanted most, what had eluded her for so long—Bonechewer himself, and everything else.

Images whirled through her head of UnNamed ones coming from all over, seeking the benevolence of the Named, of Thakur teaching UnNamed cubs to herd. Of daughter tribes springing up all around clan ground, a new breed of the Named arising, flourishing. And of all paying her honor for her vision and generosity, a leader not just respected but beloved.

She took one last step to Bonechewer, boldly extended her head for the nose-touch, and was shocked with delight when he met it. His scent was deep, wild, and so rich with promise that her head spun.

Ratha shook herself. She couldn't get carried away like this. She needed to meet with Bonechewer's companions, listen to their needs, and make her offer.

"Where are your friends, Bonechewer?" she asked.

He stared at her with an expression she had never seen, while the moon seemed to bleach his eyes from amber to steely white.

"Here," he said.

Shadowed forms leaped from the bushes on either side and were on Ratha before she could move. Stunned by disbelief, she felt teeth sink into her nape while a clawed weight on her hindquarters flattened her.

"Bonechewer, what are you—" she tried to cry, but a set of jaws closed over her muzzle, cutting off her scream.

She felt as if she'd been flung off a peak into a chasm. She sought refuge in a thought that her enemies were attacking him as well, and the pair must fight to defend themselves. She jerked her head madly to free her teeth, but the jaws around her muzzle bit down hard. She felt a trickle of blood run into her mouth.

Half expecting to see Bonechewer fighting off attackers, she shoved her assailant around until she could see Bonechewer with one eye. With horror, she noted that he was standing free, looking on. She was the only victim in this hunt.

With her jaws clamped shut, she could only scream in her throat and through her nose, squeezing her eyes tightly shut.

This had to be a bad dream, like her dreams of the Firecat. When she opened them, she would be lying by her campfire, Ratharee curled up against her.

But the teeth still dug into her muzzle and fastened in her neck. Sudden rage made Ratha writhe and buck, but her captors subdued her by sinking their teeth deeper.

Her mind jumped around, seeking any answer except the terrible truth. Any answer, no matter how crazy. This must be a trick of some sort, to fool other UnNamed ones who were watching. Yes, that was it. When the ruse was over, Bonechewer would release her, explain to her, lick her wounds, comfort her. . . .

When she caught sight of him again, the bottom of her world fell out. Not only was he free, he was jerking his head at her captors, signaling them. Her cry turned into a maddened shriek that tore through Ratha. Crazed with rage and grief, she went into a wild frenzy and nearly broke free before her captors secured her again.

She heard Bonechewer's footsteps as he moved off. Her captors hauled her after him, taking her across the boundary and away from clan ground.

At last Ratha's assailants flung her down, pinning her and keeping her jaws shut. Bonechewer circled the struggle, shadowing her. Again Ratha fought, but only exhausted herself.

"We have come far enough that the Named will not interfere." His voice was still silky, but it held a chilling note. As she watched him through the one eye not blocked by the UnNamed ones who held her, he stopped his circling and stood over her, his eyes narrowed in scorn.

"I know what you are thinking, clan cat. You are hoping that this is a trick. That I'll release you, lick your wounds, and lie with you as I did once long ago." He spat. "Well, it isn't."

He put a paw on her side over her ribs. She was startled by the gentleness of his touch . . . before his claws drove deep and raked her. She gasped at the pain.

"That," he hissed, "is what I feel for you."

He stepped back from her, his foreclaws stained with red. A strange amusement came into his moon-pale eyes. "You made it too easy, leader of the Named. You gave me one of your vine ropes you use to lead your wretched herdbeasts. You wrapped one end around your neck and laid the other in my jaws."

Again Ratha struggled, but her rage drained into despair.

"Do you know what that tether was, leader of the Named?" he asked. "It was hope. Hope that I, once and perhaps again your beloved, could bring you a precious gift. That I care so much about you that I would help you turn the UnNamed from foe to friend." He paused. "How reckless you were, chasing your dream. How deluded. How blinded by your ideals."

Ratha wrenched her head from side to side, trying to free her jaws from the enclosing teeth. She subsided, heaving, wishing she could go deaf. Or die. Anything not to hear the tearing words, but Bonechewer pressed on, relentless.

"Do you want to know the truth, clan cat?" He stared down at her. "You thought I cared for you. You thought what I felt then was more than the mating lust." He opened his jaws in a heart-killing snarl of derision. "I fooled you, clan cat. I used you. I never cared for you, then or now. I hate you and that bunch of animal-drivers you call the Named. I also hate the UnNamed ones you sought to help. They are savage, mindless, drooling beasts."

No, you are the savage, Ratha thought, shaking. *I only wish you were just a beast.*

"Don't fear that I will kill you," Bonechewer sneered, "even though your clan nearly killed me. No. It is easier to kill what lies inside of you. The foolish hopes. The cub-dreams. Reaching a kind paw to the UnNamed, *ptahh*!"

Ratha knew that he was not lying or posturing. She smelled his contempt and derision. Its strength dizzied and shook her. She thought she knew how deeply he could care when they laid together and created Thistle-chaser. Now she knew how deeply he could hate.

Not only had he slain her hopes and present happiness, he had reached into the past and murdered her joy there as well.

The wound was as deadly as a suffocating bite to the throat. Already she felt herself withering.

"I will leave you to lie here, to die or not as you choose. I suggest you die, as you will no longer be of any use to the Named."

Ratha felt her captors pull back from her, but she only lay as if paralyzed. Her strength and will had died, along with her hope. He had ripped out, torn out, burned out her core.

The Ratha that had been was gone, leaving only this. Spent. Empty. Worthless. And the one who struck her down was too cruel to grant death.

A sudden shrill voice screeched from the bushes. "No, no, no! Get *away* from her!"

It startled Ratha out of her sinking lethargy. She tried to lift her head as Thistle-chaser crashed from the underbrush and flew at Bonechewer.

"Not him! Not Bonechewer. Not my father!"

Bonechewer tried to fend Thistle off, but Thistle's fury thrust her past his guard. She raked his face, tried to pull off his ear, then gave a strange gulp and dropped off.

From the surrounding brush, the Named poured in to save their leader. Fessran and Bira, swinging torches and leading the Firekeepers. Thakur, leaping after Thistle, his tear lines crumpled by a snarl of rage.

Dimly, Ratha saw him take a fierce swipe at one of her captors, sending the UnNamed one end-over-end into a thornbush, squalling. Fessran and Bira dealt swiftly with the others. Thakur jumped to Ratha's side.

She had never seen him so gallant, but he was too late. Bonechewer had already administered a poison no one could counteract.

He laid one forepaw under her cheek, cradling her head. His whiskers trembled as he licked her face. "Easy, yearling. We're here. I'm here."

But there was a deep cold creeping through her that even he couldn't drive away. The knowledge that she had turned away from him to Bonechewer. He might care for her now, but he would soon hate her.

"I'm sorry, Thakur," she tried to say, but her tongue lay limp in her mouth.

"Stay quiet, Ratha." He paused. "Fessran," he called. "We reached her before . . . well, she doesn't have any severe wounds."

Not on the outside, Ratha thought. *Just the one inside that is letting me bleed to death.* She felt her senses fading, giving in gratefully, even eagerly.

Then Thistle's high, clear voice pierced through the dark walling Ratha inside herself.

"Knew my father," Thistle screamed. "Would never be so cruel. You are not him, not him, not him!"

Somehow Thistle's words penetrated, wriggling through crevices, forcing their way through chinks in the blackness.

Dully Ratha heard sounds of fighting mixed in with Thistle's yelling.

"He cared for Ratha-mother. Would never have hurt her like this. Was there. I knew. I know!"

A thought trickled into Ratha's mind. Could Thistle be right? That the one who had tormented her, had broken her hopes and cast her down . . . wasn't Bonechewer? No. He had to be Bonechewer. He knew her far too well. Who else could have seen her fatal weakness, her foolish dream? Who else could have used it so well against her, luring her so skillfully that she had no idea it was a trap? Who tricked her into exhausting herself in pursuit of an illusion, so that she would be open to his attack? Who had no ideals, no conscience, and thus had no qualms about turning her own against her?

Faintly she heard more fighting, scuffling, and the crackle of torches. Soon, she hoped, she would hear nothing. The scuffling ended.

"They've got him," came Thakur's growl. "Now . . ." Ratha felt his paw sliding from under her cheek fur. Thakur paused, both in words and in motion. "Bira," he called. "I need you to stay by Ratha. Give your torch to someone else."

Then he was gone and the paw slipping under her head was Bira's. "I'm here," said the soft voice. "You will be all right, Ratha. Just lie still."

Thakur's voice was thinned by a growing distance. "Hold him, Firekeepers. I need to look . . . Arrr, I thought so. Bring him over here. Ratha needs to see."

I don't want to see anything. Everything is a lie. Why should I believe in words, or even in life? Even ideals and dreams are only bait for those who would prey.

Dully she felt the sudden tension in the paw under her head, and Bira's voice, strained with worry. "Thakur, she won't wake up."

Then Ratha felt Thakur's teeth take her nape. He shook her gently. "Ratha. Ratha?"

Something in her wanted to respond, but she had gone down too far. Even if she wanted to come back up, she couldn't.

"Ratha!" The shake was harder, but she barely felt her head flopping and rolling. Then came lighter footsteps and Thistle's voice. "Ratha-mother. Hear me. This one is not Bonechewer. I was there and I saw. He cared for you. Even after you got angry, bit me, chased the others away and chased him, he cared. I lay in his paws, heard his words. He cared. More than cared, but no word for it." Thistle paused. "No matter what you did. Would never have hurt you. Not like this. Believe, Ratha-mother. Come back."

It was if a crack of light had broken through the wall isolating her. She summoned the only thing left in her: her will.

Now she began a battle against an enemy greater than any she had faced, even the terrifying Firecat. It was as if she were clawing her way out of a pit, fighting a clawed shape that struck her down repeatedly. Each time she crawled and fought back, sinking her claws into the earth walls and dragging herself up to the light, only to be beaten down and begin the struggle once again.

Only Thistle's words, held close inside her, gave Ratha the determination to keep fighting.

Ratha didn't even know she was winning until her paw jerked itself up to her face and curled around Bira's paw, which cradled her head. No, it wasn't just Bira's. Many paws helped support not only Ratha's head, but the rest of her. Other paws lay on top of her. She could feel them all—Thistle, Bira, Fessran, Cherfan, Mondir, Chikka, Mishanti, Ashon, Bundi, even Ratharee's small hand. Then last, Thakur.

Their touch, their mingling scents gave her the renewed strength and will to climb the rest of the way out of the abyss.

"Ratha," said Thakur's voice in her ear. "Wake and see. . . ."

Ratha's eyes slowly opened. Her sight, at first blurred, began to sharpen.

"Bring him here. Turn Ratha's head. Gently."

Ratha blinked. All she could see was a close-up view of someone's flank with dark coppery fur. A paw came into her vision. The paw pressed, then swiped down the fur. The trail it left was no longer copper but shiny black.

Despite herself, Ratha felt her eyes widen.

"Pull him back so that she can see his face," Thakur ordered. "But first, Ratha, feel this."

Thakur's paw met hers. She felt something slick, wet, and slightly gritty on her pawpad. When she hesitantly lifted her paw to her face, she saw a dark copper-colored stain.

"Colored clay," the herding teacher said. "Thistle is right, Ratha. He rolled in it to color his fur. He even broke off part of a fang. To fool you into thinking he was Bonechewer."

Ratha managed to turn her head and gaze at the prisoner's face. He stared back defiantly. His eyes weren't amber. They were a green so pale that they looked white. Firelight and her own imagination had disguised them.

"Who are you?" she heard her voice ask weakly.

"Why should I tell you? You'll discover soon enough," he said, his face surly.

"Why did you trick me and hurt me?"

The prisoner paused before he answered. "Pain."

"Yours or mine?"

"Both, Named leader." He fell silent, ducked his head, and would say no more, despite shakes and pokes.

Perhaps the two herders who held the false Bonechewer relaxed, thinking he was completely subdued. Perhaps it was because everyone was distracted, trying to comfort their stricken leader.

Only Ratha saw the sudden convulsion of his face and the tremor in his shoulders. Before she could croak a warning, he erupted into a flurry, tore himself from the two herders, and was gone.

The two herders, their faces scratched and their claws full of copper-stained black fur, looked at each other, then at Ratha.

Fessran yelled an order, sending the Firekeepers charging after the escapee, torches flaming.

Fessran crouched down briefly beside Ratha, her voice and scent fierce. "I'll bring you that son of a bristle-mane's painted pelt, clan leader. With a few burned holes."

"No . . . don't kill him," Ratha said. "If you can . . . catch him. I need to know . . . who he is."

"All right, but—"

"Catch him. Alive."

Fessran hissed in distaste but galloped after the Firekeepers, yelling Ratha's instructions.

"Don't think they will catch him," said Thistle, reminding Ratha that she was there. "Too fast. Too clever."

"Does it really matter?" asked Bira. "If he isn't Bonechewer, the nasty things he said don't mean anything."

"I need . . . to know . . . who he is . . . and why he did this."

Thakur interrupted, "But not now, yearling. You need rest and food."

And you, Thakur. Can you ever forgive me?

"Cherfan and Mondir will carry you back to clan ground and your lair. I've got your treeling. Here she is." Ratha felt the familiar little hands on her fur as Ratharee curled up on her neck and laid her pointed muzzle against Ratha's cheek.

Ratha felt herself being lifted by gentle paws and mouths, then being laid across the two big herders. Other paws steadied her as the pair began to move off. Many more touched her, giving comfort as the Named bore their leader back to clan ground.

It took more days than Ratha expected to recover. The mental and physical violence done to her wouldn't easily be shaken off. Her wounds healed, but the pain inside lingered. Who was the imposter? She didn't know anyone like him, did she? What had she done to make him hate her so?

She wondered if he might be an UnNamed one who had barely escaped the clan's attack with fire and had vowed revenge. Or could he possibly be a cub whose parents were killed or driven out by the Named? Or even, somehow, one of True-of-voice's people?

Then the last possibility entered her mind. Bonechewer had sired four cubs, not just Thistle-chaser. Could this possibly be one of Thistle's brothers? Ratha remembered how Thistle had once hated her and tried to slay her on the wave-swept rocks beyond the shore. She had to come to terms with her daughter. Was there another cub that had been stunned and angered by her rejection and desertion of her first litter?

She nearly groaned aloud at the thought. Would she have to go through with a male cub what she had gone through with Thistle? Even worse, there were three brothers in the litter. Was there now a small pack on her trail, seeking revenge?

The thought was so wretched that it was almost funny, but her jaws and face still hurt too much to loll her tongue out in a wry Named laugh.

Then she grew somber, thinking that the false Bonechewer had accomplished one of his goals. But in this he was right. Never again would she have the foolish dreams and ideals that led her down the path to suffering. That set her up to be vulnerable to such schemes and attacks. She would look after herself and her people. The UnNamed would have to do without her.

It was many days closer to winter. This evening, Ratha had invited Thakur, Thistle-chaser, and Quiet Hunter to join her at the evening fire. She still did not sit as close as she once had, relying more on the warmth of Thistle-chaser and Quiet Hunter curled up against her to shield her from the night's wind. She hadn't mentioned either the false Bonechewer or the attack since they had happened. Thakur lay a short distance apart from Ratha. She also found it very hard to respond to him, since she wondered deep down if he hated her as much as the false Bonechewer did. He had asked her not to trample on his feelings and she had run all over them, without thinking. When the mating season came, he would probably go away again, as he had always done, but this time, it would not be just for fear of siring witless cubs.

Now he kept apart and silent before the evening fire, letting Thistle and Quiet Hunter do most of the talking. She didn't say much either. She listened to the young couple, wishing she were their age again, with the path before her open and promising.

Thistle nudged her gently. "Haven't heard you talk much, Ratha-mother."

"There isn't much for me to talk about," Ratha said softly.

"Miss you talking about . . . idea you had once. That clan could help UnNamed ones, not hurt them."

"That is a stupid, foolish idea. Forget it, Thistle."

"No, not stupid. Not foolish. Already did it a little with me, Quiet Hunter, and True-of-voice."

"I won't ever think of doing it again," Ratha growled.

"Because he—"

"He was right."

"But he wasn't . . . my father."

"It doesn't matter. He showed me that ideas like mine just bring trouble. If I hadn't been chasing them so hard, I wouldn't have been such easy prey."

"That dream," said Thistle. "Made you more. Don't chase it away."

Ratha fell silent.

"Ratha," said Thakur's voice, startling her because he had been so quiet lately. "Fessran and I found out something today. Do you remember the smell the stranger left? How strong it was?"

"I don't want to remember, but yes, I do. It wasn't a body smell. It was more like the fleabane plant."

"We found the source. It *is* a plant. Fessran crushed some and sniffed it."

"What happened?" Ratha asked, curious despite herself.

"I'll have to tell you since she won't. She's too embarrassed. She was sillier than I was the time I ate fermented fruit." Thakur paused. "He used it on you, Ratha, to lure and confuse you. You have no reason for the shame I smell in your scent. He used a strong medicine plant, not to heal, but to harm."

Slowly Ratha blinked. "Then it wasn't . . . all me?"

"No," Thakur answered.

"Only a little?"

"Enough so that you believed it was Bonechewer."

"I thought you were hurt. I thought you were angry and hated me."

"How could I?" Thakur moved nearer. "You didn't disguise yourself by rolling in colored clay. You didn't rub yourself with a mind-twisting scent. You didn't bring enemies to attack. Stop wounding yourself, yearling. It wasn't your fault."

"But I turned away from you . . . to him. How can you forgive me?"

Thakur lifted up her drooping head with his nose. "Because I know how much you cared for the real Bonechewer. And I know how much you care for me."

Ratha raised her head, her feelings again in confusion, but this time the whirling in her mind was centered on hope.

"Who was he, Thakur? How did he know me so well? He spoke . . . just like Bonechewer."

"If we ever find him, we'll know. And I think we'll find him someday. It doesn't matter now. He wasn't Bonechewer. Thistle screamed out the truth. Bonechewer would have never done such a cruel thing to you. He wasn't Bonechewer, so whatever he said doesn't matter."

"I will try," Ratha said slowly.

"I know. When you have been harmed like that, it takes many days, even seasons, to recover."

"Why did he hate me enough to . . ."

Thakur soothed her. "Whatever his reason, he saw things as wrong and twisted. He hated something in his own mind. Not you. Not the real Ratha that I see."

Then Thistle spoke. "Hated something in my own mind too. Attacked you. Now know better. Know you better." She paused. "You haven't lost Bonechewer, Ratha-mother. Have him still. Inside."

And you have given him back to me, Ratha thought. She bent her head and licked Thistle's nape, catching in Thistle's fur an echo of Bonechewer's scent. *The real Bonechewer. I have him still. In you.*

She knew then that she had started to heal.

"Do one thing for me and Thistle," said Thakur.

Ratha cocked her head at him.

"Don't chase away your dreams."

"Why not? They're foolish and they get me in trouble."

"Difficult, perhaps. Trouble, maybe. But not foolish."

"I don't know. . . ." She faltered. "Part of me doesn't want to give them up. But part of me is still afraid."

"Then he wins," said Thistle simply. "Or he will."

Ratha's growl was very low. "No, he won't. Whoever he is."

She felt Thakur beside her. Even though he didn't speak, she heard her thoughts in his voice.

Ratha, you wouldn't be who you are without your ideals and your dreams. Someday they'll happen and I'll be there to help. Don't let angry minds and empty hearts pull you from this trail. Be careful, but be strong.

"Thank you, Thakur," she said aloud.

He looked at her knowingly. "I knew you'd come back, clan leader."

They all fell asleep against each other in the warmth from the fire.

CLARE BELL was born in England and raised in the United States. She is best known as the author of the Books of the Named, about a prehistoric clan of self-aware intelligent big cats who herd their former prey. (Before and while writing, she worked in such diverse fields as mudflat ecology, test engineering, and electric vehicles.) The first four titles—*Ratha's Creature, Clan Ground, Ratha and Thistle-chaser,* and *Ratha's Challenge*, were reissued by Firebird in 2007. E-Reads (www.ereads.com) has published the fifth book in the series, *Ratha's Courage*; it is available in paperback from Imaginator Press (www.imaginatorpress.com).

Visit Clare Bell's Web site at **www.rathascourage.com**.

AUTHOR'S NOTE

This first Ratha short story took me onto new ground. I had done short fiction in *Catfantastic* and *Witch World*, but all the Ratha tales were novels. The first element of "Bonechewer's Legacy" was Bonechewer, from *Ratha's Creature*. I'd always regretted his death. With his mix of irreverence and wisdom, he was my best character.

Second came the theme of the idealist who is manipulated by those who exploit or use her passion. This comes from my work as an electric car engineer and journalist; I ultimately left the field after too many bad experiences with certain companies. Not surprisingly, this second theme is strong in my mind.

Ratha is becoming an idealist. Urged by her daughter, Thistle-chaser, Ratha has extended understanding and friendship outside the clan (*Ratha's Challenge*). Along with Thakur, she envisions helping the struggling UnNamed. This new idealism leaves Ratha vulnerable when a strange cat uses her dreams and her memory of Bonechewer to attack her. He even makes her believe that she deserves this cruelty.

The "legacy" is Thistle-chaser's true memory of Bonechewer. She realizes that the strange cat is not her father; in fact, he is her brother, one of Ratha's other children with Bonechewer. With a similar voice and physique, he can convincingly re-create his father, and use that presence to hurt his mother. Thistle-chaser's passionate intervention exposes the fraud and saves Ratha—not just from the attack, but from her own self-condemnation—and helps Thakur heal the damage.

Elizabeth E. Wein

Something Worth Doing

"You feel like Henry the Fifth in armour and
Joan of Arc tied to the stake at the same time."
—*anonymous Spitfire pilot*

Theo lost her younger brother in the spring of 1940. Kim died a month shy of his eighteenth birthday. He was knocked over by a van loaded with infantrymen not much older than himself, bound for France, as he cycled through the lanes on his way home from the grammar school in Canterbury, which he would have finished with in less than a month.

"What a waste. What a tragic waste of a young life," the parishioners kept telling their bereaved vicar, Kim and Theo's father. It made Theo want to smash their sorrowful faces in. It was so nearly what the policeman had said when he brought

Kim home the day after Kim and his friends had tried to drink a pint in each of the ten pubs along the seafront at Share, or what Kim's headmaster had said when Kim had not turned up for his exams last year. Everyone made Kim's death sound like one more failure to live up to expectations. It had not been Kim's fault he had been hit by a van, had it? All of Europe was at war. Wasn't the vanload of soldiers on their way to the front a tragic waste of young life, too?

Theo's own record was about as third-rate as her brother's. The pressure to set a good example for the wayward Kim had only made Theo want to join him in his escapades. She liked reflecting the glow of his artless magnetism and being counted one of his crowd. The threat of war had caused her parents to pull her out of a Swiss finishing school the previous spring, very unfinished, and Theo had flatly refused to start in an English girls' school halfway through her final year. So Theo had spent most of the last year hanging about at the Manor stables, wheedling her brother into going riding with her when he should have been in class, or getting Kim to bring his twelve-bore out to the churchyard so they could take potshots at pigeons.

There had only been a year and a half between Theo and her younger brother. They had both watched with horror as throughout 1939 the Axis powers plunged the world into deeper and deeper darkness. Theo was more informed about it than Kim, because she often had nothing better to do than spend the afternoon in the village library with a stack of newspapers, but it was Kim who had come up with the idea of joining the war effort.

"Because this is really something worth doing," he had said.

Kim and Theo had gone together to enlist in the Royal Air Force and the Women's Auxiliary Air Force, respectively. Theo's application had been turned down, to her great shame and embarrassment, because she had not finished school. Kim's application had been accepted, providing he managed to make passing marks on his final exams at the Canterbury Grammar.

Theo had enjoyed her year of conspiratorial truancy with her younger brother, who seemed like her twin in age and temperament. She had dreaded the abyss the approaching war would open between them, but Kim's ironic early death was a blow Theo had not been prepared for.

She tried to find comfort in the fading echoes of her brother's existence. She bicycled to his school to pick up his cricket things, some of his books, and his examination papers. The headmaster gave her tea. His secretary brought it in; she dropped a plate of buttered toast on the carpet when she saw Theo sitting there, boyish and tall and big boned, not very tidily dressed, wearing jodhpurs and a lumpy dark green pull-over she had knitted herself.

"Miss Lyons, I beg your pardon. How like your brother you are!"

"All Kim's friends know me right away," Theo said. "Even if they've never met me."

"You gave me a start. I can't get used to the idea of never seeing him again."

"Nor I," Theo answered, willing herself not to cry, unconsciously sticking out her lower jaw in her determination. This, too, had been characteristic of her brother.

"He was such a charmer," said the secretary.

"Pity he never applied himself to anything," Theo said waspishly, beating them to it.

The headmaster and his secretary both nodded in sympathy, gazing at her with a kind of spellbound doubt, as though they were watching a ghost.

Theo did not know what to do with Kim's books and papers. She went home and began to file things in the pigeonholes of his desk, as though he might come looking for them soon. Lying open beneath a lump of flint shaped like a dove's head, which Kim had found on the beach at St. Catherine's Bay and used as a paperweight, was the letter from the RAF explaining the details of where and when he was to report for his initial training.

It was her own name that drew her eye to the letter: T. Kimball Lyons. She and her brother had shared Kimball as a second name because it was their mother's maiden name. No one had ever called Kim by his biblical Christian name, Titus, for obvious reasons.

I've got Kim's name as well as his face, Theo thought suddenly. If I turned up with this letter at the Flight Training School by Little Cherwell, would anyone know the difference? Kim's already been through the selection board and the medical. And he passed his exams.

She thought, maybe Kim can apply himself to something after all.

Theo made a quiet cull of her brother's wardrobe, and

skimmed off his mail when it arrived. She unearthed her brother's birth certificate and took possession of it. She told her parents: "I'm going to join the Women's Auxiliary Air Force. I said I'd do it, and I will. I start in May."

Theo had not told her parents about being turned down by the WAAF. Only Kim had known that.

Theo said good-bye a day before Kim's training was to begin and spent the night in an inn in the village of Little Cherwell, five miles from the airfield. It was May now: the night was warm, and the whole village smelled of lilac. Theo stood in front of a narrow, tilted dressing table mirror in her very small guestroom and surveyed her profile critically. She was tall and broad-shouldered and, taped tidily into a roller bandage and hidden by a sleeveless undershirt, flat-chested. The riding and horse work of the past year had tightened the muscles across her arms into strings and knots. She had hacked her dark brown hair convincingly short.

She looked so much like Kim at seventeen that it made her collapse in tears. She sat on the worn cushion of the vanity stool with her head in her hands, pulling at her short hair with tense fingers, and sobbed for a long time.

The Chief Ground Instructor frowned over Kim's exam results. "You've done the reading, I suppose?"

"Yes, sir." Theo had never worked so hard at anything in her life. To be kicked out because she was carrying on an insane masquerade was one thing, but she could not redeem Kim's memory if she was kicked out for failure.

"Well, you'll be tested again, anyway. Never mind. Lyons, is it? Eighteen on the eighteenth?"

Theo hesitated. She would be twenty in November.

"Yes, sir."

"We'll have you solo before your birthday."

Theo kept her head down. She forced herself awake half an hour before any of the other cadets, before the sun rose, and managed to keep out of their way in the bathrooms. They were housed in the dormitories of a school that had been requisitioned because it was so close to the airfield; Theo had a scared-looking roommate with whom she exchanged polite remarks about the weather and the work. Two young men came in once while she was taking a bath, and Theo sat bent over in the water, her knees drawn up to her ears, studiously rinsing her hair while her messmates brushed their teeth.

"Nice place, isn't it?" said one, conversationally. "I sure didn't expect the luxury of Edwardian bathtubs during training."

"Very nice," Theo muttered. The boys left. Theo let out her breath slowly and continued to rinse her hair. She did not even jump when one of them came back for his toothbrush. But she learned to dress and undress with demonic speed.

It was worth it. To hear her brother's name and see it in the rosters, to wear her brother's familiar jacket and tie when they dressed for dinner, to see Kim's reflection in the mirror, gave her the faint illusion that he was still alive. It did not occur to her that if she were found out she might be thrown into prison or accused of being a German spy. She only knew that she could not bear the world to tell her again, definitively, that her brother had died senselessly at seventeen with nothing done and nothing to be remembered for. For two days Theo lived cautiously from hour to hour, paying deep attention to the lectures, being outfitted with flying suit and goggles, playing by the rules, and quietly keeping her mournful, peculiar secret safe.

Then they put her in the pilot seat of a Tiger Moth biplane.

There were no brakes. She and her veteran instructor waited, with the control stick held back to dig the tail skid into the ground, while another brave soul swung the propeller and got rid of the wheel chocks. Her instructor sat in front of her—Theo as pilot behind her passenger, but fortunately the controls were all in duplicate—and began to work Theo through the checklist. Theo became absorbed. Even her stomach calmed down. There was no room in her mind for fear, either of discovery or of what she was about to do; there were only her hands and her eyes and the instrument panel, and Flight Sergeant Wethered's distorted voice shouting through the speaking tube and reminding her to set the altimeter.

"Want to take off?" the disembodied voice offered casually.

"Isn't this an observation flight?"

"I'll talk you through it. Taxiing this old lady is harder work than flying her," said the instructor. "She'll do anything you tell her, in the air."

Theo stuck out her lower jaw. "Sure."

Theo fought the "old lady" across the airfield, legs working the rudder pedals in a battle of will to keep the aircraft straight against the backwash of its own propeller. And then suddenly the fight was over, and they were in the *air*, now, five hundred feet above the trees according to the altimeter, and climbing, and how did you get yourself back down?

Theo laughed aloud.

"That was a nice takeoff," came Wethered's voice.

"Beginner's luck!"

"Think you can find your way to Oxford?"

Theo looked down, frowning in concentration. She was in an entirely different England from the one she thought she had left behind; she felt like Alice finding herself in Looking-Glass land. The landscape below bore no resemblance to the tidy outlines of a map. Theo could not tell the difference between a hedgerow and a tree-lined road. She could not see the undulation of the plain below her. She could not even tell the surrounding meadows from the grass airfield she had lifted off from, minutes earlier.

"Is that the Thames?"

"Spot on."

Then it all came together: Theo's perspective changed. She could picture it whole, suddenly, all the great heartland from above, with the Chiltern Hills to her right and the Cotswolds hiding in the haze far to her eleven o'clock, and the Thames Valley spread before her.

"Well, if that's the river, I reckon I *could* find my way to Oxford."

"Try it. Give me a heading. I'll fly, you navigate."

They were in the air for three quarters of an hour. Theo did not touch the controls again after the takeoff, yet by the time she successfully relocated the airfield she was as worn out as if she had been riding all day.

"Want to do a loop?" asked the casual, distorted voice of the instructor.

"Go on, then."

He plunged straight into a dive that made Theo's teeth go bare and cold. It was better than skiing full tilt down the slopes above Zermatt; better than any helter-skelter she had ever known; but like it, like the first swoop of a fairground ride, when you top the crest of the rails and your heart rises into your throat. The little biplane roared through the dive and started to climb, up, up, and up until finally there was no view of anything but sky. Then suddenly the horizon came back, only it was upside down. The engine cut and they fell in silence, the wind etching Theo's face.

"How did you like that?" Flight Sergeant Wethered shouted, looking back over his shoulder with a wide grin as he studied his student's reaction.

Theo could not speak. She gave him a thumbs-up, flourishing both gauntleted hands for emphasis.

She had never wanted *anything* as badly as she wanted to learn to do that herself.

Theo fell into routine. She did not pay much attention to the terrible things that were going on in Europe, as the Allied forces were beaten back to the beaches of France and evacuated. It never occurred to her that she might be sent there herself, one day, or be called upon to defend Britain from invasion if she scraped through her training; the possibility of lasting that long without being discovered seemed laughable. She concentrated on learning to fly. She kept her place in formation. She dropped paper parcels filled with chalk dust over a target mown in the grass beside the airfield. Theo was a good shot; her father had indulged her along with her brother, and her wasted girlhood of clay pigeon shooting and stumping after pheasants through wet woods and fields seemed suddenly worthwhile, even a natural and obvious means to an end. How could she have carried on the illusion otherwise?

She took occasional telling insults. In an impromptu soccer game on a Sunday afternoon:

"Jesus, Lyons, you kick like a girl!"

"Never bothered playing," she muttered. "Wet vicar's offspring. More interested in horses." She could not actually bring herself, aloud, to say that she was someone's "son."

But fortunately, not being able to kick straight did not matter, because she flew better than anyone on her course. The little Tiger Moth seemed to her as alive and responsive as a horse. She could feel it tugging at the control column the way a horse might tug at its reins, telling her which way the wind was blowing and how hard, and it gave Theo untold satisfaction to feel the machine fighting her less and less, then not at all, as she settled it into trim. She liked the hairline precision of being at the edge of her abilities and the aircraft's limits: turning so tightly the horizon seemed vertical, so that her own slipstream knocked the wings about when she met it again; the wires screaming and her body pressed into its seat in the high speed dive you made when you pretended your engine was aflame and you were alone in the sky with only the wind and your wits to put it out. Before long she got in the habit of closing her eyes when she kicked the plane into a spin. It was bliss.

She struggled through the ground school exams, and

was sent to Bristol for two weeks of officer training, which was not bliss. It would have been her downfall if they had not billeted everyone in private rooms in a boarding house at the last minute. Sheer determination got her through the endless drills, and Theo came back to Little Cherwell to put her infant pilot's skills to work in something more advanced than Tiger Moths, namely Harvards, American-built single-engined training aircraft, monoplanes with wing flaps and retractable landing gear. It became Theo's role to play the terrible Luftwaffe gunner on everyone else's tail. She could not run as fast as they did on the ground, but she could chase them out of the sky.

She scarcely spoke to anyone. She governed her body like a prison warden, forcing its functions into a strict and secret routine. She could not allow herself more than one cup of tea a day; she had a deep fear of being caught behind one of the mechanics sheds with her pants down. The toilet cubicles were private, at least, but she could not spend too much time there. She washed her underthings in the dark. There was an airing cupboard where she was able to dry out linens quickly, draped hidden over the back of the water boiler.

Her navigation was first-rate, her knowledge of engines and aerodynamics average. She won the right to wear the coveted wings of a pilot.

"Well done, Kim," she whispered to herself as she followed the other successes, young and sharp and proud in their smart blue uniforms, to the formal dinner congratulating them.

So passed June and July, and on came the end of August. Beyond Theo's lonely, solitary world of sky and study, the

Battle of Britain raged. Desperate and alone at the edge of Europe, British forces and civilians beat off invasion as Hitler's preparations for Operation Sea Lion rained fire from the air on them in the effort to break their strength and will. The wireless crackled daily with the evil news, and with the prime minister's gravelly voice repeating the defiance he had made in the aftermath of May's retreat:

"We shall defend our island whatever the cost may be. . . . We shall fight in the fields and in the streets, we shall fight in the hills; *we shall never surrender.*"

During the last week of August Theo was transferred to an operational squadron of Spitfire pilots, at Maidsend, inland from Hastings. It was so unexpected Theo thought it must be a mistake; could the RAF really be so desperate for fresh pilots? She stood before her new commanding officer, Leland North, as he turned the pages of Kim's log book. There lay the record of all the flying Theo had done in her brother's name.

The CO finally shut the book and tossed it across his desk toward Theo. He cast his head into his hands and muttered, "Seventy-seven hours in the air! Dear God, please tell me this is a bad dream and I'm going to wake up in a minute."

This outburst did not seem to require an answer. Theo waited. After a minute North raised his head. He was probably ten years older than she was, but looked haggard and ancient, eyes red with lack of sleep and sandy hair thinning.

"I've lost two or three pilots every day this week," he told her. "And two or three planes with them. Where am I supposed to come up with a training plan for you?" He sighed and flourished a piece of paper at Theo. "Your last CO gives you a very good recommendation, anyway. Says you're a daredevil in the air, without being a troublemaker or suicidal. Attentive with your checklists, and a good navigator. Go talk to the ground crew. Here, I'll write you a pass. They'll get you into a plane. You've got a week to figure out how to fly it."

"Can you spare an instructor?" Theo ventured.

Leland North gave her a withering look of pure disgust. "The Spitfires are single pilot," he said. "Surely you know."

She could have kicked herself for saying something so unutterably stupid.

There was instruction, after all, a great deal of it; the planes were too precious to be trifled with. Theo took it all in carefully, but she did feel like a lamb to slaughter as the fitters trussed her into the cockpit for the first time, and showed her how the oxygen mask worked. The gun sight made her stomach turn over. *This is real.*

It was a pig to taxi. Theo hardly dared use her brakes for fear she would tip herself over; the long, slender nose was so high off the ground you could not see a thing ahead of you, and you had to weave all over the place to get an idea of where you were going. There was the trick to remember about switching hands on the throttle once you were in the air, so you could raise the wheels. But taking off was, as ever, so easy, easy as falling over, easy as jumping off a cliff, only in the opposite direction. The sheer strength of the fighter took Theo by surprise. It was staggering that a single human being could master so much power at once. She had, previously, thrilled to be in the air; now she thrilled to be in control of this tremendous Merlin engine.

God, this is all worth it.

The little airplane was beautiful. It was so neat and clean and shapely, with its slender fuselage and smoothly curving wings; Theo had never imagined such a marriage of force and grace could be possible. She hauled up the landing gear and felt the drag cut away. The Spitfire seemed as eager to be in the air as she did.

She flew a neat circuit, once she got the engine to behave obediently, carefully curving her flightpath on the approach as they had advised her, so she could see the runway past that great pointed nose. She landed sweetly, with scarcely a bump on touchdown.

Two of the ground crew came racing out to her, both clearly in seven fits of fury.

"Do you know how close you came to clipping the dispersal hut?" one of them shouted. "Do you know how close? By God, I thought you were going to take the roof off. You bloody well ought to be grounded!"

"Sorry—sorry—" Theo cringed, chagrined and deflated.

"Half-trained cocksure young blood fresh out of flying school!"

Nobody grounded her. They sent her straight back up. They meant to send her into battle next week.

Theo walked into the mess hall that night in a turmoil of exhaustion and frustration. She took a deep breath and introduced herself to her new fellow pilots. They were more welcoming than anyone else had been that day, until she came face-to-face with a pale, fair-haired young man with a wispy mustache and big ears. He went gray as skimmed milk when he saw her, and almost instinctively drew back his offered hand for a moment.

"Who are you?" he whispered. In her memory, Theo peeled away the mustache, and saw behind it the face of Graham Honeywell, one of Kim's three best friends from the Canterbury Grammar. Graham had been a year ahead of Kim.

"Kim Lyons," Theo said in a low voice.

"But—" Graham said weakly, and of course he knew who she was. He gave Theo a long, searching once-over, taking in her wings, her smooth face, her challenging gaze. He had been shooting down German bombers earlier that day, and Theo suddenly felt like such a charlatan, such a time-wasting fake, that she wanted to turn and run.

Graham rubbed his eyes, then held out his hand again. Theo took it. Graham's palm was damp, but his handshake was firm and determined. He shook his head. "Could have sworn you were knocked down by a van last spring," Graham laughed.

He had always been a wisecracker, behind the milque-toast, which was why Kim had liked him.

"I haven't been knocked down by anything yet," said Theo. "Though I expect you could do it very quickly, if you wanted to."

"Damned if I'd try." He grinned at Theo conspiratorially. "That's the Hun's job." He clapped his arm over her shoulder. He was shorter than her. "Have they let you go flying yet?"

"I've been up all afternoon."

"Unbelievable, isn't it?"

"Unbelievable," Theo agreed with fervor. She did not know if he meant the war, or flying a Spitfire, or the fact that she had turned up as his messmate, or that she had only a week to train in, but it was all, unquestionably, unbelievable.

For a moment she wished Graham *would* give her secret away, make it easy for her, take the responsibility out of her hands.

I could leave, Theo thought, as she lay in bed in a twin bunkroom whose other occupant had been killed two days earlier. I could just tell them who I am and they'd kick me out. I could join the Women's Auxiliary Air Force, like I said I was going to. They might take me, now that I can decipher Morse code in my sleep. Maybe I could be a fitter. Some of the fitters here are girls.

Don't be an idiot, Theo, she told herself. If you tell them who you are, you'll be so blackballed no one will ever let you near another airplane.

Well then, *Kim* could leave. Kim could walk away from here and disappear, and I could turn up at home as Theo, and go back to doing whatever Theo was going to do with her other life, her real life.

Theo threw off the covers and sat up, pounding the mattress with her fist, enraged with herself. Oh, good plan, Lyons, fine plan. That would really be the perfect ending to all your efforts to honor your dead brother's memory. T. Kimball Lyons, who walked away and disappeared in the darkest hour his nation has ever known, and went down in the annals of the Royal Air Force as a deadbeat and a quitter! Not just a slacker, this time, not *just* a slacker, but also a *coward*! A *deserter*! That's how you're going to immortalize your brother?

⊠ ⊠ ⊠

You get sucked into things. You go with your idea, or someone else's, or the movement of the crowd, until you find there is no turning back. The pull of events, of your companions, of duty or excitement, sweeps you over hurdles that your heart and brain would never venture. Guilt and shame are stronger than fear.

Theo would sooner have cut her own throat than failed to follow her squadron leader into the air and up to twenty thousand feet, high over the white cliffs and blue waves and into a swarm of Messerschmitt 109s, escorting a band of bombers, dense as a cloud of midges.

They were twelve against a hundred. That was a guess; there were too many to count. The only shots Theo had ever fired from her loaded wings had been at stationary targets on the ground. Clay pigeons, she thought, clay pigeons. Stay high, keep the sun at your back, blind your enemy. They're just a mess of clay pigeons—nothing to it.

She fixed one of them in her sight and pressed the gun button. Clay pigeons did not go spiralling out of the sky in flame. Nor did they shoot back—Theo did not have a second to focus on either elation or regret, and for the next ten minutes did not fire a single shot, only because it was all she could do to keep her own plane from being hit.

Gosh, throwing yourself around like this burns an astonishing lot of fuel, she thought.

The Spitfires were joined by a squadron of Hurricanes. They harried their enemies back from the cliffs through sheer persistence, it seemed, or more likely the German planes were running low on fuel as well. The Messerschmitts started retreating first, and the bombers had to go with their escort or be blasted out of the sky. The entire battle lasted twenty minutes.

A parting shot from one of the German fighters landed dead on the nose of a Spitfire a thousand feet below Theo, and the aircraft bucked and dipped, trailing black smoke. She watched in horror, anticipating the inevitable dive toward the bright sea.

The voice of Theo's squadron leader burst over the radio in a blue shower of obscenities. It was impossible to tell if it was he who had been hit or if he was cursing on behalf of the stricken aircraft.

All of a sudden the sky was practically empty. Half the squadron, Theo's flight, had headed back. As far as Theo could tell she was alone above the crippled plane, which still glided gently toward the cliffs. Come on—get out, get out, get out, Theo willed the pilot, watching for a parachute. Get out! she urged him in her mind, and then woke to sensibility and screamed into the radio, "Get out! Open the hood! Roll!"

Oh, what's the matter with you, she thought with a sudden surge of irritation. I'll *show* you what to do.

She plunged after the limping Spitfire at such a speed that for a moment it made her head tingle and her vision go gray. She was unprepared for the cloud of debris the hapless plane was trailing, scraps of wire and metal and whatnot that had been invisible from a distance; something struck her windscreen with a bang and blanketed the front of it with oil, so that she was suddenly flying blind. She glanced out the side of the canopy, and through the clear Perspex there recognized the markings of the other aircraft. It was Graham's plane. Theo flew in formation alongside him, and saw him raise his head.

God help him, he's been out cold all this time, she thought. Another few minutes descending on this course and he'll fly into the cliffs, if that thing doesn't fall to bits first.

"Open your hood!"

Theo pointed aloft. She did not know if Graham could hear her, so she mimed the motions of opening the canopy and the access door, making broad, exaggerated gestures. She wrenched back her own canopy. The wind off the sea was cool and salty sweet, blowing away the stench of burning oil and cordite.

"Out of your harness—"

She kept her own harness fastened, but he was with her now, and went through the drill obediently. They were still a good couple of thousand feet above the cliffs and out to sea.

"Now follow me through a roll, and you'll be out—over you go—"

Theo had done all she could. She climbed away from the cliffs.

She could not for some reason manage to get the canopy shut again. It was so filthy anyway, and the wind so welcome, that she did not try very hard. Theo was drenched with sweat. She tore open her jacket and collar. She circled back over the cliffs and saw an open parachute floating gently toward the rock pools below.

"The lucky sod!" Theo exclaimed triumphantly. With all the English Channel to dive into, Graham had managed to come down twenty yards offshore.

Theo circled overhead, watching as the parachute folded into the water. She passed within two hundred feet of the bobbing silk and saw a figure stagger out of the sea and lie down on the flint pebbles of the beach at the foot of the cliffs. There was no sign of his plane but for a patch of oil spreading over the swells. Theo roared back toward Maidsend.

Well done, Kim, Theo told herself. *Bloody well done.*

Flying at cruise speed with the hood wide open was like battling a tempest. The goggles protected her eyes, but she still found herself flying with her head turned aside and her chin tucked into her shoulder. Her unbuttoned jacket, though held down by the life vest and harness, yanked and whipped around her neck. She could not do anything about it while she flew and the wind howled. She landed, without taking the roof off the dispersal hut, and taxied away from the runway.

After she had opened the radiator grills and switched off the electrical system Theo had spent herself entirely and sat waiting for someone to help her out of the plane.

"Bloody hell, Lyons, are you hurt?"

Two fitters and her squadron leader scrambled up on the wings and laid half a dozen concerned hands on her.

"No, no, just all out."

"What's all this bandaging, then?"

Her shirt had torn open in the wind. The men had their hands around Theo's waist, on her chest.

"Get lost!" Theo snapped, and hit their hands away.

They stared at her.

"Bloody hell." John Manston, the squadron leader, swore again. "You're not—"

"I'm not *hurt*," Theo muttered. "I need a cigarette."

There was a long silence.

"Here."

Manston held an unlit cigarette clenched between trembling lips; he could not light it so near the bullet-ridden fuel tanks of his own plane and the refilling cans. He passed it to Theo anyway. Then he and the fitters lifted her out of the plane and handed her down the wing into the arms of half a dozen other men waiting anxiously on the ground.

"Get your hands off me. I can walk." Theo pulled her uniform shut; her hands were trembling too much to fasten it.

"Lyons—" Manston began.

"Did everyone else make it back?" asked Theo. "Except Honeywell. He bailed out in St. Catherine's Bay."

They all nodded, gaping at her.

"Yes, that was nice work, Lyons, showing him what to do. A bit original, but you pulled it off. You got a 109, too, didn't you?"

"Two."

"You must be joking! On your first time out?"

"Well, there were a lot of them to choose from."

One of the other experienced pilots nodded and drawled slowly, "I saw them go down. I can't count much higher than two, but I'll confirm those."

"Feel like going back up in fifteen minutes?" Manston asked her.

Theo accidentally pinched the cigarette in half. Her lower jaw jutted out. "Sure."

"Or shall I find someone to take over for you?"

"Don't be stupid," said Theo, thinking she might as well be hung for a sheep as a lamb.

John Manston looked from one to the other of his stunned companions. "If any one of you thinks there's some reason Lyons shouldn't be flying in this squadron, let's have it now or never."

They were silent.

"Now or *never,*" Manston cautioned.

The two fitters turned away and set about industriously reloading the ammunition in Theo's wings.

John Manston gave her a thumbs-up. "Let's go have a cup of tea, then, while they patch up and refuel."

No one ever said another word about Theo's open shirt.

During the next two weeks, the German bombers were relentless, pounding London half to dust. There was no respite for anyone, no time to think of anything but defense. After four days of seemingly incessant flying and firing of guns, of slinging her plane all over the sky to avoid flame and tracer bullets and other aircraft, then coming down for a tinned beef sandwich before being strapped in to do it all over again; after four days of such constant trial and fury, and managing to do it on two or three hours' sleep, Theo could no longer report accurately on any details of these flights apart from their duration; she could not in her memory tell one sortie from another, unless her gunfire actually hit something. Nor was there any place in her log book for the names of her companions who did not land again at Maidsend; but these were fixed indelibly in her mind. Two weeks of glorious warm September weather passed Theo, and the rest of them, in a haze of electrifying tension and perpetual exhaustion, triumph, and loss.

They were winning. They were turning the invasion away.

Then came one blissful morning of thick, driving rain that let them drink tea in peace. Those of them not required to be at readiness did not even bother to put on their uniforms. After breakfast they all fell asleep in the glow of the twin fire grates in the mess hall, until the telephone rang and kicked everyone into frenzy. Sunlight was streaming through the cross-taped window panes, and Theo found her heart filling with bright and eager dread.

"It's stopped raining," Graham commented, as John Manston took instruction over the phone.

They squinted at the sky.

"How I hate the sun," Theo said.

Graham laughed. "Go back to bed, then."

"Not on your life!"

"Scramble! Scramble!" Manston shouted at them. "Get out to dispersal, you lazy oafs. We need an extra flight up there!"

"We're not in uniform!" somebody said.

"You can still fly a plane, can't you? This isn't a vicar's tea party! No offense, Lyons."

They snatched parachutes and helmets and raced for their planes, shrugging life vests over their civilian clothes as they ran.

In the middle of the ensuing dogfight over the rolling South Downs, Theo's guns ran out of ammunition, and one of the German pilots noticed it, and four of them unsportingly banded together to try to blow her to bits.

"Oh, *God,*" she gasped aloud, glancing over her shoulder, and there was another behind her.

She realized, as though this were the first time she had ever been in danger in the air, that she had no chance against them. One or all of them would shoot her down. She could not possibly outfly five armed Messerschmitts.

"Come and get me," Theo muttered, and swung into them.

She made them chase her in circles. She could fly a tighter orbit than they could, just, and as long as they were all playing "here we go round the mulberry bush" no one could do any firing; or, at least, none of the German planes could fire at her without risking hitting one another. Idiots, Theo thought, beginning to find this absurdly funny. They must be very low on fuel. Maybe I can drag this out until they go home.

She opened the throttle and widened her orbit enough to turn it into a corkscrew climb. She teased her pursuers further into England. The rain clouds were piling up again, but the English Channel was still clearly visible; the German fighters were obviously not worried about being lost over unfamiliar ground.

Not giving up yet? How much fuel have you got left? Not as much as me, I'll wager. I didn't fly here from France. And I can land in any of these fields when I run out, but *you're* over enemy territory.

They fired at her randomly.

She saw with immense triumph that one of them did have to make a forced landing, and laughed and laughed. Two others turned away and she lost sight of them, which worried her they might have got behind her again. There was a lot of cloud about now; she could see nothing in her rearview mirror. In sheer self-defense, sure the German pilots would not fire on their own planes, Theo flew headlong between the remaining two, and one of them had to bank so hard to avoid her that he sent himself into a spin. The last of them blew away her rudder. As Theo fought to regain control, the Messerschmitt circled back, turning for home with its guns blazing, and blasted off a quarter of her starboard wing.

Her plane fell into cloud with a fuel tank in flames. Her instruments were all toppled and useless, and she had no rudder and no aileron. She did not know which way was up. But she must have been upside down, because that was the only way to get out, and she was out, and falling. You felt curiously safe in a cloud; cold with the wind of the fall and a bit damp, but at least you could not see where you were falling. As Theo's parachute opened, her flaming plane fell past her, its engine still roaring reliably, a monstrous bright shadow in the white nothingness.

She landed on the side of a hill, and the cloud was so low she scarcely had time to register where she was before she was down. Then she was lying in a potato field in a tangle of cord and silk. Her helmet was askew over her face, half blinding her; she dragged it off. The downs were on fire in a copse of trees lower down the hill, two fields to the west. Theo untangled herself from the parachute and stumbled over the furrows toward the blaze. There were four people there ahead of Theo when she reached her plane: two schoolboys scavenging for trophies, a gamekeeper, and a diminutive countrywoman with a very well-bred pair of dogs. The man and woman looked up from the bonfire with white faces.

Theo plunged toward the flames, sobbing hysterically, and the boys and man held her back.

"Stay away, love," said the man. The boys let go of her, but the woman laid her gloved hands calmingly on Theo's shoulders. "You're all right, dear."

How do they all know I'm a girl? Theo wondered, until she realized it was only the gamekeeper who had recognized it. The others had just followed his lead. And she was, indeed, blubbing very childishly.

The man shook his head in pity. "Much too late to do anything for the poor devil."

Theo opened her mouth in astonishment, looked down at herself, and shut her mouth. She had pulled off her life vest with her parachute; she was not in uniform. She was wearing the shapeless old green pullover that she had knitted herself. Apart from the RAF-issued flying boots, they could not know it had been her plane.

"Did you see it? Did you see it?" the boys clamored eagerly. "There were five of them after him, *five,* and he just picked them off like clay pigeons—"

"They were out of fuel," said Theo. The boys stared at her, goggle-eyed.

"Aye, so they were," said the gamekeeper. "He never fired a shot at them. Guns empty, I expect. Forced all five of them down, though; I counted. Looked like most of them landed in one piece, so we'd best get the authorities hunting for them, eh? Can't have the countryside running wild with German pilots."

"It seems rotten," said one of the boys, speaking very

deliberately, his face red and shining in the glare. "It's *rotten* that the 109s made it down safely, and the Spitfire crashed."

"But—the parachute—" Theo began incoherently.

"There wasn't any parachute."

I came down through cloud, Theo thought. They were watching the plane. They didn't see me.

"Rotten," the boy repeated, shaking his head, and angry tears slipped out of the corners of his eyes. He scrubbed at them in fury. *"Rotten."*

"But what a hero," his friend consoled him avidly.

Theo began to choke with sobs again. She remembered Kim, suddenly, whose spirit she had meant to canonize. But it was not Kim's Spitfire that was falling to ash and molten metal in the fields of Sussex; it was Theo's.

"It's over," said the woman bluntly, and took her hands from Theo's shoulders. "He's gone, dear."

The rain held off. Theo got a lift to the nearest railway station riding pillion on the gamekeeper's bicycle. She had just missed a train. She hung around at the station for a while, then set out aimlessly to walk off the nerves and tears and ended up collecting the parachute and the rest of her gear. By the time she got back to the station, it was dark, and she had walked over twelve miles. The Victorian waiting room was locked, its windows barred and taped, the blackout curtains drawn. Theo slept deeply and soundly on a bench on the station platform, wrapped in the warm, billowing silk of her parachute.

She woke to the sound of voices whispering. She opened her eyes and saw three women with shopping baskets sitting on the bench opposite Theo, eyeing her with distrustful white faces.

My own fault for filling the woods with German airmen, she thought.

"I'm British," Theo said, and went back to sleep.

The shopping women woke her just before the train came in.

"Where are you going?"

"Maidsend."

No one would let her pay for a ticket, not even the stationmaster. One of the women managed to force the parachute into submission in a string shopping bag. On the train her companions gave Theo quantities of bread and cheese, and tea from a flask, and apples. Theo had not eaten since yesterday's leisurely breakfast.

"Oh—" She looked down at the core of her third apple. "Have I devoured everybody's lunch? I'm sorry."

"I think you've earned it, lad," said the one with the string bag.

Amazing what attention a life vest and flying helmet will get you, Theo thought. I'm not even in uniform. At least they don't see I'm a girl, like the people at the crash.

She wondered whether she would be killed before she was caught. She suspected that half her squadron knew she was not Kim. Sooner or later someone would let it slip, and North would turn her out in disgrace. And she would never get to fly again.

Theo thought suddenly: I should go home now.

She did not want to. It made her sick with shame to think of deserting her squadron.

But it made sense. Because, she reasoned, because then everyone will think Kim the pilot was incinerated in my crash. Theo could start over. It'll take longer, but it'll be a clean start, because Kim will have died honorably in defense of his country. We can be our separate selves at last.

I suppose when I change trains in Canterbury I'll have to lose my flying equipment.

That thought made Theo want to cry again. She sat with her elbows on her knees and her head in her hands, tugging at her hair, thinking how strange and unfamiliar it was to be riding on a train.

She made her way home. Her parents, who of course had not heard a word from her in five months, were overjoyed to see her. For all they knew, Theo had been deeply involved in the coastal defense all along; she explained to them that she had had a bit of a breakdown and had been given indefinite leave to recover. She managed to intercept the telegram announcing Kim's second death. She wrote a grovelling letter to the Women's Auxiliary Air Force, detailing an impressive list of preparatory reading she had done over the last year, and begging them to put her to the test and reconsider her application. Miraculously, she was given a review date.

The daylight raids stopped. The bombers kept coming by night, but the German invasion had been turned away. It dawned on Theo that she had been in the thick of it, in the very worst of the combat fighting over Britain. It seemed utterly unreal.

She dreamed about flying. She dreamed about mist in the Thames Valley and frost on the Chiltern Hills, a quiet, empty sky and an open map on her knees.

Two weeks before she was due to start all over again training as a radio operator, Theo found her mother standing on the doorstep with an official-looking letter in her hand. Gray rods of November rain came slamming down like bullets in the path beyond the open door.

"Shut the door, Mother! Whatever's the matter?"

Her mother, stunned beyond speech, handed the letter to Theo.

"It says your brother's been awarded a posthumous Distinguished Flying Cross."

The letter was from Leland North, the commanding officer of Theo's squadron, and explained to the bereaved Lyons family the heroic circumstances of their son's death. The squadron would find time to have a presentation ceremony at the airfield, now that their services were not in such fierce demand, and would Kim's sister Theodora be so kind as to accept the decoration in her brother's place?

"This can't be happening!" their mother cried, choking with sobs. "Kim as a fighter pilot, flying cold-blooded into battle? My aimless, childish *Kim*? My God, the *irony*! He never had any drive, any commitment to anything—"

"He might have," Theo said slowly. "If he thought it was something worth doing."

"What shall I do?" her mother wailed. "Now I'll have to write back, explain it's a mistake, drag it all up again—"

"I'll go, Mother."

"You can't go around collecting undeserved medals! They've got to be told—"

"It bloody well *is* deserved," Theo said through her teeth.

"How in the name of God can you say that!"

Theo drew in a sharp breath. She had left the RAF by choice; she did not deserve a medal. "I mean, it might have been. It's a way to remember Kim as he might have been."

"You can't waste the RAF's time like this!" her mother snarled at her in fury.

That took Theo like a slap in the face, for she knew all too well what little time they had.

"I'll go and tell them it's a mistake," Theo said.

She wrote for an appointment with North. She took the train from Canterbury to Maidsend. She wore a nicely cut wool dress in a dark green paisley print, and a green felt hat decorated with two sharp pheasant feathers, and Graham picked her up from the station in his MG.

"Miss Lyons," he said blandly, shaking her hand. "I'm Flight Lieutenant Honeywell. Maybe you remember me."

"You were at school with Kim," said Theo. "Of course I remember you. How do you do?"

He escorted her to the CO's office.

Leland North of the gaunt look and red hair shook Theo's hand as well. He dismissed Graham. Theo gave her little speech, which was not exactly the same speech she had rehearsed for her parents the night before.

"Suppose," she began, "suppose Kim Lyons was knocked over by a van last spring."

Burning with shame, for in her heart she could not help thinking of herself as a deserter, Theo laid her brother's alternative history before Leland North; and her own.

"You see why I can't take the medal," she finished.

"I . . . see."

They were both silent.

"It makes no difference to me, you know," North said at last. "From where I stand, I've just lost one more decent, dedicated pilot. I'm damned if I won't see the name T. Kimball Lyons, DFC, put down on my squadron's roll of honor."

He did not accuse her of cowardice. He understood why she had had to pull out.

Theo had been so in awe of him as her commanding officer, and so wary, that she had never thought of him as a human being. "Thank you," she said, with relief and gratitude. "Oh, thank you."

"I don't suppose you ever put much thought into what you'll make of your own name, did you?" he asked.

"I'm training to be a radio operator."

"Wouldn't you rather be flying?" he challenged her, point-blank, and Theo's mind suddenly flashed with a vision of the high, quiet England of her dreams, and her eyes filled with tears.

"You could join the Air Transport Auxiliary," North said. "They already have a few women pilots doing ferry work for them, and I don't doubt those girls'll be delivering us fresh Spits and Hurricanes within the next six months, if the war goes on."

Theo said carefully, "The ATA doesn't train you, though. You have to have two hundred fifty hours of flying before they'll consider you."

Leland North dropped all pretence and exclaimed, "For God's sake, Lyons, have you not got two hundred fifty hours yet?"

"Nowhere near," Theo said. "And anyway, I haven't got a log book to prove it."

"I'll see what I can do for you," North said. "Suppose I saw you fly as a civilian, before the war, before your log book was destroyed in an air raid. Suppose we flew at the same club. Suppose I taught you to fly."

"I'd say you did teach me to fly, sir," said Theo.

North smiled. Theo realized she had never seen him smile before. It made him look younger.

"Come be introduced to your brother's squadron," he said. "I'm sure the lads will all want to meet you."

He led her through the mess hall to the favored spot in front of the double fires, where the warmth and the arm chairs were. Some of the faces were new, and some were missing. John Manston, Theo's old squadron leader, was not there. The ones Theo had flown with stood up and saluted.

"Don't be silly," Theo told them.

"They all recognize you," North said. "You have your brother's face."

They made her toast over the fire and laced her tea with whisky.

"What are you going to do now—I mean, what are you doing?" Graham asked her.

Theo smiled slowly. "I'm going to be a Spitfire pilot, of course," she said. "Like my brother. I'm going to join the ATA."

"There must be more to you than meets the eye," Graham said gravely.

The tired, haunted, familiar young men burst into merry laughter.

Elizabeth E. Wein has looped the loop in a Tiger Moth in real life, though not at the controls. She has, however, flown a couple of loops herself in a Cessna Aerobat with a very brave instructor.

Elizabeth is a member of the Ninety-Nines, the International Organization of Women Pilots. She was awarded the Scottish Aero Club's Watson Cup for best student pilot in 2003, of which she is inordinately proud. She has never had to work so hard for anything in her entire life.

Her most recent novels are *The Lion Hunter* and *The Empty Kingdom*, which together make up the two-book sequence called The Mark of Solomon.

Her Web site is **www.elizabethwein.com**.

Author's Note

Why did I write this story? I was *ready*. For a few reasons.

1. For *forever* I'd been an admirer of Deborah Sampson, the young woman who disguised herself as a man so she could join the Continental Army.

2. For some time, a Battle of Britain story had been niggling at my brain.

3. I'd just got a private pilot's license. I'd written a couple of flying stories ("Chasing the Wind" in *Firebirds,* and "Chain of Events" in *Rush Hour: Reckless*). But I'd never written a story from *the pilot's* point of view.

But mainly, 4. I was in love. I was upside-the-head head-over-heels weeping-as-you-read-the-operations-manual (I am not kidding) in love. I was in love with an *aeroplane.* I was in love with the Spitfire.

It all came together into "Something Worth Doing."

There is one place in the story that always makes me cry. It's Theo's dream: she dreams she's flying in winter, in peacetime, though in fact she's never done either. But for me, the fire in the sky is history and fiction, and the quiet, open sky and valleys of frost are real. I am privileged to be able to do my flying in an empty sky.

I had a little help with my fact-checking. Arlene Huss, whose U.S. Army career brought her to Scotland on Mother's Day in 1944, after a two-week-long ocean crossing, gave me lots of tips on military life in England during World War II. I am also indebted to James Allan of the Scottish Aero Club, who trained in Tiger Moths with the RAF. I'm proud to say I was there to witness his victory flight on the sixtieth anniversary of his first solo.

acknowledgments

This is one of the most satisfying parts of any Firebird anthology—giving credit where credit is due. Many of the people listed below are rarely thanked in life, much less in print.

So, my fervent ongoing thanks to:

Firebird

The editorial boards, especially the teens all over the world who weigh in

Geri Diorio and the folks in Ridgefield, Connecticut

Grace Lee, my assistant, who doesn't even like genre fiction

Puffin

(Note: Firebird is an imprint of Puffin)

Eileen Kreit: President and Publisher

Gerard Mancini: Associate Publisher (and Mr. Patience)

Tony Vernal: Associate Managing Editor (who can look into my office from across the hall and be very very scared)

Pat Shuldiner: Production editor

Deborah Kaplan, Linda McCarthy, Nick Vitiello, Jeanine Henderson, Tony Sahara, Christian Fünfhausen, and Kristin Smith: Art directors and designers

Amy White and Jason Primm: Production

VIKING

(Note: Other than these anthologies and the Firebird short novels, all of the other fantasy and sf books I edit are published by Viking first.)

Regina Hayes: President and Publisher

Gerard Mancini and Kim Wiley Luna: Managing Editor and (very patient) Assistant Managing Editor

Denise Cronin, Nancy Brennan, Jim Hoover, Sam Kim, Kate Renner: Art directors and designers

Janet Pascal, Harriet Sigerman, and Nico Medina (in absentia): Production editors *par excellence*

Laurence Tucci and Andrea Crimi: Production

PENGUIN GROUP (USA) INC.

Greetings to the new: Don Weisberg, Felicia Frazier, Shanta Newlin

Doug Whiteman: former head of the children's group (who still watches our exploits from across the street)

Mariann Donato (in absentia), Jackie Engel, Mary Margaret Callahan, Mary Raymond, Holly Ruck, Annie Hurwitz, Allan Winebarger, Ev Taylor: Sales

Jill Bailey, Colleen Conway, Nicole Davies, John Dennany, Biff Donovan, Alex Genis, Sheila Hennessey, Doni Kay,

Steve Kent, Todd Jones, Nicole White: Field Sales reps

Diane Burdick, Vicki Congdon, Jeanne Conklin, Kathy Space, Diane Quattrocchi, Bob Talkiewicz, Carol Thatcher: Inside Sales

Emily Romero, Erin Dempsey, Rhalee Hughes (in absentia), Jessica Michaels, Gina Balsano, Lauren Adler, Ed Scully, Casey McIntyre, Julianne Lowell, Lisa DeGroff, Allison Verost: Marketing and Publicity

Scottie Bowditch, Kimberly Lauber, RasShahn Johnson-Baker, Leila Sales, Leslie Prives, Rachel Moore: School and Library Marketing

Courtney Wood and Jillian Laks: Online Marketing

George Schumacher and Camille DeLuca: Contracts

Helen Boomer (in absentia): Subsidiary Rights

Alan Walker: Academic Marketing

Susan Allison, Ginjer Buchanan, Anne Sowards: Ace

Betsy Wollheim, Sheila Gilbert, Debra Euler: DAW

Paul Slovak: Viking Adult

Sean McDonald: Riverhead

OTHER ROCK STARS

If you're reading this book, you have my thanks. I don't think I'll ever stop being surprised and pleased when people e-mail, come up to me at cons, and otherwise invest themselves in the Firebird imprint.

Special thanks to Charles M. Brown, Liza Groen Trombi, Amelia Beamer, and the staff at *Locus*; Renee Babcock; Alan Beatts and Jude Feldman at Borderlands Books (www.borderlands-books.com); Jack Dann, Ellen Datlow,

Gardner Dozois and Susan Casper, Cat Eldridge and the *Green Man Review* folks; Jo Fletcher and Simon Spanton, Diana Gill, Gavin Grant and Kelly Link, Anne Lesley Groell, Eileen Gunn, Jaime Levine, Elise Matthesen, Shawna McCarthy, Farah Mendlesohn, Patrick and Teresa Nielsen Hayden, Stella Paskins, Bill Schafer, Christopher Schelling, Jonathan Strahan, Simon Taylor, Rodger Turner, Juliet Ulman, Jeff VanderMeer, Gordon Van Gelder, Michael Walsh, Jacob and Rina Weisman, Duane Wilkins, Jason Williams and Jeremy Lassen, and Terri Windling, among *many* others.

Thanks to FACT for ArmadilloCon, HRSFA for Vericon(s), and SSFFS for ConBust. An "alas" thanks to Chris Bell, Dave Devereux, and everyone in the ill-fated Convoy. Special aside to Travor Stafford: One day, I swear.

I want to again thank all of the authors in this book and their agents.

A special word to Mike Dringenberg: *Thank you* for the art and the cookies and hitting your deadline. Brilliant genius.

Thanks to our cover artists—especially Cliff Nielsen, who always comes through.

There are so many librarians, educators, and teachers who have gotten behind Firebird, and they all deserve applause.

BOOK NAMERS

Here's a list of everyone who suggested I name this book *Firebirds Soaring*, in the order in which I received their e-mails.

Rod Lott (in his review of *Firebirds Rising)*
Joe Sanford's daughter
Raina Zheng
Peter Shor
Amanda Race
Nicole Jurceka
Heather Putnam
Olivia Pham

Thank you so much. Who knows what this book would have been called without you.

About the Editor

Sharyn November was born in New York City and has stayed close by ever since. She received a B.A. from Sarah Lawrence College, where she studied and wrote poetry. Her work has appeared in *Poetry, The North American Review,* and *Shenandoah*, among other magazines, and she received a scholarship to Bread Loaf. She has been editing books for children and teenagers for close to twenty years, and is currently senior editor for Viking Children's Books, as well as the editorial director of Firebird. Her writing about her work with teenage readers (both online and in person) has been published in *The Horn Book* and *Voice of Youth Advocates*. She has been a board member of USBBY and ALAN, as well as being actively involved in ALA, NCTE, and SFWA. She was named a World Fantasy Award Finalist (Professional Category) in both 2004 and 2005—in 2004 specifically for Firebird, in 2005 for editing. *Firebirds Rising* was a 2007 World Fantasy Award Finalist for Best Anthology.

She has played in a variety of bands (songwriter, lead singer, rhythm guitar), and maintains an extensive personal Web site at **www.sharyn.org**. She drinks a lot of Diet Mountain Dew and likes to cause chaos in her wake.

The Firebird Web site is at **www.firebirdbooks.com**.

About the Illustrator

Mike Dringenberg was born in Laon, France, and grew up in Salt Lake City, Utah. (He is not a Mormon.) He is probably best known for his work as co-creator of DC/Vertigo's *Sandman* series, with Neil Gaiman; he is responsible for the iconic representation of many of its principal characters. His work appears in the Sandman collections *Preludes and Nocturnes, The Doll's House,* and *Season of Mists.*

He currently illustrates book jackets and CD covers, notably for various books by J. R. R. Tolkien, Kij Johnson, Kage Baker, and San Francisco's Big City Orchestra.

Mike Dringenberg lives in Portland, Oregon, where he rides his bicycle everywhere.

—I'd like to extend my deepest thanks to Sharyn and Xenia (who posed) for their patience and friendship.